BLUNT BUT IMMINENTLY FATAL PROJECTILE

MOLISIA
BAUSTIC MOUNTAINS
GAROBANSUROV
RIFTOLEN
DEEP
HO
INFERT
DESERT
N
W
E

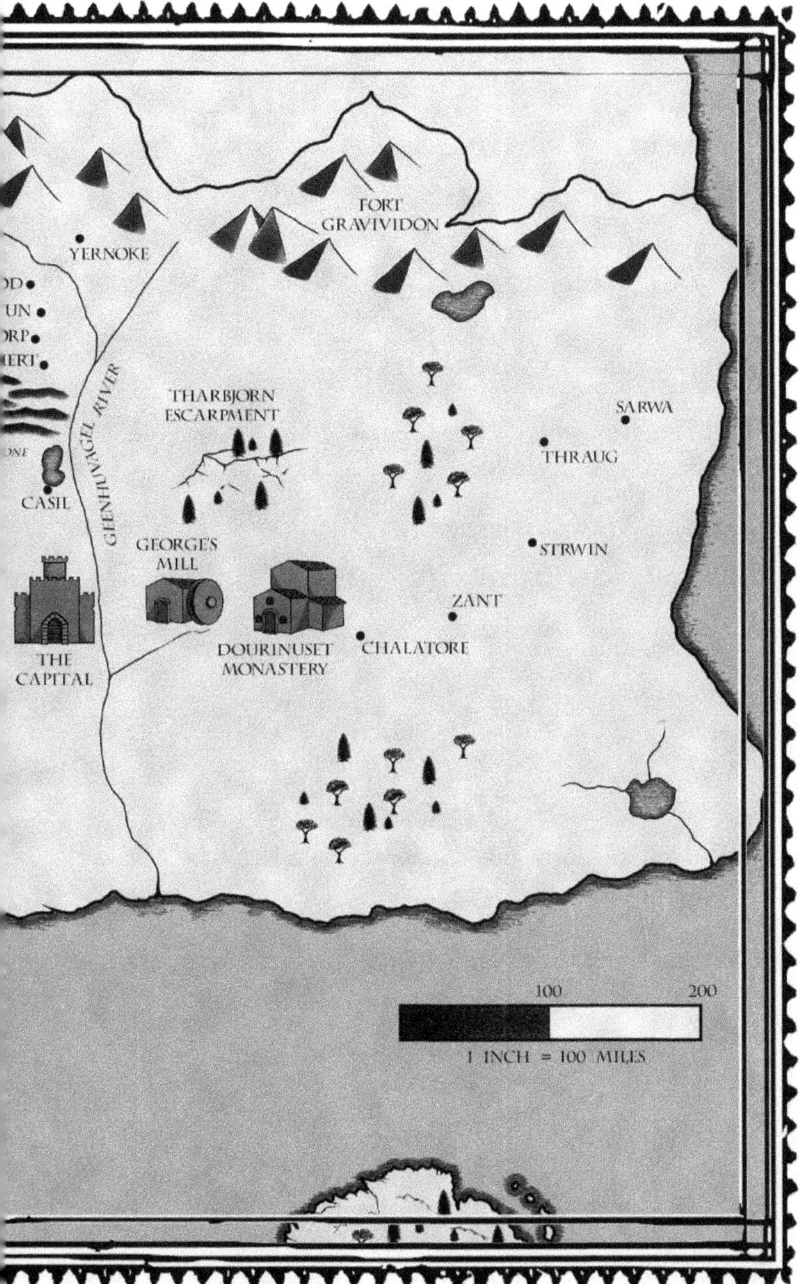

YERNOKE
OD
UN
ORP
ERT
ONE
CASIL
GEENHUVAGEL RIVER
THE
CAPITAL
GEORGE'S
MILL
THARBJORN
ESCARPMENT
DOURINUSET
MONASTERY
CHALATORE
FORT
GRAVIVIDON
SARWA
THRAUG
STRWIN
ZANT
100
200
1 INCH = 100 MILES

ALSO BY NICHOLAS WUDTKE

—NOVELS—

Black Needle, Book One: Parabolic, Magnetic Key

Black Needle, Book Two: Blunt but Imminently Fatal Projectile

Black Needle, Book Three: Deserved, Contorted Relics

—SHORT STORIES—

The Swords, Friendships, and Winds of Far Off Places:
A Collection
~ FREE copy available at website below ~

Find out more, join our list, and purchase your next
great read at www.NicholasWudtke.com.

Black | Needle
Book Two

BLUNT BUT IMMINENTLY FATAL PROJECTILE

NICHOLAS WUDTKE

BLACK NEEDLE BOOKS

For Lifeson

CHAPTER 1

BACK IN THE pack, far from lightweight, were Mick and Dave's awkwardly shaped, homemade tents. The burden of the tents was more than compensated by indisputably proving themselves over the years, having outlasted every hazard Mother Nature decided to throw at them. The time-proven tents were the infrequent brand that screamed imperishability so loud that no one could ignore.

Like always, the tents had been the first things shoved inside Mick and Dave's backpacks, followed by tarps, clothes, and food. After this bulky quad of items were levered into the travel packs, the compartments themselves were full. So, everything else needed to be externally strapped onto the backpacks' frames, including: armor (the new armor they'd recently received from Brom Quintaga); sleeping bags; fishing poles and nets; weapons (not the *black needle* swords, for they were sheathed and waist-strapped); and a few other miscellaneous items. This time around, total combined weight was 192 pounds.

Dave and Mick's hometown of Chalatore, if anything, needed its roads repaired, for they were notoriously well-rutted. The traffic lanes saw traders, tourists, vagabonds, and everyone else of whom you could think come and go daily. Town was normally asphyxiated, even during non-armwrestling tournament days. But along with the traffic came a bustling economy.

Chalatore annually hosted a renowned armwrestling tournament, which saw participants from all over eastern Garobansurov. It was an important strength event which Mick and Dave—previous winners—would more than likely have to miss this year because, as it turned out, General Ulfenkerki was right in telling Mick and Dave last winter to expect a medal or such for their heroics at Fort Gravividon and the Battle of Sarwa. A month ago an emissary from the King himself came to Chalatore to inform Mick Thraiker and Dave Ghrere they were each to receive Garobansurov's highest honor: the Knowing Circle.

The award ceremony and presentation for the Knowing Circle was at the Capital. It was a long journey, which was why the bags were packed and the tournament would be missed. Despite disappointment from the event's organizational committee, Mick and Dave expected to leave days before the tournament's opening bouts. Yet again, the distant winds were calling to Mick and Dave, unignorably beckoning.

Overnight, a fog of no consequence had crept into Chalatore and into its town square, where Dave Ghrere stood busy. Including the potatoes he'd just bought, and the rabbit he trapped earlier at first light, Dave threw all the ingredients of his mother's acclaimed rabbit stew recipe into the town square's large, community cooking cauldron. A company-loving, older man named Gadzud watched Dave heave his ingredients into the cauldron. Waiting for an opportunity to help, Gadzud stood poised for conversation.

Dave said to Gadzud, "Remember ten years ago when Old Man Johnson had to patiently wait for two whole months for a wood trader to come into town, so he could buy the wood needed to fix the hole in his barn roof? Had any more moisture gotten into his barn, it surely would've started to rot. Now, from where I'm standing, I can see three separate wood traders lugging plumped full timber wagons, aiming to sell their wares. I'm glad they're here, but three is superfluous to be sure."

Gadzud took a giant sniff from the pot, and responded, "Well, my friend, if you and Mick would stop putting on such outstandingly entertaining shows during the finals of our armwrestling tournament, people would stop flocking to our town like ravenous vultures on fresh carcasses."

After hearing this comment, Dave couldn't help but nearly fall into the cooking pot laughing. "We should halt the apparently entertaining shows, eh? I'll be sure to tell Mick. I think the townsfolk may be a little upset about it, though."

"Tell me what?" Mick snuck into the conversation and the group from behind.

"Evidently, our armwrestling skills," Dave stated, "are responsible for the boom in traffic."

"I bet those skills are accountable for a lot more than that," Mick let out.

Gadzud chuckled at Mick's bold, but obviously wrapped in humor, statement, and said, "And I don't think the two of you bringing back Knowing Circles will help out the traffic matters any further.

"I think you're probably right."

Gadzud voiced, "I don't mean to change the subject, but who exactly is going to eat all this stew you're cooking here?"

"Whoever wants to," replied Dave. "When it's done, anyone can just come right on over here and eat up."

"How will they know to do so?" asked Gadzud.

"Oh, trust me, they'll know. They'll just smell the aroma wafting through town, and they'll know."

It appeared Dave was right. Once the stew was done half the town showed up to partake in the all-around goodness that was both stew and goodwill. The stew wasn't abundant enough to feed everyone, but no one cared. Everyone had the feeling the cookout was Mick and Dave's way of saying goodbye for a while. No one said anything about it, though, because they all knew what'd happened the last time Mick and Dave left town. The villagers just hoped Mick and Dave's path this time would be safer and a little more war-free. They didn't want to jinx anything by mentioning it.

The war with Molisia still waged on. Mick and Dave's audacious retaking of Fort Gravividon at the onset of the past winter had kept battles and any new invading armies out of their corner of the country for the time being.

At the end of the gathering, Mick, Dave, and their longtime friend Gadzud, cleaned everything up, and went to their homes to sleep off the excitement of the night.

The next day, the one leading up to their departure, Mick and Dave ventured to Old Man Johnson's cabin to bid him farewell. They knocked on the door, were greeted, and entered.

"Glad to see you, youngsters," said Johnson.

"Same to you, old timer."

"Now, you guys do know that there are a lot of people—including myself—who can recite by heart all of the receivers of the Knowing Circle."

Mick unleashed a quick grin and a joke, "Does that mean there've been few recipients, or there are many old men attached to a great deal of time on their hands?"

Old Man Johnson was getting old—as his name suggested—and a little slower at quipping, so it took him a few moments to put together the fact he'd just been on the receiving end of a wisecrack. When he finally understood, he loosed his distinctive, nasal laugh. "I guess it's a little of both, but I'll tell you what: one day, you'll be glad all us old men sit around remembering seemingly useless information."

"Maybe we will."

"All kidding aside, hopefully I'm still alive when you return. I want to see them. I've never actually seen a Knowing Circle up close."

"Oh, I'm sure you will be. We aren't going to be gone that long."

"I hope so. I don't think I'd be very good at explaining to the townsfolk why you've been gone so long. And with any luck, you won't have to use that new armor of yours on the trip," said the old timer.

Dave responded, "I don't think we will, but you never know. Speaking of which, I know we've said this a million times already, but you giving the third set of armor to Jason like that was one of the most honorable things I've ever seen done."

"Not honorable… wise. Our army needs all the help it can get, and him possessing it keeps all of us alive just that much longer."

"You and your modesty. It was *honorable* and you know it."

"Hmmmph." Old Man Johnson shrugged. "Have you heard at all where Jason, General Ulfenkerki, and his army are currently stationed? Sometimes their whereabouts are as mysterious as the existence of the Icytryxis."

"I wouldn't go that far; but, nope, nothing new," answered Mick. "All we know is what you know. Before leaving Chalatore, last winter, Jason expressed planning to rendezvous with the army, either at Zant, Thraug or Strwin. The army very well may have already moved westward, since remnants of war are now showing up in all sorts of unexpected niches of Garobansurov."

"Dangerous times indeed," said Mr. Johnson, as he struggled in hoisting an un-split, hulking log into his fireplace. Mick and Dave knew he liked lifting the logs himself, so they didn't help. "I savor the big ones. They're fun to watch burn, if in fact they do decide to burn."

"To each their own," Dave remarked.

"Will the two of you be leaving tomorrow, then?"

"Yes, sir, that's the plan," replied Mick.

"Say hello to Tim Warmane for me," requested Johnson.

For no real reason, Mick poked at the big log in the fireplace with the available fire rod. "We certainly will do that. Had Dave or I ever told you that when Tim was forging our swords all those years ago, he barbecued over the fire more nights than he didn't?"

"Yeah, he sure liked to barbecue," Dave blurted.

Johnson replied, "No, I can't recall you guys ever bringing that up. Good times."

Mick and Dave stayed for half the day at their great friend Old Man Johnson's cabin. Ironically, barbecuing had transpired. They went home only after eating enough to hurt their stomachs.

Later that day, Mick and Dave stopped at their friend Mrezil's house. It was something they did from time to time, since she was a nice, interesting lady. Plus, she maintained a large collection of books they liked to look over. As for this day, she had a book they particularly wanted to peruse. On their way to the Capital, Mick and Dave intended to stop at the Dourinuset Monastery, a place they'd always yearned to visit. They never got around to doing so because it was built on the top of a large, hard-to-navigate hill and once one made the long journey they weren't necessarily allowed admittance.

Because the monastery was along the way to the Capital, and Mick and Dave were feeling extra-adventurous, they decided to leave early to summit the hill and visit the monks—but a visit that would only transpire if they were indeed permitted entrance by the holy dwellers, a chance they were willing to take. The book they wanted to study at Mrezil's house contained a chapter specifically concerning the Dourinuset Monastery. They thought maybe by knowing a decent amount of data on the subject, their chances of being allowed visitation would be slightly enhanced.

Mrezil reached for the book in her bookcase she was kindly asked to retrieve. After handing it to Mick, she said, "Go ahead and take your time reading it. I'll just be over here, peeling potatoes."

"Thank you so much."

Dave emitted, "I'll help you peel, while Mick reads. Only one person can read from it at a time anyways."

Lacking any inefficiency, Dave and Mrezil finished off her two pails of potatoes, coincidentally in the same amount of time it took Mick to finish reading the chapter on Dourinuset—a long chapter.

Mick voiced, "Well, by reading this, I'm certainly not any more informed on how we can increase our chances of being welcomed into the monastery, but I do know a lot more about elements correlated with them, one of them being that although they're generally a silent monastery, they do speak sporadically, between scheduled activities and such. It seems like a good place to leave you at, Dave. Maybe they'll teach you how to be less chatty."

"That very well may be a good idea, but if I get left there for that lesson, we'll also have to stop at Warton's tavern. There, you can learn how to drink properly. Lately, you've been drinking like a lightweight."

Mick laughed, having realized how fast Dave's comeback was, and responded, "Touché."

Mrezil joined in: "I'm just glad we're all working to improve ourselves."

Three people expressing amusement filled the house, drowning out the all-too-familiar sound of citizens in the street arguing about produce prices.

Mick continued speaking on Dourinuset. "Apparently, parts of their living structure and church are thousands of years old."

"Did it mention if their beliefs go back that far on the timeline too?"

"No, it didn't go into detail about that. I was hoping it would, but it didn't. The chapter did discuss some of their specific beliefs. I'll fill you in more on that along the way, Dave. We wouldn't want to bore Mrezil any further."

"The two of you are way too charismatic to ever bore me with anything."

"Oh, Mrezil, you're too much."

Eventually, conversation ran its course. Dave and Mick left Mrezil's abode, knowing it was a day well spent and most edifying. Thankfully, for Mick and Dave's sake, the streets were now free from annoying produce price-debaters.

Twilight approached all but itself. The city didn't exude much animation, so the previous year's Chalatore Arm-Wrestling Tournament champs went home to bed for much needed sleep for traveling. For no doubt, Dave and Mick were going to journey far—unmistakably reminiscent of countless times before.

MANY MILES FROM Chalatore, a man, a monk, coasted through the motions of life. Brother Alfonso Alardo, for the millionth time, found himself having to break the woeful trance induced by the saddest, most powerful memory of his life. It was a memory where he constantly dwelled, and one from which he constantly had to escape. It was the memory of his wife, who inexplicably left him. Before joining the monastery, Alfonso was happily married, for his part, of ten years. He'd put every ounce of his heart and soul into that love, and never foresaw an ending to the great romance. But guided by the unpredictability of love, Alfonso's world came abruptly to an end. Like lightning on a virtually cloudless day, he never saw it coming, no foreshadowing in the slightest.

After a year of the visceral pain caused by the breakup, he found himself being moments away from killing himself from the despair. But he was miraculously saved by the hearing of God's calling, and as a result, joined the Dourinuset Monastery. It was the best place he could be, to find meaning after such a loss.

Brother Alfonso tolerated existence. He found occasional happiness at Dourinuset, but as soon as memories of his wife flooded in, the happiness washed away. He endured a wound that time could not, and would not, heal. An excruciating burden, from which he was never free. The man had a heart of gold, something that most who knew him surely saw. But they also could see the manifestation of pain in his eyes, and couldn't help but feel immense sympathy.

Momentarily free from the trance and mental anguish, Alfonso pulled out a chair from underneath the large table, and joined the other monks for breakfast, bringing along his contagiously wonderful smile.

For no reason, Abbot Ferdinand (the head monk) liked to fashion his three eggs and toast geo-symmetrically on his plate. Next to Alfonso, Ferdinand carefully sat as to not disturb his creation, and addressed all at the breakfast table: "Good morning everyone."

As aforementioned, the monks spoke only rarely—a degree of peace all twelve monks appreciated. They listened as Ferdinand continued.

"I give you all the credit in the world, Brother Dimetriev, for your attempt at negotiating with the Smiths at their farm for water. Much recognition for your effort. I'm afraid, however, our predicament concerning our well running dry last month is more serious than previously expected. Due to either a water shortage everywhere or nobody wanting to contract with us, things are dire. I'm so confused about nobody wanting to help that I'm at a loss for words. If we're unable to procure a water source soon, we may lose our blissful, hilltop existence here. We're unquestionably in great jeopardy."

Brother Dimetriev bowed his head and voiced, "You're welcome, sir. The Smiths gave no reason as to why they didn't want to negotiate. They just seemed to be uncouth and unaccommodating. I wasn't able to figure out why exactly they didn't want to sell us water rights."

"I guess some people are just like that. We have one more chance, of which I'm aware, to get the water. I'm fairly certain Savata Dearer—a young, single man—has a well at his farm." Ferdinand stood up. "And by no means is it implied that if whoever volunteers for this mission were to fail, they'd hold sole responsibility for our demise. Don't think of it as the last chance. So, knowing that, do I have any volunteers to make the journey to Mr.

Dearer's dwelling and parley with the young gentleman?" Brother Ferdinand sat back down and couldn't help but hold his breath.

Even though Brother Ferdinand had just got done saying the volunteer would hold no ultimate way-of-life-ending accountability, the brothers were in no hurry to step forward to bear the enormous load at hand. They all looked at each other with the uncomfortable stare of unanswered request. Time momentarily stood still, the room silent. The high-pitched whistling of wind was heard channeling through the outer monastery walls, a mystical sound. Finally, Brother Alfonso Alardo figuratively stepped forward.

HAWK AND LEOPARD—MICK and Dave's respective childhood nicknames—having started their westerly walk at sunrise, were ecstatic to be on another heartland crossing. These deep runs were what truly gave them identity. Eventually, they would be returning with Knowing Circles, making them the only folks from their town or neighboring towns to ever do so.

By suppertime, they reached a point fifteen miles away from Chalatore, a fairly decent day's walk by their standards. They had crossed one river, two creeks, and many forests and fields along the way.

Dave flipped the poultry burgers and said, "Too bad the creature that was once these burgers wasn't any larger. Then we could've ridden it through the air all the way to the Capital."

"Keep dreaming, but don't dream too hard and burn my burger."

"You'll never let that go, will you? I burn your burger once, and the whole world comes to an end."

Mick emitted, "Ah yes, the incident at Falbasert. Well yeah, anything could've happened after the Falbasert incident."

In a good mood, Dave laughed. "We're just lucky there were no casualties or collateral damage."

Mick laughed, shook his head, and took a deep breath. "Intriguing phenomenon: a lung full of cool, spring air has the ability to bring back countless memories of old."

"Intriguing indeed. And true. Sure is magnificent to be out here in the untamed wilderness again."

"I wonder if it thinks the same of us."

"Of course it does, Mick. I thought it was common knowledge that the untamed wilderness loves us."

"That very well could be."

Mick and Dave chuckled, ate their burgers (un-burnt) and for the first time of the trip, set up their tents. For them, sleeping in tents were cozy experiences, always summoning feelings of utmost gratification.

Gazing at his tent, Dave said, "Maybe we should just live in these things year-round."

"I wouldn't complain."

Early the next morning, Mick and Dave witnessed rain wash away a weak-rooted bush in lamentable surges. "Well, that's sad," produced Dave. "What a big waste of a little bush."

When the rain subsided just enough for comfort they put down the tents and continued walking. The trail was soggy, but not unbearable. Wetness added a few pounds to the total load weight, but a condition that was only temporary.

A few miles from the previous night's campsite, Mick pointed at a dilapidated farmhouse and said, "Remember the time when we were kids, and we spent a couple days at that house?"

"Oh yes. I don't remember why we did it, but I remember doing it."

"I haven't committed to memory exactly why either, but I think it had something to do with a rampant disease in town or something."

"Makes sense," said Dave. "I remember staying up all night, playing hide-and-go-seek with that one guy."

"I think his name was Dan."

"Yup, Dan. Dan was fun. I wonder whatever happened to Dan."

"Me too."

Run of the mill walks and campouts were all that ensued during the few days of the expedition's opening stage. Mick and Dave didn't typically like that sort of boredom in their lives, but they had no choice in the matter. Every now and then, monotony declared itself the winner of the day, and there wasn't any manner of creative thinking, wild imagination, or prudent planning that could say otherwise.

BLAZINGLY FOCUSED, Brother Alfonso Alardo, still wearing full monk garb, advanced to the front door of Savata Dearer's house. Abbot Ferdinand had supplied him the numerical parameters by which to negotiate for water, with a little wiggle room. Alfonso knew precisely what he was going to say to Savata. He knocked and waited patiently.

A man opened the door, looked at Alfonso, and said, "Now here's a surprise. It's not every day one sees a monk at their door. One hailing from Dourinuset, I presume?"

"That is correct. Hello, nice to meet you. My name is Alfonso." The two shook hands.

"And mine is Savata. Very pleasurable to meet you. Welcome to my home on this fine day. Please, please come inside."

Humbly, Brother Alardo went inside the house, and sat in the chair, at which Savata had kindly pointed. "Lovely home you have here."

"Thank you, sir. So what can I do for you?"

"Well, I'm guessing you know, since you live in the area, the Dourinuset Monastery sits atop a barely traversable hilltop. You might as well call it a mountaintop for as isolated as we are. It's arduous to say the least to import anything at all to such heights. Furthermore, we'd been presented the unfortunate occurrence of our aquifer running dry. I guess for as long as we've been dipping into that well, it was bound to happen at some point."

"How long is that?"

"I'm not sure exactly, but I do know it's been longer than anyone else in the area has been dipping into theirs—over a thousand years."

Savata replied, "I once heard the age of the monastery, but the number was so farfetched that I assumed it was a jest."

"Oooh, it is that old, believe me. Our documentation goes back quite a ways. So, anyways, I see you have a well, yourself. Does it work?"

"For the most part, yes. The block and tackle system I use for hoisting jugs doesn't want to cooperate half the time."

"Yes, apparatuses with moving parts can be finicky." Alfonso unintentionally held his breath for a moment, and put forth, "I'm here to make a proposal. The Dourinuset monks are prepared to offer a sum of 300 gitis for every standard load of water delivered to us, more or less, indefinitely."

"That is an extremely generous offer, but I'm afraid I just don't have the time for that, with all my farm work and all."

Brother Alfonso stopped himself from holding his breath again. "I understand, but, respectfully, I must say that what I'm offering you is much, much more than what your crops are worth."

"That may be true, but I didn't make a promise to my deceased father to deliver water to a monastery. I did promise him that I would farm his cherished land to the best of my abilities, for as long as it was my land to farm."

"What if we hired someone else to do the delivering? All we'd need from you is use of the well."

"I wish I could help, but I use most of my water for irrigation," returned Savata. "I'd hate to risk running it dry. And as you said, wells are running dry these days."

"I recognize and honor your wishes and appreciate your time and attention. I wish you all the best, and since we can't come to an agreement, I must bid you farewell."

Savata showed Alfonso the door, and said, "Good luck to you and your quest. I really hope you do get your water."

Forlorn, Alfonso walked away from the Dearer farm, his mission unsuccessful. He was slightly confused about what was said about the irrigation, since all the land in the area was both fertile, and exhibited high moisture retention, rendering any form of irrigation virtually unnecessary.

Just like everything else in my life, a complete failure.

CHAPTER 2

"I THINK THAT'S it, Dourinuset," said Mick, looking at a far-off hill on the horizon. "What do you think our chances are exactly of being allowed passage into the monastery?"

Dave scratched his chin. "My guess is about ten percent, in light of the fact they rarely receive visitors."

"But why as high as ten percent then?"

"Because of our charm, Mick, obviously,"

"Obviously."

A wall cloud eerily loomed in the northwest like a giant tidal wave preparing to break over the countryside. As Mick and Dave walked, the dark cloud slowly advanced across the entirety of the sky. In the end, it turned out to be not as dangerous as it looked.

Mick howled, "Bbrruuuugg!"

Dave looked back at Mick in astonishment. "Now what in the heck was that?"

"You couldn't tell? I'm in a good mood and feel like communicating with the *soderths* in the woods."

"Why don't you talk with the crows instead? There are plenty of them to answer your call. I haven't seen a soderth fly overhead in weeks."

"That's part of the reason why I did it. I feel like calling some in."

"Only you." Dave chuckled and shook his head, expressing amusement.

Under no circumstances did Garobansurov harbor a way for its inhabitants—none humanly known of, to be exact—to speak telepathically to each other. But for some peculiar reason, Dave and Mick were sometimes able to nonverbally communicate to each other when and where to stop for the night, this being one of those nights.

The tents went up so fast a farmer off in the distance was slower in completing three entire laps of field planting. You could call it *journey beginning energy* or you could call it a slow farmer, if you chose to look at it from that perspective. Either way, Mother Nature wove her tapestry of will, and influenced Mick and Dave to set up camp in a particular place, one of great past significance next to an ancient Machergrair wayshrine.

It was said the seven ancient wayshrines of the Machergrair held certain mystical powers. Only four of the seven were ever actually found, including the one Mick and Dave were at. According to legend, whoever prayed at all seven would receive a gift of immeasurable power from the deity in honor of whom the wayshrines were erected. The name of the deity was lost in time. Nobody of the era was known to have ever received the gift, for all seven were never prayed at. Even if all seven were found, the proper prayers were long forgotten.

The primeval wayshrine was clearly worse for wear, due to having seen its share of weather. Half of it was now underground; geological forces made their own rules. The visible part consisted of stone structures at the perimeter, covered in vines. Moss was strewn everywhere. An oval shaped, central structure dominated the site, more intact than the erections at the periphery. A person could take refuge inside the central structure if it rained. People always liked to hold get-togethers within the central hub of the holy place, because they foolishly rationalized themselves being important when they did. Today was no exception.

Hawk and Leopard had technically stumbled across the wayshrine years ago, so their current visit wasn't their first time being there.

This time, they chanced upon individuals conversing in the central structure. Thanks to experience, Mick and Dave knew when voices were heard in suspicious places to stop and listen first, before making their presence known. It was wisdom that'd saved their lives in the past. Mick and Dave listened in cautiously from behind a stone pylon.

There were two voices, one deep, one nasal. The man with the deep voice said, "Everything is coming together. Every single person in the area turned them down."

"Splendid, now that that is settled, we can move to phase two of the plan: swoop in and charge as much as we want. This is the part where we make money," the man with the nasal voice stated.

"They won't expect a thing. The plan is genius."

"I feel bad for hustling such a dignified organization, but these are hard times, and we all need to do what needs to be done to survive," said the nasal voice.

"Indeed."

Mick and Dave had no idea as to what was being discussed. Distinguishing the pair of strangers presented no peril, Mick and Dave returned to their campsite for the night. They were in no hurry to explore what they'd already explored before, although they didn't remember what the ruins accurately looked like, since it was so long ago, and they'd seen so many others in the past.

Waking up with cheerful countenance, Dave shook Mick's tent. Mick apparently didn't sleep as well. "Wake up in there! We've got shit to do today."

Mick mumbled a few words bearing no resemblance to anything in the reasonably large Garobansurovian dictionary.

"I'll just assume you meant something comprehensible by that, and go ahead and start cooking breakfast," returned Dave.

Halfway through the cooking of the morning meal, Mick ungracefully staggered out of his tent. "So we've got shit to do today, eh?"

"We sure do."

"Well, alright then. Let's get at it," said Mick, feeling a bit more jovial, owing the upgrade in disposition to the fresh morning air. Contributing to the morning routine, Mick took his revitalization and began gathering more wood for the cooking fire.

Mick dropped an unwieldy batch of dry, gnarly wood near the firepit and said, "Do you think our Knowing Circles will be made of solid gold, or gold plated? I've never read any literature describing that particular aspect of them. Paintings portray them as being gold, though, that much I know."

"I couldn't say, but I do know they're inscribed with all past recipients."

"Which means our names will be on every medal henceforth."

"That they will. Kind of exciting isn't it?" Dave changed the subject. "Do you think the King will decree another general? There's always been at least four. The Nighteagle's passing—bless his soul—and Rayton's lethal defection opens up a couple offices."

"You'd think that would be the case, but I have no idea. Maybe we'll know the answer to that when we reach the Capital."

"Maybe we'll meet one of the other generals when we get there."

"Yes, it's possible Generals Dalarginta and Wiotweisten will be stationed at the Capital when we arrive. Who knows? Hopefully, they're still alive. The unpredictability of war is ever present, causing complete chaos to whatever it touches."

"Unfortunately, true. I think, Mick, we'll undoubtedly learn General Ulfenkerki's status when we reach the Capital."

"I agree. I do suppose that if something negative had happened to him or his army, we would've already heard."

"Probably," said Dave.

Mick ended the discussion of generals to go into his tent and sop up the water he'd spilled the night before.

Dave put out the campfire in preparation of heading to the Machergrair wayshrine. He projected, "Should we set the tents down now, or when we get back? And completely unrelated, Jason Thorncat's visit to our hometown sure made a lot of people blissful."

Mick stuck his head out of his tent to reply. "Yes, that was completely unrelated, and yes, it sure did. As for the tents, let's put them down when we get back. It'll give mine more time to dry out."

As he did once before, Dave laughed at his pal's clumsy misfortune involving the water spillage. "Sounds good."

Mick laughed, knowing full well what'd made Dave laugh.

Mick and Dave arrived at the wayshrine for a small bout of exploration, and noticed the locale was now void of people holding meetings. Silence covered the area.

Rubbing his hands across one of the stone edifices, Mick said, "Wasn't the Altar of Gerpardis we saw a few years ago also built by the Machergrair?"

"I believe it was. But it wasn't an official wayshrine."

"I see."

The pair refrained from taking up a lot of time to see the sights, being on somewhat of a schedule.

Having finished up investigating the wayshrine, they headed back to their campsite to pack up the tents and continue trekking. Being only twelve hours away from Dourinuset, they hoped to reach it by nightfall.

Pleasant to the senses, the morning was nice and cool, thanks in part to a slight breeze.

Having made good time by afternoon, the duo decided to rest their legs near a fallen tree, propped up on what looked like an old outhouse. "While we're here, do you feel like taking a dump?"

Dave laughed, and answered, "I would, if it had a roof and more than two walls."

"It's better than most of the things we use as bathrooms."

"That's true."

"This sure is one resilient privy, though, to have completely outlasted the accompanying dwelling of whoever lived here."

"That's true. Now, Mick, quit making me say that's true."

"Yup, that's true, I do keep making you say that."

Mick and Dave laughed, and searched their backpacks for a quick snack.

Dave stopped his search, grew in attentiveness, and uttered, "Did you hear that?"

"No," replied Mick, craning his neck to listen better. "I hear it now. It's coming from *over there*."

Mick pointed at a dense copse of Balsam trees fifty yards away. "What does it sound like to you?"

"I can't say I have a guess. It could be anything. Let's go over there and investigate."

"Oh, what fun are you? Go ahead and guess."

"Alright, Ill guess. I'll say it's a squirrel stuck in a live trap."

"Good guess. I'll say it's a child's kite that got away and landed in a tree. And it's now banging around against the tree trunk."

"Well, let's go see who's right."

The pair sauntered to the thick grove and realized they had to duck underneath limbs to enter its depths. There was much to be concealed within the thick vegetation.

After performing some probing, they realized both their guesses were wrong, and not just a little wrong. The sound was a man working with great fervor, trying to draw water from an aged, seemingly dry well—a robed man.

Dave spoke to the man. "I don't think the greatest of commitments will draw water from that particular well."

"I can't fail—not this time," voiced the stranger. "I'm sorry, it's just that it's imperative I locate a water source for us."

Mick looked at Dave, raised his brows in interest, then, looked back to the robed man, and said, "By 'us' do you mean you and the rest of the monks at the Dourinuset Monastery?"

"Yes, that is correct. My name is Brother Alfonso Alardo. Pleasure to meet you."

"My name is Mick Thraiker, and this is Dave Ghrere. It's a delight meeting you too."

"I know it may seem out of the ordinary to see a monk in the middle of nowhere, attempting to draw water from a broken well, but you could say our future depends on it."

"How is that? That appears fantastically implausible."

"You'd think that, but since our own well ran dry a while back, we've been trying to negotiate with everyone in the area for access to a water source, failing miserably at every attempt. If we don't procure an affordable water source soon, Dourinuset will be doomed."

Sometimes Mick grasped concepts faster, but this time it was Dave. As testament, his jaw dropped first. Mick's jaw dropped moments after. With dropped jaws, Mick and Dave stared at each other in astonishment.

Dave picked his jaw back up, and said to Alfonso, "You're never going to believe this, but coincidentally we sort of know what happened concerning your negotiation failures. By chance, we'd overheard a couple shady individuals speaking privately back at the Machergrair wayshrine. We can only now assume it was about your predicament. At the time, we had no idea what they were talking about, but now that you shared your little narrative with us, it all makes perfect sense."

Mick jumped into the dialogue. "Yes, we'd heard much of their conversation. These were the key points verbatim that apply: *Every single person in the area turned them down; phase two of the plan: swoop in and charge as much as we want; I feel bad for hustling such a dignified organization.*"

Brother Alfonso Alardo sat on a rock, feeling overwhelmed. "I think you're right. That sounds like it altogether relates to our dilemma. I couldn't imagine someone coming up with a plan like that for spite."

"Maybe it's not too late, maybe there's something we can do about these intransigents yet."

"Yes, Mick, this is your area of expertise, making a plan," Dave communicated.

Alfonso stood up with the look of hope in his eyes. "I'm all-in. Let's intervene in this treachery."

It occasionally took a while for Mick to conceive flawless plans, so in the meantime, Brother Alardo shared his tragic story with Mick and Dave. He spoke of how his wife left him, how he'd been moments away from killing himself, and how he'd heard God's calling—effectively, joining the monastery. Every time Alfonso imparted the account—he didn't do it often, for it was too sad—his eyes glossed over at the end. This time was no different.

Feeling great empathy, Dave said, "I do wish Mick, or I could do something to help ease your pain, but I'm afraid that realm of healing is something you must summon alone."

"Thank you, Mr. Ghrere. Every day, I face the process alone. Well, almost alone. God stands beside me," acknowledged Alardo. "I routinely ask the Infinite Lord for serenity."

"That's about all you can do," Dave stated.

Mick laid his hand on his new friend's shoulder. "Well, I don't have enough information to come up with the quintessential plan right now, but I've got a start."

"Sounds good, how do we begin?"

Mick paused, paced back and forth a few times, pondered for a moment, and responded, "First, in order to prevent any illegitimate, disagreeable deals with these untrusting characters, you must hurry back to the monastery to inform your brethren of the situation. Next, Dave and I will inconspicuously visit the biggest company in the area and try to ascertain some information. Fundamentally, the most prosperous business of a particular rural area holds great influence over people's everyday lives. The odds are good that sort of influence is related to your predicament, Alfonso. And I'm guessing the most prosperous is the hefty sawmill on the river."

"I do believe you are correct," Alfonso said. "I can't think of anything in the neighborhood more instrumental than the sawmill. If I remember correctly, I think it's called George's Mill."

"How creative," Mick blurted.

Since meeting Hawk and Leopard, Brother Alfonso's face revealed its first smile. "Yes, quite the creative name indeed. Excellent, I will hurry back now to enlighten my brothers. Hopefully, everything turns out. It would be a great tragedy if my brothers and I end up having to abandon the monastery. Godspeed, my friends."

"Same to you. We will see you soon."

"Farewell, for now."

Having already distanced himself from Dave and Mick, Brother Alfonso stopped abruptly. He turned around, and jogged back to Dave and Mick to say, "Whenever you encounter a fork in the road on your way up the hill to Dourinuset, look for the way marked with triple cedar trees. They will guide you in the right direction. We planted them like that, so certain people would know the most efficient way to the top."

"That's handy! Thank you, good sir," said Dave.

"You're welcome," yelled the monk, jogging away.

Mick and Dave intended to head in the opposite direction as Alfonso, but before starting the walk to the mill, they needed to grab their gear still situated back at the dilapidated outhouse. They inched their way through the thick vegetation, ducked under the same limbs, and found their equipment right where they'd left it.

The mill wasn't far. Since they walked fast, it didn't take long to arrive at George's Mill's array of large and small wooden buildings. The first thing they noticed was the large building containing the massive saw, conveniently situated on the river. The saw was connected to a giant waterwheel, currently in laborious motion. Nothing supplied power for mechanics better than the might of a river.

Mick's presumption of the sawmill having a huge influence over its part of Garobansurov was more-or-less correct. Other than influence, the mill supplied an area within a twenty-mile radius with valuable lumber and wood products. In addition, the mill enjoyed a greater range to the south, due to the ability to float wood down the river on barges for delivery. The other delivery method was far less efficient: a long drudging walk with a cart. Nobody liked that particular job, but there always seemed to be someone willing to do it.

Fifty miles up the river to the north in Bertradia was another sawmill, posing as George's Mill's greatest competition. It was a smaller mill, but it could undercut many wood bids north of George's mill, since they could obviously also float wood downstream.

Selling lumber was fiercely competitive, no different than every other aspect of life.

"So how do you want to do this, Dave? Should we devise a speech, or should we just wing it?"

"Since we've no idea what exactly we're facing, I suggest winging it."

"In that case, you can do the talking."

"I would, but you know as well as I you'll just jump into the conversation anyways, like you always do."

"I was hoping you didn't notice that."

"Oh, please," Dave responded, and joined Mick in cackling. "Alright, my fellow adventurer, let's go start the show."

Spread seemingly unsystematically throughout the property, the diversified buildings offered no indication as to which was the main office. So, the pair had to guess where to go. Their first guess was wrong, having entered a storage room. Thankfully, avoiding further embarrassment, the second building they tried was indeed the one they desired: the office.

They walked up to a half glass/half wood counter, behind which stood a tall, bearded man.

Mick followed Dave's lead. "Good afternoon, sir."

"Hello, what can I do you for?" asked the clerk.

"We're in the process of building customized church pews and need to make an order."

"Will it be a delivery, or will you be hauling it yourselves?"

"We will be hauling it ourselves," answered Dave. "I'm not really looking forward to hauling it, but we didn't get paid very well for the job, so we have to cut as many corners as we can."

"I hear you on that," returned the bearded fellow.

Realizing where Dave was heading with his rationale, Mick joined the exchange, "We have the main pieces, but we need enough oak boards for legs and trimmings." Mick expatiated on the sizes of the boards he and Dave needed, or at least pretended to need.

"I'm pretty sure we've plenty of that. I'll have to double check, but I think we'll be able to accommodate you post-haste, and for a reasonable price."

"Excellent. The more room for profit, the better," noted Mick.

"That's the name of the game," replied the clerk.

The employee left the building to round up the wood, leaving Dave and Mick behind. While patiently waiting, Dave reached into his pocket and pulled out some change, which he put into a jar sitting on the counter. Finishing the transaction, Dave grabbed a drink off the nearby shelf, a convenience offered by the mill to those waiting for their orders to be filled.

Mick blurted, "What is it?"

"Apple juice."

"Do you have any more change in your pocket? I wouldn't mind some of that juice. All my change is deep within my pack."

"I believe I do." Dave dropped some more coins into the jar, echoing a clinking sound, and Mick grabbed a tasty beverage for himself.

While Mick and Dave were finishing their drinks, a couple new faces brought in boards, followed by the man originally working the counter.

The bearded man lowered his boards to the floor, looked at Dave's apple juice, and said, "It's fresh. I squeezed and filtered it this morning."

"It's undeniably first-rate."

In the matter of minutes, all the boards ordered were stacked on the office floor, ready for Mick and Dave. The three workers stood behind the counter, two of which had no real reason to.

"The total comes to eighteen gitis."

Dave paid the balance,—an easy balance to pay, for Dave and Mick had plenty of gitis left over from their last adventure.

"Now we can finish the work for the annoyingly frugal monks," noted Mick. "I can't wait to be done with this job and be rid of them."

The tall, bearded man commented, "You can say that again. We are currently in the midst of working out a sort of deal with them too, but they are being awfully stubborn."

"How so?"

"Oh, it's a long story, but it involves the owner of the mill wanting financial payback for an incident that happened a long time ago. It involves the monastery and the mayor of some town somewhere. I guess he bribed everyone in the area to back off so he could hike up a bid for water delivery."

Mick nodded in understanding. "Well, hopefully we can get our job done without incident."

"Good luck to you and have a good day."

Dave had an idea, so he spoke: "Before we leave, there's actually one more thing. Is the owner of the mill around at all? We know someone who is interested in buying the whole place and would like to speak to him about the matter on our friend's behalf."

"I think he may be available." The tall, bearded man turned to the other two employees, who apparently both were out of shape, still catching their breaths from bringing in the wood. "Will you go and see if you can round up George?"

"No problem."

Two employees left the building, while the bearded man, Mick, and Dave remained. They exchanged pleasantries, while waiting. Mick wasn't quite sure what kind of idea Dave had in mind, by requesting a get-together with the owner, so as soon as the bearded man wasn't looking, Mick shot Dave a confused look, hoping to get some answers. Dave responded to the confused look with a cheesy grin, and emphatic thumbs up. Mick found no answers from Dave, but he did find himself having to cover up a laugh through a snort, due to the comical, cheesy grin.

One of the workers who had left to find the owner returned, and said, "Come with me, I'll show you where George is."

Mick and Dave were escorted forty yards away into another small building, adorned by a fancy interior. A man sat whittling a chunk of wood into what looked like a sailboat. "Come on in guys, have a seat. I'm George, the owner of this sawmill."

"Hello George, my name is Mick, and the fellow next to me is Dave."

George wasn't much of a talker, so he got right to the point. "So, I've been told you wanted to speak to me about business?"

Dave responded, "That is correct. A friend of ours, who goes by the name Darmaga Gethitz, the mayor of Bertradia, asked us to offer you a sum to purchase your mill."

George set down his whittling project, leaned back in his squeaky chair, and grew a weird look on his face. "First of all, why did he send you two, instead of stopping in himself?"

Dave replied, "He couldn't make the fifty-mile trip. His father is gravely ill. He wanted to strike a deal as soon as possible, figuring Mick and I talking to you instead of a courier doing so would be more personable. Darmaga requires a huge supply of wood, both at the present and indefinitely. Buying the mill outright he said would be the most efficient way of accomplishing this."

George interceded, "Another thing I'll bring up is it seems a twist of bizarre fate Darmaga wants to buy my mill now, when a while ago, he inconveniently canceled a wood order, the biggest I've ever gotten. I lost so much money because of it."

Just prior to replying to George's statement, Dave quickly turned to look at Mick with that same unforgettable, cheesy grin. "He never did tell us why he did that."

George stood up, enveloped by passion. "It was those blasted monks! Darmaga told me he wanted to build a church. He ordered all the wood from me as opposed to the closer mill, saying he wanted it from me because he was feuding with that mill's proprietors. I went ahead and had my employees spend hundreds of non-refundable man hours getting all the wood together for shipment and at the last moment Darmaga canceled the order, telling me the monks at Dourinuset convinced him not to build a church because of some sacred reason, some holy mumbo jumbo. So because of the monks, I lost all of the money I had spent putting the order together."

Dave shook his head. "My loyalties lie to the righteous, and I have to call Darmaga out. You got swindled by the seemingly underhanded Darmaga. I'm surprised you haven't seen for yourself, but we've been to Bertradia lately and there is a huge, extravagant church there. Also, there's a large increase in the size of Bertradia's sawmill."

"You have got to be kidding me! He specifically told me he wasn't going to build a church!"

"Wouldn't it seem more plausible a group of monks would promote, not hinder, the building of churches. I'd bet he wasn't actually feuding with the nearby sawmill, but acting on its behalf, trying to sabotage you. By doing that, he probably got a fabulous deal on the wood for his town's new church."

"That makes perfect sense. I just can't believe nobody has told me about the church before. I guess everyone I know never goes anywhere. And you're right, monks don't usually condemn the building of churches. In fact, they hardly ever meddle with other people's business. It's not their way. How could I have been so blind? Here I came up with this magnificent scheme to swindle the innocent monks, and it turns out I was the one that was swindled. I'm such a fool! Out of curiosity, what sum was Darmaga offering?"

"After negotiations, 16,000 gitis with an initial offer of 18,000."

"Interesting. I certainly wouldn't have accepted the deal. Maybe I would've gone as low as 22,000, but even if it was an agreeable offer, I still wouldn't have sold to that unscrupulous prick. By the way, you couldn't have been too good of friends with him?"

"Not best of friends. Sometimes you go with your gut, and side with the moral high ground."

"Good point, I would've done the same," said George. "So, I understand that you're currently doing a job for the Dourinuset monks?"

Finally able to rejoin the conversation, Mick voiced, "Yes, we're building pews for them."

"Will you be going up to Dourinuset to deliver them?"

"Yup, that's the plan."

"Tremendous. That means the two of you will be seeing the monks a lot sooner than I'd get a chance to. Will you do me a great favor when you see them, and describe to them everything that had transpired here today? And can you extend the sincerest of apologies for the misunderstanding, and tell them we'd be honored to deliver barrels of water to them, weekly or whenever needed, for the price of the lowest offer they gave to anyone in the area, first year free."

Mick replied, "We will certainly do that for you. I'm sure they'll understand the circumstances and will be thankful for your newfound generosity."

"Excellent! I'll send a cart up next week. I'd send one today, but the person I'm going to have do it won't be available until then." Delicately, George reached into one of the drawers in his desk. "As a token of my sincerest apologies, I would greatly appreciate it if you would give this wood carving to the monks. It's the best one I've ever done, taking me just over a year to complete."

"Sure, we'll do that." Dave grasped the carving and admired its exquisiteness. "Is this an exact replica of the King's Castle at the Capital?"

"Not exact, but close. I have only been to the Capital twice, so I whittled it by memory. It's carved to scale as much as I could."

"The detail is extraordinarily impressive. It has a majestic feel to it. I'm sure they'll love it."

George thanked Mick and Dave one last time, bade them farewell, and picked back up his sailboat. He then carved it with a smile.

On their way out of the mill, Hawk and Leopard were sure to grab their wood—boards which had no purpose other than giving Mick and Dave a reason to visit the mill in the first place. The pair started for Dourinuset, their arms loaded with uselessness.

When out of earshot of anyone at the mill, Mick said to Dave, "What are we going to do with this heavy, awkward lumber?"

"I'm sure the solution will present itself along the way."

"Hopefully sooner than later. Carrying this isn't the most fun thing in the world."

"Agreed."

Mick looked back towards the mill to double-check, making absolute certain there wasn't anyone around to overhear. "I just have to know, how in the world did you know there was a big church in Bertradia? We haven't been there in a long time. And how did you know that that was what George was mad at the monks about?"

Dave put on his cheesy smile, the one he'd learned to love rather quickly, and replied, "I had no idea what George was mad at the monks about, before going into his office. That part just worked out. My whole plan revolved around my knowledge, and I'm sure yours as well, chances were low the monks actually carried out something unprincipled. I used that to my advantage going in. I knew something was shady, hoping we'd get lucky and stumble upon the source. But most importantly, I calculated Darmaga Gethitz to be the only person of power on this side of Garobansurov exploitative enough to do something as underhanded as frame monks. It was the key to my plan, and thankfully it worked."

"What if there actually is no large church in Bertradia?"

"I'm sure, once we get to Dourinuset, the monks will validate the fact they never persuaded Darmaga not to build a church. That'll be all the proof I need there is one, or at least some sort of large, wooden building."

"It'll be all the proof I need too," stated Mick. "It's possible Darmaga just used the monks as a way out of something, having in some situation bitten off more than he could chew."

"Yes, it's possible Darmaga used the monks in that regard, but unlikely. Nobody wants to exploit a group of monks for something minor, whether you believe in a God or not. It's not worth it."

"I agree."

Dave and Mick would soon learn there was indeed a large, relatively new church in Bertradia.

CHAPTER 3

BY THE TIME the two were five miles from the mill, their arms had gotten unbearably sore, having carried the wood for so long. Mick declared, "I'm spent. Either we camp here and burn this wood in our nightly fire or we start knocking on doors to give it away."

"I say we burn it," Dave replied. "It's not worth the risk to give the wood away to the wrong person. You never know who could piece together our ruse."

Mick dropped his armload of wood like it was already on fire. "Oh, that feels so good. I'd hate to burn eighteen gitis worth of wood, but I'd hate to lose my arms even more."

"Me too. I figure at about noon tomorrow, we'll reach the Dourinuset hill and start the ascension."

Mick added, "And summit around 4 or 5 o'clock."

The campsite was established rather fast that evening, mainly because they didn't have to spend any time looking for firewood. Over the fire, the companions cooked a meal fit for the wealthy.

"This is one tasty bird."

Fairly sweltering rays of sun poked through the branches of an uncharacteristically large aspen tree, reminding Dave to open one of his tent's flaps to let the heat of the day escape. Improving sleeping conditions through temperature regulation was never a bad idea. Mick didn't need to be reminded, he had already opened a flap.

It was harder than usual to quarantine the fire. The wood from the mill was exceptionally dry and burned extremely violently. Any side trips away from the fire were out of the question that evening.

It took a while to burn all the wood, so Thraiker and Ghrere stayed up later than typical. Normally, that time of year, they never made it far enough into the night to see the Frayity Constellation, but that night they witnessed the eleven-starred wonder.

"Have you ever considered why the middle star of the Frayity Constellation seems to spin in circles?"

"I've noticed it too, Dave, but I've never given it any conscious thought, nor have I heard or read anything about it."

"Neither have I. I'm going to now, though."

"So much wonder in the night sky. It'd be hard to put to mind all its mysteries."

The coolness of night enveloped the twosome. The pleasant weather coupled with the viewing of the Frayity discussion sparked the pair to stare adoringly into the night sky for over an hour. Dave and Mick searched for new and overpowering sensations. They found some and slept wonderfully.

Refreshed, and raring to go in the morning, Dave and Mick packed up and hit the ground running. They were really looking forward to the day and couldn't help but think a lovely one was just waiting to happen. The trail to Dourinuset got rockier the closer they got, making the walk arduous, but only slightly.

Dave observed the stones in the trail. One caught his eye, so he bent over to pick it up. "It's crumbly and gray. This stone sure is far from home."

"You're right. I'd bet it's from the Cadmiust formation, which surfaces a hundred miles from here, I believe."

"Glaciation at its finest."

"Yup. The tremendous sheets of ice like carrying rocks more than I do."

Noon approached, and as predicted, the massive shadow of the Dourinuset hill was cast upon the ground before Mick and Dave. The hugeness of the shadow foreshadowed just how intense the climb up to the monastery was going to be.

Dave looked up at the hill. "Just envision having to make this ascent with a water cart once a week."

"I don't think they're getting a cart up this hill very easily."

"Unlike what George thinks, it'll probably take the efforts of more than one person."

"True," said Mick. "Well, let's start climbing."

The lower slopes didn't force too sharp of an incline upon the pair, but eventually it'd give way to a much steeper gradient.

"Maybe we should stash our gear somewhere, lightening our loads for the climb," suggested Dave.

"You can if you want, but I'm not risking losing anything."

"Good point, me neither."

Having been on the hill for an hour, they reached the first trail divergent.

"Triple cedars are what we want."

"Here they are, Mick. We take the *right* path."

"You'd think, since we're going clockwise around and up the hill, we'd always take the right-sided path."

"Unless, the right path is a dummy path, and it dead ends."

"I guess that's possible. If that's the case, then the monks, or somebody else would have to come to the hill often to perform upkeep on the dead-end trails."

"True," answered Mick.

The duo looked into the distance through breaks in the canopy and saw they were halfway up the hill. No signs of civilization anywhere. It was truly a sight to behold.

The sword-wielding pair came to another fork in the road and looked for the triple-cedar marker. Upon locating it, Dave voiced, "I guess someone does come here to groom trails, this time we do go to the left."

"Well, I'll be darned."

"Or maybe Brother Alfonso wanted to lead us on a wild goose chase, for the fun of it."

Mick laughed, "I highly doubt that."

Eventually, Dave and Mick were coerced to demonstrate how strong their legs were, for the uphill climb got crueler and crueler. Along with the steeper gradient, the upper division of the hill presented more of a diverse population of birds. The creatures of wing happily dispensed their harmonious composition to the backpackers. Mick and Dave appreciated the concert.

After six more forks in the trail—four going to the right and two to left—Dave and Mick finally caught a glimpse of the stone monastery's towering eastern side. "Twenty minutes, and we'll be there."

"Looks like you were right, Dave. Five hours to climb the hill."

"We've also positively confirmed that men of the cloth don't lead travelers on wild goose chases."

"For sure," agreed Mick.

"At least not ones they want to easily locate the monastery."

"Too true. That sure was quite the maze system. Just imagine the view the monks get to wake up to every morning."

"Oh, yes. Panoramic to its fullest."

The twenty minutes passed quickly.

The front doors of Dourinuset had a grand, stone staircase leading up to them. At the top of the steps, looming mysteriously, the vine-covered heavy-appearing doors looked almost as if they required four people to open them—two for each side. The pair ascended the staircase with excitement and nervousness.

Dave took hold of the rusty knocker, pulled it back, and let it slam back into the door, three times in total. For a minute Mick and Dave waited before Abbot Ferdinand and Brother Alfonso came to the door. Brother Alfonso was happy to see Mick and Dave again, and spoke first: "Welcome to Dourinuset, our home on high. Come in, please, and sit on one of those couches, there." Alfonso pointed. "Your legs must be sore from climbing the brute."

"Good to see you again, Brother Alardo," extended Mick. "Thank you so much for the hospitality. And, yes, sore legs indeed."

On the quartet's way over to the red couches just off to the right of the front doors, Brother Alfonso introduced Brother Ferdinand. The two facing couches sat in an alcove with no windows of its own. Along with mystifying darkness, the alcove exhibited a thick rug, and a few tables with eye-pleasing, artful statuettes atop.

Sitting unexpectedly cross-legged, the head monk said, "I hope you found the triple cedars well enough. We'd calculated it takes those who don't know the trick an hour and a half longer to reach us than those who do."

"Yup, they certainly came in handy," answered Dave. "On the way up we wondered, who does the upkeep of the trails? They were rather nice trails."

"We actually do. Every day we take a few hours out of our daily prayer routine to perform the anonymous labors required to keep things running smoothly. Once in a while these labors take a few of us to the hill for maintenance. It's actually one of our more favorite tasks—well, it is for a lot of us anyways."

"Brother Alfonso chuckled, and to his superior said, "How can a task be more favorite?"

Without hesitation, Abbot Ferdinand joined in on the laugh—monks of Garobansurov were known to reveal an excellent sense of humor. "Oh, you know what I meant. I suppose we should get to the point and talk about why you're here. Brother Alardo told me all about your run-in with him, and about what you found out about our water situation."

Having just finished chuckling himself, Mick responded, "Actually, to tell the truth, we were already on the way here to see if we could visit, before we'd run into Brother Alfonso, and learnt about your water crisis."

"Coming *here*, even knowing we rarely receive visitors?" emitted Ferdinand.

"Yes, we've always wanted to make the trip, taking the chance on admittance, but we'd never gotten around to it, so much going on with the war and what-not. If we'd gotten turned away, at least we could say we tried. We're on our way to the Capital, having left a week early to venture here along the way."

Brother Ferdinand inquired, "Nice, from where have you come? And what beckons you to the Capital?"

Dave answered, "We are from Chalatore, and you might not believe it when I tell you, but we're headed to the Capital to receive the Knowing Circle, both of us, one for each."

The abbot's expression became animated. "What the heck did you guys do to merit such an accolade?"

Mick replied, "We re-captured a pivotal fort and helped win the Battle of Sarwa."

Brother Ferdinand was awestruck. "Really! that was you two? We don't hear much about the outside world here, but we have heard about that. I'll be darned. And here you are, also helping us in our time of need. What *don't* you guys do?"

"Well, let me think. We don't rescue cats from trees."

Dave interrupted, "Wait, Mick, what about that time Gadzud's cat jumped from his roof to the tree, and you jumped from the window to the tree to get it down?"

"I guess I stand corrected. We do indeed do everything." The quartet laughed. "Now to get to the important stuff." Mick expounded on everything that'd transpired at the mill. He described in detail the whole confrontation, how a man named Darmaga Gethitz blamed the monks for a deal gone awry. He concluded the telling with how George came to his senses, and how is now going to supply the water, cheaply.

Brother Alfonso stood up and paced away to avoid anyone seeing his pale complexion from the overwhelming good news. Brother Ferdinand clapped once, pumped his fist, and spoke. "Yes, I have never even heard of a man named Darmaga. And that is true, we wouldn't ever try to persuade anyone away from building churches, no matter the denomination."

Brother Alfonso found his way back to the alcove to add, "I just knew when we parted ways the two of you would solve our problem. Sometimes in life, you just know people."

Ferdinand asserted, "It seems you guys *are* deserving of Knowing Circles."

Dave smiled. "We're really not that nice and helpful, we just get bored a lot."

The monks laughed. "Sure, sure. I think you say that to everyone."

Mick Thraiker attached, "George said he'll deliver the water at the cost of the lowest offer you gave to anyone down the hill, with the first year being free. And as a further token of his apologies he asked us to give you this. He said it was his best work ever." Mick handed over the wood carving of the King's Castle.

"It's beautiful. I know just where to put it." Ferdinand placed the carving next to the other artful pieces on the tables of the alcove.

"It fits in seamlessly," noted Alfonso. "A fine addition."

"Splendid," Ferdinand responded. "Now to change the subject, you'd mentioned you were on your way here in an attempt to accomplish the rare feat of being welcomed inside?"

"Yeah, we were. No guts, no glory."

"Well then," the abbot emitted, "I'm pleased to announce you'll be our first overnight guests in almost six years."

"Wonderful," erupted Mick.

"I'm curious," said Dave, "who was it that'd visited you six years ago?"

"A few priests from afar had spent the weekend. Something that happens more frequently is priests from relatively nearby coming to join us in mass, but they'll only stay for the day."

"Fascinating."

The abbot stood up. "Let's retire from the drawing room, introduce you to the rest of the Dourinuset monks, and tell them the good news."

Alfonso said, "Yes, they will be ecstatic. Up to this point, our very existence here has been in jeopardy. Mick, Dave, your intervention has been our saving grace."

Plain would be an understatement. A bed, rug, end table, candle lamp, desk with parchment and pen, and a wardrobe were the only things in each and every one of the monks' monastic cells. Mick and Dave's would be the same. They met all the monks, told them the good news, and were about to be shown their individual sanctuaries.

Standing in a cool, still hallway, Ferdinand pointed to two unoccupied bedrooms. "Monks go to bed early and wake up early. We encapsulate highly meticulous schedule keeping. It's been like that for thousands of years. You're not expected to maintain such a schedule, Mick, Dave, while you're here, but if you did, we'd be appreciative beyond measure."

"I'm sure we'll align our schedules with yours," returned Dave. "We want to get the most out of our visit."

"Great," returned Ferdinand. "Good night. Sleep well."

Dave had fallen asleep, and Brother Alfonso paid Mick a short visit in his room, just before he too fell asleep. "After first service tomorrow, I'll show the two of you the grounds, and the rest of the building."

"Excellent, sounds fascinating. I really can't express how amazing it is to be here."

"I'm glad to hear that," said Alardo. "We don't really strive to be amazing here. But if it happens, all the better."

"Indeed."

"I'll see you tomorrow. In the morning, you and Dave can fill your wardrobes' basins with wash water, which will be situated just down the hall. We warm up a fair supply for all. At 5 o'clock, morning bells will ring, at 5:30, first service will commence."

"See you at dawn, Brother Alardo. Good night."

"Good night."

Brother Alardo retired to his room while Mick opened up his wardrobe to see what else besides the water basin lurked within. What he expected to see was all he saw—seven robes, one for each day of the week. *They must do laundry exactly once a week. Good thing I've my pack containing my own clothes, I'm not really the robe type. We'll see tomorrow if Dave is.*

To ensure all the monks heard the alarm, the predesignated morning bellringer walked through the hallway of the bedroom wing a total of three times, waving the bell emphatically. It was the same routine every morning, probably the most regular bell ringing on all Garobansurov.

Mick rose to the alarm, and went to fill his water basin, without delay. Dave did the same but was a step behind Mick, Dave having slept a little more soundly, finding it hard to remove himself from such a superb doze. Both made themselves as presentable as possible for their first full day at Dourinuset.

Both with the trajectory of the church, Mick met up with Dave. They'd intended to adhere to the monks' strict schedule but didn't intend to adhere as much to their strict silence regiment. "Awe, that's disappointing. I was hoping to see you in a robe this morning," Mick said to Dave.

"It's just as disappointing for me. I was thinking a robe would suit you better."

"You know, I think you could be right, Dave. Though, I'm still going to pass."

Fittingly, the church was the biggest, most extravagant part of the monastery. It had a high, arched ceiling, supported by massive, wooden beams. The walls were amazingly decorated, conceptualizing through murals many years of their religion's history. Twenty pews, ten on each side of the main aisle, highlighted the floor. The monks sat in the left-side, front two pews, in front of the altar—a stone-cutter's masterpiece which looked even more ancient than the monastery itself.

Mick and Dave sat just behind the monks. The rest of the church was empty. Being head monk, it was Abbot Ferdinand's responsibility to say mass. On rare occasions, priests from surrounding locales would come to perform the service, but this particular service wasn't one of those infrequent circumstances. Along with all the monks, Brother Ferdinand was ordained proper, so mass would be the same as if given by a visiting priest. Any of the monks could lead mass, but they customarily didn't.

During the service, Hawk and Leopard did something they'd do only on the most uncommon of situations: sing willfully. Despite their lack of ability to sing on pitch, they still tried their best, hoping no one would notice their tone deafness. Dave and Mick couldn't help but think the monks had heard their erroneous notes, since they didn't receive any compliments on their singing after church.

After the church service, Thraiker and Ghrere stepped out of the main church doors, and as promised Brother Alfonso approached to supply the grand tour. "So, how was your first service?"

"It was rather enjoyable and enlightening," replied Mick.

"Good. Glad you seized benefit. There will be four more today."

"Hopefully, in forthcoming services we'll sing better."

"You guys sang just fine," Alfonso declared.

"You're just saying that to be nice." Mick chuckled. "I'm sure all the monks are at this moment discussing my and Dave's poor crooning."

"How much do you want to bet they're not?"

Dave joined in. "I thought monks couldn't gamble?"

"You're right, we don't gamble, not with money anyways. But we bet chores all the time."

"Well, in that case, I'll bet a chore," Mick said. "What chore do you have to do today, Brother Alfonso?"

"We'll have an assortment of chores throughout the week. Some are better than others. I propose that if I win, you have to do a chore of my choosing, one that I don't like, and vice-versa."

"That sounds fair. You're on." To finalize the bet, as was customary fashion, Brother Alfonso and Mick shook hands. Mick continued, "Now, how is it going to be possible to figure out the winner? Are we going to run around, asking everyone if they talked about our singing after church?"

"We won't have to do that. I have already won."

"How do you figure?"

"Easy, I know none of the monks held discussion about your singing after church, because during that particular time slot resides one our silent mandates, so I'm quite positive no one talked in the slightest. You can either take my word for it, or when the mandate expires we can ask them individually if they'd talked, your choice," said the monk, smiling like a man who knew he'd just won a bet.

Mick knew he'd been defeated. "I hate pulling weeds. Please don't let it be that."

"No, it won't be that, but I do think I've just the job for you, assuming there's no major amending of this week's task agenda. And trust me, it isn't going to be pretty."

"Fair enough. You win some and you lose some."

The trio walked outdoors, down the path heading towards the main courtyard, where Brother Alfonso desired to begin the tour of the grounds. It was so early in the morning the grass was still wet and cold to the touch, grass so cold the birds prone to delicacy stayed clear, perched on whatever high ground of the courtyard they could find—benches, statues, trees, bushes. The locale also contained paths, flowers, and a plethora of anonymous odds and ends—the monks spared no expense for landscaping. Plus, the courtyard offered many isolated places, perfect for meditation and prayer.

Taking in the beauty, the threesome noticed Brother Azoundaja praying silently next to the statue of Sartinhal, a life-size monument commemorating the revered healer of old. Focused on his craft, Azoundaja kneeled motionless, not paying any attention to the courtyard's newcomers. Not wanting to bother Brother Azoundaja, Alardo ushered Mick and Dave through the courtyard quickly, talking only sparingly.

Having passed the confines of the courtyard, Alfonso escorted Mick and Dave to the trailhead of one of three hiking trails meandering through the woods adjacent to the monastery. The three hiking trails were completely removed from the trail network connecting the bottom to the top of Dourinuset hill.

Alfonso voiced, "Dare I ask, how are you enjoying Dourinuset thus far?"

"I haven't seen too many things equal in majesty."

"I'm glad to hear that, Mick. Obviously, you've seen the trails coming up the hill, but there are three additional scenic hiking trails here at the top of the hill, each one offering something different. We are standing at the trailhead of the shortest trail. It's three-quarters of a mile long, and pretty much just circles the monastery. You start here, walk the little lip, proceed to circumnavigate the building and courtyards, and then end back up at the lip. The trail is surprisingly beautiful for how short it is, maybe because it's the one most thoroughly groomed, or maybe only because it's the one least taxing."

"I think I've seen parts of it already," voiced Dave.

"The second trail starts 200 yards to the east. It's a pretty fierce, hilly trail, dispensing a mile and a half of unavoidable rocks. Stepping on all the rocks lodged in the trail really does a number on the old ankles. You can try to steer clear of them, but there's just too many. But there is one rock alignment near the far end that makes the trail a standout. You'll know it when you see it."

"Sounds fascinating."

"The third and longest trail starts fifty yards to the west—two miles worth of vistas, trees, rocks, and serenity. It's an easier walk than the second trail."

Dave jumped in, "Before we continue onward, I have to ask something that is rather important to Mick and I."

"Sure, ask away."

"By chance, on an excursion through the woods, have you or any of the other monks ever come across the rare sight of a pine tree containing black needles?"

"Oh my, wouldn't that be quite the sight. I have never known of such an anomaly. I'd never heard the others speak of something like that either. I must say, why do you ask?"

Mick replied, "When we get back to quarters, we'll show you the proof, but believe it or not, a long time ago, Dave and I stumbled across a single black needle pine tree hanging off the side of a cliff. Mysteriously, it hung there by nothing but sheer will—not a single root had dug itself into any part of the cliff-face for stability, as if it was magic, magic like in the tales of old. Taking advantage of the miraculous properties, we cut off two limbs and used them to construct two swords. The swords, which are back in the rooms, have a gripping capability that only seeing for yourself can explain effectively. So that's why we're always on lookout for other black needle pine trees. One day, we'd like to solve the mystery of how in fact such a power can exist."

Amazed by what he'd heard, Brother Alfonso replied, "Is that how the two of you captured Fort Gravividon by yourselves?"

"No, that was done on Dave's physical prowess alone."

Dave laughed. "*My physical prowess alone*, you're too funny."

Mick tried to hold back laughter, but failed. "In all seriousness though, yes, the swords helped, but mainly it was teamwork that blazed the trail to victory. We also received a lending hand from a prisoner we freed during the capturing."

"Way to fight the good fight. I definitely would like to see the swords."

"Of course, brother. They'll astonish, I'm sure."

In the midst of imagining what the swords looked like, Alardo remembered something else in the area he wanted to show his guests. He led them to a steeper part of the hill and pointed. "Speaking of mysteries, that right there is one to us. Do you see it, the two noticeable, parallel, earthen embankments that go all the way down this part of the hill?"

"Yup, I see them," answered Dave.

"Me too."

Alfonso continued, "The bizarre thing is we've no idea why they're there, or what they're there for. We have no record of them anywhere, which is odd, since we've detailed records of everything, records that go back into history a long way."

Mick and Dave inched up to the unexplainable mounds for a closer inspection.

After a few minutes of study, Mick returned to Alfonso, and said, "Do you think it may be possible they were constructed even before the monastery was built, which would've been a very long time ago, since the monastery is already ancient?"

"Some of us think that, since almost everything that'd happened here at Dourinuset had been written down with great perfectionism. There's no mention of the linear mounds anywhere."

Dave dropped the rock he was inspecting and straightened back up. He sauntered over to the conversing duo to join their discussion. "One might think it was a way to slide felled trees for timber down to the bottom of the hill, but that's unlikely, because there's never really been a need in Garobansurov to labor so hard for lumber. We've always been endowed with a substantial amount of trees. Sliding them down the hill seems overly arduous."

"That's true," agreed Mick. "It also could resemble a child's sledding hill, an extremely dangerous one. If it was a sledding hill, all it would take is one mistake and instant death would result. So, on further thought, I'm positive it wasn't a sledding hill."

"We've been through that same thought process," stated Alardo. "Someday, the enigma will be solved, but for now, it'll remain a mystery, for there are other things to see. Go ahead and keep thinking about it though."

"I'm sure we will."

Brother Alardo led the tour through another courtyard and brought the men to one of the more instrumental parts of the monastery—the farming section. It was huge, and where all the food for the monks was grown and corralled. The garden was massive, containing every plant imaginable. On the periphery were many fruit trees. Chicken, goat, and pig pens were positioned on the eastern side. Milk was gotten from the goats, some of which was made into cheese. The monks also maintained a small aquaculture pond, obviously used to farm fish for consumption.

At the time, two monks were tending to the garden. "I'm sure at one point or another, the two of you will experience farm duty," voiced Alfonso.

"I'll look forward to it," returned Dave.

"I'm confident your designated work will be impactful, but I'm more so convinced the chore I choose for Mick will be especially impactful." The monk unleashed a rare chuckle.

"Oh boy," let out Mick.

"We are pretty much self-sufficient here at Dourinuset, except of course for the water lately. The small amount of gitis that we do need, we earn by selling wine. Our plentiful fruit trees supply the ingredients for that tasty treat."

"Where do you make the wine?"

"I can show you that, but it's nothing special, just a large room housing various wine apparatus."

Alfonso guided the procession to and through the wine room. They stayed for only a few minutes, but before exiting, Mick and Dave were given a sample. "Delicious."

"Now for the best part, other than the church—the library," emitted Brother Alfonso, closing the wine room door behind him."

Dave stated, "Last year, we saw another grand library, which contained every classic book imaginable. It was at a forest-dwelling hermit's home. The benign bibliophile also wrote the thickest book we've ever seen, but unfortunately we didn't have the time to read it."

"Thicker than the Feroestithe?"

"Considerably," returned Mick, frankly.

"That is impressive. I bet that's quite the read. The defining aspect of our library, expectedly, is our collection of holy books, including three copies of the Feroestithe."

"From which book do you preach the most, the Feroestithe or the modern Bible?" asked Dave, as the three stepped within sight of the library.

"That is a good question. Each one suits different purposes, but I have to admit we're taught not to favor one or the other. Together, the two include all known religious history, but between you and I, I'm predisposed to the modern Bible. There are a lot more parables in it that have helped me get through the tough time of my wife leaving me. One in particular of Bagoyatrad presents the fable of a young man and his lost love. The more times I read it, the more I get out of it, wisdom that helps me stitch back together my torn soul."

Dave's lips formed a thin line, and he put his hand on Alfonso's shoulder. "One day, my friend, you will get ultimate closure."

"Thank you," said the monk, fighting with all his might to push back misery, as memories flooded in.

Standing before the doors to the library, Mick whispered, "So many words."

The trio went into the library, and saw another group same in number reading, and hard at it, swelling the room with the exhaust of concentration.

Leopard and Hawk noticed right away the library wasn't as impressive as the hermit's in terms of sheer book numbers, but it was a larger space. The locale was exceptional in terms of setting a scene, picture-perfection straight out of a child's storybook. Mick and Dave observed the library was designed to resemble the church. The wood carvings of the library's bookshelves and benches were geometrically the same as the church's pews and artwork frames.

They didn't spend too much time in the library, as to not bother the monks reading. Mick and Dave figured there'd be plenty of time to examine the books in full detail.

Alardo showed the rest of Dourinuset's key aspects, and ended the tour back at the bedrooms, where Mick and Dave expressed appreciation to Alfonso for his efforts.

As promised, Mick went into his room to retrieve his black needle sword to show Alfonso. The monk took it in his hands, swung it as powerfully as the hallway allowed, and said, "The gripping properties are even more remarkable than I imagined. It's as if the magic of the ancient world decided to finally return. The bygone power grew weary of dormancy, yearning to awaken, to perform. And it chose *your* swords as its opening act."

"You painted quite the picture there, Brother Alardo," communicated Mick. "Maybe the black needle pine tree was just some fluke, some evolutionary mutation just wanting a place to grow. We've been on a quest ever since to find another."

"Nevertheless, I certainly wouldn't tell too many people about their origin, otherwise, you'll find yourselves confronting would-be thieves morning, noon, and night."

"Many know of our swords, but not too many know their real story," stated Dave. "A few folks back in our hometown know the story. The swords' maker knows. And a company of soldiers and their leader, the Black Bear, knows, whom we fought alongside during a few battles last year. We trust them greatly."

Alfonso produced, "Yes, I've heard of General Ulfenkerki and his superb repute."

"We'd actually spent a good chunk of our childhood with his second in command, Jason Thorncat."

"I do believe, then, those are the kinds of people you can trust with your secret."

Mick noted, "There are actually a few more interesting things we could show you, if you like curiosities?"

Alfonso replied, "Who doesn't."

Mick opened his wardrobe to show Brother Alardo his armor. "There's a long story that accompanies this armor, but I know church starts soon, so we'll tell you that later. Dave has an identical suit."

Dave went into his room, brought out the parabolic, magnetic key, and handed it to Alfonso. "Same too with this magnet, the account is long."

"I imagine."

The monk looked over the magnet and the armor, sticking one to the other. "Fascinating. I can't wait to hear the stories. The day's second church service starts in ten minutes, so I must be going now. I've a few preparations to attend to. I'll see you there."

"See you there, and thank you so much for the sightseeing," extended Mick.

Dave and Mick had no preparations, so they dawdled for a bit. Eight minutes after Alfonso parted ways, they moseyed into church.

After second service, Mick and Dave were assigned their morning chores, along with all the monks. Mick and Dave were to fix a shed door, but before they started Brother Alardo approached with a big, cheesy grin, similar to the one Dave grew to love at George's Mill. "That's a mighty pleasant chore, getting to fix a door. I should say a mighty pleasant task for Dave and me. Mick gets to do what I was assigned—outhouse duty."

"And what is it I'm doing with them?" Thraiker inquired with a half-smile.

"There are three. All you have to do is wash the walls and scrub the floors. It sounds easy enough, but trust me, the smell will get to you after a while."

"Fair enough. A bet is a bet."

Mick Thraiker cleaned outhouses to the best of his ability, learning rather quickly how to better maneuver a mop. He also became more proficient at dexterously keeping his nose inside his shirt while swinging a stringed implement.

With enjoyment, Dave and Alfonso successfully fixed the door. They also had learned a lesson, but it wasn't as valuable as Mick's. It did, however, make their job easier. The small saw was sharper than the bigger one, therefore it worked better.

The three met back up when chore time was complete. Dave and Alfonso looked identical to when their chore had begun, while Mick looked worse for wear. The exchanging of well-chosen facial expressions effectively communicated the humorousness of what'd just transpired. "Next time, I'll give a little more thought, before making bets with monks," uttered Mick in good humor.

Meals, church sessions, and the afternoon chores indicative of a monastery were past Mick and Dave for the day. The free time occurring just before lights out was upon them. Yearning for relaxation, Dave searched out a comfortable chair. He found one in the small common room of the monastic cell wing. He intended to split his time between reading and just sitting and thinking. Risking looking ridiculously out of place, Dave pulled another chair to his frontside, and propped his feet on it. *Worth it*, he thought. He contemplated the scene. A ray of inner meaning was cast upon him, triggering a bliss reflex.

Looking at the beautiful, hand-drawn cover of the book he'd chosen to read, Dave wondered if the story inside was as good as the cover art.

Having worked up a necessity for a lot of food by laboriously washing outhouses, Mick made his way to the dining room for one last quick nibble. He sat on one of the chairs next to a counter and grabbed an apple from a bowl, which also contained bananas and pears. *Maybe I'll eat a banana or pear tomorrow, if they're still here.* Halfway through eating his apple, Brother Norbe joined Mick in the dining room, apparently also hungry.

After grabbing a few pieces of cheese, freshly made that day, the monk asked, "How are you enjoying your time at Dourinuset so far, Mick?"

"Growing up in Chalatore, we learned of Dourinuset, our young imaginations trying their best to capture what life would be like up on the hill. To be honest, that adolescent approach to picturing it never gave it justice. A locale like this has so many intricate components that one truly has to see it to believe. I'm having a wonderful experience, and I'm sure so too is Dave," replied Mick, who realized an apple just wasn't enough. Making sure the monk wasn't reaching for it first, Mick grabbed a perfect banana out of the bowl.

Brother Norbe beamed. "So, you're going to stay permanently then, and swear the vows?"

Mick chuckled, "It's not that wonderful. But you never know, anything can happen in the next few days."

"The more monks, the merrier, you know."

"I don't doubt that."

"Well, my friend, enjoy the rest of your banana, and have a good night's sleep."

"You too, Brother Norbe."

"And remember, always trust in who you are."

Mick thought deeply for a few moments on Brother Norbe's profound utterance, eyes closed. He opened his eyes back up, more content.

He finished his fruit, and left the dining area, satisfied his stomach was full enough to make it through the night.

Mick ambled to the common room, where Dave was nestled. He sat in a chair near the opposing wall. "Brother Norbe and I just had a nice chat."

"Glad to hear. Are you going to stay awake for a while yet?"

"Nope. In about five minutes, this guy is going to sleep. Hopefully, I don't dream about outhouses."

Dave loosed an out of the ordinary silly laugh. "I'll probably stay awake for another half an hour, yet."

"Enjoy."

Mick went into his room and noticed the moon outside his window. For a few minutes, he pondered from where the moon came. Realizing his mind was too tired to come to any scholarly answers, he opted for bed. Thankfully, he didn't dream about outhouses. Instead, he dreamt about some woman he'd never seen before.

Dave forgot what he'd dreamt about.

A group of three showed up at the monastery with a rather large cart containing four huge wooden barrels of water, confirming the validity of the arrangement of which Mick and Dave spoke. One of the deliverers said they'd return once a week and that delivery could be more or less frequent. Before they headed back down the hill with the empty cart, Abbot Ferdinand thanked them, gave them some food for the road, and told them about the triple cedar way markers.

Dave and Mick's morning chore was to carry each barrel to where it needed to be in the building. The empty barrels would be sent back, as full ones came in. One barrel went to the kitchen for drinking and dishwashing, one sat by the sleeping quarters for bathwater, and two went to the farm for the animals. The bathing water would be warmed by fire as needed. During rainy years, they'd need less water; drought years, they'd need more.

In the afternoon free-time, Hawk and Leopard decided to go hiking, curious about the rock alignment that made the mile and a half long trail a standout. Passing through the main courtyard to get to the trail, they noticed Brother Athentra sitting on a bench and praying. When the monk looked up, the three exchanged smiles and waves.

Brother Alfonso wasn't kidding when he said the trail was rocky. A hundred yards into the trail the pair was forced into rock hopping. But, according to Mick and Dave, when someone needed to rock hop for a trail hike, nine times out of ten it'd turn out a high quality experience by the end.

The rocks in the trail displayed a higher degree of slippery dampness than usually shown by other Garobansurovian hilltop rocks. Dave and Mick had to maintain perfect balance in order to keep from receiving face-fulls of hard, jagged rock. Plus, they couldn't avoid the trail entirely by walking next to it, since that course presented an even higher level of treachery. "Good times," remarked Dave.

Mick noted sarcastically, "At least we'll enjoy sore ankles tonight."

"I can think of worse things," Dave said, as he big-heartedly held a face-level branch, so it didn't slam back into Mick.

"I know getting hit with that branch would've been worse."

Dave chuckled, and because he was in the lead, he was the first to see why Brother Alfonso referred to the trail as consequential. "Now if that isn't a sight!"

"Remarkable!" Mick followed.

They got closer. "Do you recognize the species, Mick?"

"I can only speculate, but I think it's a *beraxalaton*, partly because of the shape of its head, and partly because of its enormous size."

"I do remember reading a little on them. You could be right."

"One thing I do know is that complete fossilized skeletons of this ancient species are rare—actually complete skeletons of any prehistoric species are rare. In all Garobansurov, and all Taraosk, this would be a remarkable discovery."

"Yes, that is true," agreed Dave. "I don't think it was preserved exactly like this in this Dolostone formation. My assumption is the monks thoroughly brushed and cleaned it, beautifying it, so it looks its very finest for onlookers."

"Probably. I'm sure they needed a rather large ladder to do so," stated Mick. "At any rate, even vestiges of forty-foot-tall, carnivorous death-bringers are ominous. Imagine being chased by one."

"Chills. It really is quite a magnificent sight."

"They should put a bench here," Mick emitted.

Dave scratched his chin. "Maybe one of these days we could build one for them, perhaps during chore time or free time."

"We'll inquire about it when we get back, eh?"

"I suppose we better start walking back now, or we'll risk being late for the next church assembly."

"Yup, my ankles are rested up enough to assault the rock-strewn path again."

The duo backed away from the cliff-face and its colossal relic, not wanting to look away. They turned around and entered the rocky gauntlet, head-on.

After mass, Dave and Mick asked Abbot Ferdinand if they could build the bench by the fossil. They also asked if, in fact, the impression had been cleaned and scraped by the monks to look showier. The answer was yes to both questions.

The dark, spacious halls connecting the different wings of Dourinuset were a spectacle in themselves. Giant stone arches and intricate, pebble infused floors were only a fraction of the beauty contained within. Once in a while, one of the monks would sit or kneel to pray in the vast corridors. For them, the emptiness offered solitude, silence, and uninterrupted inward thought. Having time to themselves, Mick and Dave sat in the northeast hall, admiring the superb masonry and architecture.

The monks made a ham for supper, which wasn't a customary dish, because the Dourinuset farm's pig supply was limited. Pigs tended to break fences and wander down the hill, a real inconvenience. The meal was looked forward to by all, including Mick and Dave.

Brothers Ferdinand, Alardo, and Norbe sat next to Hawk and Leopard, trying to talk over the large dining room's rabble. Voices were louder that evening for some reason, echoing throughout the large space.

To the small group sitting around him, Dave said, "The sheer impressiveness of the giant fossil on the trail is going to stick with me for a while. Seeing such an unexpected sight caught me completely off-guard. I never asked—are there any other huge, fossilized skeletons up here on the hill?"

Brother Norbe replied, "I'm afraid not, but there is a cave on the north face. There aren't any big fossils in it though. There might be some smaller ones."

Brother Alfonso commented, "If you pay it a visit, you might see remnants of three, young men who once lived in it."

Dave emitted, "Interesting. For how long did they live in it?"

"I think for about seven months. They abandoned it when winter approached."

"Smart in their timing," said Dave. "We might check it out."

After pouring himself a glass of grape juice, Abbot Ferdinand added to the conversation. "When you guys were at the fossil cliff, did you notice that when standing on top of it, you can see the Stragan's windmill down below?"

Mick answered, "Actually, no we didn't."

Ferdinand said to Dave and Mick, "Tomorrow, I'm going to have the two of you build your proposed bench over there, so maybe you can spot it then."

Brother Alfonso, having eaten too much, backed his chair slightly away from the table, making room for his bloated belly, and said, "You know, one time I stood on that cliff on a very windy day. The wind usually isn't noticeable there, due to the cover of trees, but that day it was. I could hear it all around me. I stood watching the windmill, as it was exacted to revolve violently. Then, surprisingly, I witnessed one of the blades get completely torn from its base."

"That must have been quite a sight."

"It sure was, Dave. But, thankfully, that was the only part of the windmill that'd suffered damage. I do know it didn't take the Stragans very long to repair it."

"Well, that's good," replied Dave, imagining how unusually strong wind must be in order to ravage a structure whose entire purpose in life is wrestling with it.

Everyone who had room for it ate dessert as the scintillating dialogue continued. They all talked jovially right up until they departed the room for their prayerful rendezvous with God at the next church service.

Night came, and the two future recipients of the Knowing Circle found themselves in, what they had just recently decided to be, their favorite part of Dourinuset, the cozy commons room of the sleeping quarter's wing. They each hunted for a book from the bookcase—a great assortment from which to choose, ranging all genres. Mick picked one on astronomy, and Dave resumed reading the one with the beautiful cover he'd previously started.

Before reading, they speculated a bit on from where they thought the books were acquired, a pointless conversation, really. They halted the topic and opened their books.

Mick skimmed through his book and got to a part that caught his attention. "Dave, did you know that according to this book, there are at least five times on record that a mysterious straight line had been seen in the eastern sky?"

"No, I didn't. Does the book say how long the straight line was, and if it was a light source?"

"It says that it was as long as half the moon, but it doesn't say if it was indeed a light source. You'd think it'd have to be, though, in order for us to see it."

"Odds are yes, but it could just be reflecting light."

"Then," noted Mick, "the line would have to be really close, which I doubt it is."

"I'm really curious about this. Let's go outside and take a look. Besides, I'm not really tired tonight. This sort of intrigue really gets my mind churning."

"I'm not very tired either. I'm game. Let's go see if we can spot this wonder in the sky."

In the biggest courtyard stood a sort of elevated platform, just high enough that whoever perched on it received a good view of the night sky, especially the eastern part. Subsequent to climbing the steps to get to the top of the platform, Mick said, "Sure is a lovely, still night. Quite the unobstructed view from up here."

"Yup. The air is nice and cool too," responded Dave, scoping the panoramic view. "We're in luck! There isn't a single cloud in the sky obscuring any wondrous sights the heavens have to offer." Dave took a deep breath. "Why me, why you, why is anyone even here?"

"You go ahead and try to answer those yourself. I'll wait patiently for the answer."

"Sounds good," noted Dave. "So, did that book of yours mention any constellations in the eastern sky to use as guide marks in finding this straight line?"

"I wish it did, but it didn't."

"I guess we just stay focused and stare."

Looking for the sky anomaly intently, Mick voiced, "I have a question. Do you think the rest of our trip is going to go as smoothly as it has thus far?"

"To answer that, I will use the law of averages. Plugging in our history, I must respond to your question by saying *of course not.*"

"Blunt, and to the point. I like that."

An hour's worth of enjoyable conversation elapsed, and Dave finally emitted, "I don't think the straight line is going to present itself tonight."

"Maybe some other night it will. Now that we know to look for it, we may possibly see it in the future."

The duo stepped down from the platform, found their way back to their respective bedrooms, and fell asleep.

Since they were handed just a short amount of sleep due to the unscheduled stargazing, Thraiker and Ghrere hoped lethargy would stay at bay.

Morning chores arose. As desired, Mick and Dave began construction of a bench adjacent to the giant fossil. Benches were easy to build with pre-milled wood and proper tools, so it didn't take them too long to fashion the perfect bench. Luckily, the monks had a supply of wood. One could now sit comfortably while gazing upon the memento of the past.

Before once again battling the rocky path leading to the monastery, they made a point to climb to the top of the cliff, and find Stragan's windmill, like Abbot Ferdinand had suggested. They located it spinning majestically far off in the distance.

Time passed and with only a couple of full days left with the monks, Mick and Dave endeavored to make the best of their time. They searched out conversations with every monk and searched out all available points of interest, including the cave Brothers Norbe and Alfonso had talked about during mealtime.

The cave expedition ended up being a memorable side trip. They even saw a few things left behind by its temporary inhabitants.

As seemed to be habit, the heroic duo ended the penultimate full day at Dourinuset in the commons room. Maximum relaxation seeped into their bones.

"Do you think you'll get that book with the neat cover finished before we leave?"

"Yes, I've been pacing myself to do so," replied Dave. "The plot is turning out to be as intricate as the cover. Hopefully, it's the same with the ending."

Mick's attention went elsewhere. "I just realized that painting on the wall depicts a view from the small trail here at Dourinuset."

"You know, you're right. I can't believe I didn't see that before. It's the tree in the center that gives it away."

"That it does. Specifically, the lowest branch of it."

Contently, the pair sat and read for an hour; and then, went to sleep.

The next day, they both made a point to walk the small path, trying to confirm the fact the painting portrayed what they'd thought. They were correct, and asked Brother Alardo who it was that painted it. They learned it was an old painting, and that it was done by a brother of whom they've never heard. They also discovered from Brother Alardo that on the next day, Mick and Dave's last moments at Dourinuset, the monks were going to throw a going away feast in the main courtyard, honoring their pair of visitors. Mick and Dave half expected it.

After all the day's church services, chores, meals, and prayerful moments were past, Mick and Dave sadly faced their last evening at Dourinuset. Despite the innately depressing tone the last evening presented, they were still able to enjoy themselves.

Uncharacteristically, Dave aimed to finish up the last thirty pages of his book in two segments, usually finishing the last few chapters of books in one uninterrupted segment. Between the two segments, he paced in circles within the common room, trying to guess at the ending.

Dave closed his book and stood up from his chair of tranquility. To Mick, he said, "I had no idea. The main character wasn't even human. He was from outer space."

"Maybe he hailed from the straight line." The pair laughed, and Mick joined Dave in standing. "I think it's another weary-free night for me. How about you?"

"Yes, me too. I don't think I'll fall asleep very fast, knowing it's our last night and all."

"I suggest we walk the monastery's periphery and close out the evening by playing rocks."

"I've a propensity to agree."

Not all the stones needed to play rocks were still in their packs, so they looked to gathering on their nighttime stride.

Amongst the animal sounds of night, Dave grabbed a pebble from a damp ground, and said, "I wish a temporal displacement field would manifest itself now. That way we could have a few more days here."

"Aim high, my friend."

A near full moon illuminated what was normally hard to see on the path they chose to walk. The moon was bright enough to outline the incredible shelf-cloud approaching. "We may not be able to traverse the space-time continuum, but at least we get to see sights like that," commented Dave, pointing at the beautiful cloud.

"Regardless of the amazing time we've had here, I'm no doubt looking forward to our journey to and at the Capital."

"Me too. I'm hoping they put us up in the castle."

Mick chuckled, "Still aiming high I see. Though I undeniably wouldn't turn that experience away."

Pleasantly surprised, Mick and Dave were visited by Brother Alfonso in the dark. The monk voiced, "Taking advantage of the cool night air, eh?"

"That's right," noted Dave. "It's lovely out here, to be sure."

"I like to come out to this part at night, because I look at this locale as being the one sparking the most memories."

Mick inquired, "Do you think about anything in particular?"

"Usually just memories of the one that left."

"I see. Your wife. If you don't mind me prying, do you actually know where she went?"

"The strange part is I've no idea where she went. When I met her, she told me she had traveled far to get to where we were. So, I can only assume she traveled far to get back. She always kept that part of her life secret, and I respected that. When she left, she told me she loved me, that she would always love me, and that she had to leave for a reason that had nothing to do with me. I never did find out what that reason was."

"Hypothetically speaking, what would you do if she ever miraculously returned? I do know your religious vow as a monk is eternal," said Dave.

"That really is a good question. I think about the situation of her returning quite a bit, especially when I'm out here. Though she's been gone so long that I just don't consider it realistic to see her again. If she did come back, it'd be possible that she'd find me here, because I always did hint to her that I would consider monkhood, if she died. But, you're right, my vow is forever, and it's not something we take lightly."

"I couldn't imagine how hard it would be to go through what you did. A love like that is irreplaceable."

"That it is," remarked Alfonso. "I'll let you two get back to your activities, and I'll see you tomorrow. I'm definitely glad to have had this time with both of you."

"Same with you. See you later, brother. We really do hope you find your much-deserved solace here."

Hawk and Leopard concluded their nighttime stroll about the building and went inside with their game pieces. For one last time, they settled into their spots within the comfortable common room of the bedroom wing. They played rocks well into the night, discussing the highlights of their week at Dourinuset. Fittingly, the winner of the game slept slightly better than the loser.

The next day, before attending the farewell get-together, Dave and Mick made sure their bedrooms were cleaned spotlessly, and all their gear was packed and ready to go.

"Looks like we're trading bedrooms in for tents yet again," Dave said to Mick.

Not counting the food, everything for the farewell party was made and set up the night before. It was quite the lovely spread: tables with tablecloths; vibrant streamers; vivacious, anonymous decorations; and a dead pig cooking over a fire, rotisserie style. Excluding none, the monks enthusiastically contributed to the occasion. Lovely flowers were pinned to every robe.

Mick and Dave walked into the courtyard for the festivity, and cheerfully greeted each monk. They were honored such a function was put on for them, they truly were.

The meal was fantastic, and the post-dinner conversation was just the same. A half hour into lighter topics, the dialogue switched to the serious theme of war.

Abbot Ferdinand vocalized, "So, Mick, Dave, how long do you think the war with Molisia will last?"

Mick responded, "Judging by the longevity of Garobansurov's last war, I would say at least another few years. Things have been pretty quiet lately here on our side of the country, due to the nearly impenetrable Baustic Mountains."

Brother Alfonso Alardo interrupted, "And, of course, due to yours and Dave's fort capturing."

Mick chuckled. "Of course. I'm almost positive the other half of the country is facing tumultuousness right now, the far-western side, nearly a month's journey from here."

Brother Norbe emitted, "Are there any other dangers we might expect to face?"

Dave replied, "Nothing obvious comes to mind, but one thing I do know is that the Molisian, General Gamald, and his first lieutenant escaped Sarwa after the battle, and hasn't been seen nor heard from since. He could be anywhere."

Norbe said, "That's just two men, hardly much to worry about."

"Maybe so, but Gamald is incredibly cunning, having the capacity to organize much atrocity."

Ferdinand added, "I think with the Black Bear's army hanging around somewhere on this side of the nation, Gamald will think twice before causing a scene."

"That sounds like some solid reasoning to me," responded Mick. "As far as we're aware, the Capital has been free from danger up until now."

"Let's hope it stays that way for your ceremony," declared Alardo.

"Hopefully."

Conversation rolled effortlessly. Time rolled quickly. The feast needed to reach its end, for it was nearly time for the next church service to begin. They talked as long as time permitted, and sadly the room emptied.

Having grabbed their gear from their rooms, Dave and Mick were met at the front door for the final farewells from all the monks. Each monk supplied a hug and words of kindness.

Brother Norbe said to the departing pair, "May your receiving of the Knowing Circles be joyous and unforgettable. It's been a real pleasure getting to know you guys."

Brother Ferdinand's final words were, "I want to thank you one last time for compassionately obtaining the water. Without it, we were sure to be lost. We owe you so much. I hope your stay at Dourinuset was as grand and remarkable as you envisioned. For us, memories of meeting the two of you will pleasantly stick in our minds for a very long time. Please come back for a visit some time."

A hawk went soaring by. All watched it glide over air currents as if without exertion.

Brother Alfonso was the last monk to extend departing words. "That hawk flew past with the grace of a thousand perfectly timed muscle contractions. It's the same grace the two of you exhibited in coming to our aid. It's no wonder they're giving you medals. If I could, I would be right there in the audience, watching the medal ritual with a huge smile on my face. I'm sure the two of you will give one heck of an acceptance speech. Enjoy the moment. Your benevolence is commendable, and I wish you nothing but the best in life. And don't worry about me, I will be fine concerning the loss of my wife. Stay safe, Godspeed, and don't forget to look back."

After all of Dave and Mick's personal farewells to the monks, Mick addressed the monks as a whole. "This experience has been something that both Mick and I will carry with us forever. All of you exhibit true class. Life at Dourinuset exemplifies everything that is genuine and honorable. I wish you all the very best."

Dave added, "Honestly, we had an extremely great time all week long. There wasn't a single mediocre day in the lot. The farewell feast went above and beyond. I sincerely do hope to come back someday. Thanks for everything, praise God, and a heartfelt goodbye to all."

Each monk said and waved good-bye one last time, as did Mick and Dave.

The pair depressingly stepped down the monastery's grand, front-side staircase, but they were sure to remember what Brother Alardo suggested: after fifty paces, the duo turned around for one final look. They were pleasantly surprised by what they saw. A huge, finely-constructed banner hung overhead, which read: LONG LIFE FOR THE KNOWING CIRCLE RECIPIENTS. Both Mick and Dave raised a lone hand into the air, and in a demonstration of style, they loudly clapped each other high-five, without looking at the other in the process. The maneuver nearly seemed practiced.

They all shouted and waved good-bye one more last time.

Pivoting their heads almost all the way downward, Dave and Mick started the long descent of the steep hill.

81

CHAPTER 4

"THEY AREN'T the biggest in the known world, but looking up at the fabled Baustic Mountains can really make a person feel meek," said General Ulfenkerki, to his second in command, Jason Thorncat.

"I bet they're pretty close to the biggest, though."

"Maybe. I'm not sure about the technical minutiae of it all, but I do know they are among the oldest mountain ranges in the world, and certainly Taraosk."

"I heard that from somewhere too," commented Lieutenant Thorncat."

"That was quite the card game last night, Jason. I can't remember one lately that has kept me so much on the edge of my seat. By the way, during that last hand there, how in the heck did you know Gregg was bluffing?"

"I wasn't positive, but what'd given me the feeling was the look in his eyes, the look of a child whistling in a dark forest."

The Black Bear laughed. "That's a good one. How much did you end up winning?"

"Enough to buy a few rounds at the next tavern we run across."

"I'll hold you to that," remarked General Ulfenkerki, walking towards the entrance/exit flap of a nearby army tent. "See you later."

Ulfenkerki's army had spent the rest of the winter at Strwin, post Battle of Sarwa. And after that, had since made camp at the foot of the Baustics, guarding against any further Molisian armed intrusions. There wasn't much action for the soldiers at their current position, except for the occasional heated card game. But the view was nice. Some liked it that things were moving slowly, some didn't; but all were fond of the fact they'd waited until snowmelt to set up the garrison near the Baustics and their bitter influence on the climate.

Jason searched out Gregg Hogarty to rub in his victory over him, a pretty much mandatory part of a soldier's card game. Jason found Gregg and the pair shared a few laughs.

Jason went back to his tent—officers got their own tents—and poured himself a cup of apple cider. More than most, Jason liked to polish and admire his armor, which is exactly what he'd decided to do before aiming to fall asleep.

He picked up the breast plate, and couldn't help but think of the fond memories he had of getting the armor, how he delightfully shared almost a month with his childhood friends Mick Thraiker and Dave Ghrere, and how when the three went to visit Old Man Johnson, he was unexpectedly given the extraordinary armor set that he was about to polish. A priceless set of which he, Mick, and Dave all had nearly identical copies. Lieutenant Thorncat also thought about the man who'd made the armor, Brom Quintaga, and how happy Brom was at being reunited with his son. The three suits of armor were a gift to Mick and Dave for making the father/son reunion possible. Jason's suit was a gift from Old Man Johnson, who initially received the suit from Mick and Dave in exchange for being responsible for making possible the transformation of Mick and Dave's miraculous black needle pine tree limbs into the handles of their one-of-a-kind swords.

He finished his trip down nostalgia lane, put his freshly shined armor away, drank his cup's last drop of cider, and crashed into his semi-comfortable bed for the nightly power sleep.

Without any militarized provocation, Jason spent the day exercising. *An in-shape soldier is a living soldier*, was one of his mottos. Gregg joined him for the finishing run up a foothill.

Before running back down the hill, the pair stopped for a breather. Gregg Hogarty stretched his calf, and said, "I'm surprised nobody lives up here."

"It would be easier said than done. But I think it'd be worth it."

"If I was living way up here, I'd hate for my well to run dry, and have to haul water up here, or try to hire someone to do it," commented Gregg, not thinking about cosmic irony at all.

"I would probably try to hire someone to do it. There's always someone wanting to make a giti," said Jason, also not thinking about irony. "I just remembered, I think in about a week, Mick and Dave will receive their Knowing Circles."

"Oh yeah, that's right. It's too bad our garrison isn't any closer to the Capital, allowing us to attend the observance."

"That would be nice."

Weariness past them, the pair took one last look at the far-off horizon and jogged back down the foothill with ease and into camp. Gravity made downhill running pretty undemanding for anyone with strong front leg muscles.

Jason and Gregg changed their clothes and graced the nightly drill session with their presences.

BEHIND THEM, IN THE DISTANCE, stood the hill the Dourinuset monastery called home. From where they were, Mick and Dave tried to spot the monastery, but couldn't. Too many trees got in the way. In fact, you couldn't see the monastery from anywhere, other than standing right in front of it. It was a situation unlike that of the Werite Labyrinth, a stone structure far from where they were. The Labyrinth also sat atop a hill but was unmistakable from a dozen miles in all directions. An eerie sight, because of all the sacrifices that took place within its depths many eons ago.

Their minds veered away from Dourinuset and onto the path ahead.

"Isn't it odd that even though the Capital has other names, a different one depending on where you're from, most people still just call it *the Capital?*"

Dave replied, "You're right. I can't think of any other towns that are like that."

"I wonder if King Rowlangiv dubs it the Capital, or if he calls it Myothraces like many from central Garobansurov still do," stated Mick.

"Good question to ponder. Maybe you should ask him that just as he bestows upon you the Knowing Circle."

"I will in return for something from you." Mick half-smiled.

"We'll see, maybe I'll think of something to trade by then. I imagine it has to be something more valuable than item carrying, though, in order to risk such embarrassment."

"That's true."

While exuding steadfast spirits, they covered their conventional daily mileage, then, pitched camp. For not seeing any action in a week, the tents appeared astonishingly dust-free and without any sign of moldy besmirchment. Tents could gather mold if left unattended, but that'd be the last thing that'd be allowed to happen by those who lived and died by their tents. Mick and Dave were always sure to not let any unnecessary dampness accumulate.

Their yearning to make good time beseeched them to wake up early and get a head start. You never know when a daylong rainstorm would present itself, rendering for a traveler possible delay. Though, that way of thinking was bilateral. Sometimes an early start made for lethargy. It was all a matter of chance.

By midday, Hawk and Leopard decided the early rise was worth it, for their vigor levels were as high as when they'd woken.

But they weren't the only ones in the area overflowing with energy.

Inconspicuously lurking behind a few trees, some thieves (who'd been rather successful in the past) waited for a target. Times were tough, so the three bandits behind the trees had collectively decided to rob from people carrying large loads, which wasn't particularly good news for Mick and Dave. Their provision supply was just large enough to make them a target.

Just like opportunistic carnivores, the three waited until their quarry passed and snuck up from behind. Dave was walking point and Mick was in the rear. Because of his hawk-like peripheral vision, hence his nickname, Thraiker was able to spot a raised sword coming at him, before it was too late. "Dave, draw your sword!"

Dave ripped out his sword from its scabbard as fast as a snake strike—the resemblance was uncanny. Dave joined Mick in the fight, already blocking enemy swords with his own.

The three thieves were similar in height and weight, but one was a considerably more accomplished swordsman, having a much broader skill set.

The clanging sound of metal hitting metal drowned out any other noise in the area. To witness the battle was to witness an unmistakable blur of motion.

The metallurgical quality of the black needles compared to the thieves' weapons facilitated a substantial advantage for Dave and Mick. The black needles' gripping capabilities supplied a much larger one. But adding even further yet to the advantage were Hawk and Leopard's sheer skill levels.

Mick and Dave had been outnumbered in the past and knew exactly how to overcome dangerous three-versus-two circumstances. Though, they had to find a key to unlock their way out of being flanked. They searched for it high and low.

Eventually they found the key hiding in the form of a swift kick to an enemy shin, by Dave Ghrere. Through the maneuver, Dave's opponent was deprived just enough balance to lose the ability to block Dave's sword plunging into his gut. The thief was legitimately debilitated.

The brawl was now evenly matched. Beneficially, Hawk and Leopard didn't have to watch their backsides anymore, creating a much easier clash. They tried their best to not kill the bandits. *Does anybody really deserve death?*

Not that it was anything to look forward to, Mick received the opportunity to face the best sword handler of the thief-group head-on. Fighting aggressively, Mick tried to lure his adversary into an un-advantageous position. Waiting for the proper time for an adrenaline surge, Mick studied the man's movements carefully. When the best time came, Mick stutter-stepped and positioned himself into perfect balance. He vehemently swung his sword at all the right angles. As the finishing move, Mick pierced his opponent's lung. The finishing move was so fast that even the wind created from it had enough force to rustle nearby leaves. The leaves teetered delicately across the ground, though nobody but Mick noticed.

Fifty yards from Mick's battle, the fight had separated drastically, due to terrain. Dave faced the less-skilled opponent. Because of the uncomplicated swordplay of the enemy, Dave had no problem devising a stratagem to catch his foe off-guard. He unexpectedly threw a dagger at his combatant's head. The handle side of the dagger hit, dazing the man just enough so Dave could knock him unconscious with an elbow blow.

With the fight over, Leopard and Hawk ran to the nearest group of houses to explain to those within what'd transpired so the thieves could get medical help and proper punishments for past larcenies. The folks to whom Mick and Dave talked sprang into action quickly.

Mick and Dave didn't stick around the scene very long—the rural citizenry had no problems in dealing with the thieves themselves. Thankfully, the thieves were given a proper hearing.

"So much for a trouble-free journey," commented Dave, as the pair resumed their trek to the Capital.

"At least we know the swords are still sharp."

"Sharp and extraordinary. It's too bad we didn't have enough time to put on the new armor though."

"Yes, it would've been nice to try it out. Did you sustain any injuries at all?"

"Nope, not a scratch on me. Moreover, my headache went away."

"That all worked out pretty well then," replied Mick.

"Were you on the receiving end of any damage, Mick?"

"I think I hyperextended a quadricep during a lunge, but overall, I'm fine."

"That's good."

The day silently wore on. The day's path proved to be without further treachery, the heroes' grasps on safety once again restored. If a traveler didn't have a grasp on that, they didn't really have anything at all, or so the old adage stated.

At the nightly stoppage, the tents went up quickly. In unorthodox fashion, they'd made camp in a field, barely a tree around. Field erections were usually avoided because the open space provided much ground for wind to pick up speed and wreak havoc on the tents. A tent flapping in the wind made for unpleasant conditions. It was loud and just outright annoying.

Owing to the field's abundant, waste-high switchgrass, time had to be spent trampling a swath, in order to create a more comfortable camping experience. In the process, Dave found an artifact. "Mick, take a look, an arrowhead. I wonder to which of the many ancient cultures it belonged."

Mick took hold of and studied the intricately carved stone. "It's always hard to tell, there having been so many. This particular shape and rock type were used by so many ethnicities."

"True. I might as well keep it and add it to the collection."

"I can't think of a reason not to. It's not like it'll weigh you down much."

Mick and Dave got lucky that evening, for the wind changed its mind and calmed significantly, and by morning it was as still as could be. A feather dropped would've fallen straight down, whereas twelve hours previous, it would've practically been swept to the sea.

Other than the arrowhead, noteworthiness was sparse at the field campsite, which sometimes was a good thing. In fact, things of great magnitude were light all around on that leg of the trip to the Capital.

The pair continued to walk steadily and sleep soundly, no enemies reared, no hurdles materialized.

A FEW DAYS HAD PASSED since Mick and Dave spent the night in the field. They were certainly getting close to their destination. "Are you excited at all yet about the medal ceremony, Dave?"

"The tension is so prevalent it has its own gravity."

"Really?"

"Well, maybe not that much unbearable anticipation, but yes, you could say I'm animated."

"Me too."

The next day, Hawk and Leopard passed through a small settlement named Fuirk, which had a populace consisting of mainly the aged. It was a place for them to get away from the hustle and bustle of the Capital and live their lives in tranquility. There was one saloon, one church, and many gardens: some flower, some vegetable/fruit, some a little of everything.

One house in particular of Fuirk caught the eyes of Dave and Mick. It wasn't built on the ground, but in a large Oak tree. "Now there's as good a place as any to spend a large amount of time."

"I sure would like to lodge there some night," declared Dave.

"Who wouldn't?"

"I think I'm going to build my next house in a tree."

The agrestic community wasn't very large, so it only took them six minutes to traverse the length of it, including the sixty-second gawking of the treehouse, after which the duo continued on their way.

They traveled a few hours past Fuirk, before resolving to make camp.

As someone would expect, the closer they got to Myothraces, the wider and better quality the roads became. Relatively speaking, it was unquestionably Garobansurov's vastest metropolis. Dave and Mick didn't mind the nice roads, it was a pleasant change to the walking conditions to which they were normally accustomed.

Mick and Dave were drawing near their destination. One more day and they'd finally be there. They walked excitedly.

"Barring the treehouse, Dourinuset was pretty much the only sight we hadn't seen before on this trip to the Capital. It's been a pretty monotonous hike since leaving the monks."

Mick replied, "You can say that again. You could count the attempted robbery as a hiccup, but that's all it was."

"That's true," said Dave. "The Capital will be livelier, I think. Technically, the last time we were there, we didn't see too much of it—shops, businesses, whatnot."

"Correct. We spent most of our time focused on the construction of the swords and with Tim. We didn't venture into the town's innards too much."

"The sword-making process definitely stole most of our attention."

"That it did," commented Mick, while kicking a lone branch out of his footpath. "I still wish they had informed us of what our accommodations will be."

"You win some and you lose some."

"You know, tonight will probably be the last night we spend in the tents, before the trip back to Chalatore."

"Well then, we had better make the best of it."

By evening, the pair reached a new part of road, a part with smooth cobblestones. It signified they were really close—ten miles away exactly, or one river and two small settlement crossings. If you're the sort to judge distances like this.

"This segment of road must be utilized for sheep crossings. The sheep carcass lying over there gives it away," stated Mick.

"It being lined with dried mud chunks is another clue."

"Maybe we'll soon encounter a herd of sheep or two along the way."

Dave added, "That may liven things up."

Ghrere and Thraiker didn't come across any sheep within the hour, but they did come across a traveler coming from the opposite direction.

The friendly traveler waved, walked closer, and spoke. "Hello there, sirs, how goes it?"

Dave responded, "Fairly well, and you?"

"Can't complain."

"Anything new or exciting at the Capital, if that's indeed from where you're coming?" inquired Dave.

"It is, and nothing new really, other than all the hubbub centered around the Knowing Circle festivity."

"Oh yeah, that's right, that's happening soon. Exciting," Dave said, pretending to be unfamiliar with current events. He didn't entirely want to draw attention to himself, seeing as though the festival *was* in honor of him and Mick and all.

With ulterior motives on his mind, Mick jumped into the conversation. "By chance, you wouldn't happen to know where at the Capital the recipients of the medal usually spend their nights?"

The traveler looked over Mick and Dave a little more thoroughly. "You're them, aren't you? I heard the other day the Knowing Circle beneficiaries would be arriving soon and from the east. And here we are, east of the Capital, a single day's journey away. And the biggest giveaway: questions about where the recipients are going to lodge. I mean, really, do you expect me to believe you care about that? Tell a new friend the truth." With hands on hip, and suspicious smile, the traveler stood patiently awaiting a response.

Mick and Dave were caught off-guard but enjoyed the moment of being so, for it was something that rarely occurred. Smiles slowly crept onto their faces. "You caught us. I'm Mick Thraiker and this is Dave Ghrere, future recipients of the Knowing Circle. Your capacity for observation is commendable to be sure."

"I guess you could say that. I'm glad to have crossed paths with you. To be a hundred percent honest, last night, I coincidentally told my children the action-packed bedtime story of your fort capturing, and of how you and your crew turned the tides at the Battle of Sarwa. The kids were enthralled."

"I bet those youngsters slept fantastically last night then," Dave said.

"I left before they woke up to know, but I bet they did too," returned the traveler, whose name was Jim Tradel. "I must be going, for I have a deadline to meet, but before I go, can I ask of you a huge favor?"

Mick answered, "Sure, we can try to comply."

After stating the favor to Mick and Dave, Jim said goodbye and continued his mission.

Prior to resuming their journey to the Capital, Hawk and Leopard peeled the rotting sheep corpse off the road, so no one further had to be subjected to its egregious stench.

Carrying the carcass with a stout stick into the woods for disposal, Dave noted, "Evidently, one of the shepherds of the area is down a head."

"That's too bad. Times are tough enough the way they are."

The duo unloaded the carcass fifty yards from the road and walked on. They didn't walk too far though, because it was time to make camp, the last camp before arriving at the Capital. They intended to keep their tents in stow for the extent of their stay at the Capital.

The portable sleeping quarters were set up on the banks of a crystal-clear spring pond. So clear the fish within could be seen from shore, even at dusk. "I bet you're just itching to pull some of those babies out of there, eh Dave?"

"Yes, normally I would be, but I'm virtually positive we'll be fed generously throughout the days of the ceremony. So, there's no need to. Although, the massive sizes of some of those beauties aren't helping me resist the urge to have a go at them."

"Same here, I'll admit."

Having just completed the final tent-related task for the evening, tarp fastening, Dave commented, "It sure seemed like a long day today for some reason, even for a couple of *nemophilists*."

"I agree. Despite the word *nemophilists* sounding dirty."

"I guess it would, to someone not knowing it only refers to appreciators of trees."

"That be true," said Mick.

"I'm probably going to go to sleep early, just to end this lengthy day. Maybe in an hour."

"Good plan, Dave."

Like always, the sun fell below the horizon. In the dark, Hawk and Leopard stood beside the clear pond, staring at the moon's reflection, a mystical and hypnotic display. Caused by a cool, northerly breeze, the pond's surface rippled, adding to the mysticism. "I wonder how deep it is."

"Maybe it's as deep as the pond that one guy we met a few years ago said had no bottom."

"I don't know if I necessarily believed that guy. I think he just said that because he didn't possess a depth-gauging anchored line long enough to reach the bottom of the pond."

"I think you're right about the line. I didn't believe him either. I bet this pond is forty feet deep."

"Yes, it's probably about that."

As previously planned, the pair went to bed early, and rose early to finish off the trip to the Capital.

Unexpectedly, the final leg of the trip was interrupted by a short, twenty-minute hailstorm, during which Dave and Mick took refuge under the roof of an abandoned shack-like structure. Surprisingly, waiting out the hailstorm in the dilapidated shack had ended up making their top twenty-five list of most memorable moments of the walk to the Capital.

The hail stopped and they resumed. As they got closer and closer to town, Dave and Mick were met by a cornucopia of people coming and going. Some of the folks greeted Mick and Dave vocally, some used hand gestures, and some felt comfortable enough just ignoring them.

The pair finally reached the marker representing extreme closeness to the Capital—the iconic bridge over the Geenhuvagal River. It was a place where they always liked to stop, due to the fact they deduced it was the river that once long ago flowed over the cliff in the Tharbjorn Escarpment, the very cliff where they found the black needle pine tree responsible for the greatness of their swords.

"I wonder if the river ever freezes enough for ice fishing."

"I bet it does in the backwater areas."

"True. Ice fishing is great," said Mick, pondering some of the many great days spent fishing over frozen bodies of water. "Shall we continue on?"

"Yup."

CHAPTER 5

FROM A DISTANCE, the duo could tell the Capital was bustling with enthusiasm. The eve of the Knowing Circle ceremony was almost as much of a party for the inhabitants as the actual day of the celebration itself. It was early afternoon. The streets of town were full of those types who liked to get revelry going early. Many were already drunk and rowdy—good, clean fun.

Mick and Dave were approaching the Capital from the east side. To no surprise, this side of town was lavishly decorated for the Knowing Circle event. But the middle of town, the epicenter of festivity, was where things were truly decorated. It was where the most impactful statement was made, the statement that the Knowing Circle celebration was a big deal.

Mick and Dave's two-week journey was finally 500 steps from being complete. Amid the view of town, Mick said to Dave, "I do say we deserve a drink or two."

"I say I deserve three or four."

"Thirsty, are we?"

"You could say that," replied Dave. "Ravenous thirst seemed to have snuck up from my blind side."

"It does that sometimes."

Dave skipped over a pothole in the road, and commented, "I wonder how far we'll make it into town before we're recognized."

"I have no idea. That isn't something easy to guess at. I think Jim figuring out who we were was just a fluke."

"That may be. We'll find out soon enough, I suppose."

The east-side gate, along with all the others, was loosely guarded. It was determined at some point in the past it wasn't exactly cost effective to flood the gates with guards. Posting sentries at the gates to question every single person who decided to come or go would've taken far too much time and manpower. So, Mick and Dave walked right through the east gate, unquestioned. They received a nod of the head from the lone guard, who was oblivious as to whom he was nodding. It was, however, a fancier greeting than most got.

Mick and Dave took their first steps inside the Capital, and since the trip was long, they sighed relief. The sight of the Capital was certainly nostalgic for them, bringing back many pleasant memories. Emotions surged over them both.

Mick spoke. "I can't say I've ever seen decorations quite like this before, moreover, that statue of the Knowing Circle over there sure looks like a lot of effort had been put into its creation."

"It even looks as if names of past recipients have been meticulously etched into it, just like on a real Knowing Circle."

"A list of outstanding individuals to be sure. The band I can hear in the distance sounds pretty good too."

"Well, Mick, we may as well head in that direction."

"Sure, but first, I want to take a closer look at that water feature." Mick pointed. The pair of friends sauntered forty paces to where the finger had been pointed. "I like how the two streams of water cross and come back together."

Dave added, "It's very interesting how the water flows the way it does, before being scuttled away in such detailed wonderment."

"Yes, very."

Compelled by strong, intangible evidence they were going to enjoy the rest of the day, Hawk and Leopard left the water feature behind, and headed in the direction of the music.

The Capital was a reasonably large place. There were roads, passageways, dead-end alleys, buildings, and people in every direction. Mick and Dave thought it'd take weeks to see every nook and cranny in the vast city.

Ornate columns stood tall on both sides of the street that Mick and Dave were walking. Behind the columns were multiple sets of stairs leading to a lower-level walkway. Various shops and homes were scattered about the lower level of the Capital, a curious place, where as many things as possible were squeezed into as small a space as possible. "Things to see on a different day, down those stairs."

"Not for me. I think I want to explore the lower level for a bit, you can go on ahead, Dave, and I'll catch up with you."

"Alright. I'll continue heading towards the music." Dave pointed at a moderately traversed passageway and separated from Mick.

Mick ventured down the stairs to the lower tier, where a myriad of sights awaited. For no particular reason, he went inside the very first shop door he saw. Hawk closed the door behind him, and realized he was in a clothing store. He didn't need any new garments at the moment but told himself it wouldn't hurt to look around. Surveying all the latest fashions was something he rarely received a chance to do, not that it was something he ever considered doing daily.

A beautiful woman came out of nowhere, intending to voice the usual sales pitch. She began her attempt at making a sale, sputtering all the tried and true pitches. Mick listened politely, and realized that what the woman exhibited in beauty, she lacked in knowing a lost cause.

The woman finally realized that unless she switched gears with Mick, any sales commission would be lost. She resorted to the oldest trick in the book: flirting. "Has your morning been filled with any man-related excitement at all?" she asked in a soft tone, delicately brushing her long, blonde hair away from her striking, hazel eyes.

Mick answered, "I guess you could call waking up at the side of an unnamed pond, after sleeping in a tent sort of manly. But between you and I, that sort of thing could be done by one and all just the same, not particularly the province of only men."

"I love camping, but it's been a while since I last strolled through camping land. I certainly would like to again soon. Maybe you can take me?"

Mick registered a flirt session was transpiring. He liked the thought. He'd nary an intention of putting a stop to it. "I wouldn't say no to that. There's room for another in my tent."

"That sounds lovely."

"It does indeed." Mick didn't want to change subjects, but he did anyway. "Do the owners of your shop plan on keeping the store open for the duration of the Knowing Circle presentation and ensuing celebration?"

"Gratefully, no. We'll be open tomorrow morning, but then we'll be closed for the rest of the day, and half the next day. I'm glad, because I was hoping to see firsthand the two recipients deservingly get their medals. I heard the amazing story of what they did to earn them, and really wanted to be a witness of the moment."

"Yes, that is also why I'm here. My friend and I traveled a long way to be here and be a part of the same moment." Mick chuckled inside his head at his words.

"I actually have a friend who told me he'd heard Dave and Mick had camped for weeks on a mountain in preparation for the Fort Gravividon onslaught. And that their campout was during that huge snowstorm we had last winter. I couldn't imagine being in a tent during such conditions. Have you ever been that manly as to do something like that?"

"Yes, that is one interesting story. Waking up by a pond is one thing, but doing so within a shell of snow enclosing the entirety of a tent is something else completely."

The store worker took a step closer to Mick, almost close enough to be inside his personal bubble. "From where exactly did your journey begin?"

"Have you ever heard of Chalatore?"

"The town way east of here, which holds the renowned, annual armwrestling tournament?"

"Yup, that'd be the one," said Mick, hoping that divulging the name of his hometown wouldn't give him away.

"You aren't kidding, huh? That really is a long way. That must've taken you weeks."

"It did. We also stopped somewhere for a time along the way. It was an enjoyable couple of weeks."

Purposefully forgetting about any possible sales commission, the lady was now practically standing on Mick's toes, practically breathing in his exhaled air. Many would've called it an erotic moment. The lady had been bitten by the smitten bug. "So, will I be seeing you at the ceremony?"

Mick had also been bitten and was having a hard time keeping in character. It wasn't entirely easy to pretend a vast commotion throughout a city wasn't centered around you and your past deeds. He replied, "I will be there indeed. Will you be going alone or with someone? Because I would love to accompany you."

"I can't say that I would, because I don't usually go on dates with men whose names I do not know. But if you were to tell me, perhaps I'd consider your proposal."

"If I tell you, do you promise not to laugh or be mad?"

"Why would I laugh or be mad at hearing your name?"

"Out of serendipitous irony, I guess," replied Mick.

"Okay, I promise. But I can't say I've ever been told that before."

Mick said his full name, and quickly blurted, "May I ask you your name?"

Rebecca said her name, but not until after doing so did the realization of to whom she was talking set in. She was instantly overwhelmed but kept her composure. She looked into Mick's eyes for the briefest of pauses and spoke: "So, how deep was the snow on the mountain actually?"

"Where we were, not as deep as you'd think; the surrounding hillside created a wind-wall, which kept away a lot of the snow. In locations away from our tent pod, the snow had ended up being chest-high; by us, only stomach-high. Believe you me, it was a pain to walk through."

"Fascinating. Are you really allowed to take dates to the commemoration?"

"To tell you the truth, I have no idea. I don't even know where Dave and I will be staying the night. I imagine, though, we have a lot of say as to what we are and are not allowed to do. So, henceforth I proclaim that

Knowing Circle recipients are allowed to bring dates to all formal and informal procedures involved therein."

Rebecca chuckled. "Let the proclamation be heard far and wide, and by those big and small. By the way, where is Mr. Dave Ghrere?"

"He continued on ahead to one of the bands, while I hung back to look around some."

"Good thing you did, otherwise you wouldn't be here to hear me saying yes to your invitation."

"Yes, good thing I hung back."

"Do you think Dave would mind if I introduced my best friend to him at the ceremony?" Rebecca asked nervously.

"Better yet, I'm sure I could convince him to be her blind date for it."

"Are you serious? That would absolutely make her day."

"Yeah, I have a lot of sway with him, you could say. As he does with me. We've known each other since childhood."

Rebecca put her hand delicately on Mick's back, followed by Mick putting his hand lightly on her hip. "Superb, just superb," emitted the shop employee. "I suppose I better get back to work now, but can I see you tonight, after I get done here?"

"I would love that. What time are you done?"

"I'll be done at six o'clock, and I can meet you somewhere at seven o'clock. Actually, I'm sure I can drag my friend along this evening too, so Dave can meet her.

Which in essence would mean the blind date would be tonight."

"Yes, that it would. Dave will love it, I'm sure. It all sounds like fun. We'll meet you back here at seven o'clock."

"Alright, see you then, Mick. We'll have fun at the celebratory activities, I'm sure."

"I'm sure too."

Mick left the shop, and decided to further explore the vicinity a bit before meeting back up with Dave. All around, there were many shops and businesses, many narrow alleys, many hidden places, all of which he was excited to spend a little time exploring.

Mick tried to see as much as possible in the least amount of time, although for the moment he refrained from going into any more shops. He figured more of that would come later on, some other day.

Responding to the natural flow of the area, Mick eventually came to a spot that opened up slightly to reveal one of the holy shrines in the city. The monument stood tall and represented divine greatness. At the moment, Mick was unsure as to the specifics of the shrine. He'd ask someone about it later.

Finished with the curiosity-driven exploration, Mick found his way back to the main thoroughfare of the upper level and headed towards the music and Dave. The music wasn't coming from as far away as Mick had thought, due to the acoustics of the area, so it barely took Mick any time to find Dave. The area where the band was playing wasn't the Capital's main square, but it was still one of the busier locations.

Playing just outside the tavern that'd hired them, the band (a local ensemble) performed all their own music. Exhibiting the carefree look of no purpose, Dave stood near the band. "How was your sightseeing tour, Mick?"

"Productive."

"In what way?" asked Dave.

"I procured us dates for this evening."

"Even for me?"

"Yup, my friend. Even for you."

"Well that's some good news. Sometimes I do come to be dumbfounded at just how good you can be with the ladies."

"Well, thank you, my good man." Mick was glad Dave was all in. Though, he assumed he would be.

Mick went on to talk about the experience at the clothing store. Despite it being a short tale, Dave listened to the telling with enthusiasm. What guy wouldn't, knowing the story detailed how he obtained a date.

Having stood by the band long enough, the duo decided it was high time to present themselves to the Knowing Circle officials. They knew someone, somewhere was eagerly waiting for them.

Because it seemed to make the most sense, they figured the castle district was where to head in order to find dignitaries. It was the easiest district to find, in view of the fact that one could see the castle looming from almost anywhere in town.

Walking through the crowd, Dave voiced, "You know, Mick, since you found me a date, I'll have to return the favor and procure one for you someday."

"I guess you're right. I'll look forward to it," returned Mick, after threading the needle, squeezing in between two people who'd practically walked straight at him. "I've never seen so many people. There's got to be nearly five thousand people in town."

"Yup, there's a lot, and they're all walking the streets."

There were a lot of interesting places to check out along the way to their destination, but they had dawdled enough. They'd sightsee some other time.

Mick and Dave were correct in their assumption to go to the castle district to check in, for once they were virtually within the shadow of the King's Castle, they were recognized.

A young, wiry gentleman approached, donning an outfit exquisite enough to be worn at the fanciest of functions held within the castle. He reached out his hand in greeting, and said, "Hello, Mick, Dave, my name is Charlie, your liaison. I'm to escort you to your rooms, instruct you on the ins and outs of the ceremony, and answer any questions you may have. Speaking of questions, do you have any for me, before I go on?"

"It's good to meet you, Charlie," said Mick. "I guess my only question for now, before you actually show us, is where will we be sleeping?" He just couldn't wait any longer to know.

"In the castle, of course."

"Well, that seems intriguing."

"I could imagine it would be, but I've never slept in the castle myself, so I wouldn't know how intriguing firsthand. Technically, there aren't very many people bestowed this privilege."

Mick emitted, "Lead on then, Charlie, my good man." He chuckled in his mind, having become aware of the fact Charlie was the second person in five minutes he called 'his good man.' Mick noticed he was in quite a good mood.

On the way to the castle gate, Dave asked, "How did you recognize us so fast?"

"It was easy for me. I was assigned this position, partly due to my uncanny ability to pick out people from a crowd using written descriptions."

"That makes sense. I'd like to see these writeups of us sometime," Dave chuckled.

"Sure, I'll show them to you," said Charlie, keeping a steady pace as he guided Mick and Dave. "All the important buildings of the Capital surround the castle. They're unquestionably the most illustrious in town."

"We intend to go sightseeing at some point, no doubt," Dave voiced.

"You won't be disappointed when you do."

The front and only gate of the castle was at the end of a long, raised walkway (a causeway), which spanned over a deep trench encircling the entirety of the castle. The elevated pathway was guarded by fifty men, who stood in pairs symmetrically. For a would-be invading host, the fifty men guarding the causeway wouldn't be the primary obstacle preventing the host from getting into the castle, that station would be held by those in the twenty-four raised archer platforms surrounding the causeway. Each platform had protective barriers and housed three archers, some among the best marksmen in the country. Given the belief the guards on the walkway would considerably slow an invader coming down the narrow causeway, it was said the archers could fend off a force of a thousand strong. The defensive system had never failed.

The threesome walked past the guards of the causeway, stoic defenders dedicated to duty, country, and king. Charlie and his accompaniment were allowed passage across the walkway, as he was acknowledged as someone of importance.

Charlie greeted the two huge men standing guard beside the gate, and escorted Dave and Mick into the castle. Once inside, they noticed another thirty guards scattered within eyeshot. Mick and Dave were told there were many more guards hidden about. Although he wasn't currently in the castle, the King and any other dignitaries that might be present were well guarded.

Charlie ushered Dave and Mick up a few staircases and down a few corridors, and eventually arrived at the VIP quarters. "These will be your rooms for as long as you decide to stay. If there is anything you need, just ask any of the staff. Or ask me, if I'm around." Charlie unlocked the doors of two rooms, opened them, and handed over the keys to Mick and Dave.

Mick put forward, "Thank you very much, Charlie. Will there be anything formal arising tonight, for which we must prepare?"

Charlie replied, "Nope, nothing ceremonial is to occur this evening. Go ahead and enjoy yourselves tonight, live a little. Or live a lot. Your choice, heroes. We will perform a small rehearsal for the ceremony in the morning. During the ritual itself, you will probably be asked to say a few words, not entirely mattering how many or what they are. It's completely up to you, it's your moment."

Dave inquired, "Will there be any times when the castle gate is locked, preventing us from getting back in?"

"Guards will be stationed at the gate at all moments, so re-entry is possible whenever. \Stay out as long as you want, tonight or any night. You're also allowed guests, within reason of course."

"Good to know."

"I will take my leave now, and I will see you in the morning. Congratulations, by the way. I am truly honored to have met you both."

"Thanks, Charlie. Enjoy your night too," Mick extended.

Mick and Dave went into their respective rooms and started to put their stuff away.

Dave looked around and was quite taken aback by the enormity and extravagance of his room. I guess I should've expected such lavishness, it *is* where the King lives. You could probably fit six Dourinuset monastic cells in here.

There were all kinds of places in the bedroom to stow gear, so Dave unloaded almost everything from his backpack and stored it all away. He placed his armor and weapons in the most secluded spot of the room, the closet.

In the next room over, Mick was doing the same, except he decided to keep his armor and weapons in the large corner wardrobe. He set his nearly empty pack in the closet. There were a number of extra pillows and bedding in the closet, conveniently placed in case guests needed some.

When Mick was done unpacking, he went over and rapped on Dave's door to see if he was done as well, which Dave was. Enthusiastically, they made their way down the ornate hallway and down the multiple stairways.

"What did the paintings in your room depict?" Mick asked Dave.

"A couple were forested scenes, and a couple more were of pretty people I didn't recognize. What did yours portray?"

"I didn't get any portraits, but I did get the forests. I also got one of what I'm guessing to be the grand dining hall in the castle here."

"We'll find out soon enough, I suppose. Not right now, though. Let's just get something to eat downtown for supper," proposed Dave.

"I agree. We might as well eat with the ladies."

"Hopefully, they come hungry."

The pair walked past all the castle guards, as still as statues and out the front gate. They were excited about exploring the castle further, but at the moment they were more enthused about being a part of the after-dark merriment going on in town. Technically, Mick and Dave *were* the exact reason for all the Capital's animation that night. Who wouldn't be enthused by the masses celebrating their accomplishments?

Having reached the end of the raised causeway Mick said, "We are to meet the girls back at Rebecca's shop at seven o'clock, so since that isn't for a couple hours, we might as well join the exultations downtown."

"Did you catch what her friend's name was?"

"No, I don't think she said it. Her friend might not even be pretty, you know."

Dave smiled. "I don't necessarily care what she looks like. "Any date will add to the enjoyment of tonight."

"If I were in your shoes, I'd think the same thing. All women look good in a dress anyways."

They headed to a different part of town than where they were earlier that day. It didn't really matter to what segment they went, the party was practically everywhere. But they were sure as to not stray too far away from Rebecca's shop. Such an action would've been counterproductive for the most part.

The first door Mick and Dave decided to enter since leaving the castle proved to be a wise door to choose. Inside, armwrestling was transpiring, a sport of which the pair couldn't get enough. They had entered a raucous bar—though it wasn't really a bar. It was more of a makeshift restaurant, currently doubling as another place for citizens to get wild.

The armwrestling didn't take place on an actual armwrestling table, instead, on a regular eating table. It got the job done.

A lot of the time these sorts of things ended in fights (boys will be boys), but luckily not this time. And it wasn't because Dave and Mick were recognized. It was just a friendly, fun-loving crowd.

The time went by fast, and twelve minutes before 7:00, Mick and Dave left the bar and its armwrestling to go meet up with their lovely dates.

The ten-minute walk to Rebecca's shop was just long enough for Hawk and Leopard to realize twilight was almost upon them, an appreciation of which seemingly was a daily occurrence. Twilight for Dave and Mick contained a certain magic.

From a distance, Dave could see the beautiful hourglass silhouettes of two women standing gracefully in front of a shop. His heart practically skipped a beat. "I sure hope that's our meeting place and our women there," said Dave, before pointing discreetly towards the clothing store.

Mick responded, "Whatever happened to not caring how attractive your date is?"

Post-chuckle, Dave stated, "I still don't care, but it doesn't hurt once in a while to be blessed with good fortune."

"No, it certainly doesn't. And, yes, my friend, today good fortune is smiling upon you, for your date is the one on the left."

"Most opportune, to be sure!"

Trying not to accost the elegant ladies, Mick nimbly walked up to them, followed closely behind by Dave, smiles a' blazing. "Wonderful to see you again, Rebecca. You look sensational."

"I'm glad to see you again too. This is my friend, Olivia."

"And this, as I'm sure you've already guessed, is Dave."

Dave stepped forward and lightly hugged both ladies. "Delighted to meet you."

The quartet exchanged pleasantries for a few moments, as nervousness subsided.

Mick posed, "Shall we go join the jubilation downtown?"

"I'll be ready for a heaping load of social interaction, just as soon as I lock the shop door," answered Rebecca.

The pairs walked hand-in-hand towards the part of town where crowds were loudest, the part where the Knowing Circle commencement would occur officially. They arrived, and looked around at the sumptuous display of decorations, wide-eyed and awed. No expense was spared ensuring the Knowing Circle event was the most superlative of all the land. Mick and Dave were astonished by the sheer grandeur of the outdoor auditorium itself, it really was quite the sight. *So many chairs.*

"I bet all the buildings that surround the stage supply the perfect acoustics," commented Dave, trying his best to speak above the crowd without shouting.

"They certainly do," voiced Olivia. "The concerts here are amazing. I went to one last summer and loved it."

"The whole area is adorned by the greatest of ornaments—a real manifestation of sheer elaborateness," Mick said, looking up.

"The decorations team plans months in advance for this," Rebecca noted. "I remember once my grandmother telling me her grandmother (my great, great grandmother) had led a Knowing Circle decorations team many, many years ago."

"Fascinating," said Dave. "These teams certainly know what they're doing."

"That they do," added Mick.

Darkness was upon them. Multiple fires, candles, and torches (strategically positioned in symmetrical, aesthetic patterns) illuminated the whole area. Nocturnal splendor abounded.

Olivia was elated to have met Dave, and vice versa. "So, what happens when the two of you are recognized?" Olivia asked.

"So far on our trip, it's only happened twice, both times being pleasant. One time was by Charlie, our greeter, and the other time was by a traveler, just outside of town. The traveler deduced by context clues who we were. So, staying optimistic, if it happens tonight, hopefully it'll occur with the same sort of amiability."

"Well, hopefully only bright outcomes prevail then."

After purchasing customarily high-priced drinks, the four walked to one of the lovely candle pods for a place to stand and talk.

Dave said, "There is one person in town who will surely recognize us. A while back, we came here to get something important constructed by a blacksmith named Tim Warmane. We will certainly pay him a visit while we're here, unless he finds us first."

Rebecca remarked, "I've heard of him. Most in town consider his work to be the finest around. What did he make for you?"

"Dave and I both had him fashion unique, custom swords for us."

"That's a long trek just to get swords made. Aren't there blacksmiths closer to Chalatore?"

"Yes, there are, but we needed the best. The whole thing is a long story, of which I'll save the long version for another time perhaps. You could say the trip was worth it though, no doubt."

"Sounds interesting. I'll hold you to that," said Rebecca, as she caressed Mick's shoulder.

A burly man walked past the foursome, glancing their way. He took three steps, stopped, and reversed to face the quartet. "Please excuse my interruption. You probably don't know me, but my name is Dan. I fought with you at the Battle of Sarwa under the Nighteagle's command. After the battle, a lot of us made a point to discover who it was that finally defeated the monstrous Molisian warriors Grunt and Roar. Maybe it was a bit peculiar of us to join your fan club of sorts, but oh well."

Outstretching his hand for a handshake, Dave said, "You're right, I'm not familiar with your face, but I'm definitely glad to see it. It's not that peculiar, by the way. What brings you to the Capital?"

"Just my scheduled leave. I'll be going back to Ulfenkerki's army next week, a few others and I."

"We were actually wondering about that. I take it that General Ulfenkerki is relatively near then?"

"Kind of. The army is camped out about seventy-five miles northeast of here. The army had spent some time close to the Baustics. We had moved to the new location just before my leave began."

"That's good to know," returned Dave. "I have to go refill our costly beverages. What are you drinking, Dan?"

"My wife will never believe this—tomorrow's Knowing Circle recipients want to buy me a drink! What a story this will be. I'll take a beer, any kind. It's all good here."

Dave chuckled, and right before walking to the beer stand, he said, "Just tell her if she doesn't believe you, she can come ask us if it happened."

Dan replied, just before Dave left earshot, "I'll be sure to say that to her."

Mick suggested, "Let's move this party over five feet. A guy staggered past just now and spilled half his drink, and we're downhill from the spillage. We'll get wet feet standing here much longer."

"Say no more," blurted Dan, as he began shuffling to the side. The women followed suit, along with Mick. They all watched the puddle of beer slowly trickle down to where they'd been standing—cheap amusement.

Dave returned with the drinks, and the five of them discussed topics including Dan's family, the Battle of Sarwa, and the Knowing Circle.

At the end of the five's discussion, Dan declared, "It was a wise decision regarding the giving of Knowing Circles to the two of you. The recapturing of Fort Gravividon alone was heroic enough to warrant Knowing Circles, even without adding in what you did at Sarwa."

"Thank you, Dan," expressed Mick. "Your service to Garobansurov is praiseworthy as well."

Dan aired, just before parting, "I'll be at the ceremony tomorrow. Maybe I'll see you at the pre/post-ceremony festivities."

Mick responded, "Yes, hopefully we run into you again."

Dave added, "And hopefully it's not on the battlefield. It'd be nice for this war to end. But if we do see you on the battlefield, we now *will* be familiar with your face, and we'll be glad to see it."

"Perfect. Enjoy your day tomorrow, fine sirs," put forth Dan, before turning to walk away, his recognition of pure class in Mick and Dave entrenched.

When Dan left, Olivia observed, "Now that's three people having recognized you that turned out well."

"That does appear to be the case," said Dave. "Hopefully, it's a pattern that sticks."

The four of them paced away from the ornate candle pod and ended up standing next to a trinket shop, which happened to be open for business. Many of the shops on the main thoroughfare had stayed open, taking advantage of the obvious high potential for tons of business.

After five minutes of standing next to the shop, Rebecca and Olivia started unconsciously expressing desires to go inside, looking within often. So eventually they all went in. Rather than finishing their drinks before going in, they'd just brought them with. *Why not, everyone else was doing it.*

Looking over the wares, Rebecca noted, "I think I've only been here a couple times, and even that was many years ago."

Olivia added, "A while ago for me as well."

The four looked around meticulously at all the charms and baubles for sale, not forgetting to keep the whole of their beverage inside the cup, something that couldn't be said for almost everyone else in there. The floors were wet in some places and sticky in others. The mop bucket wasn't far away. It wasn't the first Knowing Circle celebration the shop had seen. And it wouldn't be the last.

They left the shop empty-handed. If they had bought something, they'd have had to carry it around the rest of the night—*who wants that?* Not that Mick and Dave didn't want to buy the ladies something shiny and pretty.

The quartet realized the alcohol was gratifyingly starting to kick in. *About time.*

"I'm in the mood for dancing," exclaimed Olivia. She grabbed Dave's hand, and pulled him towards the music in the distance.

Being dragged, Dave looked over his shoulder at Mick with a silly look on his face, and said, "I guess we're going dancing now."

Mick raised his brows and replied, "That looks to be the case."

Rebecca and Mick followed.

The dance floor was crowded. Nevertheless, the four squeezed their way in. They danced to the music of a five-piece band until their feet were sore. Hawk and Leopard weren't the greatest of dancers, but with the women's help they successfully went through the motions with what one could call *mediocre poise.*

Afterwards, they took advantage of an open table and sat for a while to rest their tender feet.

They sat and talked at the table for half an hour. Then the foursome decided to leave the hubbub of town and spend some time back at the castle. The women were mainly responsible for the decision, for there weren't very many Capital citizens who wouldn't have wanted to take advantage of the opportunity to step foot in the castle. Besides, they were all hungry, and there was an entire staff to prepare food at any given time. *You only live once,* thought Olivia and Rebecca.

Having successfully weaved their way through the late-night crowd, they reached their destination. With a nod of the head from one of the guards at the gate, the quartet entered the confines of the castle. Hunger was priority, so they headed to the guest-wing kitchenette, as opposed to the main kitchen/dining hall. The group could've just as easily gotten the staff to do it, but they fixed some hulking sandwiches themselves to save time.

They sat to eat in the small dining space adjacent to the kitchenette.

Subsequent to the meal, Dave and Mick switched into the most charming versions of themselves and allowed the enchantment of the moment to take control. They paired off and went into their respective bedrooms for the rest of the night, succumbing to the same advice mother nature regularly gives virtually all living things.

In the morning, the women ate breakfast with Mick and Dave, and left the castle just before rehearsal began, but not before promising to be at the celebration.

Again, Charlie was dressed to kill. He, Mick, and Dave walked to the Knowing Circle grounds, which surprisingly had already been spotlessly cleaned. "The cleanup crew seems as proficient as the decorations team," commented Dave, impressed.

"We're blessed with quality crews here at the Capital," stated liaison Charlie.

Rehearsal went off without a hitch, lasting about an hour and a half. They had walked through a condensed version of the ceremony. Mick and Dave had also been given time to practice their acceptance speeches, at the end of which many people told them how much they enjoyed listening.

Mick noted, "It seems the ceremony will be a couple hours long."

Charlie reminisced. "The last one, if my memory serves me correctly, took an hour and forty-five minutes."

Dave asked, "How many people usually come to watch?"

"All of town comes, and much of the countryside. Each and every one of the seats gets filled. The rest stand anywhere they can get a halfway decent view."

"And do they party as hard afterwards as they did last night?"

"Oh, for sure!"

"That's the Myothraces I know and love," declared Dave.

"Some are even partying already."

For supper, the ceremony committee planned a gigantic feast for Mick, Dave, and other dignitaries which was to take place just before the actual ritual. A less extravagant lunch was also organized. Both meals were to be held in the grand dining hall. Lunch was designated as being the time when Mick and Dave were to first meet King Rowlangiv.

They went to their rooms to clean up a bit, after which Ghrere and Thraiker sauntered to the main dining hall for the ceremony luncheon. As was the case for any event in the castle—formal in the slightest, seats were assigned, and Mick and Dave were shown theirs.

While the waiters started to bring out food, the King appeared. King Rowlangiv was forty-five years old, had a neatly trimmed beard, was average in height and weight, and was known to be pretty soft-spoken. He approached the honorary guests and said in his customary soft tone, "It's my pleasure to meet you, Mick, Dave. Of course, your heroic deeds have been detailed to me, and I must say, it really intrigued me."

Mick returned, "Thank you, sir. I'm glad to meet you as well."

"As am I," Dave emitted.

"Are the two of you fully recovered from yesterday's intense festivities?" asked the King, humorously.

"It was a long night, but we're good to go." Mick produced the first smile he'd ever supplied a king.

Rowlangiv continued, "I'm aware the two of you are very free -spirited, but even so, I still must try to convince you to join my Castle Guard. These are dangerous times, and I would love to have you aboard. I would go as far as to say I'd even offer officers' positions to grease the wheels a bit."

Dave replied, "I am quite taken aback by this generosity. I can honestly say I didn't expect to be presented with such an admirable proposal."

"Nor I," added Mick. "I guess I half expected more recruiting from anonymous army personnel while here at the Capital, but I didn't expect it from the top. It really is a praiseworthy bid."

"I'll let you sleep on it. For now, let's eat, and we'll converse further, later." The King sat, and everyone partook of the meal. Stomachs were satisfied without delay.

In the time between meals, Hawk and Leopard first took naps (having not received enough sleep the previous night), and second, went to explore the castle's arboretum. Adjacent to the castle's western main wall was the renowned arboretum, which contained tree species from all across Taraosk. Each and every tree was labeled and manicured scrupulously. The arboretum also encompassed many artificial and natural water features.

Dave looked high into an oak canopy and said, "Most of these species I've seen in the past, but some I have not."

"Same here. The ones I've never seen before sure are wondrous."

"You can say that again."

The two of them sat on a bench next to a particular water feature. It caught their attention, because the rocks surrounding the invitingly crystal-clear water were massive, and obviously brought in from afar. "Quite the display of manpower," said Mick.

"I wonder how they keep this water so algae-free, plus, I wonder from where these rocks come."

"I guess we'll have to ask somebody."

Having enjoyed their time on the bench as much as one could enjoy time on a bench, they stood and continued strolling. In their walk, they endeavored to not miss a single one of the arboretum's highlights.

The locale's crowning tree, according to Mick, Dave, and many other visitors, was a certain non-indigenous cedar tree. The tree's label didn't say from where it came, nor were Mick and Dave familiar with the species, Brethyn. Towering higher than the castle's loftiest point, the treetop was well acquainted with birds of the sky. The cedar's branches were spread out imposingly for all to see, observable from both ground and castle window.

"The colossal trunk sure is a real eye-opener."

"Cedars are famously slow growers," noted Dave, "so I'd say the most impressive part of this tree is certainly its age."

"I'd estimate it to be over five hundred years old."

Dave supplied the tree a final scrutiny, and commented, "I concur. This gnarly old man has been around for many sunsets."

"And hopefully many more."

The last thing to see at the arboretum for the pair was an orderly assortment of bushes, which were surrounded by a wide array of bird feeders and bird houses. The locale drew in birds of all shapes and sizes.

"It sure is noisy here amongst these bushes."

"You'll have that," stated Mick. "Birds will always go on doing their thing, no matter the circumstances."

After leaving the arboretum, Hawk and Leopard caught sight of the fact there was still half an hour left before the giant feast. To kill time, they relaxed in their rooms. They knew it was going to be another long night, so reserving energy was a force spent sensibly.

Compelled by punctuality, the duo left the comfort of relaxation and headed to the grand, pre-ceremony banquet, wearing the fanciest outfits the closets in their rooms had to offer.

"I didn't know you cleaned up so well."

Mick replied, "There are a lot of things you don't know about me, Dave."

"That would seem to be so."

When Mick and Dave arrived at the dining hall, the seats were only half occupied. The fashionably late trickled in as minutes ticked by, all dressed in their best. Garobansurovian women especially knew how to look beautiful on the day of the Knowing Circle event.

King Rowlangiv arrived, followed by his most trusted adviser, Yori Rothlin, who approached the honorary recipients and shook their hands.

The King introduced Yori to Mick and Dave. In a pleasing voice, Yori spoke: "King Rowlangiv and I have spent quite some time talking about your noble deeds. It's been a while since we've bestowed the medal upon anyone. I must say the two of you are certainly deserving. I'm glad to be here to witness it all."

Before either Dave or Mick could respond, they found themselves having to shove aside innocent thoughts of how incredibly attractive Yori was. She was wearing a tight fitting, lavender silk dress. Her hair was high, and her makeup alluring.

Dave uttered, "I am glad you're here to witness it too, and I'm delighted to meet you."

"How has your stay here at the Capital been thus far, guys?"

Mick responded to Yori, "It couldn't be better. The sights, sounds, experiences, thrills have all amazed without intermission."

Yori let a smile creep onto her face. "You've even found some thrills, eh? I'm ecstatic to hear it. May your stay here at the Capital continue to thrill."

King Rowlangiv cleared his throat and emitted, "I hope tonight the two of you eat so many crab legs it hurts, but hurting in a good way."

"That's the plan," Dave returned.

"Good." Rowlangiv raised, "Has anyone ever told you the story of why it's called the Knowing Circle?"

Mick replied, "Not precisely. I know the medal is round, so I've always figured that's from where the circle part comes. And for the knowing part, all I've heard was that a long time ago a great warrior named Thurengule won an important battle, but what he *knew* during it, I have no idea."

Dave added, "That's all I've gathered about the subject as well."

Yori gave the King a look suggesting that she'd like to be the one to tell the story. Since he knew how much she liked telling it, he was more than willing to allow her the privilege.

She began the execution, all smiles. "Yes, the circle part is pretty self-explanatory. But I bet you didn't know they are actually made of platinum, but gold-plated?"

"Nope," answered Mick. "Interesting."

Yori continued, "Indeed they are. And the carvings on them take months to complete. The medals truly showcase Garobansurov's highest level of craftsmanship.

"So," Yori continued, "the story detailing what Thurengule *knew* all started hundreds of years ago, during a time stained by blood—*too much blood*. Our country sure has had a plethora of enemies over the years. The King at the time was Frederick the Second, who had wisely appointed the stalwart Thurengule as his guard captain.

"At the time period of my chronicle, Myothraces had been facing attacks from countless barbarian hordes, but one horde in particular was of great size, strength, and formidability.

"The battle with this horde multitude lasted all day and into the night. It was presumed the horde was only fighting for financial gain, killing everyone in their path in their quest for riches. To the guards, the King was top priority, so as guard captain Thurengule never let him out of his sight. Still, the enemy ominously closed in around them. In fact, things were so treacherous that according to most sources, an arrow had missed Frederick's head by mere inches and embedded itself into the wall behind. This is shown by the nick you see right over here," said Yori, as she walked ten paces to point at a deep, eye-level notch in the wall.

"I'll be darned," uttered Dave. "I wouldn't have even noticed that."

Yori resumed, "Frederick wanted to surrender—an action in his mind that would've surely saved the lives of the soldiers protecting him. Thurengule, however, was all too aware that surrendering in situations such as that didn't boast a very good survival record.

"Having seen the look of defeat in his King's eyes, Thurengule strongly counseled not to capitulate. It was said the guard captain in this moment somehow *knew* the overwhelmed Castle Guard would receive help from the least likely of places.

"Even though he was moments from a barbarian axe in his skull, the King heeded his personally chosen guard captain's advice, and abstained from yielding to the barbarians.

"Forever etched in stone is Thurengule's *knowing*—the miraculous knowing that an earthquake was going to strike.

"The vibrations from the earthquake were vicious, forcing an entire wall to crash down upon the enemy horde, who were closing in on the King and Thurengule. The fallen wall also provided an escape route for Fredrick and Thurengule. They were able to get themselves out into the open air, gaining enough time to stay alive, and for reinforcements to arrive.

"If not for Thurengule's bravery, King Frederick surely would've been captured and killed. In two months' time from the day of the earthquake, the very first Knowing Circle (which wasn't yet platinum) was bestowed upon Thurengule. Frederick the Second proclaimed henceforth anyone exhibiting the noblest of heroism would be honored with the same award. So here we are, many hundreds of years later, doing that very thing."

Dave scratched his chin, and said, "Wonderful story, Yori, wonderful indeed. How big was the first Knowing Circle celebration? Was that recorded anywhere at all?"

"I couldn't really tell you how big the celebration was, but I can tell you attendance has been increasing more and more every time we have one."

Mick asked Yori and King Rowlangiv, "So, if I may probe, who was it that decided Dave and I would receive medals?"

Rowlangiv replied, "We have an entire committee for that. There are ten of us on it, Yori and I included. My vote counts for three. A seventy-five percent positive vote is required for there to be a recipient in the given year. That's why there can be many years between receivers. This has been the first time since I've become King we've had a vote be unanimous. The last ceremony, five years ago, we'd voted in favor at seventy-five percent exactly."

"Well, I'll be darned," blurted Dave. "It's humbling to hear we were unanimous."

The quartet of Mick, Dave, Yori and the King conversed until the servers presented the first dish. Heavenly aromas immediately filled the air, all the guests who weren't already seated sat, and all partook in the bountiful meal. Everyone enjoyed the notable moment, Mick and Dave especially.

Chapter 6

AMONGST A GREAT ARMY, General Ulfenkerki's army, two soldiers sat leisurely sharpening swords. "It won't be long now before Mick and Dave's ceremony."

"Yup, too bad we're not forty miles southwest, otherwise we'd be near enough town to see it," Gregg Hogarty said to Jason Thorncat.

"That would've been nice," replied Jason, as he reminisced. He pondered the last time he'd seen his friends, Mick and Dave. He thought about how when he was visiting Mick and Dave, he was given his great set of armor. *Old Man Johnson, what a guy!* Piling onto Jason's reflection, he couldn't help but think about how he pulled his shoulder muscle trying (and failing) to beat his childhood friends at armwrestling on a picturesque winter's night. Mick and Dave both were in fact

Chalatore Armwrestling Tournament champs at the time, so he wasn't too embarrassed by the losses. The pulled shoulder had since healed, thankfully. Good thing too, because it was his sword arm. Jason snapped out of his fond memory just in time to hear Gregg speak.

"I wonder if we'll be sent to the western side of the country soon, since this side has been so quiet lately."

"I don't think the King will arrange that because he knows according to the law of averages if he were to dispatch us to the west, the eastern side would then become overrun."

"I suppose that's logical. It just doesn't seem natural for us to be so dormant during wartime, not that I'm complaining or anything," said Gregg, just before the pair finished the task at hand.

They got up from sword sharpening, and walked towards General Ulfenkerki, who was cleaning fish nearby—his day's catch from the nearby stream.

Jason pointed to a fish and said to the General, "That one there is a pretty nice-sized one."

"I suppose it is. I almost lost it too. I had to jump into the stream to dislodge it out from underneath a log."

"It ain't a battle unless you get wet, my old man always used to say," declared Gregg.

"Too true." The General looked around at the landscape, was struck by realization, and said, "Jason, do you remember the time we camped out in this very same clearing, a while back?"

"Now that you mention it, I do remember. It sure has changed though."

"Yes. The trees are obviously older, different species of grasses have since become dominant, and those rocks over there were moved for some reason."

"That is odd. I wonder who would've had a reason to move them."

"I guess we may never know."

Later that evening, Jason and the General sat around a fire and played cards, enjoying the cool night air. It was one campfire of many and a two-man card game. They played with chips representing small amounts of real money they'd someday exchange. Jason was leading monetarily in games between the two, but not by much. During the game, they discussed some things that mattered, and some things that didn't.

On most nights, army camp was an upbeat place. Almost every soldier was doing something enjoyable.

Jason threw his cards down emphatically, knowing he was bested that round. But the night was young, and there were many more hands to be played.

SINCE SHE ENJOYED THEIR company, Yori accompanied Dave and Mick to the Knowing Circle grounds, which as expected was swarming and raucous. The official bestowing would soon commence. Conveniently, there was a back way into the backstage area for the trio. It provided a way for recipients and presenters to remain hidden until it was time to reveal themselves.

The backstage area was full of guards, mainly because King Rowlangiv was at hand. He was expected to say a few words before and after the medals were presented.

Standing amongst the hubbub of the backstage area, Yori said to Mick and Dave, "Relish the moment, men, you've earned it."

On stage, the event was just about to begin. The lead stagehand stood tall and hushed the crowd. Impressively, a roar instantaneously switched to silence, like the stagehand held some magical power over the spectators.

Sitting in the front row, Rebecca and Olivia watched on with great enthusiasm. Mick and Dave were given authority to apportion seats to anyone, the girls being their first and only conferring. They would've liked Tim Warmane (the maker of their swords) to sit up front, but since being at the Capital, they hadn't yet had the time to pay him a visit. Everything was happening so fast, though they'd surely make the trip to his blacksmith shop soon.

The moment everyone was waiting for finally arrived: the ceremony had been initiated. It all started with the singing of the official Knowing Circle anthem, entitled "Thurengule's Knowing." It was a short song with a pleasing melody.

Post-anthem, the first two to take the stage were members of the Knowing Circle Committee. They summarized what the award stood for, along with a woman representing a governmental position. Mick and Dave weren't exactly sure which governmental position—there were too many to remember. She recited from memory all past recipients, and what they all did to merit the award.

For lack of anything else to do while waiting to go onstage, Hawk and Leopard listened to the opening speeches through the partition separating stage area from backstage area.

When it was time, Mick and Dave were signaled to go out onstage. Upon their appearance, an unrelenting blast of thunderous applause sprang forth from the audience. All but those who couldn't stood, clapped, and cheered loudly. During the ovation, Dave and Mick spotted Rebecca and Olivia in the audience and projected smiles their way. The sight of so many people was overwhelming to Mick and Dave, but they held their composures.

Looking out into the crowd, Mick and Dave also took note of a rather large, curious assemblage of local youngsters taking advantage of the unique conditions. Multiple groups of children were perched atop the giant-sized stone fountains at the periphery of the audience. If their mothers had seen them doing this, the children surely would've been scolded. *Kids will be kids, especially on occasions such as the one present.* Mick and Dave loved it.

Mick and Dave remained standing centerstage when the applause finally subsided. They stood idly as a couple more people spouted speeches.

After the speeches, Yori, King Rowlangiv, and the rest of the Knowing Circle Committee came out with the medals. The sight of the iconic medals glistening in the sun triggered another burst of cheering from the onlooking multitude. The arena became so loud some had to cover their ears.

The King delivered a small but memorable speech, then placed Knowing Circles around Mick and Dave's necks. Mick and Dave eloquently said a few words to the audience—not too many, just enough to articulate how much they appreciated the high honor, and everybody coming out to join in on the festivity.

At the conclusion of his speech, Dave made a point to follow through on a promise—the one he and Mick had made on their journey into town, a promise made to the fellow traveler, Jim. Dave came out from behind the wooden podium, stepped to the edge of the stage just in front of the crowd, and said, "I don't know where in the audience you are, but Seth and Derek Tradel, the two of you have got what it takes to one day receive Knowing Circles too. Stay brave, guys, just like your father, Jim."

Standing somewhere in the middle of the audience the Tradel family beamed with joy. Jim was ecstatic he'd run into Mick and Dave on the road. The kids looked up to their father a little more that day.

Subsequent the medal presentation and the acceptance speeches, King Rowlangiv had a few more things to say to conclude the ceremony. Standing five feet away, Mick listened to his King speak with utmost attentiveness. However, this attention of Mick's suddenly averted to the audience. He noticed a man a hundred feet into the audience had snuck a mini crossbow into the event grounds. Instantly, a high-velocity bolt was shot straight at King Rowlangiv.

Half a second before the trigger was pulled, Mick acted fast and instinctively, doing what seemed best at the time. He'd ripped the podium from its base and whipped it to a point right in front of the King. Due to adrenalin, the podium was as light as a pillow. Mick's quick thinking stopped the bolt from assassinating the King. The bolt sailed right through the first board of the hollow podium, and luckily embedded itself in the second board, inches from Rowlangiv's face.

The would-be assassin, seeing the failure, whistled, signaling an armed host scattered in the audience to come alive. It seemed right then and there the war had reached the Capital without the slightest bit of warning.

Both Mick and Dave reacted flawlessly, rushing the King back into the backstage area. As fluently as possible, all available members of the King's Guard joined Mick and Dave in escorting the King back to the castle.

Along the way to the castle, a couple guards handed swords to Mick and Dave, but disappointingly, they weren't their trusty *black needles*. The borrowed swords would have to suffice.

It didn't take long for a pursuing group to catch up with the escaping King and his company, which led Mick and Dave to believe the band was strategically positioned to cut the King and company off from reaching the stronghold of the castle—a good idea on their part, because it'd delay the escapees just enough for other pursuers to catch up—though a problem that wasn't without some anticipation on Garobansurov's part, a squadron of troops was dispatched to the scene from the barracks near the castle. The Capital had an impressive network of audio signals for just such an occasion.

Mick and Dave took part in the battle that ensued. Not without a bit of humor, they fought while still wearing their medals around their necks. They hadn't yet received the chance to take them off.

All around, villagers became frantic, just trying to survive. Some ran past Dave and Mick's fray, screaming. Chaos was everywhere.

Mick made do with the borrowed sword, slashing and stabbing with precision. One of Mick's adversaries for some unknown reason yelled annoyingly, every time he swung his sword. The yeller managed to draw Mick's blood (nothing perilous), before being defeated. Another warrior tried to sneak up behind Mick, but it took a lot more than that to outclass Mick Thraiker—he had seen it all.

Dave had easier foes, disposing of them rather quickly. The only one who made Dave break a sweat was a tall man strong enough to wield a massive war hammer. The hammer was so immense it probably could've been used to pound trees into the ground. However, the tall man was barely able to swing it fast enough to shoo pigeons. Dave was no pigeon. Two sidesteps, a fake, and a lunge was all Dave needed to slay the tall man.

Both Mick and Dave were well aware their party had an advantage once reaching the castle's causeway, where all the archer towers awaited.

Mick said to King Rowlangiv, "Stay low, sir. You never know when an errant arrow will come screaming out of nowhere."

"Indeed, I will." The King stayed calm. It wasn't his first battle. He had unwavering faith in his guards—official guards and unofficial guards, Mick and Dave being the *unofficial* guards.

Battling and moving at the same time, the Garobansurovians reached the causeway and the first archer tower. From the tower, bow-wielding snipers one-by-one picked off the assailants presenting the safest shots. Of course, nobody wanted to be the one to accidentally hit the King.

The skirmish progressed down the causeway, resulting in more archer towers being put into play. Arrows from above were plentiful.

The enemy soon knew they were outmatched. Enemy survivors acted quickly, took advantage of the town still being frenzied, and disappeared into the confusion of the crowd, back into hiding. The assassination attempt had utterly failed.

King Rowlangiv and company made haste to the fortress of the castle. Looking at Dave and Mick's necks, the King said, "Wonderful! Your medals remain unscathed."

Dave responded, "Yeah, good thing. We would've looked pretty silly going back to Chalatore with tattered medals."

Most of the guards stayed on high watch, in case further transgression transpired. Mick, Dave, the King, the officers present, and the guard captain (Raymond), went into one of the castle's meeting rooms to discuss what happened, and what now needed to be done about it.

Rowlangiv voiced his thoughts. "I believe the conflict was a sign of things to come. We will have to ascertain all the details—who they were, for whom they were fighting, and where others could be hiding. From now on, everyone coming and going Myothraces will be scrutinized."

Yori spoke: "Yes, sir, we will immediately form a crew skilled in the art of questioning and post them by every exit and entrance."

"Excellent. Mick Thraiker, without your impeccable reaction time today, things may not have gone so well. I owe you the greatest of appreciations. It seems like you and Dave don't need to join the King's Guard officially— you already perform their functions anyway."

Mick half-smiled, and responded to the King, "That does appear to be the case, and thank you, sire."

"You're most certainly welcome. And it's too bad your celebration ended so abruptly. Later tonight, the townsfolk will probably get gutsy and come back out into the streets to further their merriment. All is not lost."

"That's good to hear." Mick's half-smile turned into a full one.

Yori commented, "I think they'll try another assassination attempt in the future, whoever they are, so I hope you stay as cautious as possible, King."

"I probably won't leave the castle until more intel is gathered."

"Good, sir. We also have to be extra wary of everyone inside the castle. You never know if anyone in here switched allegiances," said Yori.

Everyone in the room took a moment to brood over the incident as a whole, Yori's words, and who they knew who could've possibly switched sides.

"We'll make sure only those most loyal serve as Castle Guard during the upcoming days, possibly weeks," declared Raymond.

"I'd like a head count of how many guards we lost today, so we can replenish ranks as soon as possible."

Responding to Rowlangiv, one of the officers stepped forward and said, "I'll go get those numbers, sir, and report back."

"Thank you. Also, can you bring me a list of all their names."

"Yes, sir, will do."

Once it seemed all the important matters were finished being discussed, Mick left the room to wrap the small wound he'd sustained and Dave left to make sure Rebecca and Olivia were alright. Last he saw, the ladies were successfully fleeing the scene.

Dave found the two women and was relieved to see they'd made it through the pandemonium of the conflict, and to the safety of their homes. To them, he shared the account of everything that'd transpired from his perspective. Afterwards, he went back to the castle to inform Mick (who'd finished attending to his wound) the women were safe.

Later that night, Hawk and Leopard discussed the future. "So much for this trip being hazard-free, eh Mick?"

"They never are."

"What do you think we should do next?"

"You mean in terms of whether we stay or leave?"

"Yup. Should we head back home relatively soon, or stay longer in case there's further incident here?"

Mick stood up from the chair on which he was sitting, thought for a while, and replied, "Well, our initial plan before any of this occurred was to stay a few more days, see the sights, visit with Tim Warmane, then leave. But I know I personally would like to heed my curiosity and see what's exactly going on here. Frankly, the mysterious appearance of the aggressors has confounded me."

"I too was thinking of staying longer, maybe aid in trying to get to the bottom of the enigmatic attack. These are dangerous times, especially for our King. He needs all the help he can get. But as for signing up for permanent guard duty, I'll pass."

"Same here. Our freedom to roam is the armor protecting us from the monotony of life."

"True. We'll tell the King as soon as possible," said Dave.

Good fortune had blessed the Capital, for there were no further attacks on Knowing Circle commemoration day. Celebrators came out into the streets eventually, but not at full force, as the night before. Nevertheless, good times had rained down. Bands played, peddlers sold their wares, street performers executed routines. And of course, drinkers drank.

The citizens were unquestionably rowdy. They made a mess, broke many things, and walked the thin line between legal and illegal. But in doing so, they never forgot they loved their country through and through. They'd die for it. It was the way of things, the same as it always was, and the same as it would always be.

Mick Thraiker and Dave Ghrere went out amongst the commotion but now, since everyone saw them at the ceremony and recognized them, they only stayed out on the town for a couple hours. *There's only so much attention a man can take, so many handshakes, so many free drinks, so many requests from women for dances—well, not so much that last part.*

Nonetheless, they were pretty spent, and went back to the castle. Activities of a more leisure nature were calling their names.

They decided to visit a section of the castle they hadn't yet seen: the lower level. There were actually two parts they hadn't been to. The other was the catacombs/dungeon, even lower yet. This, they'd save for another day when more time was available.

On the lower level, and peering throughout, Dave said, "All these rooms are elegantly furnished, as if they're being used, but there's nary a soul around."

"True, Dave. I wonder how often they are utilized."

"We'll add that to our list of questions."

Mick walked into one of the larger rooms and shouted to Dave in the hallway, "I bet at least three people could sleep comfortably in this particular bed."

"A kinky mind today I see."

Mick chuckled. "I wasn't even thinking that."

"Sure, you weren't."

Dave wandered aimlessly into a different large room. He took some time to admire the curious paintings. I bet much time was spent on these. Fascinating.

Other than a handful of large bedrooms, and a couple of small ones, the level housed a huge recreation area, where one could go to engage in an assortment of leisurely activities. There was a court on which an individual or multiple people could participate in pretty much any sport they desired. Also scattered throughout were various wooden contraptions, games probably constructed by some of the Capital's more creative tinkers. Mick and Dave occupied themselves with the wooden devices for a few well-spent hours.

"We really should organize a game of some sort to play on the court, at least a four-on-four match. The court is rather inviting."

"Definitely, Mick. We'd need six more participants."

"We'll locate them some other day."

"Agreed."

The pair eventually grew tired and went to their respective rooms to turn in for the evening.

NESTLED IN AN out-of-the way nook of the world, as humanly unreachable as one could imagine, the naturally-shielded island of Swyrove aged gracefully. Swyrove was part of an archipelago containing a few other smaller islands, some of which were forested, some were not, but all were beautiful and inhabited. This was the veiled home of the man-like race known as the Icytryxis and has been since their first breath many eons ago.

The number of years the Icytryxis had been in existence was a number higher than most folks of the time could comprehend.

The Icytryxis were like humans in a lot of ways, but were unlike them in just as many. As far as physical appearance went, for the most part, they looked like humans, however their eyes were slightly smaller, but they boasted better vision. Their ears were shaped a little differently, and their hearing was about the same as humans. Their arms were a bit longer and stronger than humans. Their hands (in only the men) resembled pointed weapons, though they were still dexterous enough to perform three-fourths the tasks humans could—exceptions being things like threading needles and plucking the strings of musical instruments at great speed. The men's individual fingers were pyramid-shaped, coming together symmetrically. Adding hard, sizable fingernails, their hands could penetrate a myriad of substances. However, they hardly ever used their weapon-hands for confrontations, because they could still grasp the handles of conventional weapons. Icytryxis scholars postulated their weapon-hands were a part of their evolution benefiting them greatly before the invention of metallurgy. Wielding a rock or pointed stick could inflict a lot of damage to prey or an attacker, but having hands that could penetrate hide and muscle tissue with great precision presented more of an advantage, or so the scholars postulated. Female hands were more human-like and correspondingly more dexterous.

Where the Icytryxis were the most diametrically opposed from humans was in their approach to politics—they didn't have any. None at all. Unlike for those living on the rest of the planet, the concept of politics was illogical to the Icytryxis, serving no purpose in their daily lives. In fact, they had no government, nor money, and nobody had official jobs. They all worked, but did so only at their own will. The system worked and had been working for many, many generations. It was a successful lifestyle for them made possible by one main reason—the Icytryxis virtually never lied. Only one in a hundred thousand of their statements were determined by their greatest thinkers to be lies. Factuality was in their genetics. Their truth begot their manner of living.

Most of their reality was spent away from the other peoples of the world, but on very rare and/or important occasions, it wasn't.

CHAPTER 7

WOODENLY, THE CASTLE GUARDS stood as Mick and Dave walked past and opened the door leading outside. It was a fine day. Any undesirable morning heat was pleasurably shielded by a cool breeze. In addition, town smelled like baked goods—an agreeable aroma for almost everyone.

Ghrere and Thraiker were on their way to Tim Warmane's blacksmith shop, toting along their seemingly magical *black needle* swords, which Tim had cast for them many years ago. They figured he'd want to see how the swords were holding up. Truth be told, *magnificently.*

The shop was all the way on the other side of town, the part of town less traversed by most, for it contained less of the archetypal shops the bulk of the populace took pleasure in so much.

"I'm sure Tim was in the audience at the commemoration and made it out safe and sound when the melee began. Just a gut feeling of mine, Mick."

"I'm positive of that too. He was always a resourceful fellow."

Dave admired the stone architecture of a few buildings as he walked past them and produced a comment having nothing to do with what he was looking at, not that he didn't think the stone buildings were worth commenting about. "I'm anxious to see what kinds of projects Tim is working on now."

"I'm curious to see the look on his face when he sees the *black needles* again. He really was proud of them, deservingly so. They truly are quite impressive metallurgical constructs."

"Mine is. Yours has been slow lately."

"Oh, you just watch where you're going, you might trip over that large opinion of yourself."

Dave laughed, "Good one."

Having reached eyeshot of their destination, Mick noted, "Thankfully, there's smoke coming out of his chimney, and the front door is propped open. Tim mustn't have run into any danger yesterday."

"Yup, a resourceful fellow indeed."

They walked into the front room of the shop, a space serving as a small area for Tim to display and sell his wares. Weapons and armor of all shapes and sizes were hung on the walls and propped up on racks. Both Mick and Dave noticed Tim was elsewhere. *Excellent weapons and protective gear, just like always*, they thought.

The duo breezed through the front room and back into the foundry itself, where Tim usually spent most of his time working. A place Mick and Dave had spent considerable time in the past, watching and helping their swords get made.

Tim looked up, set his hammer down, took off his mask, and enthusiastically said, "Well, if this isn't a day of days! I just knew you guys would be stopping in here soon."

"It's phenomenal seeing you again too," exclaimed Dave. "We're relieved to see yesterday's scuffle didn't cause you harm."

"Yes, yes, I was indeed present at the ceremony, standing proudly in the back. And because I was in the rear, I was able to get out easily. You know, you wouldn't believe it, but this old man here even ran. I didn't think I had it in me."

"I would've paid to see that," Mick returned. "Never in my wildest dreams would I have thought such violence was going to happen yesterday. This war is everywhere already."

"And I have a feeling it's only the beginning," added Warmane.

"History does show that wars here in Garobansurov do tend to be perplexing and drag on for years," said Dave.

"Yes, a gloomy reality," voiced Tim, as he stepped away from the forge. Tim took off his apron and pointed at what Mick and Dave were carrying on their waists. "Those are them, aren't they?"

"Indeed, they are. The steal is as sturdy as the day you finished forming it." Both Mick and Dave took the swords out of their scabbards, and handed them to Tim. As soon as Tim grasped them, his face lit up, and the memories he had of constructing them flooded in.

"Apparently, they slice with exactitude, for here you are, having just received the nation's highest award by using them—or so I'm guessing you've been using them."

"Yes, that we have. The black needles accompanied us into every battle last year," Dave stated. "We used them so much that we had to get another sharpening stone."

"Speaking of which, I'll give them a good sharpening while you're here, a professional one."

"Have at it. A sharpening done with perfection goes a long way." Mick glanced around the room. "So, what do you have keeping you busy these days?"

"Over here." The trio walked over to Tim's foot-activated grinding wheel. "I'm finishing up a privately-contracted dagger for a local resident right now. But mostly my contracts are with the Castle Guard. They keep me busy with odds and ends. Occasionally, I'll get to make a sword or two. None of them very extravagant though." Tim eyed the black needles. "These two swords are and always will be my most paramount construction. I knew when I was making them, I'd never make anything better. I enjoyed every second I spent on them."

"There's not a swing taken that isn't done so in complete appreciation of your painstaking work on them," said Mick. They've no doubt been responsible for winning many fights for us." Dave shook his head in agreement.

"I hold those words in high esteem," Tim declared. He finished sharpening the first sword and started on the other. "Did Rowlangiv discover who it was that spearheaded the attack?"

"Not yet, but as we speak, he has teams of people tirelessly working on ascertaining their identity."

Tim responded, "That's good. By the way, Mick, I don't think I've ever seen anyone move a podium that fast before."

Mick laughed. "I didn't know they could be moved that fast either. I was also unaware they could even be used for that reason."

Dave added, "That podium sure was sturdy, I'll say that much."

"That it was. Podium: The Protector of Kings," said Tim, as he finished sharpening the second sword. "There you go, sirs, two weapons with edges as good as new. They should last quite a while before needing another sharpening."

"Excellent, thank you very much."

"Yes, much appreciated." Dave blurted, "And of course, Old Man Johnson says hello."

"It's good to hear the old man is still alive. Too bad he couldn't make the trip too, it's been far too long since he and I raised any mischief."

"Maybe next time he'll walk along," noted Mick. "Actually, you should hear what he did last winter. Long story short, in exchange for his help in getting the *black needles* made, Dave and I gave him a priceless set of armor we had acquired. But knowing his generous nature, he turned around and gave it to Jason Thorncat, who was with us at the time."

"Yeah, that sounds like something he would do. I know Jason of Ulfenkerki's army. He's been in the shop here before, multiple times. A real stand-up guy. Wise decision to bestow superior armor onto him. He'll wear it with honor, defending Garobansurov with every ounce."

"Yup, that's exactly what Old Man Johnson said too. Everything worked out well."

"I don't think he's had to use the armor yet. Last I'd heard, Ulfenkerki's army hasn't seen any action since fighting the Battle of Sarwa with the two of you," said Warmane.

Dave produced, "We'd heard the same as well, but we did spend much time on the road, so we didn't hear many details about anything."

"There hasn't been much information making it here from the western front either, only whispers of sporadic encounters, and nothing at all from Riftolen," emitted Tim.

Mick spoke: "The situation on the western front has certainly been on our minds lately. Let's hope the front holds."

"Yup, let's hope." Tim asked, "Would you guys like anything to drink?"

"Yes, I do believe I'm parched. I'll take a beverage— any kind."

"Me too," replied Dave.

As Tim was retrieving the beverages, Dave came within inches of excruciatingly slamming his knee into an anvil, the sort of interaction one tries to avoid at all cost while aimlessly walking in circles. For no real reason, he wasn't paying much attention to anything other than the ground at the time. The close call compelled Dave to momentarily lose his balance and stutter-step.

"I saw that. Good save," Mick chuckled.

"Yeah, that would've ruined my day for sure."

Tim came back with three tall glasses of orange juice—one for each of them. "These should hit the spot. By the way, have you guys had any luck in locating any more of those black needle pine trees, of which the swords' grips are made?"

"Disappointingly, no," Mick replied, "and that surely hasn't been for lack of trying. No new information either. The quest for that continues ever on."

"That's too bad. Every time I run across a book on botany, trees, or even cliffs I scan the pages for information on that rare tree of yours. No luck, however."

"Someday that mystery will be solved."

"I sure hope so. I've never encountered anything more fascinating in my life than the wood from which your sword handles are made."

"Neither have we, Tim, that's for certain."

The trio talked for a couple hours more, catching up on many things, and had themselves a fine morning. Tim even made sandwiches. Previous to Mick and Dave leaving the shop, Tim Warmane promised he'd pay them a visit at the castle, before they headed back to Chalatore.

Back at the castle, the men searched out what news, if any, had been gathered about the day of the Knowing Circle aggression. A few discussions were had, but no new information had been learned.

In the evening, after visiting with Rebecca and Olivia for a while, they had a lot of time on their hands, so Mick and Dave decided to check out the storied catacombs lurking far below the castle.

Armed with lit candles, and a few extra unlit ones, they opened the well-worn, ancient catacomb door. It was so old that it was surprising it even opened. Throwing caution to the wind, they descended the creaky stairs into the deep, dark unknown.

Five hundred years previous, the crypts saw occasional funeral service attendees, but now, the only to visit the darkness were brave souls and rats. In fact, when Mick and Dave asked around, nary an individual was able to be the slightest descriptive about what they were going to find in the depths. They were told it was easy to get lost, and that they could re-light some of the old candles placed at irregular intervals along the walls, as long as they put them out on their way back.

Strolling within Dave's long shadow, Mick stated, "I don't know what we're going to find down here, but it sure is thrilling."

"I concur. There aren't too many things more exhilarating than the unpredictable backdrops of the universe, the ones that have never seen the light of day. I just hope no breeze appears out of nowhere and extinguishes these candles. I'm trying my best to paint a mental picture of where we're going, but I'm not positive I'm capturing it accurately enough I could find the way back out in utter darkness."

Dave commented, "I'm trying too, but I'm afraid I'm doing about as well as you."

They approached another set of stairs, and followed them to an even lower level, which had narrower passageways and visible tombs, ominous visible tombs.

Looking at a particular sepulcher, Dave gasped. "Hey, Mick, come look at this."

"Well, I'll be darned! I was unaware of there being any Thraikers buried here at the Capital. I can't quite make out the first name. I guess you learn something new every day. It could be a relative."

"Could be."

They moved on, and having walked through a narrow tunnel for five minutes, they reached a point wide enough for a gathering. The pair hypothesized the locale was where some of the funeral services were held. A lot of the chairs were even still there, along with an altar, and an ornate priest's chair, adorned with what were probably fake jewels. Any real ones would've been plundered long ago.

Lit candle in hand, Mick walked up to the altar. "I think if I opened up this book sitting on the altar, it would disintegrate into dust in an instant."

"Same with these decayed chairs here. I know I'm not going to try to sit in one."

"Good thinking." Mick looked down. "The designs carved into the floor are pretty unique. Very interesting."

Dave walked over to Mick. "I wonder what the pictograms are supposed to depict."

"My guess is as good as yours."

"Unless there's translation text in the library somewhere, we'll never know."

Having finished checking out the area, they continued on, and reached yet another flight of downward sloping stairs, which presumably led to a third crypt echelon.

Once to the new level, they found more tombs, and the actual dungeons themselves. They decided the new environment was definitely the creepiest yet. They couldn't help but imagine all the suffering that'd taken place there so long ago. One room even looked like a torture room, due to the fact there were chains bolted to the wall, and blood stains everywhere.

"There aren't exactly very many reasons for there to be chains attached to a wall, and a floor strewn with dried blood," stated Mick. "Torture."

"Sinister indeed."

Dave drew together some nerve and stepped inside one of the ancient cells. "This is just enough to drive a man insane. There's barely enough room here to successfully perform a pushup."

"Don't accidentally lock yourself in there! I don't see any keys lying about."

"That would be the day."

The pair examined as much as they could and realized the third level was the last and lowest part of the catacombs. It was probably the lowest point in all the Capital—perhaps the lowest place for one to step foot in the entire country. No way to tell for sure.

Since they no longer felt compelled to linger in the terrifying dungeon plane, Dave and Mick headed back up, remembering to extinguish the wall candles along the way. It took them half an hour to get out of the catacombs, walking relatively straight.

Standing beside the ancient door they'd opened to enter the catacombs, Dave voiced, "Taking into consideration the average distance we travel in a given amount of time, I calculate the shafts we just traversed were a mile and a half long."

"Including all the side shafts, I bet altogether there's probably over four miles worth of tunnels."

"Sounds about right. Such a massive network. It must've taken over a hundred years to laboriously excavate it all."

"I'm glad I didn't have to do it."

"Same here." Dave digressed, "I think we've now officially seen every part of the castle."

"It's too bad we can't say that about Garobansurov," responded Mick.

"I wonder if it could be done in a lifetime.

"I doubt even half."

Evening rolled around. Mick and Dave ended up winding down with Yori Rothlin in one of the relaxing living rooms. She'd been at the castle per request of Rowlangiv to discuss matters. The discussion with the King didn't take long, since there wasn't much new to discuss.

With her feet up, Yori noted to Mick and Dave, "We never thought these assailants would be this hard to track. They must either be getting help from the inside, or are capable of a degree of inconspicuousness one would deem nearly impossible."

Mick commented, "Maybe they gave up and went away."

"Hopefully, but I doubt it. The sentries and their bookkeeping counterparts we've posted by every city gate haven't reported any suspicious comings and goings whatsoever."

Dave spoke. "I bet if something is going to happen, it'll happen fast and soon. They won't risk getting prematurely discovered."

"That's right," noted Yori. "In the name of surprise, we've secretly doubled the number of archers inside each tower."

Mick scratched his chin. "Good thinking. I've also spent some time thinking on castle defense, and I'd propose greasing the causeway for the time being to prevent any 'no guts no glory' mad dashes to the castle door by assaulters."

"That's actually a good idea, but there's no way we have enough grease at hand to cover the whole causeway," said Yori. "We probably have some stored away somewhere, but not in the amount of which you're speaking."

Mick smiled and remarked, "With the King's permission, you can just leave that to Dave and I."

Curling her lip in bafflement, Yori half-chuckled. "Go right ahead. I'm positive he'd agree to it. I have no idea where you're going to find such a supply, but more power to you. I'll inform Rowlangiv the causeway will be a bit slippery for a time. If he happens to be against it, I'll let you know asap."

"Excellent," said Dave. "Tomorrow, consider yourself stunned–stunned, alongside your usual stunning self."

Standing up, Yori replied, "Oh, you guys! I'll see you later."

Dave and Mick hung out in the living room for a while, discussed their grease plan, and played a few rounds of low stakes poker before going to bed.

The King ended up liking Mick and Dave's plan. Though, Adviser Rothlin was correct in saying there wasn't much available grease, only enough cart axle grease stored in canisters in the sheds to cover one-fifth of the causeway. Mick and Dave used half of the grease in the sheds, and kept the other half in storage, saved for the official governmental carts and wagons of the Capital. Mick and Dave had something up their sleeves to acquire the rest of the grease they needed.

Taking advantage of his close proximity to the castle ground's storage sheds, Dave borrowed a wheelbarrow; he'd need it later.

Lugging the wheelbarrow, Hawk and Leopard headed to Myothrace's busiest business district. It was 9:00 in the morning, so town was pretty empty yet. The Capital normally didn't liven up until at least 10:00.

Mick and Dave knew they wouldn't procure enough axle grease for their mission, so Mick's plan all along was not to search out equipment-type grease, but animal fat grease, the kind found in restaurant waste piles.

They entered the biggest, most prominent restaurant in town (the Regal), and searched out the owner. With the obliging guidance of a young waitress, they found him in his office, going over numbers.

Mick wrapped on the half-open door, approached the man, and said, "Good morning, sir."

"Well, hello there. I never thought I'd see the two of you in my office. My name is Mike. What can I do for you, misters Thraiker and Ghrere?"

"Nice to meet you, Mike. We are actually here to ask something of you."

"Ask away, gentlemen."

"I like the ink drawing you have posted on the wall, by the way," Mick stated. "Hopefully, it's not too much of an inconvenience, but we'd like to ask you for as much of your kitchen grease as you have currently available."

"Thanks, I drew it myself a couple months ago. And I can't say I ever would've expected a request such as that." Mike laughed. "But I can certainly comply. What's it for? If I may ask strictly out of curiosity?"

"Don't tell anyone because you never know who's listening in, but a certain causeway made slippery would greatly enhance the safety for our King."

"Say no more. Follow me." Mike showed them to where the waste grease was stored before it was permanently disposed of underground. "Will this be enough grease?"

"This should be much of what we need. Thank you very much, Mike," answered Dave.

"I'm glad to have been able to help. Hopefully though, no more attacks on the King ensue. By the way, if you guys ever get a chance, come back and enjoy a meal on the house. We have the best farm-raised shrimp in town."

"We might very well take you up on that. Thank you so much for the generosity and the grease."

Dave and Mick emptied the grease into the wheelbarrow, a process which didn't take long.

Holding the exit door open for Mick and Dave, Mike said, "Enjoy the fine weather. Hope to see you soon. Goodbye."

"See you later."

Dave wheeled the heavy grease to the castle's causeway, while Mick went to parley with the next restaurant owner. Each eating establishment Mick visited was a success, being as easy to acquire the grease as at the first restaurant. Overall, it took five restaurants and six wheelbarrow trips to get enough.

Standing at the foot of the causeway, Mick uttered to Dave, "Now to spread it all out."

"Hopefully, we don't trip in it while doing so."

Dave and Mick dispersed the grease evenly over the causeway, which took half an hour—easy, fresh-air abounding labor.

"Granted," vocalized Mick, "some of the Garobansurovian infantry will have to fight on the greased causeway to keep any possible enemies in front of the archer towers, but it'll be worth it."

"Yes, I believe so too."

They left a small part right in front of the castle gate ungreased, so that way a few warriors had a good place with firm footing to stand, fight and defend the gate, just in case a few assailants made it past the archers.

"Now that's one slippery causeway, Dave!"

"Hopefully, the wrong person doesn't trip and fall in it, a dignitary or such."

"True. Though, it would be funny."

"Yeah, I'm positive it would be." Dave chuckled. "Let's get supper."

That evening, Mick and Dave decided to spend some time downtown to see if they could overhear anything on the streets about the mysterious Knowing Circle day attackers. Finding their hideout/hideouts would surely solve a lot of problems. Everyone who was looking for answers was coming up with nothing but dead ends.

And by the conclusion of the night, Thraiker and Ghrere came up with the same.

They had paced around the streets for hours, but all they heard were stories about pets, two-layer cakes, and Bo Fisk's incredible performance at yesterday's game. What kind of game exactly, they never did end up hearing.

Solving naught, the pair sauntered back to the castle.

"We'll try again, tomorrow," Mick said, disappointingly.

Back at the castle, Ghrere and Thraiker grabbed a snack, and sat relaxingly in a different living room than the one in which they sat the night before. This living room was probably the most lavishly decorated in all the castle. The more-than-adequate array of furniture was visually stunning and comfortable. So comfortable, in truth, Dave never made it back to his bed that night. He fell asleep sitting in an armchair. He stayed there till morning.

The new day brought with it a new assemblage of activities for Mick and Dave.

They'd intended to head to the streets to engage in detective work again, but first, on impulse, Hawk and Leopard stopped at the guard training grounds near the castle. Practicing a little archery, the duo felt it was valuable to keep this particular skill honed and locked down.

"Well, I'm satisfied my aim hasn't lost a step," Dave declared, setting the practice bow he used into the nearby rack.

"Same here." Mick placed his bow next to Dave's. "We better return to the castle to clean up, before hitting the streets for reconnaissance. I believe I may have broken a sweat."

"I believe the same to be true for me."

After the washup at the castle, Dave and Mick felt renewed, and were ready to hit the ground running.

Venturing out the front gate of the castle and onto the slippery causeway, they felt optimistic.

"Let's go inside some of the bars this time. Maybe alcohol will have loosened the tongues of the attackers."

Mick returned, "That way of thinking may turn out prosperous. But going into taverns, we may have to talk about the Knowing Circles to all sorts of people."

"I think it'll be worth it."

Heading downtown, the two of them traversed the causeway gingerly. A fall into the grease would've surely resulted in embarrassment, and the requirement of an additional washing. *Who wants to do that twice in an hour?*

They made it halfway across the causeway but suddenly stopped in their tracks.

Dave uttered, "I don't have the signal-flag system memorized, but seeing them being waved in the distance when they're otherwise still can't be a good thing. Are you thinking what I'm thinking, Mick?"

"If it's that we're not fighting another battle without the *black needles* again, then yes, I am thinking what you're thinking."

"Exactly, let's hurry and go get them."

Dave and Mick made it back across the causeway and ran as fast as they could to their bedrooms to grab their trusty swords, plus their bows and arrow quivers. They also slipped on the parts of their armor sets that were able to be slid on quickly and easily.

By the time they made it back to the causeway just outside the main gate, they could see arrows flying from the further towers.

Some of the castle guards (including an officer) were also standing on the causeway trying to get a look.

The officer said to Mick and Dave, "Rowlangiv is upstairs, three flights up, in that level's main living room. He is immediately guarded by twenty good soldiers, including Captain Raymond. My company and I are about to go back inside to link up with the castle interior's front line. We will protect against any foes stepping foot inside the castle. I see the two of you are ready to fight. You're welcome to fight alongside us, if you wish."

Mick replied to the officer, "Thanks for the offer, but we'll defend the front gate by making a stand on the ungreased portion just in front of it. We intend to not let anyone step foot in the castle. Furthermore, if by small chance they have a force with grappling hooks foolishly trying to ascend the castle walls, we will surely inform you."

"Okay, good," returned the officer. "The backside of the castle—a blind spot for you—can be viewed from where Rowlangiv and his guard team are right now, so that point is covered."

Dave emitted, "Alright. Excellent. Godspeed to you and your men."

"Same to you. And good luck in your mission of keeping them out."

Mick and Dave shook the officer's hand, before he and the other soldiers went back into the castle.

The force attacking the crown this time was double in number than the one during the Knowing Circle presentation. Myothrace's permanent infantry engaged the raiding party head on. The defenders tried mightily to keep the fight as far from the castle as possible but the infantry was showing signs of being overwhelmed and the conflict drew near the castle's causeway.

This was where the cleverly versatile layout of the Capital would come in handy. Any power trying to get into the castle could only do so by braving the causeway, or descending into the watery pit underneath the causeway and climbing the castle walls with grappling hooks. Wall climbers could be easily cherry picked by archers from the above castle windows. Due to the ingenious layout, any aggressor trying to cross the causeway or pit underneath were subjected to arrows from the towers, and most of those firing these arrows had excellent aim.

Battling bravely, but fewer in number, the Garobansurov infantry exchanged blows with the (presumably Molisian) squadron trying to assassinate the King.

During the early stages of the battle, a few attackers made it past the infantry and onto the causeway. But due to it being greased, they couldn't run very fast, and were easily shot down by the archers from the towers. Eventually, though, as the Capital's infantry wore down, more and more invaders were able to break free from the melee and attempt the mad dash across the causeway.

Mick and Dave's grease plan was working splendidly, for dozens of would-be assassins met their demises, as they lost traction in the grease. However six did make all the way across, but only to run into the unmovable wall that was Mick Thraiker and Dave Ghrere guarding the door. Four were shot down by Mick and Dave, while two made it to close combat.

If the two invaders were a little quicker-witted, maybe it wouldn't have taken Mick and Dave less than a second each to dispose of them. But the world wasn't built by maybes, so a quick defeat was what resulted. A more intelligent duo would've used better teamwork. The fools had faced the masters guarding the gate independently instead of cooperatively.

In the end, the raiders weren't even close in getting at Rowlangiv, but what they did accomplish was incapacitate practically all of the Capital's available infantry. Half were killed, and forty percent were injured and held up at the infirmary. The wave of invaders fared even worse, having been ninety-nine percent eliminated. Five individuals were secured for questioning.

Mick and Dave saw all was clear and went back inside the castle to inform everyone the battle was over. Going upstairs, they aimed to search out Rowlangiv.

"It's over, sir," said Dave in the presence of the King. "Not a malicious soul stepped foot inside the castle."

"That's good to hear, but this is getting ridiculous," emitted the King, sheathing his un-bloodied sword.

"At least you can get a few answers now. Five were captured for interrogation," emitted Dave.

Rowlangiv erupted, "Excellent! We possess certain personnel especially trained for extrapolating information. I'm confident we can syphon some data from the five."

Captain Raymond spoke. "Were the two of you from your post able to see how much of our infantry was left standing in the end?"

Mick replied to the guard captain, "We could only vaguely see what was going on across the causeway, but unfortunately we did see a large portion of the infantry go down. They fought valiantly and held strong, only allowing a few dozen to get through and onto the causeway."

"The two of you were positioned by the front gate, I was told. Is that right?" asked Raymond.

"Correct," replied Thraiker.

"Did any make it all the way across the causeway to you?" inquired Raymond.

"Six did, having survived the arrow onslaught from the towers. We shot four of the six down with arrows, and two we destroyed by sword."

King Rowlangiv declared, "Let's all meet bright and early tomorrow to discuss matters. By then, we should have more information."

All present agreed and left the King alone to his thoughts.

Dave and Mick ventured to the battle scene to see if they recognized any of the deceased. Many bodies of all shapes and sizes were being hoisted out of the dirt to get ready for funeral. Even though Mick and Dave had traveled far and wide, having seen much grotesqueness, nothing could ever prepare for such an unpleasant scene.

Having not recognized any of the dead (they thought surely they would've), Mick and Dave headed back onto the castle causeway. On the way to the castle gate, they pulled the arrows they'd shot out of the dead foes. They planned to scrub them off and insert them back into their quivers. They were good arrows, no point in letting them go to waste.

"We're missing one. You must've missed."

Dave laughed. "Yeah right, you must've."

"I guess we'll never know who missed."

After supper, Mick felt like going for a run, taking advantage of cool, long shadows and overflowing energy. Dave sat in the commons area by his room to read, taking advantage of rare silence and a clear mind.

There was a wide swathe of moderately-level terrain encircling the castle, perfect for Mick's laps. Fifteen half-mile loops were what his legs wanted to do that night.

After the refreshing run, Mick washed up, changed, and sat by Dave.

Dave put his book down, and asked, "How far did you run?"

"I covered about seven and a half miles, I'd say. My pace seemed equal to that of my last run."

"Out of this world, Mick!"

"It felt good." Mick grabbed himself something to read, and enthusiastically joined Dave for the rest of the evening. There weren't too many things in life more agreeable than a good read after a run.

Plants rejoiced as the morning sun appeared.

Someone thinking ahead had brought a bunch more chairs into the first-floor conference room for the King's morning meeting. If they hadn't, it would've looked pretty funny, some people sitting around the giant wooden table, and others standing around it.

Both Mick and Dave sat in the provided chairs, and nodded to all who were already present: Rowlangiv, Yori, Captain Raymond, the officer Dave and Mick talked to yesterday, and a few more they hadn't talked to yesterday, but more than likely had at one point or another in the past.

Another of the King's advisors and the captain of the archers showed up and sat down.

Rowlangiv stood up and spoke. "Thank you all for coming to my war council. My interrogators were hard at work all night on the five enemy soldiers we'd captured. They were certainly burning the midnight oil. Even though we didn't get all the information we sought, I'm pleased by the result. We learned the assailants are indeed Molisian of origin, and that they thought an assassination would produce a swift victory in the war. However, we failed to ascertain who within the city is helping them, if in fact someone is, which I'm fairly confident someone is. We also haven't learned where within the city they've been hiding, and how they've been getting into town unnoticed. Other things to which we need answers: if there are any more Molisians currently within city limits, and/or if more are expected to be.

"We plan on continuing the interrogation procedure, but I've come to an important decision. As soon as this meeting is adjourned, I'm dispatching my fastest messengers to General Ulfenkerki to inform him of everything transpiring here. Plus, I'm ordering him and his army to come to the Capital, post-haste, to assist in its protection. I'm not taking any chances—the infantry is too depleted."

Yori added to the round-table discussion, "I was told this morning he's currently camped thirty miles northeast. They moved recently."

"Excellent, which means he could probably get here as soon as four days—three and three-quarters days for the army's march, and one-quarter day for the messengers, a team light of foot, who will no doubt run the whole way. Our messengers are usually handpicked from the best runners in town and paid well. We risk leaving the eastern and northern outlying villages defenseless for the time being, but I feel this is the right call."

Captain Raymond commented, "Yes, sir, it is good judgement."

The party discussed less important matters for a time and concluded the meeting. Soon after the conclusion, Rowlangiv's messengers were sent off. They hurried towards the Black Bear, practically sprinting.

Mick and Dave were animated by the King's announcement to summon Ulfenkerki's army. Seeing Jason Thorncat, Gregg Hogarty, General Ulfenkerki, and others would be an unexpected pleasure. Dave and Mick now had no intentions of leaving the Capital soon.

Subsequent to the meeting, breakfast, spending a few hours practicing swordcraft at the nearest training grounds, and lunch, Mick and Dave decided to take the rest of the day for themselves. They endeavored to go uptown to piss around for a bit. There were areas with which they hadn't yet gotten familiar. One area in particular was a district harboring Garobansurov's largest cathedral. Since they liked touring noteworthy churches and learned it was open to the public daily, they planned to pay the cathedral a visit.

But before doing so, they ambled through a residential stretch. It was mainly dull, except for a park containing a lovely pond.

"I'd say this pond was hand-dug, judging by those earthen mounds over there."

Mick turned to look at where Dave was pointing, and said, "I'm inclined to agree. The hills are surrounded by primarily flat terrain, and older trees. The only thing growing on the hills are bushes and young trees, younger than I imagine the pond to be. That's enough evidence for me."

"I doubt there are many fish in it, because it's probably not that deep in the middle."

"Right," agreed Mick. "They'd succumb to winterkill."

"There might be chubs and suckers in there though, they tend to be hardier species," noted Dave.

"Possibly. If the sun was out, we'd be capable of telling exactly what mysteries lurk within. With the sun penetrating such a transparent pond, we'd be free to gaze at the illuminated depths."

"Yes, too bad clouds are winning the day."

After peering into the pond's opaque shallows, Hawk and Leopard made a quick circle around the rest of the park.

The only thing during the loop worth a second look and discussion was a picturesque stone wall on the south end.

Dave postulated, "This wall looks as if it's been here much longer than the city itself has."

"It does. Upon close scrutiny, it seems every stone was laboriously placed on top of a larger one. A pattern," stated Mick.

"There has to be tens of thousands of stones here!"

"You don't see endeavors as ambitious as this very often."

"Indeed." Dave slipped into his robe of philosophy, figuratively. "In the end, ye who nature decides mattered most is ye who had the courage to withdraw furthermost from the ordinary."

"Yes. No arguments here. May the creator/creators of this wall be considered in that decision."

"Definitely. Let's head to the cathedral."

CHAPTER 8

THE EXPERIENCE-WEATHERED General (the atypical sort who not only was wise but also looked the part) climbed down from a tall tree, proving that even older members of the army had the dexterity to perform the widest array of challenges. Sometimes, due to lack of conventional places, amongst the heights of a tall tree was the best position to spy distant scenes for possible enemies.

Confident the coast was clear for the time being, General Ulfenkerki (the Black Bear) hiked back downhill to his camp.

The General approached his first lieutenant, Jason Thorncat, and said, "I told you I'd be able to get to the canopy of the large tamarack without hurting myself. That's exactly from where I just came."

"You're going to have to prove it, I say respectfully, before I actually eat my words. How many lakes can you see from up there?" Jason knew the only way someone would know the answer is if they had climbed the tree.

"Excluding the undersized pond next to the hilly, oval-shaped field to the east, there are two," answered the Black Bear.

"Consider me impressed, sir," noted Jason, honestly. "You never cease to amaze."

"You should see me with a sword."

"I have, and you aren't kidding, old-timer. I'd hate to run into you on the battlefield—I might break a sweat."

"You'd break more than that," the pair laughed.

After the laughter, Jason caught a glimpse of some out of the ordinary movement in the nearby wood. He craned his neck for a better view. "Did you see that, General?"

Ulfenkerki raised his eyebrows, and replied, "See what?"

"I saw something wiz between the trees. It moved too fast to be a furry mammal, and it hit the ground too hard to be a bird. I'm going to go check it out."

"Right behind you."

As soon as the two of them broke the tree line, they spotted Gregg Hogarty fifty paces to the right-front.

Gregg saw his compatriots, advanced towards them, and said, "I suppose you guys ventured into the forest here, because you saw one of my misses."

"Misses?" Jason looked baffled.

"The other day," Gregg answered, "I woke up, and for some reason I felt like I could be good at knife throwing. So, I tried it out. Low and behold, I was fairly decent at it. So here I am now, practicing. You probably saw my last throw, which missed the tree at which I was aiming."

Jason asked, "Mathematically speaking, how good are you really?"

"Not as proficient as I'd like to be, but maybe with practice I'll get there. My knife will stick pointed end first more than half the time. I'm shooting for three out of four. And even better than that in the long run."

The Black Bear joined in, "How far away do you stand from your target-tree?"

"Usually, anywhere from twenty-five to sixty feet away."

"Impressive, Gregg. Keep it up. Having a solid knife thrower would be a very beneficial addition to the army."

Ulfenkerki and Jason let Gregg to his practice and began walking back to the main part of camp. Before their arrival, a soldier approached.

Many were looking for Ulfenkerki, but the soldier looking hardest finally tracked down his mark. There was news for the Black Bear.

The soldier who'd tracked the General down blurted, "General, sir, messengers from the Capital have arrived at camp, and wish to speak with you."

"Thank you, Ribowitz. Where are they at?"

"By the catapults."

Both Jason and Ulfenkerki moved at speed and found the messengers right where it was said they'd be.

The ever-stoic Black Bear asked the messengers, "Before we proceed, may I see your credentials?"

"Definitely, sir," replied Theaphane, who produced documents displaying the King's official seal, signature, and current code phrase ("May all be blessed with power and justice.").

Ulfenkerki perused the documentation. "Excellent, I'm satisfied. Go on."

Theaphane went on to describe eloquently everything that had happened at the Capital since the Knowing Circle incident. Anything he missed was filled in by the other messengers. The report was concluded by the relaying of Rowlangiv's decision instructing Ulfenkerki and his army to aid in the defense of the Capital.

Ulfenkerki said to the messengers, "You can depart, and tell Rowlangiv we'll pack with urgency, and leave here as soon as possible. The packing procedure should take three hours' time, while the march itself should take three and a half days. We'll be to the Capital just before nightfall on the fourth day."

"Will do, sir." The messengers headed back to the Capital. Winded and sore from the run to Ulfenkerki, they had no intentions of running all the way back, for there was no real need.

Ulfenkerki had been correct, it took three hours to take down all tents, convert all war machines from operational status to mobile status, and pack personal/battle gear.

Defining efficiency, the army was on their way.

Ulfenkerki desired to cover a fair amount of ground before having to again set up camp. The soldiers were grateful the time-consuming and laborious procedure of setting up the big tents didn't need to be performed that night. Only the smaller ones were to be erected. Dealing with the big tents twice in a single day was a hassle to be sure.

An hour into the march, Jason passed on to Ulfenkerki, "It's too bad all this didn't happen a week ago. If it did, we could've made Mick and Dave's Knowing Circle ceremony."

"Yeah, that would've been nice. I could've used a little ceremonious jubilation."

VISITING HOURS AT the basilica tended to draw only a couple of guests per opening, Mick and Dave's appearances doubling the usual head count for the day.

"This church is definitely larger than the one at Dourinuset, but its large scale takes away from coziness, which Dourinuset certainly was no stranger to."

"I agree. Dourinuset sure supplied an ambience of comfort," Dave said to Mick, before digressing. "The overhead decorations are eye-catching, no less."

"Same with the woodwork. I bet all these candles probably take someone plenty of time to light."

"I'm sure they do."

One other guest was present at the church at the time, an elderly lady. She sauntered towards Mick and Dave. "Hello, gentlemen. Lovely place, isn't it?"

"That it is," replied Dave. "I bet it has quite the complex history too."

"I'm not familiar with much of it, but I do know there was a point about a hundred years ago when half the town took refuge here during a great battle. I think they all survived too."

"Indeed, it would be a stronghold during times of war," commented Mick.

"And during times of despair," added the lady.

Mick nodded courteously, and replied, "Well said, ma'am."

The lady smiled, and voiced, "Enjoy the rest of your day, I insist."

"And the same to you."

Hawk and Leopard explored the rest of the cathedral and in doing so, heeded the lady's bidding by enjoying their day.

On their way out, they supplied the donation box with a hefty amount. "Somebody has to help pay for all these candles."

Dave and Mick spent a couple days continuing to ascertain the truth behind the Molisian invading force, but like everyone else, came up empty-handed. Having searched high and low, they both wondered how the Molisians amassed so quickly and without detection.

Though, Dave, Mick and the townsfolk were happy the Capital was currently battle-free. Ulfenkerki and his army weren't expected for another day and a half. The townsfolk knew the army would provide a sense of security of the greatest magnitude.

Taking advantage of a previous offer, Mick and Dave got all dressed up in preparation of a night on the town and a free meal. It was one of those evenings with no shortage of high spirits.

The restaurant owner was happy to see Mick and Dave again, as were all the staff. Knowing Mick and Dave eating there could only drum up business made the owner even happier.

Dave told the owner how handy the grease was during the attack. He was ecstatic to have helped.

The meal was superb, and the waitresses were friendly. Plus, it wasn't ignored that the waitresses were utterly ravishing in their black, skin-tight pants. All in all, it was a very fine experience.

Back at the castle, adding to the fine evening, Mick and Dave received a visit from Yori Rothlin, an always pleasant occurrence.

Sitting in the common room adjacent to Mick and Dave's rooms, Yori commented, "It'll be wonderful having Ulfenkerki and his army here at the Capital. I suppose the two of you are quite familiar with them, since you fought in a battle with them."

"Actually, we fought two alongside them: Sarwa and Strwin. And Ulfenkerki's first lieutenant, Jason Thorncat, was our childhood friend. In fact, just this last winter, he made the trek from Sarwa to our hometown of Chalatore with us. The whole thing was rather enjoyable," shared Dave.

Mick added, "We've established a pretty good rapport with the Black Bear too. We've bled together. Also, we've become good friends with a soldier named Gregg Hogarty, among others."

"Then I guess you are familiar with them. I know Jason as well, he and I go way back. We were great friends at battle camp."

"I never knew they had those."

Yori returned, "They sure do, Mick. They're for teenagers."

"That sounds like fun," noted Dave, before turning to look at Mick. "Too bad we didn't get to go to that, eh!"

"Yes, too bad."

Yori said, "And of course, I know Ulfenkerki. He and I have sat together at many a wartable, countless stratagems discussed at desperate hours."

"I imagine you have," emitted Mick. "Those dangerous moments are when you realize how truly important it is to fashion human bonds."

"Ever the case," agreed Yori. "I know having him here will certainly put Rowlangiv's mind at ease. These last few days having a less than adequate infantry available have really taken a toll on him."

Dave declared, "The King's fine. He's got us here."

Yori was tickled. "That he does. I know I'm glad you're here. What the two of you can do with those swords of yours is a story unto itself. I bet you didn't know I'm not too shabby at throwing stars. My throws rarely kill in battle, but they sure can be a nuisance."

"No, I didn't know that," replied Mick. "Did you unleash any at the Knowing Circle attack?"

"I wish I could've, but I didn't have any on me at the time."

Dave proposed, "You'll have to show us your star set some time, Yori."

"No problem, as long as you show me those swords of yours that I've been hearing so much about."

"That's a deal."

"Sounds good. I'll make a point to come visit tomorrow, after supper, and bring with my throwing stars," put forward Yori, enthusiastically.

"Excellent."

Yori stood up out of her chair, aimed for the door, and said, "Until then."

Subsequent Yori egressing, Mick got up to stretch. Dave did the same, walked across the room, and stated, "That sure is one intriguing lady."

"A fact truer than most others," returned Mick, just before pacing away.

Having ended up in the recreation room, Mick spent some time exercising.

The next day, it rained profusely. Everyone had hoped the rain wouldn't delay Ulfenkerki's arrival. He and his army were expected later that evening. If the Molisians had another wave of attack in them, now would be the time. King Rowlangiv, more than everyone, spent the day on edge.

Mick and Dave couldn't help but gaze constantly out the high castle windows in patrol fashion. Trouble off in the distance was the last thing they wanted to see. Luckily, all they kept seeing were raindrops.

To kill the time of a boring day, Mick and Dave went for walks out across the causeway. And after every time, they re-entered the castle soaking wet.

The day dragged on like that of a prisoner's.

Because of the long day, the kitchen staff of the castle decided to make a larger and tastier meal than usual to brighten spirits. It worked, especially for Mick and Dave. Their moods picked up.

As promised, Yori (the advisor Rowlangiv trusted above all others) showed up after supper, carrying a small case. Wet, she met Mick and Dave in the living room closest to their bedrooms.

"Good evening, guys."

"Hello there, Ms. Rothlin. I see you're not very good at dodging raindrops," Mick said, with a beaming smile. He offered to take her overcoat.

Yori handed over the garment. "I think I was being pretty successful for the first leg of my hike over here, but eventually the raindrops became too overwhelming, and I had to surrender to inevitability."

Dave commented, "If anyone could become good at it, I'm sure it'll be you."

"Besides, the wetness only adds to your beauty," Mick piled on.

Yori chuckled and began opening up her wooden case. "Maybe you're right, Dave. But, Mick, I doubt you're right. Well, here they are, my cherished set of throwing stars."

Dave and Mick handled each one of her throwing stars with precise observation.

Mick communicated, "These are rather impressive and functional looking. Who made them? Throwing stars are pretty hard to find, I know, especially ones this ornate."

"About ten years ago, a trader came into town. He didn't exactly say where he was from. But I know a segment of his trip was by sea, since he imparted to me how an individual aboard his same ship came down with a rare illness and died. He explained to me the stars were actually made for a nobleman. But the nobleman ended up in jail before payment was secured. The stars went up for auction, at which point the trader from whom I purchased them ended up being the highest bidder. After pleasant negotiations, we both became satisfied with a price. He made a profit, and I paid what I thought they were worth. I've yet to see better quality stars lower in price."

"I too can't say I've ever seen their equal, they really are unique," noted Dave, rolling the best one over in his hand. "Most I've seen are made from inferior metals, a trick some fabricators use to be more cost-effective."

"True. I practice almost every day. And who knows, one day they may save my life, or the life of someone whom I care about."

"How much velocity can you generate with them?"

"I'd say enough to cut all the way through a watermelon."

"Impressive," Dave voiced.

"And now, let's see those swords of yours."

"Coming up."

Dave and Mick went to their respective rooms, pulled the steel weapons out from their resting places, and came back to show Yori.

She grasped Dave's sword, and ran her fingers scrutinizingly from pommel to cross-guard. "So, it's the grip that makes them unique, eh? I can certainly tell that just by touching it."

"Indeed," answered Mick. "The grips come with a story too, but it's long, and I'm sure you have more important things to attend to tonight than sit around here and listen to a lengthy narration."

"Technically, I'm sure the net effect of hearing your story would be far greater than that of what I really need to do tonight. But nevertheless, my task needs to be done. But promise me you'll tell me the story some other time."

"Oh, you know I will," proclaimed Mick.

"Marvelous."

Mick blurted, "Actually, I'll share this quick: Tim Warmane from town here was the blacksmith who forged the weapons, the grips we brought to him."

"I might have guessed," stated Yori. "He really does most excellent work."

"For sure. The man sure can *smith*."

All of a sudden, curiosity and animation leaped onto Dave. He bolted to the window and craned forward to listen and look out. He emitted, "They're here. The low-end bass sound of towable war machines rolling in the distance is unmistakable."

Mick and Yori quickly joined Dave at the window and listened. "I believe you're right," Yori concurred.

"It's kind of an eerie sound, if you imagine it's an approaching enemy."

"I suppose that to be true," replied Dave.

Twenty minutes after it was heard, the army was seen coming over the horizon. It was nearly dark, so it was quite easy to distinguish the torches carried by soldiers.

"Just imagine how wet they all are," Dave stated. "I'm surprised the torches are remaining lit."

Yori commented, "At least they'll all have warm hearths in a matter of moments, and comfortable beds tonight. The Capital's barracks are adequate enough to accommodate them all. We certainly have harbored our fair share of armies here in the past."

"Oh yes, such were our bedtime stories, the powerful Myothracen armies of old."

"Mine too, Mick," remarked Yori. "The barracks may be old, but they have always served their purpose well."

"The monstrous, stone structure across the causeway, and down the hill?"

"Yes, that's them, Dave. The infantry, archery, and guard personnel who don't own dwellings here in town stay in them too. You should check them out some time, they really are interesting. Like you'd probably expect, the ancient architecture is awe-inspiring."

"We'll probably take a look at them tonight, yet. But we'll give the army a few hours to get settled. I'm sure Mick and I will meander down there and say hello to a few old friends."

Yori walked away from the window. "Sounds good. I'll see you later. I've got a few things to talk to Rowlangiv about, before he goes to welcome Ulfenkerki."

"Bye, Yori."

LEADING THE WAY into the Capital, Jason and the Black Bear couldn't help but react. They were electrified. For most soldiers of Garobansurov, defending the Capital and the King was the epitome of duty.

"You sure took a rather sizable turn on that catapult back there, I noticed."

"You bet, Jason, my man," said the General. "Climbing trees and pulling war-machines are only the beginning of my long repertoire of skills."

"Don't I know it," agreed Jason. "Getting quickly out of these wet clothes will be the highlight of my repertoire of skills."

Ulfenkerki smiled and inaudibly chuckled. "I'm going to leave all the machines right here, instead of dragging them into town all the way, so that way the men can get dry sooner. We'll come back and lug them in tomorrow."

"I'll go inform them of this. They'll like the idea."

"Thanks, Jason."

He had done it before, so Ulfenkerki had an easy time zigzagging his army through the streets to the barracks. Normally, there would be more citizens on the roads welcoming them, but the rain pretty much kept most indoors. In any event, the Capital's residents typically enjoyed and respected the coming of an army.

The rain, however, didn't keep Garobansurov's hardy King indoors. He was at the barracks, waiting to give them a warm greeting. Nobody was happier to see the army than he.

"Salutations, my old friend. I couldn't be more pleased, seeing you brave the rain to be with us tonight."

The General replied, "It's very good to see you as well, King Rowlangiv. Except for today's rainy weather, the trek was certainly agreeable."

"Splendid. I had the barracks completely fortified in these last few days. Everything the army will need is in stock. And if we missed anything, come see me, and I'll personally see to it the insufficiency is remedied."

"Your hospitality is most appreciated, and I assure you we are all overjoyed to be here to serve and protect," said Ulfenkerki, respectfully.

"Excellent, just excellent. Tomorrow morning we'll have a meeting in the barrack's conference room to discuss in detail everything that'd transpired, and our future stratagem."

"I'll be as ready as a jackrabbit in heat."

The King chuckled. "See you then, General."

"Yup, see you then, sire. And by the way, I've been practicing at cards, so don't think you're going to beat me as badly as the last time we played."

"We'll just see about that." The King chuckled again and walked away smiling.

A couple hours after the army found its way to the barracks, Mick and Dave found their way to the army. There were certain individuals from the army they were excited to see. By then, the whole of the army was in the barracks, drying off, feasting, unpacking, and resting their legs.

Mick and Dave entered the large stone barracks of the Capital, planning to marvel the architecture as they walked, though they didn't want to dawdle too much. They'd save a more thorough examination for another time.

They ran into Gregg Hogarty, first, whom they befriended last year just before the Battle of Strwin.

Shaking hands, Dave said, "Wonderful to see you, Gregg."

"Same to you two. How was the celebration?"

"The first half, you could say was great and without incident; the second half, not so much."

"Yeah, I heard about that."

"A real calamity," Mick said. "Be that as it may, things could've gone much worse."

"Very true."

To Gregg, Dave voiced, "Quite the rain today for you, eh?"

"Sure was. For the sake of all, we tried to get here as fast as possible, rain or shine."

"The will of the warrior lives on," proclaimed Mick.

"Indeed."

"You don't happen to know where Jason or Ulfenkerki are, do you?" Dave asked.

"I believe on the north end, or at least they were the last time I saw them."

"Thanks, Gregg. Enjoy the dryness of the barracks. See you later."

"Yup."

Hawk and Leopard coursed through the stone hall, heading north. Along the way, they took notice of the mammoth rocks of the corridor walls, large specimens of superior stone cutting workmanship. Along with firelight from the various fireplaces scattered about, the tunnels were illuminated by candles sitting in brackets fastened to the walls. They found both Jason and Ulfenkerki hanging up their wet clothes near one of these fireplaces.

Jason looked up and exclaimed, "There they are! Thraiker and Ghrere! Garobansurov's very own."

"Mr. Thorncat and the reputable Black Bear, how in the heck are you?"

Ulfenkerki responded, "Good, now that we've escaped the rain and wet attire."

Jason added, "We practically spent the last decade and a half barely seeing each other, and now in the last year and a half, the complete opposite."

"Weird how things work out," said Mick.

Ulfenkerki threw a gnarly log into the fireplace, and noted, "You guys will have to bring those Knowing Circles by me one day. I've never actually seen one up close."

"No problem, they really are a sight to behold," responded Dave.

After placing a pot of stew over the fire on the rack positioned for doing so, Jason emitted, "I suppose you guys have seen more action than us, since we last saw each other."

"We very well may have," replied Mick. "Two conflicts, here, at the Capital—a thwarted robbery attempt on the walk here, and a successfully settled dispute between some monks and the owner of a rural sawmill."

Mick checked out the innards of Jason's pot for no real reason, other than habit, as Jason returned, "You don't say. I guess you have been busy. We pretty much have been spending most of our time scouting the countryside for Molisian armies. With Gravividon back in our hands, who knows where they might try and cross the border."

Ulfenkerki observed, "They've got to be getting across unnoticed somewhere. The skirmishes you've had, here, are proof of that. It's a mystery, since we've been in constant contact with the soldiers operating the central Baustic Range lookout towers, and they've confirmed there hasn't been any out-of-the-ordinary foot travel coming or going within their viewing radiuses. These radiuses cover practically the entire length of the central border. There are some pretty secluded areas in the mountains, though, that nobody frequents."

Mick scratched his head. "And the King's other two armies have the western side covered, I'm assuming. So, it really is quite the conundrum."

"Will the two of you be attending tomorrow morning's strategy meeting?" Ulfenkerki asked Dave and Mick.

Dave responded, "We attended the last one by request from the King. I'm not sure about the one tomorrow. We'll see if he invites us again."

"I'd invite you, but I wouldn't want to undermine Rowlangiv's aspirations."

"That's fine. It's easy enough for him to say something, we are still staying in the castle."

"Okay, good."

Stirring the large pot with an axe handle, Jason said, "You guys want to stay for some stew?"

Mick chuckled at Jason's ingenuity, and replied, "No, thank you. I ate already."

"Me too," added Dave. "We'll let you guys finish up unpacking, and I'm sure we'll see you tomorrow at some point."

"Okay, see you later."

While walking back to the castle, Hawk and Leopard were surprised it was actually still raining. But they weren't surprised seeing notes on their beds informing them of the morning tactical meeting.

Not until the sun was up the next day did it finally stop raining.

Chapter 9

IT TOOK A WHILE, but a good place to dock the boat was finally found. Most of the Geenhuvagal River of the area was lined with either rocks or steep embankments which under most scenarios made for rough beaching. They would've liked to take the rowboat further upriver, and closer to their destination, but the river was starting to get too shallow for their hull. Risking damage to the boat wasn't worth avoiding a little walking.

All of the boat's occupiers stood and stepped foot on solid ground. All of them were a long way from home. They traveled far with a mission in tow. It wasn't often constituents of the Icytryxis race traveled away from their island archipelago.

In fact, most humans were completely unaware of their existence.

Although they were human-like, it would've been easy to tell they were of a different race, at least the men, anyways. About ten percent of the time, if an Icytryxis male wore gloves, hiding the weapon-like hands, he could've been mistaken for a human. The percentage for the women was much higher, even without gloves.

The quartet had rowed a lot that day, and decided to make camp near the river, close to their supply of provisions on the boat.

Two of the Icytryxis were the ones on the mission, Thyxer and Syryx. The other two were mainly along to help with the rowing and to stay with the boat when Thyxer and Syryx traveled to their destination. Back at the mouth of the river, another crew was standing guard at the much larger sailing vessel used to cross the ocean.

Thyxer was a forty-six-year-old male; Syryx was his sister, thirty-nine. Icytryxans lived nearly twice as long as humans, so their ages were misleading to most. Thyxer and Syryx were relatively young.

They both went into the nearby copse of trees to gather firewood.

Thyxer noted to his sister, "I'd say we have two, maybe three, days' walk in front of us yet."

"That'll be refreshing, after having been in the boats for so long."

"Yes, it will. Hopefully the maps we have are accurate."

"They are old, but I see no reason for them to be wrong," replied Syryx, hitting the motherload by finding a supply of evergreen branches with needles intact. Such branches were superior for fire starting.

"We follow a river for most of the way, so I highly doubt we'll get lost."

"That's true," responded Syryx, stooping down for a heaping armload of branches. "Sure was a good thing, learning their language when we were younger. I would've never guessed it to come in so handy."

"Yup, who knew. I'm glad the rain finally stopped. That would've really made for some rough trekking."

"That's for sure. We'd better put the tarps over the tents tonight. I'd rather not wake up in a puddle of water tomorrow morning. Sitting in a wet boat was bad enough."

Thyxer agreed and followed his younger sister back to the campsite. "We'll leave first thing in the morning."

"Sounds good. I really hope we are successful with this operation. I'd hate to go back home empty-handed."

"Me too. May the great Infinitum be ever on our side."

"Praise Infinitum," said Syryx, as she pulled her *atlytl* from the boat. The atlytl was the Icytryxis weapon of choice. It differed from a traditional *atlatl* in that, instead of throwing spears, it threw weighted projectiles at the end of a string. She had no intention of using it this night, but like most her kin, she felt safer with it near.

It took an hour for them to finish up camp. Afterwards, they made and ate supper.

Usually at night, the Icytryxis took part in their favorite pastime, the playing of a game they called *Fantysy-Escape*. But it was imperative they went to bed early, and leave at first light, so they didn't play the game like they normally would have.

As planned, Syryx and Thyxer woke up early and went northwest, following the river to their objective. They had no idea what to expect in the foreign land, but it would've taken a sizable act of nature to bring their spirits down.

ALL THE OFFICERS of Ulfenkerki's army, the officers of the Castle Guard, and the officers of the infantry/archer core of Myothraces were in attendance at the morning strategy meeting, including Rowlangiv, Yori, two other advisers of the King, Mick, Dave, and an out-of-place butterfly that decided to sneak in. The hindmost probably wouldn't have been noticed by anyone, if not for it being as multihued as a field of wildflowers, which was from where it probably came.

Rowlangiv began by spending twenty minutes explaining in his own words and in detail all the conflicts that'd transpired recently. The representatives from Ulfenkerki's army, especially, listened intently. Afterwards, the King changed direction and spoke of the future. "I'd like for everyone to be on their guards and listen carefully to the words of everyone in town. We still have no idea how the large forces snuck into town. Maybe we can remedy this unknowing through all the new ears we'll have listening."

Ulfenkerki added, "We are bound to hear something, sooner or later. It's too unrealistically coincidental not to."

Rowlangiv said, "I agree. It's human nature to blab about everything. We just have to be there, when they do. We should also form a team to comb the countryside for information as well."

"No problem. I'll get it done."

Changing the subject, Rowlangiv proclaimed, "In the past, I've allowed soldiers staying here two nights a week to paint the town, with a 1:00 a.m. curfew. Since this has yet to cause any difficulties, I'll remove the curfew, leaving the two nights a week."

Ulfenkerki noted, "Awfully generous of you, sir."

"The same goes to the guard, infantry, and archers from now on, or until any problems arise."

"Thank you, sir. As if it was possible, they'll love you even more," commented a tall officer.

Rowlangiv chuckled. "*A loved king is a living king,* is what I always say. We will have these morning meetings, same time, same place, same people, every morning."

"Excellent, sir," some returned, and the room emptied.

Mick and Dave hung back to talk with Jason and Ulfenkerki for a bit. The four discussed nothing of importance.

Later that day, Hawk and Leopard attended a training session with the army. A good sweat had never hurt anyone.

Different than the one Mick and Dave attended, Rowlangiv watched one of the training sessions. With his eyes on the adept soldiers, the King almost felt at complete ease; The Capital was safe and sound for the time being. Too bad he didn't feel the same way about the rest of his country.

Subsequent to the morning meeting the next day, Mick and Dave had dinner with their buddy, Yori. It was always delightful spending time with her.

Mick asked Yori, "Were you able to spend much time with Jason, yet?"

"Yes. Yesterday we enjoyed a stroll through town and talked of old times. He spoke very highly of the two of you, which didn't surprise me at all, because he did the same of you when we were younger. I nearly totally forgot about those old stories."

"Oh, yes, lots and lots of childhood memories. We all sure were carefree kids."

"I told him I was eating with you guys today, and that if he found the time, he should join us."

Dave said, "That would be great."

Yori inquired, "How long will the two of you be staying at the Capital?"

Mick replied, "Everything seems to be pretty much under control now, so barring something springing up we'll probably head back to Chalatore in less than a week, although Dave and I haven't really set an exact day."

Yori stated, "Then, I guess we had better enjoy the beloved Mick and Dave while we can. I highly doubt I'll ever make it to Chalatore to enjoy you there."

Dave smiled. "We're all yours."

"Well, then, I'll have to think of what to do with my new acquisitions."

"Be gentle, ma'am."

"We'll just see about that." The trio laughed, wholeheartedly, and before the laugh ran its full course, Jason showed up. "Glad you could make it, Jason," Yori blurted.

Jason returned, "Technically, I haven't made it. I'm on an errand for Ulfenkerki, but I figured since I was in the area, I'd stop in real quick to say hello."

Mick remarked, "A little bit of Jason Thorncat is better than no Jason Thorncat at all."

"I like to think that too. How are your meals?"

Yori replied to Jason, "Mine was pretty good. I ordered too much, though."

"You'll have that."

Dave spoke: "Mine was good too."

After the party of four conversed jovially for a few minutes, Jason sighed and emitted, "Sorry for not being able to stay any longer, but I have to run."

Yori voiced, "That's okay, Jason. Glad you stopped. See you later."

"Bye guys."

Succeeding Jason's departure, the three of them talked for another ten minutes, and left the restaurant. Yori had business to attend to, while Mick and Dave went back to the castle.

The rest of the day went by fast for Mick and Dave. At night, they found themselves outside in the south courtyard, under the stars, making a fire in the available firepit of a small gully. The night was as refreshing as a glass of water to a parched man.

Dave remarked, "I bet this hole we're in is so symmetrical that one could roll a ball down any of the sides, and it would roll back up the other side to an almost equal point."

"Suffice it to say, I doubt anyone has actually tested or even thought of that before."

"Probably not."

King Rowlangiv startlingly showed up. "I see you guys found the *hole-pit*, or so we call it."

Dave replied, "That we have."

Rowlangiv tossed a log into the fire. "Yori tells me you guys are looking at heading back home in less than a week."

"We haven't discussed the exact timetable yet, but, yup, that's the plan."

Rowlangiv stated, "Well, you know how much I would love for the two of you to stick around longer and watch my back, but I suppose you gotta do what you gotta do."

Mick replied, "We appreciate the sentiment. With Ulfenkerki now about, I'm sure the Capital is more than safe without Dave and I here."

"That may be true, but nevertheless, I like you guys, I really do."

"Same here, sir," said Dave. "The freedom you so graciously bestow upon us is for what we eternally draw our swords. We fight for you with our lives."

"Spoken like a true Knowing Circle recipient. Enjoy your night," insisted Rowlangiv, just before stirring the fire, and walking out of the hole, towards the castle.

Sitting around the fire, Dave and Mick talked much more, philosophically and jokingly. By the end of the night, just before going back inside for bed, they came to a joint conclusion: they liked winning their Knowing Circles and liked representing for what they stood.

Rowlangiv was late to the morning meeting. Nobody gave it any thought—kings are never really late to anything, everyone else is just early—though he had a serious look on his face.

The King began, "Good morning everyone. I'm glad you're all here. Today will be an important day for all of you. Early this morning, I had received visitors—visitors who'd traveled far, and are not of our race. Today, you can say to your kids and grandkids the tales of the Icytryxis are no longer just ancient unconfirmed stories, they are in fact true. During the last few hours, I've been in discussion with two of them. They are here on an important mission. I'll go get them, and they'll speak to all of you, my most trusted council. I'll be back shortly."

Everyone in the room gasped and looked around at each other to gauge reactions. A murmur emerged.

King Rowlangiv walked across the causeway and into the castle. He found the Icytryxis diplomats not far from where he'd last saw them.

To the diplomats the King said, "Alright, Thyxer and Syryx, my council is all ears. Please follow me."

"Superb. We very much appreciate this opportunity, your highness," noted Syryx.

Rowlangiv led the nervously excited pair to the meeting room in the barracks.

With everyone planning to listen as close as humanly possible, King Rowlangiv addressed the crowd, "May I introduce Thyxer and Syryx to all of you, my friends.

Please listen with an open mind, and we'll talk thoroughly upon their conclusion."

Thyxer stepped forward. "Thank you, King Rowlangiv. And thank you for your hospitality. I'm sure our emergence strikes all of you as being unexpected, but I assure you, we are here for a reason of great importance. One that will hopefully benefit Garobansurov and the Icytryxis. We're a race greatly different from yours in many ways, but we're deeply alike in just as many. I know we both value a life of security, righteousness, and morals, among countless other virtues.

Alas, we share a mutual enemy. From what we've gathered, the Molisian soldiers with whom you're currently at war don't exhibit the same sort of moral aptitude.

Syryx continued, "As some of you have guessed, we hail from islands far south of your country in the middle of the vast ocean. You ask yourself, *How could the Molisians harm the Icytryxis? The distance between the two is too significant.* The answer—the Icytryxis and Garobansurov have forged a symbiotic circle, due to our shared ethical beliefs. What affects one, given enough time, will affect the other. We fear this war of yours. Well, a lot of us do anyway."

Thyxer resumed, "The primary problem is that we haven't officially helped each other in war in ages. For the majority of the Icytryxis, the will to act hasn't arisen.

We have an army, and our soldiers have freewill. Many of them fail to see the potential threat brewing here.

Our greatest thinkers see the danger, which is essentially why we're here now. We have no government to force the army into action. It's our way, which brings us to this very room. We don't have any minds that can summon the perfect elucidation in helping our populace see aiding Garobansurov in this war would be the logical thing to do. Along with our best thinkers, many Icytryxans do see, but just not enough to get the wheels of war turning."

Syryx took the figurative baton. "The mission bestowed upon us was to come to the Capital, and see if anyone here believes they can enlighten upon our army and citizens that a collaboration between our two great societies would be a force spent wisely. A land of diversity awaits brave volunteers."

Rowlangiv stated, "I can personally attest that in our royal archives it's documented that our countries have formed coalitions long ago. The parchments are very old and crumbling, but they are readable."

Thyxer said, "We have old documentation on it as well. We'd almost brought it with, but opted not to, in the name of preservation."

Rowlangiv looked at his council, and noted, "Now, we would like to hear all of your input on this very important matter."

Yori spoke. "It's my position that the Molisians certainly are a country of barbarians with morals completely different from our own. If the Icytryxis and we share in the mindset of upholding virtuousness, a partnership between us would indeed benefit us all."

Ulfenkerki said, "Last year, we received countless reports of the brutal, unspeakable acts performed by one of their generals, Gamald, or at least by his soldiers. I see no reason not to think the Icytryxis desire an end to this.

Plus, I see no reason not to trust the Icytryxis, but we must be wary of deception. I'm not saying that's what's happening here, but as the old proverb says, *Anything can happen.* If we send someone across the sea, they must also delve into the true nature of the Icytryxis."

Syryx responded, "That's entirely reasonable, and we have the utmost confidence that your diplomats will find us of like-mind with Garobansurov in the field of morals, and that a double cross would totally go against everything we stand for."

Rowlangiv said, "And it is for that very reason I'd like to see someone from this very room go. I would trust only your judgment on the matter of allowing a foreign army onto our soil. There are too many olden stories of military deception. Furthermore, it is my stance that we must take this chance—letting a potential ally disappear would be too inconceivable.

Ulfenkerki added, "Exactly, sir. Rayton at the Battle of Sarwa is one of these examples of deception. But, yes, we must roll the bones."

Rowlangiv nodded in response. "Yes, that's right. Do any of you feel you could make a difference, and persuade the unconvinced part of the Icytryxis to see the way of solidarity?"

The pause that followed Rowlangiv's question felt like it went on forever. The uncomfortable pause was followed by another murmur.

After quietly discussing the matter between themselves, the most recent recipients of the Knowing Circle (the medal representing the highest achievement in valor for Garobansurov) stepped forward. Mick said to all, "Dave and I have agreed that since the Icytryxis and the two of us are very similar in that we both value fighting for freedom under our own approach, we feel we could give it a good shot at pleading the case of our countries aligning."

Rowlangiv smiled proudly. "Thyxer, Syryx: Mick Thraiker and Dave Ghrere are the recent beneficiaries of our country's highest award for honor, and I couldn't think of anyone else who could better represent what Garobansurov stands for. I truly believe they'd stand a fine chance at swaying your army and gaining the approval of the citizens to fight with us."

Syryx responded, "We would be honored to have you, Mick Thraiker and Dave Ghrere."

Dave spoke. "Perfect. A journey we shall make with pride."

Thyxer said, "Is there anyone else? We'll have room on the small boat for two or three more Garobansurovian accompaniments."

King Rowlangiv and Yori shared a few words with each other. Afterwards, Rowlangiv addressed the crowd, "My most trusted adviser, Yori Rothlin, and I have agreed that she would also be an excellent candidate for this mission. She knows everything about me and my beliefs. Therefore, I believe no one can embody me better. I'll miss her council, but I feel this is too important for her not to participate."

Yori proclaimed, "This is an undertaking that could impact the lives of both our countries greatly, maybe even those of all Taraosk. An undeniably historic event. I wholeheartedly believe I can aid Mick and Dave in this task."

Thyxer said, "Wonderful. I'm ecstatic. There's room for one or two more representatives, although, if nobody else volunteers, I'll still be unquestionably happy with what we got."

Ulfenkerki spoke next: "I feel this charge is one of great importance, and I personally want to see this commission be successful, therefore, my first lieutenant and I have agreed. Perfect for this assignment, Jason will volunteer to take part in this enterprise. He knows best what it's like to direct a Garobansurovian army, definitively adding much military insight to this party."

Jason Thorncat said, "And also of great importance, Mick, Dave, Yori, and I are all old friends. This cohesion will be displayed vividly. It will be a powerful tool in the influence."

Thyxer commented, "You are certainly right about that. Camaraderie is contagious and will assist significantly. Welcome aboard, Jason."

Once Thyxer realized there were no further volunteers, he said, "Syryx and I couldn't have imagined our mission going any better, a first-rate quartet to be sure."

Rowlangiv said, "If I'm not mistaken, I don't think any foreigner has stepped foot on Icytryxis soil in many hundreds of years, according to my documents."

Syryx responded, "That is correct, ours too. The islands are virtually unreachable. Our guests will see why when we get there."

Thyxer noted, "We will leave in the morning, and must rendezvous with our rowboat southeast of here on the river. Then, we'll hook up with the larger seafaring vessel. The whole voyage to get here took a few weeks but will probably take a little shorter to get back, since we'll now be rowing downstream."

Rowlangiv asked, "How are you on provisions? We can send a supply team with you to the boat, if needed."

Syryx replied, "We're geared up pretty well, and won't need furnishings. However, we wouldn't mind if you endowed us with an assortment of your local cuisine. It's not too often we get to partake in exotic foodstuff indulgences."

Rowlangiv answered, "It would be our pleasure. We'll even organize a low-key farewell banquet tonight at the castle. There will be all kinds of food for you to try."

Thyxer said, "Your hospitality is downright admirable. I cannot wait."

"This meeting is adjourned," proclaimed Rowlangiv. "I'll see all of you tonight at the feast. One last thing—I want to keep this whole story under wraps for now. We'll inform the public at a later date. We don't need anyone trying to sneak into the castle tonight, attempting to steal a peek at our visitors."

Everyone left the room and the barracks.

Yori made a point to walk with Mick and Dave. "I guess now it looks like I'll have all kinds of time to enjoy the beloved Mick and Dave."

Dave returned, "We will have a grand ole time!"

Mick added, "Waking up this morning, I would've never imagined our day turning out like this."

Yori slapped Mick and Dave on the backs, and said, "Exciting times we live in boys!"

Even though it was thrown together on a whim, the farewell banquet had a whole slew of gourmet fares for the Icytryxis to try. There were various dishes from all over the Capital's food district—a veritable taste of Garobansurov. Thyxer and Syryx were thoroughly impressed. They tried at least five different dishes that they'd never before had on their palettes. They liked them all.

At the end of the meal, King Rowlangiv said a few words, wishing the assemblage a safe and successful operation.

Following the feast, Hawk and Leopard had some packing to do. Staying in the same rooms of the castle for the last few weeks had given ample opportunity for both spaces to develop sizable clutters. It didn't take long to clean and pack, though. Like everything else Mick and Dave did, the chore was performed efficiently, and quickly. They weren't prone to pissing around.

Afterwards, they duo met up near the living room.

To Dave, Mick said, "I don't know what to expect in the Icytryxis homeland, but I'm awfully excited."

"That's for sure. I have the feeling they live a poles apart lifestyle from the typical Garobansurovian."

"I'm hoping they do."

"Me too. Immersing ourselves into a totally different culture will be quite the experience," commented Dave.

"Our project may be tough, but if we give it our all, I'll be satisfied."

"I agree," noted Dave. "I do know that it'll be sort of sad leaving these rooms behind, just like it was at Dourinuset."

"Yes, it will. Do you want to go down into the catacombs for old time's sake?"

"Uh, no."

"Me neither, I was just checking," responded Mick, laughing.

Dave returned a cackle, and reflected for a second. "So much for this journey being short and easy."

"Yup, so much for that. Our trips never are. I'm sure everyone back home is starting to understand that too."

"They undoubtedly are," said Dave. "We almost made it back to Chalatore in a reasonable amount of time."

"Almost. But *almost* doesn't count."

"Nope, it doesn't."

In the morning, Mick and Dave grabbed all their gear, and met up with Yori, Jason, Thyxer, and Syryx just outside of town to begin the trek.

Jason said to Mick and Dave, "I see you guys are bringing your Quintaga armor. I'm leaving mine here to make for a lighter load."

"We're not sure if at the end of all this we'll end up back here to pick it up."

"Good point."

Dave said, "And we're pretty used to the weight by now."

Jason replied, "I would envision you are."

Yori asked, "What is Quintaga armor?"

Jason responded, "It's a long story. But it's also a long trip, so we'll tell you along the way."

"I'll look forward to it."

Once the six had their loads ready to go (including the previously requested supply of Garobansurovian food), they started the trek to the Icytryxis homeland. They left all the worries of the Capital behind.

The first leg of the journey was to the Geenhuvagal river, and to where the rowboat and the two other Icytryxis awaited. Along the way, they talked about all the battles that had taken place thus far in Garobansurov, and which ones they took part in.

"Being in Ulfenkerki's army, during this war, I fought in the major battles of Strwin, Thraug, and Sarwa," declared Jason.

Dave pronounced, "Being freelance fighters, Mick and I were in the Battles of Strwin and Sarwa with Jason. And during the time when Jason was fighting in the defense of Thraug, we were on the northern border, recapturing Fort Gravividon, and fighting to hold it."

Jason said, "It's mainly that latter part which resulted in Dave and Mick's receiving of Knowing Circles. The recapturing of Gravividon was quite the daring escapade, to be sure. Only they would have the imagination to believe they could recapture a fort of that magnitude by themselves. I know this, because I grew up with them."

Humbly, Mick commented, "We do what needs to get done, I always say."

Thyxer said, "You guys have a pretty considerable history of battle experiences."

"Unfortunately."

The first day of walking was easy going. They covered a decent distance, before making camp. Setting up his tent, Mick said to Dave, "It sure is going to feel good, sleeping in the tents again."

"Yes, it will. It's been awhile."

Of course, Mick and Dave were pros at erecting tents, so when they finished faster than everyone else, they went to help the others. Thyxer and Syryx shared a bigger tent. Yori's was fancy, and Jason's was a portable army tent. The terrain in which they set up was sandy so, cautiously, they made sure to put the tents on high ground, just in case it rained profusely. Sometimes, high amounts of moving rainwater in sandy terrain caused bothersome washouts, but not so much on high ground. There weren't too many things worse than being in a tent as it's washed away.

The six were all settled and sitting, cooking, and talking around the nightly fire. It was a beautiful night. The harmonic convergence of everyone's good moods made their first night one to surely remember.

Jason asked, "So, how much of a culture shock are we really in for?"

Syryx replied, "Other than the trip so far, I don't have much firsthand experience with which to compare. But judging by what I've read and saw thus far, I'd say the shock may be significant. Though, hopefully in a good way. We approach life in a different way than you. For starters, we have no government and politics in any way at all."

"None at all?" spouted Jason.

"That's right. Politics, we believe, is an abstract concept conjured by man. We're convinced it was invented by those incapable of sacrificing themselves by the means of measurable, concrete tasks. Politics are illogical, and the easy way out of a harder but more meaningful existence. We never lie, so we have no need for them, both politics and government. A civilization built on the capacity for lying needs government, that much is obvious, otherwise chaos would ensue. But it's easy to lie, so most other cultures do it. For some reason, maybe coincidence, our people have just been able to refrain from falsehood."

Mick spoke. "It makes sense. Only self-sacrifice can bring forth happiness. I have to see it to believe it though. An entire civilization of individuals who never lie seems far-fetched. Lying is so prevalent everywhere you go."

Jason noted, "That all does sound interesting. I know politics were created at the dawn of man to preserve fairness for all. It works, but not as well as it should. A better system could very well exist."

Thyxer said, "Man actually spends so much time creating and covering up lies they're unaware of just how much free time there really can be in a day. We have a lot of time for a cornucopia of activities. Furthermore, we have no official jobs or money. We all just take some time in the day to do what needs to be done. And because no time is ever wasted on lying and politics, we spend little time pretending to work. In an efficient manner, we work hard physically and mentally, everything gets done. Afterwards, we have relatively much time for our cherished pastimes."

Yori said, "Intriguing. What are those pastimes?"

Syryx responded, "Our favorite one is a game we call "Fantysy-Escape." It's very complex, and involves all players bringing their own personally invented stories to each new game. The stories help you win. I'm sure you'll end up playing, sooner or later, during your stay. In fact, we'll teach you the details of the game along the way."

Dave said, "That does sound fun."

Thyxer added, "Another activity we do is called "Endurance-Battle." I never noticed it before, but I guess we like hyphenating the names of our games too."

The group laughed.

"Anyways, it's an endurance fighting game. All you mêlée-revolved personage may like this one. Throughout the predetermined game time, each participating player has complete freewill to decide with whom they want to have a friendly fight. The person who was asked can then accept or decline the invitation. The winner receives points, the loser loses them. If you decline a fight, you lose points too, but not as much if you were to lose the fight. The intricate part of it is that we really delve into the math of it. We create complex algorithms, equations where variables represent point values for each combatant, successful fighters being worth higher point values."

Dave said, "Where has that activity been all my life? I can't wait to play that. Do you play it regularly?"

"Oh yes, we play it all the time. I'm sure a match will be happening while you're there for you to take part."

"Exceptional!"

Yori asked, "How often do participants get hurt?"

Thyxer replied, "Not as often as you'd think. We quite often get injured, but rarely ever get severely injured. Endurance fighting is more about cardio than physical damage."

"Even with the pointy hands?"

"Yup, even with. Our skin has more layers than yours, so penetrating it deeply is rare."

Mick commented, "I bet those supplementary layers really come in handy during war, as a sort of shield."

"I suppose they would," replied Syryx. "We have some advantages in warfare, but some disadvantages as well. They say we see better than you too."

Jason responded, "Is that right? We'll have to test that out tomorrow."

"Sounds good. We use our enhanced eyesight, and our naturally longer arms to wield our favorite weapon, one you folks hardly ever use, if at all."

Yori noted, "I've read about it in the ancient texts. It's the *atlytl*, isn't it?"

Syryx responded, "That's right, Yori. The barrage that can potentially erupt forth from an atlytl-wielding battalion can be debilitating beyond measure."

"Intriguing." Dave said, "I've heard of an atlatl, but you pronounced it differently."

"Yes, it's different. Instead of launching spears like an atlatl would, it launches small metal projectiles attached to a string. Our enhanced eyesight helps us aim, and our substantial arm length facilitates greater power."

While mindlessly rearranging the logs of the roaring fire, Mick voiced, "So the string runs through guideposts, I understand. And to execute a launch, the projectile string is held manually during the swing, and let go at its apex?"

"That's right, Mr. Thraiker. I'll show you one when we reach the boat."

"Splendid. How fast can they be loaded in the heat of battle?"

Thyxer answered, "That's the beauty of it. When the projectiles are properly laid out, they can be loaded slightly faster than a bow and arrow. You just grab the string with the tip mechanism, and it slides right into place."

Jason said, "Sounds like a powerful weapon indeed. You spoke of battle disadvantages your race experiences. What would those be?"

"As I'm sure you guessed, our hands aren't as dexterous as yours. We can be proficient with swords and such, but we have no real masters of the craft, except for a few legendary women from the past. Our women, as you're aware, have more human-like hands. Another disadvantage: although our thicker skin helps to keep us warm in the winter, in the summer it hastens overheating, which could potentially be problematic on a battlefield."

Yori said, "Only fight wars in the winter then."

Everyone again laughed. They were all starting to rather enjoy the unrelenting jokes of travel.

Dave commented, "I bet there's a lot of strategy involved with the use of your atlytls, a complexity which I can't wait to dissect."

Syryx averted her eyes from the lovely sky, focused them on Dave, and said, "Yes, we incontestably have many strategies in atlytl usage, and will definitely welcome new ones."

Jason declared, "I actually can't wait to fire one."

"There will be ample opportunity for that, no doubt."

By the end of the night, everyone had been fully bathed in camaraderie. They couldn't wait to see what thrills were to abound the next day.

They resumed heading south along the river in the morning. They walked briskly all day, and even ran some of the way for the fun of it.

Because the party walked part of the way in the dark, they conveniently made it to the rowboat on only the second day out. Syryx and Thyxer had taken slightly longer for their version of the same leg.

The two Icytryxis who'd been waiting were introduced, and they helped with tents. Since the majority of the eight-person assembly was lethargic from having covered so much ground that day, they weren't as animated at the fire-sit as the night previous. A good time was had, nonetheless.

They all crawled into their respective tents with aching legs and feet and went to bed.

It wasn't the largest of rowboats, but it was roomy enough for a certain degree of comfortability. There were four row-pods on the sides of the boat, and storage front, back, and below. The boat and the eight were in the river by 10:00.

No doubt, the trip downstream was going to be faster than the one performed upstream.

The mighty Geenhuvagal River on which they were rowing emptied into the Dartain Ocean on Garobansurov's southernmost point.

As promised, Syryx showed Mick, Dave, Jason, and Yori her atlytl. Mick and Dave had volunteered for the first shift of rowing and looked over her atlytl while swinging oars.

Dave asked, "Of what material is it made?"

"The shaft is steel, though a different type than from what your sword's blades are made. The grabber, eyeholes, and line trigger are made from aluminum."

Jason emitted, "What's stopping you from making the whole thing out of aluminum?"

"We had looked into that at one point in the past. And, yes, it would work better, since it's lighter, but we make so many atlytls we'd never have enough of it. It's a pretty rare element by us."

"It's pretty uncommon in Garobansurov too."

Yori added, "From what I've gathered, veins of it pop up infrequently all over Taraosk."

Syryx tossed an unwanted stick overboard, one that thought it could steal a free ride, and commented, "I'm compelled to believe my atlytl just isn't perfect yet. However, don't ask what's missing, for I've yet to figure that out."

Thyxer said, "I couldn't tell you. The projectiles are missing something too."

"I'll take a look at some point. I enjoy that sort of thing," stated Jason.

After Mick and Dave's couple hour shift of rowing downstream, the next crew took over. Rowing was sort of fun for a couple-hour term. Any more than that started to get a little taxing. Each team took two turns per day. When all the turns were exhausted, they beached the boat and camped.

A good long sleep was what their moderately sore arms needed. But before they slept, they all got to experience the atlytl.

Having handed Jason her atlytl, Syryx said, "I'm sure it's obvious, but you hook the string of the projectile through here, and run it down to the trigger here. After practice, one can do that part in two seconds, and go through the entire throwing motion and start the next in three or four seconds. A little more, if you watch where it lands. When our army is going all out, each soldier fires ten to twelve per minute. It really can be quite the sight."

Jason asked, "How far will it go?"

"I'd say on your very first throw, you'll probably get it over the river and then some, perhaps between two and three hundred yards."

"And how far can you throw, Syryx, at your best?"

"Twice that, with the wind. Our longer arms really help. Our best throwers have really long arms, and the matching strength to boot."

"Interesting," said Jason, as he hooked a projectile. He swung it as hard as he could and released the trigger at the swing's apex. The stringed ball flew across the river and into the brush on the other side. Without delay he fired another, this time letting it fly up the river so that way he could see where it splashed down. "I can see how your astute eyes would help in aiming. I wouldn't have seen where that landed, if there were other people firing alongside me, which is undoubtedly vital to gauge the next shot."

Syryx responded, "That is accurate, Jason. It helps significantly."

Jason handed the atlytl off to Mick for his undertaking. Dave and Yori were already trying out Thyxer's.

After everyone's first usage of the ancient Icytryxis weapon, they more or less went right to bed.

Mick and Dave stayed up a little later than everyone else, to hang out in front of their tents and talk. Mick said, "Any ideas yet how exactly we're going to go about convincing a foreign army to fight with us?"

Noticing it was loose, Dave kicked one of his tent stakes deeper into the ground, and replied, "I don't have a sound plan right now, there are too many variables."

"Yes, I think once we arrive, we'll know more, and can devise our plan of attack better."

"Yup. I really don't know what to expect."

"That's what makes it so exhilarating," stated Mick. "Have you taken note of the enormous number of fireflies this evening?"

"I actually have been observing that. It's beautiful—a thousand points of light, suspended in a darkness that knows no sun."

"Absolutely lovely."

Like everyone else before them, Mick and Dave went to bed.

Chapter 10

<hr>

IN THE MORNING, the boat launch went off without a hitch, and they were on their way. After a day and a half of rowing, they reached the large seafaring boat. This one was powered mainly by sail, and manned by expert sailors who were there waiting and guarding the boat. There were four more Icytryxis for the Garobansurovians to meet, who had even more complicated names than the rest. The rowboat was roped to the ship—there wasn't quite enough room on the deck to bring it aboard.

Thyxer said to the Garobansurovians, "You're in for a surprise when we get close to Swyrove. There's a reason we remain hidden from the rest of the world."

Dave commented, "Surprise away, my good man."

Thyxer said, "The ocean traverse won't take too long. With favorable winds, we'll be there in a week; with unfavorable, two weeks."

Yori responded, "Exceptional. Let's hope the wind cooperates then."

Before the ship got underway, Syryx announced, "Come with me Garobansurovians. I'll give you the grand tour of the vessel dubbed the "Wevex." And before you ask, there is no captain. We are all equals here. Feel free to take the helm if you desire."

Mick noted, "As to be expected from a race with no politics."

"Indeed. Most of the sleeping quarters are below, but the two largest are on the deck here—they bookend the topside. We all take turns with the topside rooms. You'll be added to the rotation, if you wish. They really are the hot commodity, because they are bigger, fancier, and have fresher air circulating through than the ones below."

All four Garobansurovians immediately wanted in the rotation. "There really isn't too much work to do on this ship, not like the rowboat. The sailors are quite adept and efficient. You can help them if you wish. About the only work to do is cleaning and food preparation, in which you're welcome to partake. Oh yeah, you can fish if you want. It'd surely add to our food stores. There are poles and nets in the storage, over there. Also, if a bird lands on board, you can kill it for food, if that's your thing."

Dave said, "Fishing is always a force spent enjoyably."

Jason commented, "Bird killing is useful, if you have the heart."

Yori added, "I only do it when necessary, I guess."

"I think on the trip here we killed only two. Though, we have plenty of poultry farms on the mainland, and brought with a decent supply," said Syryx. "There's a bathroom next to that sleeping quarter there. Don't worry about where the waste goes, I'm sure you'll figure that out soon enough." The group laughed. "Follow me underneath, I'll show you the sleeping quarters, kitchen, dining room, and everything else."

The group opened the hatch and descended the stairs, wide-eyed. A foreign vessel really was something to behold, especially the bowels.

"The first room here is a storage closet for everything sleeping quarters related. Within, you have your extra pillows, blankets, bedsheets and such. Grab at will. Every other room in this hall is one for sleeping. Come inside."

The group followed Syryx inside, and she continued, "They're not much, compared to the topside sleeping quarters, but they get the job done. I've saved the tour of the topside sleeping quarters until last, wanting to show you the benchmark first. These beds sleep one. Not much room for hanky-panky, but it can be done." The group chuckled for the umpteenth time. "You can store the clothes you're going to use in the dresser, and your gear in the overhead compartment. Mostly everyone just leaves their clothes and gear down on this level when it's their turn at the topside rooms. Of course, that doesn't work when we have a full craft, but we're not full now. Plenty of room for everyone's stuff down here."

Mick asked, "Do you have separate ships for battle?"

"We don't have any specifically geared for battle, but we do have a bunch of transport ships. This ship here could be transformed into a transport ship too if need be."

Yori inquired, "For how many people is it set up now? And how many can a transport ship transport?"

"There are eighteen comfortable bedrooms now— sixteen down here, eight on each side of this hallway, and the two on the deck. We can convert it so it would house fifty souls, uncomfortably. Especially uncomfortably if it were to rain, and worse yet if it stormed. Then we'd *all* be crammed down here. There are rain tarps, but they only keep out so much rain."

"How does it get converted?"

"We take all the walls of the bedrooms completely off, remove all the furniture, and add cots. Topside, we erect a framework for tarps, if and when they're needed. And add cots."

Jason asked, "When was the last time you mobilized the ships for war?"

Syryx replied, "The boats we have now have never been used for war. Back in ancient times, when we last aided your country, we had different war ships. None still stand, but one of the ship's wheels is in our museum."

Yori commented, "I'd like to see that."

"Not a problem," replied Syryx. "Shall we move on?"

The party headed down the hall, past all the sleeping quarters, and to where the level opened up.

"This is the mess hall. Customarily, we make large meals for everyone. You can partake in the bigger meals at mealtime with the group, or you can fix yourself something to eat at your choosing. All the dry foods are stored in that pantry there. The meats are stored in the kitchen, and the beverages topside." The group curiously looked into the pantry out of habit. "The storage closet containing pretty much everything you can think of, other than food, is over there on the left, adjacent to the kitchen, which is where we'll go next."

They all squeezed into the close quarters of the quaint kitchen.

"Usually, no more than four can work back here at a time. Any more than that can be fairly confining. All the utensils are easy enough to find. Meats over there. Pots, pans there. Easy peasy. Now for the best part: the sleeping quarters on the deck."

The five of them walked back up the stairs, and just before they all stepped foot inside the first sleeping quarter, Syryx said, "These two up here are virtually identical. You can check out the other one if you want later, but you won't see anything new."

"Alright."

They all went in and saw a bigger bed, a window to the sea, a painting on the wall of a different Icytryxis sea ship than the one they were currently on, and a fancy wardrobe. They were thoroughly impressed.

Syryx said, "Oh yeah, I forgot, the painting in the other room is different than this one. In that one, the background is virtually identical, but the ship is different from the one in this painting."

Yori asked, "Is that one, by chance, of this ship?"

"Nope, that one isn't either. It's of one of our more ancient boats."

Dave asked, "Do any ships of your fleet have paintings in their sleeping quarters of the ship we're on now, the Wevex?"

"Actually, I do believe there is. I'm not positive, though. Hold on, I'll find out." Syryx stuck her head out the door, and yelled out Dave's question to Thyxer, who was talking to someone else nearby.

Thyxer yelled back, "Yes, it's on the Ghyged." Everyone heard the yell, so Syryx didn't repeat it.

They all took a turn, looking out the window at the gorgeous scenery. The waves were high, and the sky endless.

Jason commented, "I could get used to this view."

"It is rather breathtaking." Syryx said, "That concludes the tour. The tip jar is over there on the wardrobe."

The Garobansurovians looked for the jar, not getting the joke instantaneously. Soon enough, they realized the Icytryxis had no money, and that friends don't typically tip each other. They all laughed, though, feeling slightly wooden-headed not getting the joke immediately.

With everything all set and secure, the Wevex was underway. They took to sail in a part of the ocean that was hardly ever seen. No other continent stood between Garobansurov and Swyrove. The only other abstract landmark relatively close by was the southern pole. Ships going north out of Garobansurov rarely ever departed from the south side of it.

Mick and Dave found themselves stowing away their gear and sitting in the mess hall.

Mick asked, "Are you going to jump in, and save me if I fall in the sea?"

"Well of course, my non-swimming friend."

"That's good to hear."

"I just hope we don't get seasick on this voyage."

"I never thought of that. That wouldn't be too pleasant."

"You want to do some fishing?"

"Naturally. I've always wanted to fish the ocean," replied Mick, as he stood up from the table.

They walked over to the storage closet and grabbed some poles.

Dave commented, "We have the poles. Now, I wonder what they normally use as bait."

"Good question. I suppose we should ask someone."

Mick asked the nearest Icytryxan on the deck about the bait.

To Mick, the sailor replied, "We usually have to net the bait to use with the poles, which takes a while to do sometimes. The good news is I think Gyten netted some yesterday and has it in his room."

Mick emitted, "Oh, we wouldn't want to impose."

"I'm sure he won't mind, if you ask. Bait always dies quickly on here, so it usually goes to waste anyways."

They searched out and approached Gyten and asked him kindly about the bait.

Gyten responded, "Not a problem at all. I have more than enough for myself. Go ahead and grab a bucket out of storage and take half the minnows I have in my room—third door from the stairs on the right."

"Thank you Gyten."

Dave grabbed a bucket, filled it with sea water, plucked half of Gyten's minnows, and put them in his bucket.

Dave and Mick fished for hours. Jason eventually joined in. By the time they finished, they had enough fish to feed everyone on the boat for supper.

They asked around to see if everyone didn't mind fish for supper. After having gotten a positive response, Mick, Dave, and Jason began to scale, clean, and cook the fish in the kitchen.

While frying, Jason said, "If I knew it was so easy to pull fish out of the ocean, I would've made a point to fish in it a long time ago."

Mick commented, "Same here. I don't know where I'd get a boat from which to do it, but I'd find a pier somewhere."

Dave noted, "When we were in Sarwa we could've walked to the ocean."

Jason said, "That's a long walk to go fishing. Plus, there's a reason there are no ports over there. It's all cliffs and torrential, swirling waves. You'd never find a place to fish."

"There's no such thing as a walk too long." Dave chuckled.

Mick finished cleaning the last fish, threw it on the pile, and said, "It would've been hard to fish at Gravividon too. But I imagine it may have been possible to dangle a line from a precipice. Although, catching one too big would've presented problems."

Dave started doing the first batch of dishes and remarked, "Unless you had a really long net."

When the fish were done being cooked, they all were brought out of the kitchen and set on the tables for everyone to enjoy. There was also tartar sauce and fried potatoes to go with the fish. Almost everyone on the boat partook of the meal, and said it was tasty. Afterwards, Dave completed the dishes, Jason cleared the tables, and Mick cleaned the kitchen.

By twilight, the three of them were all done with post meal cleanup and joined Yori on the deck. They sat and looked out into the ocean, talking. Thyxer joined for a bit too. The topic of science was presented, which they all discussed passionately for an hour.

The Garobansurovians slept well that night. Even though most would get nauseous on their first night at sea, the four slept peacefully, thinking the waves were soothing.

To pass time, Mick and Dave decided to sweep and mop the deck, which took the better part of the morning. Hawk and Leopard, then, spent the afternoon playing cards with a couple of the Icytryxis, since there wasn't anything else productive that could be done.

Since he liked popping into places randomly, Thyxer made his presence known at the card table, and mentioned, "Luckily, the winds are favorable today, and we're covering a lot of ground."

Dave responded, "Sounds good."

Before popping out as quickly as he popped in, Thyxer noted, "Fantysy-Escape tonight, are you guys in?"

Mick replied, "Heck yes. Ever since you brought it up the other night, I've been dying to play."

"Excellent. It'll only be the mini version, though. You'll have to wait till we get to Swyrove to play the full-sized edition."

Dave asked, "Do we need to bring anything?"

"No, not to your first playing of the game, but subsequent ones you will. You'll learn all about that as we go along."

"I can't wait."

"We'll all meet in the mess hall an hour after supper," proclaimed Thyxer, as he disappeared from the card table.

The card game lasted another half an hour and after, Mick went to his room to read while Dave did some calisthenics.

Surprisingly, time was flying by fast for Dave and Mick, undeterred by the obvious restraint of a sailing ship. The experience was one they truly wanted to remember. A hardline proclivity for adventure and multifarious experiences worth remembrance was in their character.

Supper was interesting. Mick and Dave didn't catch the name of it, but they knew it was an Icytryxis dish. It was made with a flour of some sort.

After supper, in order to pass the hour before the game started, Hawk and Leopard went on deck to clean a few of the rails.

Back in the dining hall, everybody on the boat was gathered. The game of Fantysy-Escape was about to begin. You could say animation was flowing profusely through the air. There was paperwork scattered on every table, along with multiple, highly artistic gameboards, which resembled various landscapes.

Throughout the night, and for the rest of the sea voyage, the Garobansurovians learned just how complex Fantysy-Escape was. They would certainly be ready for the full version when they reached the mainland. On the ship, the crew tried to play every other evening; but at home, most played every evening.

The trip went on, and the winds continued to be favorable. It was estimated they would arrive in a couple days.

Mick and Dave especially favored nights at sea. In such a starry blackness, Dave put a question to Mick, "Is it just an illusion caused by the panoramic view of the sky, or are the stars more densely compacted out at sea?"

"You're right, they do seem to be more concentrated, but I have no idea why."

"With all this time for stargazing, it's too bad we haven't seen that straight line in the eastern sky, like we looked for at Dourinuset."

"I forgot about that. Yes, that was intriguing."

Yori joined them, and said, "Sure is another beautiful night."

Mick returned, "Who knew it was like this in the middle of the ocean, so much enchantment. I suppose I could've guessed at the majesty, but I would've never guessed to this extent."

"Nor I," noted Yori, turning around to look the other way, taking in a new view. "Have you guys heard if we'll all be living together, or in separate places?"

Dave replied, "I've been wondering the same thing."

"Maybe I'll remember to ask tomorrow," put forth Yori.

The trio stepped away from the rail, sat in the nearby chairs, and talked well into the night.

The next day, Mick, Dave, and Jason fished again, however, they weren't catching nearly as many as they did the first day.

Jason voiced, "I'm going to try to switch to bigger baits."

"Might as well. Even though Dave and I have yet to catch something with them, doesn't mean you won't."

"Very true."

An hour after he switched to the bigger bait, Jason was struck by luck. He found himself doing battle with a monster of a fish.

When the mammoth fish jumped, they could see how big it was, at least six feet long.

In a panic, Jason cried out, "Are there any gaffing hooks onboard?"

Thyxer responded, "No, but go ahead and use the bait net. That may work."

"Alright. I'll try it when the time comes."

Jason's arms became sore twenty minutes into the struggle. Instead of his arms, he tried to use his hips and legs more, in order to leverage the rod, but it only helped minimally.

When he saw the fish darting, Dave said, "Don't let it get around the front of the boat. The line might get caught and tangled."

"I'll try not to. The next time it runs that way, I'm going to reel in as much line as I can, to try and veer its path towards the boat. And when the fish is near, drop the net on him. Don't worry about missing, and getting my line stuck in it. It's now or never right here."

"Will do."

Jason tried his hardest to pull the fish closer to the boat. At first, it didn't work, but Jason was determined, and the fish finally came around. The moment came. Mick dropped the bait net with as much precision as he could muster.

"You got it, my man!" Jason shouted enthusiastically.

Dave and Mick both had to drag the net up, it really was that heavy. Dave yelled out, "This thing is heavier than the three of us combined."

With much effort, they successfully pulled it into the boat. They all gasped.

Thyxer looked at the fish, and said, "I have no idea what kind of fish it is, but I bet it's delicious."

Jason added, "There sure is a lot of it."

"Yes, too much for all of us here on the boat. You could make some, but I'm sure you'll be bringing most of it to the mainland. There will be plenty there to help in its consumption."

Dave noted, "It's the biggest fish I've ever seen, Jason. Impressive to say the least."

"It's the biggest I've seen too. And when I clean the fish, there will be the biggest pile of guts I've ever seen as well."

Mick commented, "You'll no doubt need a shovel to pick it all up."

Jason laughed, and said, "Hopefully the wind continues to cooperate. Otherwise, the meat will spoil while we're out at sea."

"Yeah, that would be a waste."

Mick and Dave helped to clean the behemoth, and everyone ate as much of it as they could, though barely a dent was put into it.

CHAPTER 11

DAYS PASSED, AND TIME spent in a boat was almost over. The destination was near. Syryx said to the Garobansurovians, "You're about to see just how it is we've remained so hidden throughout the years. I'm sure I don't really have to actually say it, but please keep the secret a secret."

"Of course."

Syryx continued, "All of our islands are surrounded by currents so strong that no matter how hard you row or sail, you always get swept away. We have no idea how the first reached ashore. A few have guessed we evolved on our islands, but that's just a theory. It is said that in the beginning sailors, no matter the skill, would venture out from our homeland, never to return. So, we began doing what you're about to see. If you look off starboard, you'll see a ship coming towards us."

Yori noted, "Ah yes, there it is."

"It's coming to attach the towline to us, one giant towline. When attached, they'll reel us both in. Since the tow ship crosses the point of no return to get to us, it too needs to be hauled in by the mega-winch."

Mick scratched his chin and spoke: "Two questions—how do they know when to send out the tow ship, and how do they know when to start reeling the line back in? I'm guessing they can't exactly see the ship when we're this far out."

"No, they can't, and good questions. Answering the first is easy. We estimate the arrival time of a departed ship, and within that estimation range, the tow ship comes out every hour on the hour to try and spot the target ship. The answer for the second question is a little more complex. First off, we've made the towline longer than what is necessary, because no matter how hard you try rendezvousing equidistant from the winch, contact always occurs at varied places. The large towline advantageously supplies a more sizable window for connection. If connection is missed, we'd just try again after the tow ship got reeled back."

Mick declared, "This should be a very interesting process to behold."

"It'll all happen in about an hour," said Syryx. "It's always compelling seeing it for the first time."

Many had watched the tow ship approach. The two ships were now close enough together that one could throw a rock from deck to deck. Mick, Dave, Jason and Yori all made sure they had good seats for the show.

The adept sailors of both ships were in full concentration mode, trying to get the two crafts close enough to perform the connection maneuver. They'd done it before, so this time wouldn't be overly troublesome. Inch by inch, the ships floated towards each other.

With only minimal grunting and sweating, contact was finally made.

A strong-appearing Icytryxis sailor tossed the secondary towrope across. Thyxer caught it and attached it to the special clasp of the ship's frame. The Garobansurovians were intrigued—they could see everything that was happening on both boats.

Once the rope connecting the two craft was secure, members of both ships handled long poles, used to keep the boats apart, while the drifting process was underway. Usually the poles weren't needed, nevertheless, they were ready.

As the giant winch on the mainland continued to unreel, the two boats drifted. The ships ended up drifting aimlessly for twenty minutes. It was easily noticed when the line was all the way out, for the reverse in direction was quite recognizable.

Dave asked Thyxer, "How big is the winch on the island reeling us in?"

"It's the size of a house and is supplemented with an interchangeable gear system."

"Interesting."

Since they were no longer needed, the individuals in charge of the sails started to take them all down. All that was left to do was sit back, relax, and watch the waves go by as the ships got hauled in from miles away.

Yori asked Syryx, "When will we be able to see the island?"

"Probably in about five minutes, when we're at the *twelve-mile-from-land* mark."

"I can't wait."

Wave after wave went by, some surging into the boats with impressive force.

Seeing the land of a foreign race for the first time was quite the breathtaking experience for the Garobansurovians. It was a first for all of them.

As they got pulled into port, Mick said to Dave, "I forgot to pack my things."

"Me too. I don't think it'll be a problem."

"Thyxer wasn't kidding, that winch actually is the size of a house, and not just any regular house either, a large house," noted Mick, amazed, seeing it towering in the distance.

The ship was docked successfully, which took just long enough for Mick and Dave to pack up all their gear without holding anyone up.

If the Garobansurovians had their breath taken away by just seeing it from a distance, stepping foot on Swyrove was truly almost too much to handle. Their hearts in actuality skipped beats. Everything on which they laid their eyes looked different than anything they'd ever seen. The loudest most attention-grabbing talker in the crowd of sights was the architecture. It was both astounding and diverse.

Jason asked, "Is this the largest Icytryxis city?"

Syryx replied, "Yes, it is. We call it Saraty for short. I won't bother you with saying its full name. It's quite long."

Dave commented, "I'm guessing there is no capital too, right?"

"That's right. No government equals no need for a capital."

Yori asked, "What's so significant about Saraty enabling it to evolve into your largest city, other than it obviously being a port city?"

"Excellent inquiry, Yori. I guess the best answer is thus: For many centuries, Saraty has been the home and training grounds for the atlytl corps, which many consider to be the heart and soul of our culture. People feel safe here because of it."

Mick noted, "I see that even though your islands are virtually unreachable, you have a considerable amount of sea-facing defensive apparatus."

"That we do," responded Syryx. "They've never been used in combat, but you never know. Anything can happen."

"That's right. Anything *can* happen."

Jason asked, "Where's the rest of the sailing fleet?"

"Half of it is in a cove around that point there." Thyxer pointed. "And the other half is scattered about other port villages. These ships are used for delivery purposes and such."

"Ah, I see."

Thyxer said, "Well crew, shall we show you to your new, temporary home?"

Yori replied, "Certainly. Lead on."

"After that, we'll give you the grand tour of the surrounding area."

"Can't wait."

"The good news is the four of you will all be staying together, and the even better news is that it'll be with Syryx and I."

Dave returned, "That is good news!"

"We live in a giant four-story home with our families and other siblings. You'll love it!"

"I'm sure we will," said Yori.

"It's customary for extended families to live together here. We've found it to be more enjoyable and beneficial this way."

"I would imagine it to be, since you live so long and all," said Mick.

Syryx and Thyxer led the party down a few streets to their imposing log home. Upon arrival, Mick said, "These logs are massive. The trees here on Swyrove must be epic. The logs of the house are laid out in a formation I've never before seen, too."

"Yes, the trees certainly are," Syryx returned. "While you're here, we'll have to show you some of our forests, which are teaming with trees this size. As practically a whole race of nemophilists, we take pride in our forestry, and try our hardest to promote optimal growth."

Yori noted, "We strive to do the same in Garobansurov, but we've encountered obstructions, primarily land being needed for farming. How do you alleviate that problem here?"

"Yes, farming is a mandatory practice, but we undertake to limit its over-usage by generally making note as a society to never waste food. *Food thrown away is a lost tree*, we always say."

"Makes sense," said Dave, before they all entered the house, pleasantly accentuated by the unmistakable smell of cedar.

"Thyxer said, "Everyone else, I'm sure, is in the subbasement waiting to greet us. That level is basically the recreation floor, where we spend most our nights, metaphorically enjoying the setting of the sun. The floor is also home to our giant *Fantysy-Escape* gameboards and playing area.

The floor we're on now is the one my family and I generally claim as our living space. My wife's name is Cystar, and we have a ten-year-old son named Mythys. You'll meet them in a bit. Go ahead and check out every room, and when you're done with that, we'll go upstairs to Syryx and her family's floor."

The Garobansurovians explored the span and followed Thyxer upstairs. They were greeted by Syryx, who emitted, "My family and I primarily live on this level. My husband is named Symas, and our six-year-old daughter is Byxan. Please make yourself at home. What's mine is yours, and I mean that. I want you to be as comfortable here as you would be in your own homes."

Yori said, "That won't be a problem. I'm already feeling quite at ease."

"Good. Before long, you'll be having a ball."

The group explored Syryx's abode and continued onto the next stop. The large house actually boasted two basement-type levels. The first was a regular basement; a subbasement below that. The latter was supported by behemoth wooden beams, which kept the whole thing from collapsing in. It was a real showcasing of exceptional design.

Once everyone reached the upper basement, Thyxer said, "This echelon is where our siblings Dirax and Yusyta stay: our brother, age twenty-four, and sister, age twenty-nine, respectively. They both have no other family members living with them. Two of you can have rooms on this floor. The other two vacant bedrooms are in the subbasement. The four of you can armwrestle or something to choose who gets what."

Jason said, "I do believe we've already established last winter who would win that. Mick and Dave aren't Chalatore armwrestling champions for no reason."

Yori jumped in, "That's because I wasn't signed up for the tournament last year!"

"Really?"

"No, just kidding," blurted Yori eventually, relieved she no longer had to hold in her straight face.

Everyone laughed.

When the laughter dissipated, Thyxer said, "The subbasement doesn't have a stove, but all of you are welcome to use any stove in the house, or any other appliance, furniture, and recreational apparatus. Enter any room you want. Unless we're getting it on, then that room might be a little uncomfortable to enter."

Laughter resumed.

After the four quickly discussed the matter, they agreed upon Mick and Dave claiming the subbasement rooms, while Yori and Jason the upper-basement ones.

Thyxer commented, "Go ahead and look around, and then we'll head down to meet and greet everyone. They're all anxious, I'm sure."

In an effort to move things along, the group glanced at that floor quickly. They would have plenty of time to see it thoroughly later. To give the house the attention it deserved would've no doubt taken a considerable amount of time. It seemed every nook and cranny was a point of interest of its own.

Jason and Yori threw their stuff into their rooms and followed the rest down the stairs.

The two spare rooms where Mick and Dave were to stay were right at the bottom of the stairs. The pair heaved their belongings onto the beds of their new rooms, and the party resumed walking.

Past the two rooms and through another door the space really opened up. Due to ingenious device, the subbasement was the largest level of the house. The stone walls bowed, the weight of the upper basement and the rest of the house was mainly supported by stone pillars reinforced with metal cores.

"I bet you guys didn't expect there to be a swimming pool down here."

Dave responded to Thyxer, "Can't say that I did. What a neat surprise."

Along with the pool, the area had many features, but the highlight was the Fantysy-Escape game area, laid out in an L-shape. Sitting around it were the other members of the family, all beaming with smiles, especially the youngsters. Syryx introduced the guests to the rest of the Narutyx family.

A young, handsome man spoke in an unexpectedly soothing voice. "I'm Dirax. I'm so glad you're here. I'm definitely a firm proponent of your cause and would've gone on the journey to help out my brother and sister, but we all agreed room needed to be saved on the rowboat. Your war with Molisia is a looming threat for us all, one which needs to disappear. If I can assist in any way, please let me know."

Mick returned, "Will do, my good man. We're ecstatic to be here."

With a very beautiful voice and an appearance to match, Yusyta stood and emitted, "I couldn't be happier than seeing the success of the first part of the mission. We had no idea whether or not anyone would be up to the challenge. I'm so glad you came to our homeland with Thyxer and Syryx."

Thyxer noted, "We couldn't have asked for more qualified individuals to return with us. Mick and Dave had just received the highest honor in valor their country bestows, an award given rarely. They come highly regarded by King Rowlangiv. You all will love to hear the story of what they did to receive the award. I'll tell it some night, or maybe Mick or Dave can say it better?"

"I'd love to," said Mick.

Thyxer continued, "Yori is Rowlangiv's most trusted adviser. The King unorthodoxly parted with her, because of how emphatically he believed in our cause. She is highly skilled in political, diplomatic, and social matters." Thyxer turned to look at Jason. "And the burly man here, Mr. Thorncat, is the renowned General Ulfenkerki's right hand man and first lieutenant. General Ulfenkerki, the *Black Bear* as he's known more famously, earnestly wanted to see this mission become successful. He unselfishly sacrificed his lieutenant's absence for the cause. He and the King both felt having a soldier here that knew how a Garobansurovian army operated would be greatly beneficial."

Dirax politely interrupted, "But wouldn't Mick and Dave know how a Garobansurovian army operated as well? They are soldiers, I'm assuming?"

Thyxer replied, "Normally, that would be a good assumption, given that they'd received the Knowing Circle, usually a war-related honor. But in this case, they are indeed soldiers, but not a part of the army, they are freelance fighters. Which brings up another point: because of Mick and Dave's propensity to simultaneously fight their own way while fighting for what's right, we believe their similarity with our very own army will be valuable."

Yusyta commented, "That certainly rings true. Our soldiers definitively battle the way they choose. I can see how such independence wouldn't work with some, but it works for us. I think there's an old proverb written somewhere describing this penchant."

Thyxer asserted, "I believe I'm the one who wrote that proverb, although I didn't actually write it down anywhere." It took the group a few moments to realize this was a joke. Laughter erupted.

Dave said, "Mick and I will try our best to enlighten of our battle philosophies."

Dirax stated, "Indeed. And I'm sure we will all listen diligently. I trust on the voyage over you all learned of our game, the one shown on the tables before you?"

Yori replied, "That we have. The basics anyways. I can see by scanning the whole setup here the full version will be intense."

Dirax said, "*Intense*—a very good choice of words. It'll be fun."

The group maintained an agreeable 'get to know each other' conversation for another solid half an hour before deciding to check out the nearby part of town. Everyone decided to join in on the tour.

The group of twelve left behind an empty house, and as they walked through the neighborhood, a few of the neighbors shot across friendly smiles and kind words. Those aware of the mission and who agreed with it offered the friendliest of greetings. Those who didn't, did the same, nonetheless.

Syryx said, "Tomorrow we'll introduce you to the army and others involved. But for now, we'll just see a few nearby highlights."

"Fabulous."

The road led to a certain residential area, which was so close to the sea you could smell it. From high parts in the road you could even see it. *Blue as blue could be.*

They stopped by a little creek with a decent-sized waterfall, a place that received its fair share of visitors, due to its undeniable beauty.

Yori asked, "Are there a lot of streams flowing to the sea in town?"

Thyxer replied, "There are three, but this is the only one with a waterfall, Krzenk Waterfall, as significant as this. The other two have measurable drops still worth seeing, but this one is most magnificent."

Jason noted, "I'll have to walk over here one day to descend down to the bottom by the plummet pool."

"Yeah, it's worth the trek. It really is rather gorgeous down there in the gorge."

After receiving an eyeful of the natural attraction, the party headed onward.

Having arrived at the next stop, Syryx said, "This is what we call a *food hub*. Most families grow and procure almost all their own food, but sometimes we'll crave something we don't have at the moment. So, when that happens, you just come to a food hub and grab what you need."

Mick commented, "A give and take. What a sound idea. I imagine scattered throughout town are additional hubs for other life necessities?"

"That's right. There are some for household goods, some for recreational objects, and some for miscellaneous things. If any of you want a snack, go ahead and grab something. Also, there are beverages in the back." Syryx added, "Jason, you could bring some of your mammoth fish here too. It wouldn't go to waste here."

"I will certainly do that."

Leaving the hub, Dave asked, "What food and item is generally desired the most at the hubs?"

Dirax answered, "As far as food goes, the hottest commodity tends to be the sweets. Kids will be kids. And the most sought-after non-food items are likely nails and screws. Wood and stones for building are common, easily obtainable items, but metallic nails and screws are harder to come by. Although they aren't abundant, we've never had an extreme shortage, at least for as long as I can remember."

The dozen of them walked for a few minutes, and ended up at a park, parts of which were adjacent to the sea. Within the recreational area were countless artsy displays, many of them elaborately depicting Icytryxan history.

Looking up, Mick expressed, "These ornate beams running over our heads connecting some of the exhibits are quite beautiful."

Syryx noted, "My favorite ones have always been the ones including planters."

Walking through the rest of the park, the party occasionally stole time to draw in the fresh air radiating off the sea—the deep, belly kind of drawing. It was a simple but favored pleasure.

Thyxer commented, "Our next stop as soon as we get to the other side of this commons will be our main meeting hall. If there's something important that needs to be discussed for us as a whole, it's the place where we do it. It's also where the decision was made to seek you out. We call it the Javeti Edifice."

The group, having made contact with the edifice, gasped at the incredible woodwork. Dirax opened and held the main door of the meeting hall for everyone. "Looking at it from a distance, one would see this building is shaped like a giant, elongated octagon."

"Interesting." Inside the building, Jason looked all around, and uttered, "Very imaginative architecture. How do you keep it so nice and cool in here?"

Yusyta replied, "I think it's cooler in here because it's built over a spring creek, which you'll see just around that corner."

"Amazing!" Jason realized he'd never be able to hide his love of springs.

"It flows right through the main conference hall too. Even a lot of the seating was constructed around its contours."

Dave asked, "Do you ever see fish in it?"

Yusyta answered, "I personally have never seen a fish in it, but sometimes kids will come in here to fish. I've heard they catch some sporadically." Yusyta turned to ask her niece and nephew if they'd ever fished it. They replied *no*, but said they had a friend that did once.

"I know I've never seen so many rugs in one place before," announced Yori.

Jason attached, "And walls so lavishly decorated."

Inside the main conference hall the small crowd gathered. They were indeed pleasingly stunned by the stream running through the middle. The Garobansurovians also admired all the creative seating. Some seats were practically inches from touching the water.

Before heading out, Thyxer said, "I'm sure at some point or another the four of you will be involved with one of our meetings taking place here, which I suppose is one of the reasons we came here."

Syryx commented, "We'll start heading back to the house now, but we'll take a different path, so that way you can see new sights along the way."

A few hundred yards past the Javeti Edifice, the dozen came upon another hub and went inside to check it out. The newcomers were impressed by how many goods were on stock and available for picking. They didn't need anything at the time, though.

Resuming the walk, Dave asked, "What are all these other buildings I see in front of me? They don't resemble living quarters to me."

"They are largely buildings for all our other daily needs and desires: complimentary restaurants, recreational buildings, religious buildings, museums, among others," replied Yusyta.

Thyxer noted, "Speaking of museums, that's our next stop—our biggest historical museum. We won't have the time to go through the whole thing now, it closes in an hour. But we'll go just inside the lobby. I do hope you guys come back to see the whole thing."

Mick acknowledged, "Oh, I'm sure we will."

Syryx added, "Yori, that ship wheel of which I spoke on the Wevex is in here too."

"Excellent. I'll be sure to check that out."

In the lobby of the grand museum, the group looked at and read the available displays as fast as they could, learning quite a bit. Jason remarked, "I think a person would need an entire day to soak in just a brief overview of Icytryxis history. It's impressive how far back it's been recorded."

"Yeah, we usually have certain individuals that really enjoy writing it all down and sorting it. Historically, it's always been like that," responded Syryx.

Yori stated, "In Garobansurov, our history is recorded pretty well too. But by and large, it's performed drudgingly by folks paid to do it. Otherwise, it probably wouldn't get gone. I'm starting to see the rewards regarding your whole wisdom in eliminating money. Every once in a while, these little revelations strike me."

Thyxer affirmed, "I'm glad you're starting to see that. It will truly help the mission be successful."

Closing time for the museum hastily arrived, and so the gang departed, considerably more knowledgeable on Icytryxis history.

By no means did they intend to stop at every attraction along the way home. There were a lot more things to see in that part of town alone, but day's end was approaching. Nevertheless, the tour was fulfilling and exciting.

Throughout the walk, the visitors noticed all kinds of artistic sculptures peppered everywhere. One was large with much symmetry. Another uniquely resembled a tree with gnarly, curved branches. The latter sculpture looked as if it could've doubled as a chair, but one would've more than likely assumed it was less chair and more art.

Pointing at a moderately wooded path, Syryx said, "Our last stop of the trip will be that way. It's not really anything of major significance, but it's worth the walk, and you probably wouldn't know to walk down the path on your own. I could tell you to do it later, but we might as well do it now, since we're here. It's a bunch of ancient buildings that we really don't know for what they were used. You can take a guess at their former functions when you see them. The path will curve to the left and go downhill for a bit."

Upon arrival, Dave commented, "If I hadn't previously known there were buildings here, I probably wouldn't even see them. They blend into the underbrush rather seamlessly."

Thyxer voiced, "Go ahead and step inside them. You'll notice they're appreciably old."

Curiously, Mick stepped foot inside one of the buildings, looked around, and exited. "My guess is that they're all congregated here, because it was once something along the lines of a fire extinguishing department."

"Why do you guess that?"

Mick responded to Syryx's question, "For the reason that it looks like a camp, and even though there aren't any signs of wagons, there are a lot of old tire parts lying around."

"Well I'll be darned. I never noticed that," said Thyxer. "Interesting."

After the locale was semi-thoroughly examined, the crew walked back up the hill, and to the main road heading towards the house.

Syryx spoke. "Well, all, I hope you found the tour to be at least somewhat entertaining."

Yori responded, "Oh yes, I certainly took pleasure in it."

Jason said, "As did I."

Back inside the house, Syryx said, "We got back a little late in the evening, so we probably won't have time to get Fantysy-Escape rolling, but there's a good chance we'll play tomorrow."

"Sounds good," returned Dave.

Thyxer added, "Late tomorrow morning, we'll go to the army station, and begin the important undertaking."

Mick enthusiastically stated, "I can't wait."

Taking into account how late it was, everyone more or less retreated to their own part of the house for the night.

Mick and Dave decided to take advantage of the whole convenience of it all and jump into the swimming pool.

"A man could get used to this," noted a backstroking Dave Ghrere."

"Right. I plan to take a dip every night."

"Why would you not? The water temp. is almost perfect. A little cold, but to be expected."

"To keep it clean, they must change the water every month or two," stated Mick.

"A siphon running up, out, and down a hill would do the trick."

"It's too bad chlorine is so rare."

"Yeah, that certainly would make it easier. Too bad a lot of things are so rare," commented Dave, as he got out of the pool, so he could jump back in for the novelty of it.

"Especially wonderfully assed women, excusing the improper syntax of course."

The pair laughed. "Too true. Gotta love those wonderfully assed women."

"Hopefully, we run into some of those here."

"Oh, I'm sure we will, my friend. Nice butts are universal."

The swim being past them, Mick and Dave sat around the Fantysy-Escape game tables, giving them a once over, so as to get a feel for it. "This certainly does look fun."

Dave said, "I agree and can't wait to play."

"I personally like the lighting down here. It's dim enough to radiate a cozy ambiance, while just bright enough to see."

"I almost said that before too."

They talked for a while longer and then went to bed. Their first day in a foreign land was exhausting.

Fully rejuvenated, they rose in the morning, and met up with Jason and Yori in the backyard, which was aesthetically decorated, and furnished with many lawn chairs and such. There was also a large firepit.

Yori spoke. "There aren't too many things I like better than cool, fresh morning air."

Mick replied, "No doubt."

"Well guys, I don't know what to expect today, but I'm sure I'll enjoy working with the three of you on this project," said Jason.

Dave nodded his head and noted, "Same here Jason, same here."

When it was time, Thyxer and Syryx started leading the Garobansurovians to the army stationed a couple miles away. The pace was brisk, and they arrived in no time.

Mick, Dave, Jason and Yori were taken aback by both the size of the army, and all the atlytl projectiles flying everywhere. The sky exuded synchronized pandemonium. Along with the dramatic air display, a rather interesting ground show was also taking place. Every weapon imaginable was in practice.

Thyxer said to the four, "Go ahead and look on. They all know who you are and why you're here. There's no need for any long introductory speeches. Mingle and do your thing. No pressure."

Syryx added, "Feel free to think outside the box."

Dave replied, "Good. That's our forte."

The four foreigners set about their mission, not knowing what to expect.

FOR SOME REASON, whenever the piece of paper was placed on the table, it found its way to the floor. There must've been a draft in the room. Ulfenkerki, as was his way, was the first to arrive, and waited for the rest in the barrack's conference room. Rowlangiv was expected to make an appearance. For the last few weeks, the King showed up maybe once or twice a week. Things were pretty calm lately within the Capital, so Rowlangiv felt this schedule to be adequate.

Gregg Hogarty arrived. He had received a promotion. Now an officer, his leadership skills at the battles of Strwin and Sarwa had not gone unnoticed.

He was the newest officer invited to the meeting.

Now joining Ulfenkerki at the meeting were officers of the King's Guard and of the infantry/archer corps, Rowlangiv and one of his advisors, and three more of

Ulfenkerki's officers. The room was teetering on the brink of being crowded.

Seeing that everyone was settled, Ulfenkerki spoke: "Good morning, everyone. I hope you all slept fine. I know we have yet to discover the *who* and the *how* of our attackers. But last night, I received a lead from a townsman. I'm not sure if it'll amount to anything, but when he was visiting his departed wife at the graveyard, he spotted some strangers in the darkness who came and went like the wind. My informant asserted the whole thing was fishy. I plan on checking it out when we're done here."

Rowlangiv stated, "About time we get a new lead."

Ulfenkerki said, "The guy drew a map of the graveyard for me, which pinpoints where exactly he saw the mysterious folks. I have the map right here." He handed the drawing over to Rowlangiv.

The King looked it over, and said, "I would definitely say the area he has marked is the most unlit and cluttered part of the graveyard."

Ulfenkerki commented, "I'll supply the area with hefty scrutiny, as soon as we're done here. In other news, we need to liberate some more washing basins for the soldiers. The ones here in the barracks are always being used it seems. I never have enough clean socks."

Rowlangiv chuckled. "We'll scrounge some up for you. One can never underestimated the importance of freshly washed foot attire."

The Black Bear returned the chuckle. "Wonderful. Meeting adjourned."

The last two to head out of the conference room were Gregg and Ulfenkerki.

To the General, Gregg said, "I'll come with you to inspect the cemetery."

"Good. Thank you."

After Ulfenkerki grabbed something to drink, the pair left the barracks, and angled themselves towards the graveyard. Along the way, the General asked, "How is the knife throwing training coming?"

"Excellent, sir. I'd say I'll be up to a ninety-percent stick rate in a few weeks, and hopefully ninety-five in a few months."

"That's magnificent. A man with the ability to knife throw is definitely at a strict advantage on the battlefield," remarked Ulfenkerki.

The duo enjoyed a brisk walk and entered the graveyard. "We'll investigate the quadrant marked on the map first, and search the rest afterwards, if need be."

"Alright."

After looking around for twenty minutes, the Black Bear yelled out to Gregg, who'd wandered away. After Gregg found his way back to the General, the latter said, "Do you see anything peculiar about this headstone, other than how old it is?"

"It looks to be slightly above average size and made of the typical type of stone normally used for such. I guess I'm not seeing anything out of the ordinary about this gravestone."

Pointing, Ulfenkerki stated, "Behind it, there. There's a divot in the soil at the exact point where if you were to tip the stone backwards, it would form."

"Well I'll be darned. I suppose there's only one thing we can do now."

"That's right. We have to risk being disrespectful to the deceased and lay the stone back. We'll do it together. On three . . ."

On the count of three, they started tilting the stone back, and before they could even lay it down into the divot, they were astounded by what they saw underneath the base. "Now that's interesting. A ladder," exclaimed Gregg. "It must go down pretty far. The sides of the hole are reinforced by wooden beams to help prevent collapse."

"I don't think it would be wise for the two of us to go down there on our own. Let's tip the stone back up for now. We'll descend the ladder after coming back with torches and a larger force."

"Good thinking, General."

A unit fifteen strong was gathered, and they all went back to the cemetery as quickly as possible.

Leading the way, Ulfenkerki and Gregg went down the ladder, after having again leaned the gravestone back. The rest followed down the twelve-foot shaft.

At the bottom, Ulfenkerki said, "Fascinating, a hand-dug tunnel."

"Unbelievable."

When everyone reached the tunnel floor, the General commanded, "Swords out, and heighten your focus."

Having attentively walked for five minutes, the group came upon a shovel, probably left behind by the shaft's diggers. Gregg noted, "It's not rusty yet. A clue."

Resuming to stride, Ulfenkerki said, "If we come upon any adversaries, remember there's no room to flank down here, so our numbers won't be much of an advantage against a superior swordsman or two. Judging by the direction we're going, and how long the excavation has been so far, I'm almost certain we'll end up outside the city wall. But where precisely, I have no idea."

Compounded with getting brighter, the tunnel gradually got wider. It opened up into a rocky chamber. "I think we're at the end of the road," voiced Ulfenkerki. "I'm almost positive that that is daylight emanating from between those rocks over there. But the funny thing is I don't know of any cave systems just outside of the Capital. Do any of you?"

Nobody said they'd seen or heard of any.

Gregg noted, "It may be possible that this isn't a cave, and that it's just a manmade chamber, which just resembles a cave."

"That could be. We'll find out shortly, I suppose," commented Ulfenkerki, who realized he was right about his prediction involving the daylight. The group squeezed between the rocks and faced the open air. They noticed they were surrounded by forest. "We'll worry about determining if it was a cave later. First, everyone quietly fan out, and try to ascertain where exactly we are."

"Yes, sir."

It didn't take but five minutes for one of the soldiers to report where they were. To Ulfenkerki he said, "There's a well-worn trail leading to the back of the Duntam's barn."

"I see. The Duntam farm is certainly just outside city limits. Do any of you know the Duntams?"

A different soldier replied, "It's a wedded couple, who quit farming a year ago, for a reason unbeknownst to me. The husband comes into town to drink frequently, and the wife, you could say, I've known a time or two, if you know what I mean."

Ulfenkerki broke his characteristic stoic manner, and chuckled. "I think I get the picture. Have you ever known her at the farmhouse?"

"I have not. A few times at the motel in town."

"Has it been recent enough that you could arrange another rendezvous?"

"Not too recent, but I think if I worked my charm, I could accomplish the feat in a short amount of time."

"Excellent. I think we can learn more information this way, instead of storming the place. We need to learn who's all involved with this operation, how many regularly come and go through the tunnel, if it's indeed still being used, and if there are other tunnels in use. And whatever else you can learn from her."

"Shouldn't be a problem."

"We won't go back through the tunnel. We'll all just split up and casually stroll back into the city. Gregg, can you go and set the gravestone back up, so we leave no trace of our presence?"

"Yup, I can do that."

CHAPTER 12

MICK AND DAVE decided to mainly work together for their part of persuading the Icytryxis army to fight alongside Garobansurov. Their lives' experiences were nearly identical and they could feed off each other as a result. Yori and Jason primarily worked together too. The pair got along like the moon and stars.

Mick and Dave walked around the first day and made small talk with as many soldiers as they could. They refrained from getting too specific about anything at first. Learning names at the get-go was paramount, which the Garobansurovians performed successfully by the end of the day to a degree of thirty percent. Furthermore, they mentally absorbed a substantial database of the atlytl's mechanics. In a day's span, they must've seen at least a quarter million projectiles fired.

At the conclusion of their time with the army they were satisfied with what they'd accomplished on the first day.

Thyxer and Syryx joined the quartet in the walk back to the house. Syryx said, "I've heard from many that the four of you did well today in not prying the issue. The mission will be hard, and not pushing it right away was wise."

Yori spoke: "It really is a fine fighting company. It's obvious the Icytryxis care a lot about defense."

Jason said, "Which brings up a question: Have you guys ever thought about *offense?*"

Thyxer replied, "As a rule of thumb, we don't believe in ever taking anything from anyone. But let's say in theory if our population were to ever outgrow the land supporting us, then what would we do? Do we secure more land from outside our archipelago? Do we stick to our morals by not invading? Do we interbreed with your race? There have been many scholars pondering such questions. Our answer stands as thus: If our land was ever in jeopardy of not being fruitful enough to support the population, our focus would be angled towards solving the problem through science. We'd allocate all our scientific resources. We would avoid claiming land militarily at all costs. An answer through science is always just around the corner, we always say."

Micks stated, "But to complicate it, let's say that every single space in the known universe is used up, and no more space can be made, then what? Do you invade God, defeating the purpose of refraining from conquering anything in the first place?"

Syryx replied, "It takes longer for most of us to work that reasoning out. Fundamentally, the Icytryxis believe in the Infinitum, our God of Infinity. So, to invade Infinity is to only add to it."

Mick went on, "So knowing that, how do we accomplish our task?"

"That's why we've traveled far and wide to search you out. No one here can solve it. The four of you must do it. Throughout history, there have been individuals who've justified taking lives by saying they were being threatened. But by doing so, anyone at any time can play semantics, twisting ideas around, using this axiom in their favor to rationalize eradication under any circumstances. We are not these people."

Dave commented, "No one said it was going to be easy."

Thyxer returned, "In looking at the scenario where we've helped Garobansurov in the past, nobody has been able to work out an equation as to why we did it. Trust me, we've tried. However, I have faith in you."

Dave said, "Thank you for your confidence."

The conversation ran its course. The first day of the mission was abnormally long, and so the group arrived back at the house at a rather late hour.

Syryx commented, "I doubt we've made it back in time to start this evening's Fantysy-Escape. Maybe tomorrow, we'll make it back early enough. I'm sure the rest are already down there playing."

Yori noted, "Yeah, maybe tomorrow. No need to interrupt a game."

Mick and Dave spent the rest of the night thinking. They had a lot to take in, and a lot to work out. They thought so hard they slept like babies.

Day two amongst the army saw Mick and Dave being more hands-on and in the mix. Early on, they found themselves joining a fifty-count platoon, carrying out many atlytl throws. They additionally engaged in many practice rounds of hand-to-hand combat. They really broke a sweat!

Post-sweat, and having realized they were hungry, Dave and Mick headed to the mess hall, a place where anyone could go and partake of a meal whenever they wanted. Food was plentiful and in wide variety. The locale seated a hundred at a time and was currently about half full.

Eating his meal privately with Dave, Mick said, "I think to find a way to achieve success in our task, we need to organize specific battle scenarios with many different variables."

"Yes, I was thinking the same thing, because that way we can truly assess how the Icytryxis would react in a heap of situations," agreed Dave.

"Though, we do run into the possibility they won't want to participate in our battle enactments."

"It's a chance, but I don't think that will be the case. Every mind likes to compete, especially creatively."

Mick returned, "Yes. I think it'll work. First, though, let's run it past Jason and Yori. They might have input."

"Certainly."

Later on, the four Garobansurovians converged. Mick and Dave explained their intentions, after which

Jason said, "That's a good plan. I'll help out whenever you need it. You guys go ahead and spearhead your endeavor. I'm going to put a lot of focus on the mechanics of their weaponry and see what I can do about its improvement. And by doing so, maybe we'll gain a stronger foundation of trust."

Dave said, "Great idea, Jason. And we'll help you with that any time you call for it."

Yori commented, "Same here. I will assist in anything. As for me, mainly, I will put my own attention towards the personal aspects of things and try to dissect specific relationships. I haven't noticed any politics, but I will continue to study this absence. Concentrating on relationships I believe will be beneficial because at some point, we'll need at the least a majority vote to win them over. Having a thorough knowledge of their complex social interconnections will serve us well."

Mick replied, "Right you are. I do believe we now have a pretty solid plan. Our mission is a long shot, but if anyone can do it, I believe the four of us can."

Jason said, "Definitely. This is going to be one wild ride."

"For sure."

So a diagram was set: Mick and Dave on their battle scenarios, Jason on weaponry mechanics, and Yori on relationships.

The quartet carried on into the rest of the day. Mick and Dave felt there wasn't enough time in the day left to implement one of their battle situations, so they worked with a few platoons, individually. The pair realized they were really starting to get the hang of the atlytl.

The group left the army training grounds earlier in the day than the day previous. The sun was even still up.

Arriving at the house, the visitors were introduced to a new smell. Yori said, "I do believe I've never encountered this aroma before."

Thyxer commented, "Someone decided to cook up a batch of one of our favorite dishes. It's called *frynt*."

Jason said, "It smells good. What exactly is it?"

"It's a combination of a certain spicy, pepper-like plant we have here, and a bird we'd domesticated, like a chicken, except smaller. I have the feeling enough was made for all. We always tend to make more than enough. Head to the backyard when you're ready to eat."

"Sounds good."

Mick and Dave brought their no-longer needed gear to their rooms and washed up.

Following the guidance of their empty stomachs, Dave and Mick flew up the stairs towards the alluring aroma emanating from the backyard.

Yusyta said to the guests, "I'm glad you got done in time today to eat with us. You'll absolutely love this meal."

"I'm sure it'll win me over," declared Yori.

Dirax vocalized, "And after this, you're welcome to join us in Fantysy-Escape."

Mick exclaimed, "I've been looking forward to that for a while now."

Scooping a plate full of frynt, Yusyta claimed, "It'll be a fun night, undeniably."

Everyone set to work, replenishing the day's lost nutrients.

After he scraped the last bit off his plate, and shoved it in his mouth, Dave pronounced, "You weren't kidding, that was one of the best meals I've ever had."

"Glad you liked it. I'm sure we'll have it again soon," noted Thyxer. "Now, if we're all done eating, let's begin playing the Garobansurovians first full-scale Fantysy-Escape game."

"Let's play."

The entire Narutyx family led the visitors to the game space with much pride and elation. They all spent the night playing passionately, with much focus, and wrapped in enjoyment.

During mid-game, Syryx said, "Three times a year, we have the championship, where the cumulative points that'd been gained up to it are included. Furthermore, points at the championship game are multiplied by ten."

"They just had a championship," added Thyxer, "while we were at sea. They all agreed to wait until your first game to start a new season. And if you're around long enough, the four of you can experience a championship event. We really make it into quite the spectacle." Positioned high on the wall was an enormous plaque, which Thyxer pointed at and said, "If you can win, your name will be emblazoned up there, to be remembered forever."

Dave emitted, "It looks like Syryx will be remembered for a lot of forevers."

Dirax chuckled. "Yeah, she's the best storyteller among us, and always has an advantage in that part of the game."

Syryx laughed. "I wouldn't have that advantage if you guys worked harder on your storytelling skills."

Yusyta and her competitive nature joined in. "We'll just see what happens at this next championship."

"That we will."

Thyxer commented, "And one other thing: The more you play, the better chances you have of winning in the end. You can take a night off if you wish, but while you do so, the other players will be racking up the points. So it helps to be an ironman."

Mick commented, "Sounds fair. And typically, you play every night?"

"Yes, we strive to."

For the rest of the night, the players wrote and told their stories, did math (mentally and with pencil and paper), worked out strategy, maneuvered their gamepieces throughout all the boards, and did whatever else necessary to win.

Mick and Dave loved it. They enjoyed a sense of fulfillment while playing and possessed real confidence they could win the championship.

THE SOLDIER (MARTY) who promised Ulfenkerki he would bed the Duntam wife in order to ascertain valuable information waited patiently in the back of one of the Capital's taverns. He knew precisely when to strike and when not to.

Marty waited 'till the night was old to make his primary move. Setting up the situation, he'd extended pleasantries and subtleties to her all night, but nothing too forward. He didn't want to get in the way of her ladies night, which was a big no-no for guaranteed sexual success.

Eventually, the ladies of her group were thinned out by all the randy men of the establishment, leaving the Duntam wife available for a fell swoop from a hawk named Marty. He approached her with his drink and one for her, before laying on the cliché male go-to lines as thick as he could muster. Proudly, he perceived his savior-faire was top notch that night.

After he sensed an appropriate amount of time had passed, he went in with his favorite move, the *pretending to whisper in her ear, but instead kissing her neck* move.

She succumbed to her intrinsic desires and left the bar with Marty and didn't leave his side until the crack of dawn.

After the rendezvous, Marty went straight to Ulfenkerki with all the information he had just learned from the loose-lipped, married woman. The power of hypnotic clutches of passion could never be underestimated. Marty also pleaded with the General to allow some amnesty for the Duntam wife, to which Ulfenkerki had lent a compassionate ear.

Because it was an important morning meeting, just like many times in the past, King Rowlangiv was present per request of Ulfenkerki. The usual officers were in attendance as well.

The meeting room was chilly, since the previous night had been enveloped by a cold front, plus the sun hadn't quite hit this part of the barracks yet.

With his newly gained knowledge from Marty, the Black Bear began to speak: "Thank you, everyone for being here. We've finally been blessed with important knowledge on the previous attacks. Before I begin on that, though, I'd like to first address the issue concerning the battle axes. There should be enough for all who were requesting them. Their constructions will be completed in a month or so."

One of the Capital's infantry officers said, "Greatly appreciated, sir. The weapons from the old lot aren't holding their edges very well anymore. I personally will be glad to be free of their long sharpening processes."

"I know all too well how that goes." Ulfenkerki continued, "So apparently last year, in the matter of about four months, a tunnel was dug into town, ending in the graveyard. It's presumed to be the sole mode by which the Molisians snuck inside our walls. The soldier squads were housed by the Duntams, and a few of their friends. A service for which they were paid rather handsomely, even though their mission resulted in failure. As soon as this meeting is finished, these individuals will be apprehended, jailed, and fined. The confessing informant will be placed on militarily supervised probation. If all of this is agreeable with you, King Rowlangiv?"

"Yes, sounds just. Go on, General."

"We were informed the Molisians had no immediate plans to reuse the tunnel, mainly since they'd exhausted their personnel. We learned an old friend of ours spearheaded operations, and one who more than likely has further schemes up his sleeve."

King Rowlangiv blurted, "Let me guess of whom you speak. It's Gamald, isn't it, the tyrant of the Battle of Sarwa?"

"That's right," returned Ulfenkerki. "The man stuck around and has proven to be quite the resourceful adversary. I partly blame myself for his survival. After the Battle of Sarwa, I could've sent our tracker, Mr. Thorncat, after Gamald, but I decided not to, so Jason could attend the Nighteagle's funeral. I stand by that decision, but I wish things would've worked out differently."

Rowlangiv asserted, "Don't blame yourself. You've got to look at it this way, too: It may have been possible that if you had sent Jason after Gamald, he may not have made it back in time to undertake the mission with the Icytryxis, which in my opinion is far more important."

"I appreciate that, sir. I wish we would've learned from the Duntam wife where Gamald is now. I'm sure he's not done trying to win this war. The man is presumably evil and needs to be eradicated."

The head officer of the King's Guard said, "Maybe we could form a committee to search him out?"

Ulfenkerki replied, "That may be useful. He's about as cunning as a pack of wolves. Finding him will prove to be a monumental task. He may have headed back to Molisia, him more than likely becoming aware the Capital has since been fortified."

Rowlangiv stood up to walk off a random chill, and said, "Do you think we should leave the tunnel open, possibly for our own future usage?"

Ulfenkerki responded, "That's a good question. It could go either way. You can make the decision on that, sir."

"Okay. We'll leave it open, but we'll post guards at it."

"Sounds good."

The Black Bear concluded the conference by saying, "Maybe we can accrue more information upon arresting the traitors. I won't torture them, although I'd rather sacrifice their detentions to gain information leading to Gamald's capture. He's more malevolent than all of them combined from what I hear."

DRIVEN BY COVET for thought, Mick woke early to devise a format for the first battle scenario. Before long, Dave joined in on the brainstorming. In the matter of less than an hour, they saw the completion of their day's plan.

Having arrived at the training grounds, Hawk and Leopard kicked things off with running a few miles alongside a bunch of the soldiers. Afterwards, they corralled a few platoons together.

Dave addressed the crowd, "In an effort to better understand your ways, we'd like to implement a series of battle situations. By doing this, we believe it may be possible to relate your battle idiosyncrasies with your own personal principles, therefore bringing us a step closer in uniting our realms. Mick and I feel you will thoroughly enjoy our forthcoming combat settings. If not, feel free to not participate."

A far from shy Icytryxis soldier enthusiastically stepped forward and stated, "This may be interesting. Count me in."

Everyone seemed attracted to the idea, so Mick went on: "Today we will start out simple. In the future, the configurations will get much more complicated. All who care to participate, please separate into two groups. Each team will elect a leader, one who is responsible for the security of a stone. Dave is handing these stones to each of you now. The non-leaders will support their leaders in any way possible. You win by removing the stone from the opposing leader's hands and placing it in your own leader's hands. The stone must stay with the leader at all times, and everyone must stay within the confines of the training grounds. No weapons are allowed, but you can utilize whatever else you can find. Other than that, there are no other rules. And by all means, don't hurt yourselves too much. And please, no kicks to the balls, eye gouging, or anything like that. A little sportsmanship goes a long way."

It'd worked out being twenty for one side and nineteen for the other. The extra soldier for the one side wasn't really a big deal. However, by happenstance, later on, a soldier from the larger side had to leave, forming equality. Mick and Dave would sit this one out, but planned on participating in a lot of future scenarios.

The teams picked their leaders, who grabbed and clung to their distinctive stones.

Mick yelled, "go."

Instead of either team implementing *no guts no glory* tactics, rushing in for a quick win, they both took off running in opposite directions. Mick went with one team, and Dave the other. Part of one team's stratagem was to grab rope segments, while the other team made a base-type structure to secure the leader.

After an hour-long stalemate, the teams started taking more risks, venturing off towards enemy territory. Fights were prevalent, like expected, but since the Icytryxis were used to fighting for fun, nobody got seriously injured.

The team wielding the base brought their rival's defeated soldiers back to it and guarded them, while the team with the rope segments tied down their conquered adversaries and guarded them with less soldiers. Each style had their advantages and weaknesses. The rope method saw frustration by there being more rescues, as the base method's foundering was requiring a larger crew for defending.

It took half the day for the soldiers to start wearing down. At first, there was no clear superior team.

The winning team had one particular fighter who was both agile of foot and lucky. He stole the stone from the enemy leader (chosen as leader for his adept fighting skills) by catching him at just the right moment when he and his support crew were all exhausted from previous fights.

The rope team won and celebrated accordingly.

At the conclusion, Mick said to all, "Thank you for participating in our setup. We will certainly be able to use what we've learned here. I hope most of you enjoyed your time enough to join in with us again."

Dave added, "Congratulations to the winning team, and also to you all for not sustaining any major injuries. Hopefully, those of you who are married, or such, can convince your significant other to massage those sore muscles."

An animated Icytryxis soldier commented in a deep, gruff voice, "Wouldn't that be the day! Have you met my wife?"

Everyone laughed. They had met the less-than-friendly woman.

The next day, Mick and Dave didn't stay by the army for as long as they had been during the first few days. They had other plans, desiring to check out the high spot they could see from the house. Thyxer had told them there were many points of interest up on this mountain, if they could find them, places that have been long since forgotten by most, and have been affected extensively by the slow decomposition of time.

It took half an hour of running for them to get to the lower slopes. There were trails leading up, but they weren't much more than deer trails.

Mick proposed, "Let's not let the sight of town escape our vision for too long. I'd hate to get lost up here."

"Good thinking. Who knows how far the other side of the mountain goes into the wilderness." commented Dave, while tolerating with poise the fact that since he was in the front, he bore the brunt of face-colliding spider webs.

"I don't want to find out."

The pair methodically navigated the steady incline, breaking ground and a good sweat. Every once in a while they had to climb a rock to make sure town was still within sight. In the first hour on the mountain, they saw nothing of interest other than the rocks, trees, and view. But in the second hour, they came across something noteworthy.

"Hey Dave, come check this out."

Dave stepped into the clearing, a glade which an individual would've never noticed if they hadn't headed directly towards it. "This looks to be a spring pond. It's as placid as one could conceive, but the stonework behind it is what really is of interest."

"I bet this serene pond holds some major significance. For why else would the manmade stone constructions be here."

Stepping beside the primeval stone structures, Dave commented to Mick, "These, I bet, are some of the oldest handmade monuments we've ever come across in all our journeys, judging by how far they've sunken into the earth."

"Right, only the passage of thousands of years can do that."

"And I'm almost certain this spring has been here the whole time too."

"I wonder what other mysteries are buried under here, along with the lower portions of these fascinating rock edifices."

"Well, why don't you go ahead and start digging?" Dave chuckled.

"I would, if I had a few years to do so. I wonder what we can learn about this place from our hosts."

"And from the museum in town. But I think we'd better head back, otherwise, we won't have daylight on our side to guide us homeward."

"I second that notion."

The duo orientated back down the mountain path towards the house, walking the steep terrain, and running the flat sections.

Thanks in no small part to the sun they arrived at the house, having successfully steered free from getting lost.

Grabbing a quick meal, they joined the Fantasy-Escape game already in progress.

Thyxer asked, "Did you guys find anything mystical up on the mount?"

Mick replied, "We did find an astonishing locale actually. It was a small spring pond with manmade stone configurations built around it, some of which protruding out of the ground."

Thyxer noted, showing a bit of surprise, "I'll be darned. It sounds as if you found the Spring of Stillness. Not too many people I know have ever stumbled across it."

"The water was definitely still," reciprocated Dave.

"At the museum, there are a few artifacts originating from the spring, along with a fairly detailed write-up. If I remember correctly what it elaborates, four-and-a-half thousand years ago, an Icytryxan society inhabited the place. It was said the water was home to a certain abundant, edible fish. Plentiful, because it fed on an even more abounding crustacean.

"The write-up continues, saying the crustacean was virtually inexhaustible because it fed on a certain plankton that got washed into the pool from an underground river, of which nobody ever found the source. Though, the plankton eventually ran dry. The fish, crustacean, plankton, and the source of the underground river have actually never been located in modern times. However, what has been pinpointed is the underground river in the pool. It comes in on the north side between the rocks, about fifty feet down. Legend says that one day the plankton will return, and therefore once again starting the food chain, generating an endless supply of food for anyone who so decides to live there."

"Or for whomever wants to transport fish down the mountain," added Dave.

Syryx stated, "I doubt anyone would ever have the desire to do that. That walk isn't worth it. We normally have a more than adequate supply of fish, caught from the ocean."

Mick scratched his chin. "At this epoch, you have a more than adequate army. But back then, perhaps the army may not have been so grand, consequently, needing other advantages. It's possible the profuse fish supply coupled with the fact that it was high ground, as being advantageous to defend, was the reason they dwelled there. For I'm pretty sure the fish supply in the ocean is roughly the same now as it was back then."

"You bring up a good point, Mick. That may have been the case."

Yori said, "Do you think you could find the place again, if you wanted to?"

"Although I can't be a hundred percent certain," replied Dave, "I do believe we could pinpoint it again."

"I know I'd love to see it," professed Yori.

"Maybe we'll go back up that way."

The conversation continued in its level of fascination, and the game went on well into the night. A couple laugh-loving neighbors came over and joined in on the fun as well.

Dave broke fast with Yusyta in the backyard amongst the gathering storm clouds and fleeing birds. To her, he said, "It seems as if we'll be getting a bit wet today."

"That it does. I think I'll be able to stay dry myself. I plan to do my work indoors."

"Hopefully, I can too, but you never know." Dave finished his last remaining egg. "I'd say it rains by us once every four days. Does it rain more or less here, you think?"

"I'd say a little more, maybe once every three-and-a-half days."

"You might get more, because you're situated on an island, one that approaches tropical status."

"Maybe."

Meanwhile, that day, Jason visited with the army's metallurgists at the main shop which was located a hop, skip, and a jump away from the training grounds. His fascination with the mechanical side of Icytryxis weapons and his belief he could help the mission by its focus lead him there.

Jason got into a very technical conversation with the crew, one which lasted until lunch. Jason determined he would go back by the metal workers as much as possible.

The rain put a damper on Mick and Dave's battle exercise they had planned. So, they joined the bulk of the soldiers at the indoor training facility, within which was an assortment of various weight training apparatus, weapons stations, and fighting pods. There was even a running track. Soldiers could still train outside in the rain if they wanted, but most opted not to.

Ultimately, rain days limited the army's atlytl practice capacity, since not many desired getting wet while launching. In order to build a structure large enough to house the firing of an atlytl, it would have to be astronomically huge, a building endeavor that was just too unrealistic.

Not all the soldiers went to the indoor training facility during bad weather. Some went to help build arms and armor in the respective buildings. Others helped with food, cleaning, and other anonymous tasks. A few just went home.

He craved a good sweat, so Mick ran, finding himself at even pace around the track with an Icytryxan lady named Veryx.

Currently not breathing too hard to talk, Mick asked Veryx, "How long do you plan on running today?"

"I think another half hour. Any more than that and my feet will get sore. They've been acting up lately."

"Sometimes when my feet are killing me, I'll soak them in hot water. But I haven't done it in a while."

"I've done that a few times before. It helps some."

"Nothing beats a good night's sleep, though, to remedy sore muscles."

"Yes, a time-proven medicine indeed," said Veryx, while switching positions with Mick, tucking in behind for a turn at drafting. They weren't racing, but it was always sensible to make good time.

Meanwhile, Dave went to one of the blacksmith shops, aiming to help with sword construction. During all that time spent at Tim Warmane's, watching his own sword get made, Dave picked up enough knowledge of the craft to be moderately helpful in constructing a bladed weapon. He spent some time being productive—chipping slag, working the bellows, and hammering metal.

Having just become a finished product, Dave grabbed a sword and admired its craftsmanship. He swung it a few times and gave a half smile to the nearest person. "Aah, the satisfaction of a job well done. Very much worth getting dirty."

"That it is."

At the end of the afternoon, the group walked back to the Narutyx house. It was still raining, so they did it without dawdle.

Holding her coat over her head to shield herself from the force of the rain, Yori commented, "I learned a lot today. Some things that I think will be useful in the time to come."

Dave replied, "Excellent, Yori."

Jason added, "I gathered a ton of information today as well, so much that my brain hurts."

"I couldn't help but notice how hard the four of you have been working. I'm truly inspired, I really am," exclaimed Syryx.

Mick returned, "We appreciate that. Urgent missions are no doubt demanding."

"Too true."

Relieved they no longer had to dodge raindrops, the crew got settled in inside the house. Yori, Jason, Mick, and Dave made their minds up to all jump in the pool. It was, indeed, the finest place in the house.

In no time, they were all nestled within the comforting depths of the pool.

Jason, being a military officer, said, "I think morale would be pretty high within Ulfenkerki's army if we had one of these to tow along with us everywhere we went."

Mick chuckled. "It would be too for Dave's and my escapades."

A comical chill surged down Yori's spine. "Oh, you guys!"

CHAPTER 13

A FAST MONTH went by in earnest labor, during which time the Garobansurovian quartet had continued to effortfully work on the mission. Each had done their thing and discussed scrupulously their ideas amongst themselves. It was an undeniably fruitful thirty days.

The four were walking home one day when Dave said, "To be honest with the rest of you, I wouldn't mind a few days free from thinking and working so hard."

Yori stated, "I couldn't agree more. A few days of R and R would go a long way."

Thyxer innocently overheard the conversation, and said, "You guys are indubitably welcomed to a little relaxation to recharge the mind and body. You've been noticeably exerting yourselves, and as everyone knows, over-exertion can lead to burnout, so please go ahead and take some time for yourselves."

Dave noted, "It'd be nice to get into the woods and air the tents out."

Jason nodded his head. "I too wouldn't mind a nice jaunt into the wilderness with my dependable army tent."

Yori smiled, and voiced, "I know my pricey tent needs more action than what I give it. Otherwise, I'll feel like I paid too much for it."

Mick looked around at everyone to see if they were as excited as he. They were. "It seems, then, we are in unanimous agreement: We are to go on a camping trip. Enjoyable. Let's do it!"

"I think a four-day trip would be sufficient enough to replenish us," stated Dave.

"Excellent!"

"I've got some pretty good maps of the wilderness to supply you with," said Thyxer. "There are some hotspots marked on them, but unfortunately the really interesting ones you'll have to find on your own. Technically, there are ruins out there that no one has seen. And some, like the Spring of Stillness which you've seen, only handfuls have glimpsed. The wilderness is immeasurable."

Yori curiously asked, "Are any of them magical?"

Thyxer responded, "Old texts speak of such things, but in all probability mere exaggerations."

"Yeah, it's the same in Garobansurov," conveyed Mick.

Jason announced, "Except for the *black needle* swords. Those are magical if ever anything was."

"That remains to be seen," articulated Dave. "We're still trying to solve that mystery, but until we do, we're justifiably assuming there's a perfectly good scientific explanation for them."

"Well, maybe we'll find another *black needle pine tree* along our camping journey to solve the enigma," suggested Jason.

"Hopefully. We do always have our eyes open for them."

Thyxer commented, "I do know there aren't any Icytryxan texts mentioning pine trees with black needles, or any sword/weapon handles with heightened gripping capabilities."

"I bet an atlytl could propel its ammunition much further augmented with the same gripping capacity," added Yori.

"That very well could be possible," said Thyxer, as the conversation tailed off.

At the crack of dawn, the Garobansurovian quartet left the house and started their trip. They decided to mainly follow one of the old, but still usable trade routes inland and maybe head off-trail a little, if the opportunity presented itself. There weren't very many towns inland, largely in part because everyone wanted to live seaside, the middle of Swyrove being principally dense forest. There actually was a part of the forest the group was told to try and avoid. It was known to the Icytryxis as "the viper pit." It was an area rocky enough to be the habitation of a venomous viper, known to have killed hundreds foolish enough to go poking around the sector. Gratefully, the spot was marked distinctly on the map Thyxer had provided.

The group desired to avoid the large, taxing hill Mick and Dave had previously ascended many days past. Correspondingly, they went around it. Though, the four were an hour into the trip when they realized the horizon was interspersed with too many taxing ascensions to avoid them all.

Yori said, "Sure is some mighty beautiful countryside. Good thing we're going directly into it!"

Jason agreed, "Yes, it'll also feel good to be free from seeing hundreds of thousands of flying atlytl projectiles every day."

"It is rather dizzying after a while, isn't it."

"Almost enough to hypnotize. I've found myself having to shake out of a trance on multiple occasions."

Yori noted, "Same here."

Kicking a cumbersome branch out of the path, Dave communicated, "They do seem more entrancing than arrows. I think it's because they load and fire faster, making for relatively more motion."

"Makes sense."

The foursome walked a wooded path they'd probably only travel down once in their lifetime.

They stopped for the night in the most beautiful place they could find. The locale looked down on a vista of natural treasures. The glade suitable for camping flaunted rocks of all shapes, sizes, and colors.

After the tents were set up, a fire was made, and all other nighttime rituals were completed, the group relaxed and talked.

Yori voiced, "Jason, what do you think is happening right now at this very moment with Garobansurov, the Capital, and Ulfenkerki's army?"

"Well, I'm certain the war wages on, particularly on the west side of the country, and the army is still posted at the Capital. I'd bet the east side is still secure. Of course, though, whoever it is who spearheaded the attacks on Myothraces may still be at large and could be up to anything. The calculus of war is complicated, having an infinite number of variables. To correctly guess at them all would take an equally infinite amount of time."

Mick noted, "Definitely. All of life, all species, all matter, all energy are in constant conflict, trying to be the thing that exists. It teams up if it would help. It schemes, it hides, and it multiplies/divides—myriad of possible actions. Such is war, as both nature and man know it to be."

"All four winds struggling to exist—converging and diverging—a variation of warfare in itself," added Jason.

Dave voiced, "And the same is true for love. Love and war: two provinces where anything can happen."

Yori commented, "I suppose without this unpredictability, life wouldn't be as exciting."

Dave nodded. "That it wouldn't, Yori. Very true."

"Yup. Though, I digress. I hope we see some interesting things tomorrow," stated Mick.

"Me too," said Jason, before being accosted by a nighttime yawn.

THE MORNING SUN was warm and woke everyone with its gentle radiance. Met by the highest of spirits, the group took to the day's walking.

Time went fast in the sticks, and late morning popped up as the quartet discovered a small village nestled in the wilderness. It seemed as if it was straight out of a poem, perfectly centered within very old ruins. Each home was obviously made from parts of the surrounding ruins and the neighboring forest. They were quaint looking structures, of which there weren't many, but enough to make an efficient community.

Having fearlessly walked into the rural community's main square, Mick, Dave, Jason, and Yori were hailed and approached by a pair of young women.

The taller of the pair proclaimed, "Welcome to Fyatas, travelers, foreign travelers no less."

Yori replied, "And a very cheery welcome to you."

"We'd heard your story from another traveler. Otherwise, we would've certainly been more afraid to confront you, the unknown," said the villager.

"Quite understandable. We're just out for a little four-day camping vacation."

The shorter woman said, "You guys are more than welcome to camp here in town. This way you can see all the area's lovely sights. My husband is very knowledgeable of such things and could tell you all about the points of interest, and where they are."

After infinitesimal discussion between themselves, Dave spoke for the Garobansurovians. "That would be delightful. We will do that."

"Excellent. Go ahead and make camp wherever you so choose, and we'll talk later."

The four looked around and deliberated. They decided the best place to set up their tents wasn't awkwardly in the middle of town, but also not too far away as to make it seem they were discourteously avoiding everyone. They chose an area within view of where they talked with the pair of women, and next to many ancient stone structures—in fact they'd be virtually surrounded by them.

As camp was under construction, a few villagers pleasantly introduced themselves. One in particular was exceptionally memorable, because of how old he was. Interestingly, the guy looked practically as old as the stone structures near camp. An exaggeration, of course.

After the setup, the quartet hooked back up with the women who invited them to stay, this time meeting their husbands. The shorter woman's husband, Dytin, agreed to show them the sights, also offering to show them his home. He figured they probably never saw a house quite like it.

He was right.

The outside of the house looked normal enough, made of native wood. But on the inside was an entrance into an underground channel, an old habitation for someone long ago—*very* long ago. It was still plenty sturdy for living purposes.

"We mainly use this ancient sector for storage, various leisure activities, and under certain situations a stronghold," commented Dytin.

Dave asked, "And which situations might those be?"

"Mainly only when forest beasts attack. It doesn't happen much, but on occasion, a pack of them will daringly try to eat the villagers and I."

"We have a few wild animals like that in Garobansurov. *Verids* come to mind. Rare creatures, though."

Dytin responded, "You're lucky then they're rare."

The group emerged from the tunnel, and Dytin stated, "And that concludes the house tour. Stop by in the morning and I'll eagerly show you the highlights of the forest."

"Sounds Excellent."

Daybreak burst in and the Garobansurovian bunch ate a large breakfast, before meeting back up with Dytin.

The Icytryxan led the four all over the biodiverse woods for exploration.

One place was exceptionally beautiful to the foreign tourists, a waterfall—the setting of a great bridge which once mightily spanned across the entire river-bottomed gorge. The bridge was no longer there, only vestiges remained. Impressive vestiges no less.

"I've been told," asserted Dytin, "the bridge stood strong five thousand years ago, older than most the ruins in our village, connecting two primordial forest societies."

"How do they know how long ago it stood?"

"I wish I had the answer for that. Your guess is as good as mine. Probably some geological trick, about which I'd never asked. Now I wish I would've though."

The group went to where the bridge once stood and out of curiosity looked for the evidence leading Dytin's informant/informants to believe it stood five thousand years previous. They gave up after half an hour, mainly since there wasn't much hope in discovering the evidence. It was just thrilling to revel in the mystery, and in the mist from the waterfall. Though, any more revelry and they'd be soaking wet.

Another unforgettable stop on the venture was a crypt, situated both underground and in the middle of nowhere. There were a few human bones scattered on the ground of the mystifying tomb, and a chair upon which a dead body may have once been propped.

"I'm sure someone looted this place a long time ago, liberating weapons or even jewels buried in here with the bodies," explained Dytin.

Mick stated, "typical."

The group departed the haunting crypt and performed the final segment of Dytin's circle-tour.

Peaceably, the village sat as the group returned to it.

Dave decided to take a nap, while Mick made a fire by the campsite, and relaxed with Jason and Yori fireside all the way up to dusk.

Under the darkened sky of twilight, Mick rose from his chair, and walked for a bit to stretch his legs, but when he looked to the eastern forest, he noticed something alarming. It was as if the forest came alive. Unexpected motion was everywhere. He realized something hostile was heading straight towards him.

Characteristically, Mick wasted no time.

First thing he did was run back to the campsite. To Jason and Yori he quickly hollered, "Grab weapons, we're under attack!" The next thing Mick did was awaken Dave, who was still napping. "Dave get your sword, there are beasts coming out of the forest *aggressively*."

Mick grabbed his sword from his tent and joined his three compatriots. Together they sprinted to warn everyone else.

Dytin had quickly armed himself and yelled to the Garobansurovians as they ran towards him, "This happens every few years: A herd of voracious *gnyts* decide they want to try and eat us. Follow me to my stronghold."

Dave replied, "I don't think we'll need that. I'm pretty sure we can take them on open ground with the right tactics. Although it may be best for you and your wife to get into the stronghold."

"Alright," noted Dytin. "A few villagers will accompany me, and the rest have strongholds of their own."

Jason asked, "Yori, you're welcome to go with Dytin, or you can stand beside us and test out your skills with those throwing stars of yours?"

"I'll stand and fight," replied Yori. "How many usually come?" Yori asked Dytin.

"Last time, a few dozen. They are fast, strong, and towering. Gnyts work together, but are obviously not as smart as you and I. Their skulls are very thick, so aim for their hearts," shouted Dytin, as he made way towards his house.

Having joined up with his wife and three neighbors, Dytin went into his home's stronghold for refuge and battle advantage.

Firmly gripping his weapon, Dave spouted, "It's times like fights that begin finer with prized friends."

Mick smiled at Dave's unanticipated lovely sentence and replied with wit of his own. "They end finer that way too."

There was a small hill just off to their left, which the quartet climbed for high-ground advantage. Though they didn't want to go too high on the hill and be out of sight, risking the aggravated gnyts going inside the houses.

Foreseeably, it wasn't going to be a particularly hard fight, so they weren't very nervous, as the four strategically stood nearly back-to-back on the hill.

Randomly choosing their targets, the beasts ferociously attacked the three warriors and an irrefutably brave king's advisor.

Yori, proving just how good she was with her throwing stars, stunned a couple gnyts long enough for fatal sword strikes.

It only took a few minutes for the gnyts to realize they weren't winning this one, so they retreaded as fast as the incursion began. In the end, half a dozen gnyts were skillfully killed.

"I wonder if these hairy things taste any good," blurted Dave.

"And I wonder if they could ever be tamed enough to pull a carriage," commented Jason.

"We'll have to ask if they've ever tried."

The threat neutralized, the Garobansurovians proclaimed the coast clear to the villagers.

Dytin joined up with the victors and responded to the questions they previously propounded. "They're edible but very tough, taking forever to chew. If you were starving, they would be good, but we hardly starve here. Go ahead and try eating one if you'd like. And as for taming them, many have tried. And equally as many have failed. Many Icytryxans have gotten killed this way. It's a force, we've concluded, spent wastefully."

The villagers emerged from the strongholds, sighed relief, approached the victorious combatants, and thanked them earnestly. On occasion, a casualty or two would ensue during a gnyt raid, so the townsfolk were extremely grateful for today not being one of those times. The villagers offered a celebratory banquet, and the visitors graciously accepted.

A few hours after the battle, everyone in town got together in high merriment to eat a plethora of dishes.

In a good mood, Dave sat beside the old man of the village, and discussed times passed. Mick sat beside the only attractive single lady in the village, the two conferring about her participation in the day's encounter.

After the meal, everyone gathered around the town's three musicians, and jovially listened to them play well into the night. The trio's superior musicianship was undeniable.

IN ORDER TO MAKE sure none of the mud on his boots got spread all over the castle, Ulfenkerki spent a solid two minutes stomping his feet on the entrance mat—a convenient mat put at the front entry for just this purpose, and one, thanks in no small part to Ulfenkerki, which needed to be washed daily.

Rowlangiv was waiting for the General in one of the castle's living rooms. After climbing a couple flights of stairs, Ulfenkerki, glad his boots were moderately clean, approached the King and said, "You wouldn't think it, but one can really get dirty here in Myothraces."

"For a soldier, maybe, a king, not so much."

Ulfenkerki chuckled. "Indeed. Anyways, as you know, interrogating the prisoners hasn't yielded any information on Gamald's whereabouts. But the good news is the committee we formed did."

"Is that so?" Rowlangiv perked up.

"Yes. I suppose the information is reliable, but in no way is it *set in stone* fact, like all information, I suppose. We've gathered a detailed report from a small community fifty miles north. It depicts the existence of an area near their village under constant surveillance by unfamiliar folk. Apparently, no one is allowed in this area, and if anyone tries to enter the guarded vicinity, they unexplainably disappear."

Rowlangiv responded, "Yes, very suspicious. Sounds like an excellent place for harboring a tyrannical general. It might be a clan of some sort, trying to rebel in some way, but that sort of thing only comes along once in a great while. How do you suggest we proceed, General?"

"Before we dispatch the army there in haste," replied Ulfenkerki, "I would like to personally travel there myself, and ascertain what it is exactly we're looking at."

"Not all by yourself, I hope."

"No, maybe half a dozen would accompany me, I'm thinking. With your permission, sir."

"I see no reason against this undertaking," decided the King. "When will you leave?"

Distracted by something occurring out the window, Ulfenkerki didn't respond to Rowlangiv's question right away. Once he realized it was just a huge flock of out of place turkeys, he replied, "As soon as possible. I'll form my crew, then leave immediately, probably within the hour."

"Dang, General, you're a fast packer!"

"It's a helpful skill to have in the military."

"I could imagine. Well then, I wish you safe travels, and that you learn valuable information."

"Thank you, sir. See you in a couple weeks," said Ulfenkerki, just before heading out the living room, back down the stairs.

Ulfenkerki's next task was to form his travelling squad. Seldom untrue, the General's accompaniment squads were easy to form. Mainly since trekking with the Black Bear was looked upon as not being too cumbersome of an endeavor. Overall, Ulfenkerki was a renowned good guy, and traveling with him was normally a pleasant experience.

Gregg Hogarty volunteered for the crew. He enjoyed these types of things. Four other soldiers joined in, all fond of walking far and fast.

True to the General's word, the party set forth from the Capital within an hour of his discussion with the King. Each member of the company had a travelling pack, protective gear, and weapons.

The 50-mile walk/run took three days, an enjoyable three days.

At the destination, the crew had taken refuge with a family about as loyal to the crown as it gets: a former King's Guard (Bruce) who half expected a reconnaissance party from the Capital to show up at some point. He knew all about the autonomous zone that had sprung up.

Bruce proclaimed to Ulfenkerki, "Go ahead and make the barn your base of operations. I took the liberty of stocking it previously with most of the stuff you'd need. Anything else you require, just ask, and I'll try my best to get it."

After a fine meal, Ulfenkerki and his group went to the barn for the night and were pleasantly surprised to see Bruce had supplied actual beds, even a couple extra. "He must've built these beds himself as of late," noted Ulfenkerki.

"What a guy!" announced Gregg.

"I bet supposing it was closer to winter," said the General, "he would've even brought a wood stove in here for us."

Morning brought with it another day of good moods. Ulfenkerki and his crew were ready to scout, even though they weren't quite sure how they were going to go about it. They'd take things as they come.

"Not desiring to draw too much attention, I plan to sneak up close to the zone in question alone to begin. Then, as needed, I'll call on you guys," stated the Black Bear. "So, for now, hang out around the barn here."

"No problem, sir."

Two miles from the barn, Ulfenkerki found himself peering into the suspicious sector the report had detailed. Behind the perfect tree, he kept a distance, noticing sentries in strategic positions, though not strategic enough; they failed to spot the wily veteran General lurking about.

It took half the day, but Ulfenkerki learned through inconspicuous study how large the patrolled area was—certainly, large enough to house a small army. Too bad there wasn't ground high enough to peer over the periphery trees and into the interior of the patrolled zone. It was more than likely planned like this.

Back at the barn, Ulfenkerki told his crew all he'd discovered. "The area is large and rectangular in shape, probably three thousand by two thousand feet. It's weird, though, that they patrol it. I would think they could remain even more cleverly hidden by just staying within the wooded area, not drawing attention to themselves. If there is a foreign army in there, I wonder how they got across the border unnoticed. So many questions yet to be answered. I'm not quite sure how I want to proceed. I'll have to sleep on it. If you guys want to go into town to the tavern, go ahead, but only two or three at a time. And make certain you memorize a believable story for what you're doing in the area, so as to not draw unwanted attention to yourselves."

One of the soldiers responded, "Sounds good, sir."

They all desired alcoholic drinks, but they didn't have to draw straws. Two were thirsty immediately, while the other three preferred drinks later on.

Ulfenkerki woke and was still satisfied with the plan he'd concocted a few minutes before falling asleep.

Successfully standing the test of time was always the sign of a good plan.

Ulfenkerki addressed his troops, "This is what we're going to do today men: First, we need to find out what exactly is going on within the patrolled sector that is obscured by trees. Since I'm not about to risk anyone's lives, we're going to play the patience game. We'll take turns, watching to see if anyone or anything comes in or out. If after a week, we see nothing, I'll tweak the plan a bit."

"Yes, sir."

Throughout the week, Ulfenkerki and his soldiers took turns spying. And at the end of the week, they'd learned nothing. Nobody came or left the zone. However, the sentries could still be seen.

"I wonder if there are any tunnels, like the one we found in town. For all we know, there may be a tunnel leading all the freaking way back under the mountains into Molisia," said Ulfenkerki to his squad.

"That would be one long tunnel!" voiced a soldier.

"Well, I think we'll spend one more week doing the same thing. But this time, along with watching the sentries like we did last week, we'll also watch up to a half-mile radius from the guards in all directions. It'll take more of us, but I think it'll be beneficial. Who knows, maybe it'll be a big waste of time. But nevertheless, it must be done," asserted the General.

"No problem," remarked Gregg.

On the fifth day of the adjusted plan, they discovered a lead. Gregg stumbled upon a pile of dead bodies in the woods.

Upon the news, Ulfenkerki decided not to draw attention to the fact he and his men were snooping in the area, so the only person with whom he talked about it was the ex-King's Guard, Bruce. Bruce didn't know of anyone from town (only travelers) gone missing, but he promised to ask about it to only his most trusted friends. In the meantime, Ulfenkerki and company continued the investigation.

At the end of the second week, Bruce hadn't learned anything about the identity of the dead bodies, nor did they discover any fresh information.

Holding an imperative meeting with his soldiers, Ulfenkerki stated, "I did a calculation of sorts, and I estimated that there can't be any more than three or four hundred potential enemy soldiers concealed within the forest, if indeed there's an army there. If anything, it sure is a well-disciplined army. They definitely know how to stay concealed. I've decided to advise the King to mobilize a part of our army stationed at the Capital. Once they're here, we'll infiltrate the sector. Though if they travel at full force, we risk the enemy fleeing, and more importantly, we could lose the element of surprise. So I'm going to suggest they come in a hundred small waves, grouped six at a time. It's a long shot, but maybe we can stay unnoticed until our assault on the sector. Obviously, I'm going to have the five of you stay and join in on the invasion when the time comes."

"Should we continue the reconnaissance while you're gone?" asked a soldier.

"Actually, no, I don't want to risk them spotting you, and thinking something is up this late in the game. Continue holding up at the barn, occasionally going to the tavern in small groups, if need be. Of course, keep your ears open while there, but if they've been this sly for this long, I'd be greatly surprised if the enemy divulged information now. If Rowlangiv disagrees with this plan, I'll send someone to come get you."

"Have a good trip, sir."

Ulfenkerki left for the Capital as soon as he was done talking, accompanied by a couple day's food ration.

He practically jogged one third of the way, which was an undeniably impressive feat for a man of his age. The effort surprised even himself. His mouth made it to Rowlangiv's ear sixty short hours from when he left.

The two began the planning of the invasion right away.

CHAPTER 14

THE VACATIONERS left the village of the gnyt conflict the day previous, and had one more day of camping planned before heading back and resuming the mission with the Icytryxan army.

"Well guys, what should we do today?" asked Yori. "Hopefully, we find something more scenic than last night's panoramic view of repetitive thicket."

Having pretended to think before he responded, Jason said, "I'm not sure. The three of you can go ahead and decide. I'm open for pretty much anything."

"Let's make the best of it. I highly doubt we'll ever get to this side of the world again," noted Dave.

Mick said, "I suppose we'll have to walk around to find something to do. But not too far, though. We'll have to head back in the morning."

"Sounds good."

By mid-afternoon, the party found an interesting place to make camp: a hollow nestled inside a large igneous rock formation, large enough to make for an extremely gorgeous setting for camping. It was similar to a cave, in that the walls were all stone, but it was open on top to the stars. There was also an antechamber, perfect for storage. Since there wasn't a cloud in the sky, they decided against setting up tents in the niche. Instead, they laid out sleeping bags right on the hollow's ground for full outdoorsy effect.

"Now, we'll know once and for all if any of us snore," said Yori.

Mick chuckled at Yori's remark. "And we'll also find out who among us kicks in their sleep."

Dave blurted, "We've outdone ourselves this time. This really is quite the backdrop."

"I'm surprised we're the only ones to camp, or even be in, here. There are no bipedal footprints marking the sand anywhere, especially in the side chamber, where virtually no evidence-erasing erosion could manifest," said Jason.

"That, and there's no litter either," added Yori.

"The indigenous fauna sure recognizes an interesting locale when they see it. Scat, in various sizes, is scattered everywhere," said Mick.

Jason questioned, "I know you two like geology, Hawk and Leopard, so I must ask, what would've caused this fissure in the rock?"

Dave responded, "Sometimes water, sometimes wind—any sort of natural erosion. But in this case, there doesn't seem to be any evidence of erosion. This unconventional geological feature is an enigma. Sometimes Mother Nature just does what she wants."

Jason nodded and tagged on, "The music of the spheres goes on playing."

The group removed all the unsightly animal refuse and let relaxation seep into their bones. At twilight, the four of them got all cozy in their sleeping bags. Excitement at the revealing of the stars abounded.

Mick asserted, "Perfect weather for this."

Yori responded, "Yup, this is without doubt a wonderful way to end our trip. Not meaning to digress, but we're back to thousands upon thousands of dizzying atlytl projectiles tomorrow."

"I knew our mission with the Icytryxis was going to be arduous, but I had no imagination to this degree," commented Jason.

Dave spoke: "Persuading a host to go to war when the mere concept goes against their fundamental beliefs is indeed quite the monumental task. Their army is strong and capable of doing a lot in the assistance of an ally. We need to find a way to show them that."

Yori turned over in her sleeping bag, facing everyone, propped her head up with her hand to glance at Dave, and said, "This world is full of cheats and liars. Who really knows who their true allies and enemies are? It's a game that everyone plays, and everyone tries to win. Proving to an entirely different race that we as a country, one which lies across a virtually impenetrable ocean, want to form a relationship that will endure through the ages, is in no way dissimilar than attempting to do the same with that horde of gnyts that attacked us the other day, in theory."

Mick said, "Good analogy, but we do have one thing on our side—the fact that, judging by history, it's possible. Plus, I bet with the right approach someone could get a gnyt to fight alongside them."

"I bet it's possible too, no matter how much they said they've already tried," said Jason.

Dave stated, "I don't think we can win them over with logic, theirs seems unassailable. If the Icytryxis faced danger more often, they'd need allies, but since they live in such an advantageous situation—an unreachable island—they can afford to hold strong to their principles. I don't blame them. I think in order to persuade them, we're going to have to do something with shock value. I have no idea what. We'll keep up our war scenarios, searching for the answer, while the rest of you continue doing your thing."

Yori noted, "I wholeheartedly agree. We can't win using logic against them. War is an abstract concept, only existing in the mind. To convince someone to take part in a war they don't believe in is like convincing a tree to grow tall instead of wide when there are no other trees around competing with it for light."

"Interesting, truly. You have all kinds of parallels this evening don't you?"

Yori chuckled at Jason's comment. "I guess sleeping bags have that kind of effect on me."

Dave communicated, "I like and concur with your premise, Yori. The value of war is like that of money or religion to an individual: It's all what you decide it to be. Everyone decides differently."

Mick took the baton, "More similes. You can never have enough. The Icytryxis are obviously pro defending themselves, but con invading for any reason. That's what we know as fact, and it won't change. It would be a waste of time to try and alter it. So much reflection."

"Yup. Sorry for changing the subject, but that's the second shooting star I've seen tonight."

"I saw that one too, Jason," remarked Yori. "I missed the first, though." The four continued to watch for shooting stars, discussing the mission, right up until they all one-by-one fell asleep.

Having received a great sleep in the open air, the Garobansurovians were energetic and packed up in no time, partly since there were no tents to set down. A quick breakfast eaten, and they were off with a bounce.

Because of the vitality, they made it back to the house by nightfall.

After telling everyone everything what'd happened in the far-flung wilderness, they fell asleep hard, hoping their sore legs from walking all day would be relieved by morning.

They were.

Resuming the daily routine, Mick, Dave, Jason, and Yori once again found themselves amongst the atlytl projectiles in the sun's morning glow, their noses to the grindstone. Familiarity bloomed.

Mick and Dave implemented a war scenario where the participants were separated into five groups, the Icytryxans being told in order to win they must find a way to pick the winning team themselves. There were no other stipulations. It was possible a diplomatic solution could've been reached, and sometimes it would have. But more times than not, these things were settled with physicality. Such is the way of nature. Mick and Dave had devised the idea that night in the open-air grotto and thought it would be very insightful.

They were right. Watching the events performed by the actors and actresses surely got their mental gears turning.

After an hour's discussion, the Icytryxis soldiers decided they wanted to have a distance-throwing contest in order to determine the winner.

The competition commenced. But like always there were disputes, and small arguments ensued. In a show of unsportsmanlike conduct, some teams ganged up on others. Mick and Dave saw this. But the Icytryxis were good about not going overboard.

Dave and Mick mentally stored the knowledge that the Icytryxis weren't perfectly free from breaking virtue (nothing can be absolute) and congratulated the winning team.

Meanwhile, Jason continued being passionate about the atlytl mechanics. He was determined to find a way to improve their functionality. Although, it currently just wasn't coming to him.

Yori further delved into the more personal side of the army. She mapped out in her head who liked who, and who didn't. Lots of soldiers meant a large map.

Instead of going straight to the house after training along with the others, Mick ambled around alone on the nearest beach for a while. He needed a refreshing blast of sea air to help gather focus. While there, he also studied the beach defenses. The Icytryxis sure were adept carpenters. Their war machines were rather intimidating to behold. Mick spent a few moments imagining them all in action defending from an invasion, a rather deadly blur of motion. He realized he was glad to not be pitted against such a frightening force.

Eventually, Mick regained his focus, and joined the others at the house for the usual nighttime game of Fantysy-Escape, in which both Mick and Dave found themselves being within reasonable striking distance of a title. There were a lot of games left before championship day, though.

Between going to bed and the game being over, Hawk and Leopard took some time to recline and discuss the next day's plans.

Confident in what they came up with, they fell asleep in their rooms, cozy quarters which were really starting to grow on them.

Syryx woke up early, along with Jason, and the two of them started breakfast together.

Soon, Thyxer joined, and said, "Looks pretty windy out there this morning."

"That it is," returned Jason, after instinctually standing up to look out the window. "Enough to shake the daylights out of this little maple tree in the front yard."

Just then, Jason was struck by an epiphany while staring at a bird sitting on a branch of the little maple trembling violently in the wind. "I think I may have an idea. I'm going to head to the metal shop right away and try to physically realize my vision."

"Exciting Jason!" said Syryx.

"I'll be sure to seek you guys out, if it indeed pans out. See you later," stated Jason, in a hurried voice, heading towards the door.

He walked at a brisk pace all the way, straight into the front door of the metal shop he'd been lately frequenting. Before saying anything to anyone about his brainchild, he examined all fifteen existing atlytl projectile designs, noticing once again how one third were basically awkward and lumbering, geared for structural contact. They were used to destroy wood or stone buildings and other constructions. Another one third were more aerodynamic (two had grooves and one resembled an arrow), used to achieve greater distance when fired. These were utilized for the annihilation of living man at distance.

The remaining five projectiles were anonymous designs—one was made to hold poison; one was super heavy, its function was mainly door battering; one a real cheap design for the purpose of training; another had a hook at the tip, which operated primarily as a grappling hook for climbing; and the last was very peculiar. It was a blunt but imminently fatal projectile. Jason studied each one with great focus, even though it was something he'd done many times before.

After his study, Thorncat searched out an Icytryxan he'd previously conversed with on numerous occasions. Jason asked the Icytryxan, "Which of the projectile designs is the most recent?"

"One of the training points. About fifty years ago, we discovered a metal alloy consisting of abundant materials. We inserted into the mix a new point made from it."

"It's been quite a while since a fresh one then, eh?"

"That's right," replied the Icytryxan.

"You said one of the training ones? I only see a single training one in the lot."

"Well, there's the one I just mentioned, and then there's the one we once made in mass quantities but have never actually used, not even once. They just sit in storage as we speak, gathering dust, the *blunt projectile*. Centuries ago, someone had the idea to construct it for the purpose of allowing soldiers to train under the real-life situation of being fired upon. But, like I'm sure you've noticed, they look pretty darn deadly. And nobody has ever opted to work with them."

"Oh, the one I earlier mentally called a blunt but imminently fatal projectile," confessed Jason. I don't blame them. I doubt I'd ever desire to get into the ring with such potential lethality."

"Me neither."

Subsequent to cringing a bit by the visual created by the last topic, Jason digressed, "So, let's say I had a new projectile schematic brewing in my mind right now, how would I go about presenting the proposition, and to whom?"

The Icytryxan was amazed. "You really envision a new projectile? Amazing! I've never actually seen a new one myself go into production. The prospect really is quite electrifying. Turns out, I just missed the last unveiling by a mere six months. First things first, we have a staff meeting scheduled later today, so I'd recommend presenting your design there. And if you have a tangible schematic for a prototype, or the prototype itself, they may want to see it."

Hearing the man's enthusiasm, Jason sensed how big of a deal the creation of a new atlytl projectile really was. Consequently, Jason's apprehension collided with his pre-existing exhilaration. Uncharacteristically fumbling with his words, Jason said, "I haven't created a physical schematic yet, but seeing as though the meeting is later today, I'll have plenty of time to put one together."

"Yes, usually we all gather a couple hours after lunch."

"I'll be there with my drawn up proposal."

"Looking forward to it, Mr. Thorncat. See you then."

Jason took another glance at the existing projectiles, cringed one more time at imaging training with the blunt, fatal-looking one, and then proceeded to get right to work on his design.

As Jason occupied his time crafting his blueprint, Mick and Dave held another one of their battle setups. This one centered around the idea of seeing which individual was the best with the close combat weapon of their choice, of course, a wooden weapon. They held a tournament, one where the eventual winner was a quick soldier who won the championship match impressively by not only being fast, but also having more endurance than his opponents. His name was Dyvit, who in the eyes of Mick and Dave was really proving to be quite the warrior.

In the meantime, Yori met up with colleagues and discussed a myriad of topics. She learned a little, got some new perspectives, but under her own opinion didn't discover much of great importance.

Meanwhile, back at the ranch, Jason had just finished his schematic, being very proud of its turnout. He was slightly surprised at how well he was able to draw today. Normally, this skill wasn't one of his strong suits. Not wanting to give his new artistic talent much attention at the moment, he just wrote it off as divine influence.

Jason performed one last inspection of his design, went to the bathroom for the first time of the eventful day, and entered the metal shop's meeting room. Half the crew were there, the other half were more than likely on the way.

The Icytryxans already in attendance lit up at seeing Jason. They'd been previously informed of Jason's potentially groundbreaking initiative by the man Jason conversed with earlier.

Swidyt, the eldest, shook Jason's hand, shared his name and said, "Welcome, sir. I'm delighted you've been curious about the metal works here on Swyrove. Furthermore, yours and your friends' mission certainly intrigues me, and I personally wish it the best."

"Thank you, Swidyt. I've always been one for physics. And for missions."

"Excellent," the Icytryxan reciprocated. He scanned the room. "We're waiting on three more of my associates, and then you can begin."

One man was late for some reason. However, in theory, an Icytryxan can never be late. When all were present, Jason began his informative speech. "Thank you all for allowing me this opportunistic moment. I'll be brief but edifying. I've never really seen your atlytl corps in full battle form, only in the usual practice squads, but I can pretty much imagine the greatest advantage it would have over the typical archer contingent—besides the small increase in reload speed—would be the fact that an

Icytryxan, with their longer arms, can launch ammunition farther. What I'm about to say may be hard to conceive, but I've come up with a way to gain even greater throwing distance with your esteemed atlytls. As I'm sure you know, the projectile that travels furthest currently is definitively the arrow-shaped one with its long, thin design."

Jason set up an easel, on which he placed his blueprint. He made sure everyone in the room could see it.

After producing a feather and setting it on the easel, Jason continued: "As you can see, I've altered the current arrow-shaped design to this, illustrated here. It will undoubtfully fly a greater distance, therefore gaining a massive military advantage. The science behind it is an improvement in drag. I'm sure you're aware almost all bird feathers taper off at the end, a phenomenon implemented to decrease drag, accordingly improving speed and efficiency for the bird. Applying this concept of aerodynamics to the already superior arrow projectile will be utmost gainful.

"You can see in the drawing how I taper the shaft all the way down to the tail. We then have a thin egg-shaped head for causing damage, which can come to a standard point or a broadhead for added spoil. The head is as wide as the conventional arrow-shaped projectile, but the width of the shaft at the tail will be no wider than a nail. Plus, instead of attaching the feather tailfins onto the shaft, like they're done currently, they will be transformed into inserts, and slid into tiny slits cut into the tail. And at the very tail end will be the tiny loop, where the launch string is attached. All in all, I believe this design will travel fifty to a hundred yards further than all other projectiles you possess."

Jason switched the pages on his easel. "This page here depicts a few of the new battle tactics you'd be able to employ with this new gain in distance. Of course, they've never before been used in conflict. Brand new tactics. Thanks again for listening. Anybody have any questions or statements?"

Swidyt and a few others stepped up interestedly to the diagrams to examine them.

"I've never actually consciously noticed that feathers taper for a reason," said Swidyt, while grabbing and running his fingers through Jason's feather, conveniently lying on the easel. "In this new light, it definitely makes sense that a dart flying through the air would face less air resistance with both a pointed tip and tail. This certainly seems to be a wonderful idea, Jason."

Swidyt addressed one of the other Icytryxans, "How long do you think it would take to assemble a prototype mold?"

"I would say possible completion by tomorrow afternoon."

"Well Jason, my man, I bet we'll have the opportunity to test it out the day after tomorrow. All our projectiles have names, you know."

"I was unaware of such things."

"Yes," confirmed Swidyt. "This one will be called the Thorncat Missile, unless you can conceive a better."

Teetering on the precipice of a smile, Jason returned, "I must admit I do like the sound of that."

SPEARHEADING THE militarized undertaking, the Black Bear successfully reached the destination with a throng of soldiers. He left more than three quarters of his army back at the Capital in case he was walking into some elaborate trap. The Capital itself and King Rowlangiv were always top priority. At haste, five hundred soldiers (a hundred groups of five) had left the Capital and taken off into the wilderness. They had departed in intervals and followed different paths. It wasn't the most elegant of plans Ulfenkerki had ever come up with, however, if someone was watching it from a mile in the air, they would've surely seen quite the spectacle in the countryside.

Ulfenkerki met back up with the original soldiers he left at the barn, plus an additional twenty-five. They were all waiting to strike.

To his immediate group, Ulfenkerki said, "I told everyone else to hide out as best as they could, until I begin the charge, which has to take place very shortly here. The longer we wait, the more of a chance we'll get caught. The odds of this working picture-perfectly are against us, but if we can catch them by surprise just slightly, we can come out of this without too many casualties. I timed everything so our force approaches under the cover of darkness. I told the rest I'd lead the charge a couple hours after sunset, tonight. You can trust I took every precaution ingenuity councils."

All the troops in the barn were anxious for some action. For most of them, the Battle of Sarwa was the last time their swords had received any dulling in the least. Of course, they were nervous, but it was an excited type of nervous.

The piper representing a confident soldier touts exhilaration.

Layered on top of their eagerness was the Black Bear's reflection. He was trying to figure out if there were any possible ways to improve his combat plan. Some part of him thought he was missing something, but another part was self-assured he wasn't.

All conversations faded into talk of battles of old. Ulfenkerki eventually joined in, tucking his fears of insufficient preparation into his pocket.

As tensions rose, dew began forming on the grass. All five hundred of Ulfenkerki's force were hunkered down, waiting for their General's signal. Given they were informed when the assault was to begin (a couple hours after sunset), many were still watching for the signal before sunset. *Better safe than sorry*, or so they say.

With each passing moment, the soldiers got more and more anxious. A surprise attack always seemed to be a special kind of event, not that they were common. Some soldiers were calm, maybe a little too calm. Some were playing cards. But none were stupid enough to smoke a pipe or make a fire. Many were listening for just the slightest audible sound of movement in the distance (Ulfenkerki's signal), but they only heard the countryside's lone owl. You could cut the tension with a knife, even the lone owl sensed something was up.

These were the moments that really made a soldier feel alive.

The group located closest the barn heard Ulfenkerki's signal first—In fact, Gregg Hogarty heard it first. He whispered to his group, "It begins."

Gregg couldn't wait to test out his newly acquired dagger throwing skills. He was really starting to get proficient at it. His group was spotted beginning the attack by the next group, who in turn started their offensive. The noticing of the battle's onset trickled on down the line.

After having given the initiation signal, Ulfenkerki led his party through the wood, hopping from dark spot to dark spot. Luckily, it wasn't a full moon, a condition of brightness that could've been tragic for their preemptive strike. By way of starlight, the army avoided slamming their faces into trees, for the most part.

Arrows took out the enemy sentries—deaths the Black Bear wished he could've avoided for there was no real certainty that what the sentries were guarding was indeed a war party. But he had weighed his options and knew it needed to be done. In the end, two of the sentries survived—*lucky bastards*, or maybe just good medical assistance.

All the striking groups remained spread out, a good way to flank and surround the quarry.

General Ulfenkerki, with as much power as he could muster, hoped Gamald was within reach. There were a few lights that could be seen amidst the trees, which was to where they all silently steered. *What a rush,* the soldiers thought, creeping through a dark forest to a potential all-out battle.

But inevitability eventually struck. When they were within a hundred feet of the opposition, Ulfenkerki's platoon was spotted. It's hard not to distinguish at least one soldier out of five hundred approaching your fire. Branches always broke, no matter how light of foot you thought you were.

Nevertheless, Ulfenkerki's raiding party was in good position. They advanced from many angles with swords drawn.

As the General approached the fires, he made out numerous makeshift structures situated around a large rock formation. He expected to see tons of soldiers come flying out of these makeshift structures at him, but what he did see was completely different: a handful of men (ranged from middle-aged to old) come out bearing white flags. *Funny, though, how some of the flags were just white shirts.*

Regardless, a surrender was a surrender.

In the end, two dozen yielded, all who were stationed at the camp, minus the regrettably dead sentries.

Upon inspection, it was discovered that what was going on was a rather massive weapons manufacturing operation. On this realization, the Black Bear immediately held council with his officers.

The General declared, "Even though I'm disappointed to have not captured Gamald, this seems to have been a worthwhile endeavor. We've uncovered a Molisian operation, one that seem to be helping in the preparation of a massive capital onslaught. Does anyone have a rough estimate as to how many weapons are here in storage?"

An officer replied, "We've counted nearly a thousand. Half are brand-spanking new."

"All ours now," boasted Ulfenkerki. "I suppose we got lucky the army planning to come through this staging point isn't here yet. A thousand soldiers and their thousand weapons would've surely overwhelmed our count of five hundred. We'll try to get information from our prisoners, but I highly doubt they'll give anything away. I'd bet the reason they're here making weapons is that they have an iron mine somewhere tunneling into the adjacent rock formation. We'll investigate that in the morning when it's light out. You can inform your charge that once the entire area is positively free from all hostiles, they can go ahead and call it a night."

"Yes, sir," replied a few in unison.

The soldiers all slept in the pup tents they'd brought, while Ulfenkerki and the officers opportunistically commandeered the more robust structures the Molisians had built for themselves.

The Black Bear was feeling adventurous, so he woke up early and looked for the probable mine. He found it easily. A large, worn path led right up to it. And, again with his adventurous spirit, the General and a few others grabbed torches and went right in. It was a rather beautiful mine, but obviously not real massive, otherwise the cavern system would've surely been found previously by Garobansurovians in centuries past.

"Surprising after how long people have lived in this area," Ulfenkerki thought out loud, "that nobody ever thought to check this formation for minerals."

"Yeah, that's odd," agreed a soldier.

"Judging by what's in this trusty minecart over here, this is most definitely an iron mine. With this much iron, they could easily source all the other materials necessary to formulate weapons-grade steel," noted Ulfenkerki.

The General admired the picturesque, multi-colored cave one last time on his way out. "Gorgeous. At least we've claimed a new mine for the King. It'll be quite useful, I'm sure. I don't want to be the one hauling the heavy iron around, though, that's for sure. Good thing I'm in the war business."

The group chuckled, as they exited the mine.

Considering the wild possibility that the Molisian army was near, Ulfenkerki quickly decided on the next course of action, and held a morning officers' meeting regarding this resolution. They all gathered in one of the pre-existing blacksmith tent-like structures.

Decorated by a serious profile, Ulfenkerki began, "The faster we do things the better. I have no idea what we're working with here, but there's obviously an army gathering, only God knows where. One does not just simply make a thousand weapons, store them, and guard them without having something up their sleeve. There's plenty enough iron in Molisia to make weapons for war. I'm guessing a supply line got severed somewhere. What I do know is that we must act. Half of the men will accompany me back to the Capital in order to bring back our large army tents, supplies, and maybe a few war machines, if indeed King Rowlangiv doesn't object. The other half I leave behind will search the surrounding area for the Molisian army and for General Gamald himself, because I have the feeling he's behind all of this. The latter can take turns sleeping in these Molisian structures. Most of them are furnished pretty decently. There's also the barn nearby, where up to recently I've been comfortably staying, which is also well-equipped."

"Let's say we find this phantom army while you're gone, how then do we proceed?" asked Gregg.

"I'm sure they'll learn of our acquisition of this weapons station soon enough. It's possible they come and take it back by force, but I highly doubt it will happen before I return. We have been thoroughly searching the area since I first came, and there isn't an army close by or even moderately close by. But anything can happen, nevertheless. If you find a large army, withdraw back to the Capital; a small one, just keep your eye on it."

"Okay, will do."

"We'll carry a large part of these weapons back to the Capital with us, beginning the fifty-mile trek after dinner," stated the Black Bear. "I'll try to be back with everyone and everything in under a week. You all have my permission to go to the local tavern, but only occasionally."

Comically displaying the best possible visage of bewilderment he could spontaneously muster, Gregg replied, "What's a tavern?"

The Black Bear chuckled, shook his head and exited the Molisian-made tent-like structure.

EVERYONE LIVING under the Narutyx roof currently wishing to cease hunger was in the backyard enjoying a corn roast. Jason collected his third buttery cob and continued regaling the details concerning what happened to him that day. "So, they said the mold would be done tomorrow, and we can perform the alpha test the day after."

"Your idea is valuable beyond measure. With the added distance, all kinds of new doors will open with our atlytl strategies," said Thyxer. "I can't wait to see one fly."

Syryx earnestly commented, "Hopefully this invention of yours helps persuade the army that an alliance with your country is of utmost importance."

"Yes, I hope it helps," remarked Jason. "I doubt it'll solely influence them to war, but I'm sure it won't hurt."

"That's probably true."

Fumbling because he sneezed, Jason nearly dropped his corn. "Another thing today that caught my attention was the existence of a projectile that has never been used before, ever. Apparently, there's a blunt one, designed to emulate a real-life battle situation. A volunteering participant could choose to be fired upon by these deadly projectiles."

Mick asked, "And it's generally made from the same metal as the rest?"

"Yes. The same as practically all of them, except for a model specified for training made from a cheaper metal. I must admit, just looking at these blunt projectiles seems dangerous. I'm not surprised no one has ever wanted to face the fatal-looking specimens. The ends just don't justify the means."

Thyxer responded, "I've seen them. I've also seen how many of them are actually sitting, gathering dust in a storage shed, having never been used."

Jason emitted, "Well, I don't mean to brag, but I highly doubt that'll happen with the Thorncat Missiles."

"True. Plus, I certainly like the sound of that handle."

"That's pretty much what I said when Swidyt wanted to name it that," confessed Jason.

The rest of the night maintained the same upbeat nature. Jason's good mood rubbed off on everyone.

After corn, they all trickled to the basement for Fantysy-Escape.

That night, Syryx was enjoying the lead of the game (something she did the majority of the time), but Dave was coming on strong. He'd overtaken Yusyta for second place. Still, in all the championship was up for grabs. The title would more than likely come down to the esteemed championship night. It usually did.

Everyone stayed up late, Yori and Yusyta staying up the longest to talk.

An hour after everyone else fell asleep, Yori curiously asked Yusyta, "So you're single, eh, Yusyta?"

"That's right. I was married for the longest time, but sadly that is no more. How about you?"

"Being the King's advisor keeps me pretty busy, so I haven't ever been married. Someday, maybe, but probably not any time soon, especially during these hectic, war-infused times."

"I can understand that. Being married was the happiest time of my life, and I hope equivalent ecstasy for you."

"Thank you, Yusyta."

"What's Rowlangiv like? I've overheard what you've all said about him from a professional standpoint, but I haven't caught anything regarding what he's like as a person."

"I guess you could say he portrays himself as kingly, if that's really a thing. He's very serious and adamant about the welfare of the country. He's extremely practical and has a good sense of humor. I've gotten him laughing pretty hard on occasion."

"Sounds like a fine man," declared Yusyta, sincerely. "Does he have any hobbies?"

"Not that I'm aware of, except for occasionally exercising on the recreation floor. He spends most his time holding council with the vital personnel and organizations of Garobansurov. I always urge him to enjoy his time more, though."

"Yes, that would be good for his health. Stress is a killer. Speaking of which, do you have any hobbies yourself, Yori, to ease your strain?"

"Not in the customary sense, but you could say one thing I do to gather my inner focus is hone my throwing-star skills. I've been doing this now for many years, and it's something I really enjoy."

"I would've never guessed that to be your hidden talent. I bet that facility comes in handy."

"Oh yes, you're right about that. I employed my throwing stars on our camping trip. I managed to stun two gnyts during the incursion."

"Ah yes, I remember that story about the gnyts. A woman of much ability you are."

"Well, I wouldn't say *that* much ability, but thank you," uttered Yori, humbly. "I suppose it's pretty late. It would probably be advantageous to head to bed."

"Yeah, probably. Good night."

It was so late when the ladies went to bed that a few nearby birds were considering the possibility of launching their morning songs.

Dave looked to the morning sky peppered with flying metal. To Mick he vocalized, "Mindlessly staring at all the projectiles blotting out the sky is probably more trance-inducing than listening to a church congregation going through an hour-long prayer litany."

"I agree. Sometimes it's a good thing, sometimes not. I catch myself sometimes having to shake myself out of the daze."

"One time," mentioned Dave, "I carelessly bumped into someone in front of me, as I was walking along mesmerized by the projectiles."

Mick laughed. "I can't say I've ever done that, but I guess my time is yet to come."

Changing the subject, Dave declared, "Our battle scenario is a good one today, I sense."

"Yeah, we need a good one. We haven't really progressed much lately."

"I feel the same way. Well, today things are going to turn around."

"Hope you're right. The soldiers having to choose between either helping themselves or helping their team will surely be insightful from our perspective."

"Having a winning a team amongst four, along with ranking the top ten individuals was definitely one of your better ideas, Mick. The Icytryxans will be faced with many decisions, each one teaching us something about them."

"I hope so. It'll be good."

In the end, Mick and Dave were wrong about learning anything very productive from the event concerning the soldiers' individual decisions. Results turned out to be pretty straightforward. They did, however, gather some helpful information regarding how far the Icytryxans were willing to go in order to win. The answer was reasonably far, but nothing so drastic that it staggered Mick or Dave.

After a full day of substantial physical training with the Icytryxan military, Jason went to the metal shop to see how things were progressing there. He was pleased to find out that the first mold was finished.

Swidyt said to Jason, "In an hour, we're going to pour the liquid metal into the mold, which should cool by morning. Then, we'll apply the fins and it'll be good to go. So, stop by tomorrow afternoon, and we'll give it a whirl."

"How many separate projectiles will the mold produce on the first go-around?"

"It makes eight," answered Swidyt, "so we can fire the eight and then we'll have to go collect them to fire again. They'll be easy to find in the particular throwing field we'll use."

"Magnificent. I'll see you tomorrow."

"Yes. The Thorncat Missile inaugural launching will no doubt be thrilling."

Walking back to the house with the clan, Jason announced to all, "The Thorncat Missile should be ready for firing tomorrow."

"What time about?" asked Dave. "I'd like to check it out."

"The afternoon sometime. I'll seek you out when I'm going over there."

"Sounds good, Jason."

"I believe I'll come too," blurted Mick. "I'll be sure to be conveniently within the vicinity of Dave in the afternoon, so you don't have to waste time searching us both out."

"Splendid. You're usually not that hard to find, though."

"I suppose that's true. Nevertheless, I'll be near."

After they were done eating a hearty supper, Mick and Dave decided to go see more of town. They knew they'd never see all of it, but they wanted to try and see most. Garobansurov's capital had more people living in it total, but Saraty's infrastructure was more broadly dispersed, supplying the illusion it was bigger. The distance between everything in Saraty was great and it was undeniably time consuming to walk from landmark to landmark, unlike in Garobansurov's capital. The two cities were fundamentally opposites.

Going west, Mick and Dave traveled empty-handed and open-minded.

Judged by the locals as a place with a moderate to high visitation rate, Mick and Dave entered one of the many parks. They had already seen a few parks, but at first glance this one looked the busiest thus far. Eventually, they assumed the reason why it was so hectic was because it offered a myriad of food distribution hubs. Each one offered something completely different, and all of them, of course, did it for free.

"Too bad we just ate a generous meal. All these aromas are really hard to pass up," commented Mick.

"I don't know about you, but I'm coming through here on the way back for a snack."

"Good idea, Dave."

"I've distinguished one thing for certain, and that is this park smells wonderful."

"I'm surprised we've never smelt it from the house."

"Especially on downwind days," added Dave.

"I bet we will now that we'll be looking for it. Smelling for it, rather."

"Probably."

The next stop after the food section of the park was its more secluded forested part. Multiple ancient-appearing benches were situated in extra-scenic areas. The scenery was no doubt augmented by the ambient aromas.

This dark area of the park was decidedly beautiful.

The locale within a locale Hawk and Leopard deemed most preeminent was where luminosity suffocating vines hung from most of the trees. These vines formulated a haunting situation. More than likely, the setting was void of any light whatsoever at night, especially on moon-free nights. The only available light was formed by tiny nail-sized beams of sunlight slipping through the canopy.

"This is the perfect place for a ghost story."

"I'm listening, Mick."

"Brace yourself. It all started many years ago when a young lad named Mick met another named Dave. Now that was scary."

Dave laughed. "You can say that again."

"I digress. We need to create a battle setup that will compel the Icytryxans to push themselves to their limits. Through that, I feel we could learn so much. But without any real incentive for them to do it, anything we come up with will only provide for our study a meager effort from them than what's actually possible."

"Exactly. They really do participate with much intensity, but it's missing something."

"And that something is what we need to push the river," commented Mick. "It's the key."

"We can only keep trying."

"Tomorrow, even though it won't be the experiment we're looking for, I think in an attempt to get the Icytryxis soldiers out of their shells, we'll have them play a sport of some kind. Maybe, then, they'll force the adrenalin flux to the max."

"Sounds good," said Dave. "Actually, that sounds really good. I want to play, and surge adrenalin."

"Me too. So, Dave, switching topics, I got one for you. Which one of our latest endeavors, if we were to relate them with geological features, do you think was the highest mountain to climb?"

"You're right, that is a good one. I suppose the answer isn't so simple. If I answered in terms of the highest, most arduous mountain, I must also add which one was the most worthwhile. Maybe it's the same answer for both."

"Yup," noted Mick, "maybe."

"There are other variables too, I guess, Mick. But I won't overcomplicate it for now. I'll need a longer time to think about it in order to give the perfect answer, if indeed *I can* give a perfect answer. But I guess it's a question the thinking man ruminates upon every day, anyways."

"Right, we'll set aside the ultimate answer for another day, for I really don't think either of us possess it right now. I'll weigh in too, after you."

"You're right," vocalized Dave. "Here's what I got now: All the big battles last year were high mountains, especially the Gravividon capture. There was also the reuniting of Krell-nor with Brom. In addition, we've got quite the challenge laid before us now in persuading the Icytryxis army to side with the Garobansurov army. But that hasn't been accomplished yet, so even though it has the potential to be the most worthwhile, I'm going to have to disqualify it for now."

"I would too."

"We've definitely ascended much elevation throughout the last few years, the two of us. We'd received the Knowing Circle mainly for Gravividon, so you can't deny the importance of that fort capturing. I'd probably choose this, if I had to choose now. But that's just my answer for the sake of having an answer."

"That would be my choice too, with the same attachments," said Mick. "I have the feeling in years to come the answer will be different, as things get more complicated. For starters, the war is still raging."

"Indeed. And we're both getting better with the *black needles*. Not to mention, our wisdom accumulating. It is definitely a thought process I'll keep on my mind, until the true answer strikes me."

"As will I. We'll revisit the enigma, as time goes on," declared Mick.

"Yes, it was a good one. Who knows, maybe the elaborate answer is much more intricate than we think."

"That very well could be the case, Dave. Philosophy is the most convoluted of all the sciences, I always say."

"I agree, despite those who remove philosophy from the scientific spectrum."

"My butt is sore. Time to mosey on from this deathly still abode."

"Mine too," said Dave, standing from the bench amongst the dark, vine-infiltrated milieu.

Having left the park altogether, the tourists, Mick and Dave, continued west through a residential area.

The next spot of interest was a trail that meandered along a stream. The three-quarter mile trail showcased a few small waterfalls and fishing holes. One could clearly see many colorful, decent-sized fish swimming around in the stream. Some of the trail had a woodchip pathway, and on three occasions it crossed the stream via trusty stone bridge, and on one occasion via not-so-trusty stone bridge.

Reversing course when the sun was just about to hide, the pair headed back to the house. But first, they were sure to go through the food park and grab a delectable snack along the way.

Most things in the food park had a long name, dishes they'd never tasted nor heard of before. They were all delicious to be sure.

Back at the house, Dave and Mick made a point to mention the excellent park they stumbled upon to Jason and Yori, so they could one day partake. It was certainly an experience one couldn't have back in Garobansurov.

Yori and Jason did eventually visit the park and were very appreciative to Mick and Dave for informing them about it.

Hawk and Leopard went to the training grounds, and the sport they chose for the soldiers was football. There were more participants than normal for this setup, so instead of having multiple games, which Mick and Dave couldn't all scrutinize, they tweaked the rules and parameters a bit, allowing for everyone to play in a single, large game.

Overall, the alterations worked well, everyone having played hard. Both Mick and Dave ended up scoring and breaking a good sweat. However, there just wasn't anything helpful enough to guide Thraiker and Ghrere towards their much sought-after epiphany.

Unintentionally exhibiting perfect timing, Jason showed up at the end of the match to gather his buddies for the Thorncat Missile presentation, in the midst of Mick and Dave being thanked by many for the enjoyable competition.

Jason queried, "Well, are you two ready to see something awesome?"

"I sure hope so," replied Mick. "It's been a long day."

The trio met up with a handful of people at the metal shop, who seemed just as anxious and jittery as Jason.

Swidyt pointed, and said, "Everything is set. Take a look, sir. They are quite the sight to behold."

Having anticipated the moment for a while, Jason enthusiastically picked up a Thorncat Missile for the first time. "They sure do look rather aerodynamic. I like the feathers you chose for the fins. They indubitably add flare."

"We have a couple of our best throwers present to execute the launches," mentioned Swidyt. "So that way we have a fair chance of bettering the already established benchmarks. We've painstakingly recorded history's best launches."

"Do these benchmarks take into consideration wind speed and direction?" asked Jason.

"That they do. We have an astute 'calculations woman' present and ready."

"Excellent. I'm prepared if you are."

"Yup. Here we go."

The group walked tall to the premium south throwing-field. Each and every one in attendance had the feeling history was about to be made. Perhaps there'd be a new writeup for the Icytryxan history museum. The two talented throwers toted their favorite atlytls, stretching along the way, while Jason proudly lugged the eight projectiles, four in each hand. Mick and Dave walked in the rear, radiating anxiety and gladness to be a part. The south field was customary for these types of showcases since it came stocked with the utmost wind breakage. The tallest trees one could imagine surrounded.

Having arrived, the group noticed an already gathered additional audience: A large murder of crows decided to stand about on the field. Though they flew away impatiently at seeing the biped company take residence at their temporary domain.

Some justifiably deemed the crow to be the smartest bird in Swyrove, wisely abandoning the field when they did was testament to this.

The field was pretty isolated, so there weren't many onlookers other than the ones that made the walk. There would have been, if the news had spread, but the affair was pretty much kept under wraps for the time being.

An experienced volunteer went into position far on the other end to gather and mark, while Jason handed some Thorncat Missiles over to the two adrenalized throwers.

Jason stood back, and called out to the three, "Have fun."

The first burly Icytryxan locked, loaded, and flung the projectile with as much might as he could muster. The splendor of the fully extended swing of the pendulum was almost poetic.

The weight rocketed into the air. All eyes watched it soar to the heavens, arcing far above the highest reach of any nearby tree.

Amazed, Swidyt let his lip curl into a near smile, and said, "I do believe I've never seen any solely man-powered object travel so far."

Jason pumped his fist. "Now that was breathtaking. I have to see that again."

"I don't know exactly how far it went," divulged Swidyt, "but I can tell you I've never seen one clear the treetops by so much."

"A pure commanding of the sky," revealed a member of the team, "if I do say so myself."

"Unadulterated grandeur," said another.

The next thrower heaved with the same vigor as the first, resultantly achieving the same mind-blowing result, proving the former pitch was no fluke.

After all eight projectiles were methodically unleashed unto the atmosphere, the whole of the group began the long walk to the landing zone to see just how far they went.

The calculations lady was still doing her math along the way. She announced, "Seeing as there's a moderate headwind of fifteen miles per hour, we can also add a bit of distance to the formula."

The group arrived at the normal landing area. Judging by how worn and stamped the grass was, it was obvious they arrived to where the projectiles usually landed. Beyond this was nothing but thick, barely touched by anything grass. Grass so thick that it may have been difficult to even find the embedded Thorncat Missiles, if there hadn't been someone present for gathering and marking.

Having gone clear of the *old landing zone* by a good seventy-five paces, the assemblage came upon the gatherer, who was still standing aghast. The gatherer broadcasted, "Four of them are right there, the other four are marked with those red flags."

"Thank you," Swidyt said. He turned from the gatherer to Jason, who was now free from his miasma of uncertainty. "Well, here it is, Jason, unequivocal proof you were right. We'll do a bunch more tosses to confirm officially, but it is clearly apparent your design is worth precisely what you said—a hundred to a hundred fifty-yard gain."

"Astonishing," replied Jason. "Partly since my distance figures were half stabs in the dark."

"I'd hate to be stabbed by you in the light, seeing how well you do it in the dark," said Swidyt, chuckling.

Jason joined in on the good-hearted laugh.

When laughter dissipated, Jason examined the field, and voiced, "This is a pretty compact cluster of projectiles here. It's almost as if they were aiming right here."

"They may have been," returned Swidyt.

Having grabbed all the projectiles, the party trekked back to the launching pad, and began anew.

By the end of the day, they managed to get off a total of eight groups of eight. All sixty-four Thorncat Missiles had landed in roughly the same area the first grouping had.

Patting Jason on the back, Swidyt stated, "There's the full evidence my friend, indelibly in the books. Now for the next thing to discuss: how to notify the rest of the army and the public of such a monumental occurrence."

"To me, this is virgin territory," responded Jason, "so yours or someone else's experienced recommendation would be much obliging."

"I did actually have one heck of an idea brewing in my head," blurted Swidyt.

"Head-brewings are always the best."

"I don't know if you're aware, but the *Conceptual Naissance* is next week, an event which is our equivalent of your Independence Day. It's a celebration on the anniversary of the origin of our most fundamental premises, theories, and beliefs."

"I've read about it, but I didn't recall it being next week. I don't know too much about it, though."

"It's a spectacle on the grandest scale, our scale here anyways. The bulk of the celebration occurs at the festival grounds, which we've dubbed the *Reflection of Light Grounds*, being called this for what happens at hand. There are crystal clear pools there, surrounding an equally clear river, which flows all the way through the middle of the thirty-acre setting. The water coupled with a plethora of mirrors and other reflective surfaces provide a beautiful presentation, as it mirrors all the various fires and other light sources we construct."

"That does sound rather lovely."

"Here's where you and your innovation come in, Jason. The highlight of the grand finale includes a point where a bunch of projectiles are fired over the lights along the riverside. The projectiles have many mirrors tied onto tail strings. The shimmering aerial display is always the crowd favorite. The spectators like to bet pushups on how far the farthest one will go. Every year the projectiles pretty much land in the same general area. I'm sure you can now imagine where I'm going with this. Just imagine the disbelief and awe when this year's grand finale projectiles all land way beyond where they're expected to."

"A longshot guess would surely win the bets," said Jason. "That does sound like a very splendid head-brewing you had going there. So, we would keep the Thorncat Missile a secret until then?"

"Yes," replied Swidyt, "I think it would really make the unveiling extremely memorable. Plus, I think doing it this way is what would help accomplish your mission the most."

"I agree. I think the surprise factor will definitely enhance the missile's introduction. I'm excited," said Jason, letting a smile creep onto his face, "let's do it."

"Alright then, excellent. I'll run it past the festival's key organizers. I'll update you as things progress."

With the day drawing to an end, Jason started to walk back to the house in the company of Mick and Dave. He told them all about Swidyt's plan. Mick and Dave loved the idea and couldn't wait to witness the upcoming spectacle.

CHAPTER 15

∾

"WE FINALLY FOUND General Gamald!" Leedle was relieved.

MANY MILES from Gamald, Ulfenkerki shivered as if someone had just said something he desperately wanted to hear. Unfortunately for Ulfenkerki, this wasn't the case.

LIEUTENANT LEEDLE was looking for Gamald all morning. One of the Molisian soldiers found him sleeping on a couch.

Leedle waited for the General to wake, and as soon as he did, went to say what he had to say: "Sir, we just received another heavily-armed and battle-ready platoon. The bad news, though, is that we're running out of room here in these ruins to bed everyone. I'm afraid if we start to sprawl out of here with tents, we'll get spotted."

"You know, Leedle," emitted Gamald, "when we first discovered the hidden entrance to these ruins, they appeared so large that suffocating the environment with soldiers would've seemed utterly inconceivable. We've come a long way since the setback with our assassination failure."

"That we have, General."

"I'm thinking I should send a few platoons to our forward base at the iron mine, the weapons manufacturing facility. I'm sure Rowlangiv will then become aware of our hidden base there. But this will serve as an advantage for us. The army at the base will essentially be a decoy army, favorably drawing all of his attention, while our massive army here swells to numbers so great that a raiding march to the Capital will certainly be victorious."

"I agree," vocalized Leedle. "With this decoy and the presumable disarray on the western front, Rowlangiv and Ulfenkerki will never expect such a force. Technically, we haven't heard anything lately from the forward base, though."

"I'm not too worried about that," said Gamald. "We did just get a shipment of weapons from them last week. I'm almost positive the forward base is still secure. I'm going to go ahead and dispatch the platoons. Well-fortified platoons of course, since it won't take long for Rowlangiv to make the discovery and send one of his own to knock it out. It is possible he won't send one, though, remaining held up in the defensive confines of the Capital. Which will actually be even more advantageous for us, because the forward platoons can, then, join us in our offensive rally. All-in-all, things are looking good."

"Just imagine, sir, the surprise those of the western armies would feel when they learn the Capital has been taken before they could even organize themselves enough to think about a march," put forth Leedle. The Lieutenant let a funny smile creep onto his face.

"Yes, it would be priceless," said the General. "I'll get my revenge on Ulfenkerki for Sarwa, and for him generally being such a know-it-all, if it's the last thing I do. I know that prick is looking for me right now, I can just tell. Plus, I want my vengeance on those two supposed heroes who defeated Grunt and Roar—Mick and Dave, I think their names were, if I remember correctly."

HAVING ARRIVED BACK at the iron mine with the supplies and additional men, Ulfenkerki said to one of his officers, "So, no information on the whereabouts of Gamald yet, eh?"

"Nope, nothing. No signs of anything."

"Okay. I brought a few hundred soldiers more than with which I left. I figured they may be needed in case of a battle. I have a team of scouts on constant guard, scanning a broad periphery of the Capital. They can report to me soon enough in case we need to get back quickly to defend. Moreover, I needed more hands to help bring back some additional supplies as well as the war machines."

"Excellent, sir. We've had no problems while you were away, other than one small scuffle between two of the soldiers."

"Ah, yes, that happens," shrugged Ulfenkerki. "Good thing it was just a small fray."

"Yup. It was over something so stupid I won't even waste your time telling you about."

"Okay good. Talk to you later."

The Black Bear, having seen to the unloading of all the carts, performed a few rounds of camp. Things looked to be in good working order.

At dark, he found himself in a card game inside the mine itself, a good way to wind down after a long day.

Gregg Hogarty (along with three other soldiers) took part in the game as well.

Subsequent dexterously dealing out the cards, Gregg asked Ulfenkerki, "Anything stirring in Myothraces since we've left?"

"If you consider villagers being loud and soldiers bitching about having to run laps to be noteworthy, then, boy, let me tell you!"

Gregg laughed. "Indeed, I don't."

"Didn't think so," spewed Ulfenkerki. "I don't know how I ended up here myself, but why are we playing cards in a mine?"

"For the same reason that," replied Gregg, "a herd of goats decides to cross a river to graze in a pasture no greener than the one they're about the leave."

Ulfenkerki chuckled. "Makes sense. A good scenery change is always outstanding. It definitely is refreshingly quaint down here, that's for sure."

"The climate is certainly nice and cool," said Gregg, supplying those around the table with another card. "So, what exactly was on all those carts you brought with, General, other than obviously tents and general living gear?"

"Some of the materials for an undertaking sure to peeve everyone off."

"Oh boy, dare I ask?"

"You and they will thank me when the time comes, I promise. Since we are going to be here a while looking for their army, we should dig in, lest that army finds us first. I brought a supply of nails and just enough lumber, compounded with logs from nearby felled trees, to build a defensive wall—not a large one, but one good enough to aid. We'll also dig trenches. As you know, a good trench works wonders."

"That does sound like a lot of work," grunted Gregg, "but I suppose it may save some lives."

The General emitted, "We can't sit around and play cards all day, now can we?"

One of the other soldiers called out, "I know I would like to."

Ulfenkerki confidently laid his cards down. "You may want to rethink that, as I keep kicking your butt with these straight flushes."

"I just might do that," replied the soldier.

During the next hand, Gregg dropped a leaf for a reason known only to him, and divulged, "I was just now wondering something. Given that there's no noticeable wind at all in this mine, I'm curious as to what exactly is causing the waves of refracted light in that little pool over there. You can't see it when you stare at it from any other angle than the one I'm looking from now. There's a minute, observable disturbance. It's very peculiar. I wonder if there's just enough of a breeze in here to cause it, or if it's vibrations caused by some other weird source, like maybe something from further underground."

One of the soldiers replied, "One day a long time ago, maybe a decade or so, I noticed the same thing. I was outside on a calm day. I never did come to any conclusions, though."

Ulfenkerki stood up, ambled around the table, and looked at the pool of water from Gregg's perspective. He squinted his eyes accordingly. "That definitely is an odd phenomenon. Maybe it's vibrations from the planet itself."

"That very well could be possible," said Gregg. He revealed his hand and announced, "Can any of you weaklings beat my straight?"

Smiling, the General strolled back to his side of the table where his cards were sitting face-down. He picked them off the table, looked at them, slapped them on the table face-up, and won with an even higher straight. For no apparent reason other than whimsy, the General blurted, "Cards!"

A week after the Black Bear beat up on his soldiers at the poker table, he disappointingly realized he was no nearer pinpointing his nemesis, Gamald. But he was proud about the progress his soldiers were making on the wall and trenches.

The General had spent some time working a shovel in a trench and did so as skillfully as some of the soldiers half his age. He drank the last bit of water from his canteen and went to look over the day's work on the wall.

At the wall, he surveyed. The forest was noticeably thinner, but by no means was Garobansurov hard-pressed for trees. The logs of the wall were piled on top of each other one-by-one and held together by the planks that Ulfenkerki had brought by cart. There was no walkway or parapets on top for archers, but it was sturdy enough to withstand quite the tempest of physical damage. Spyholes were peppered along the length for archers. The wall could be set afire, but not without many brave men of the opposition losing their lives trying to ignite it. The trench was being dug on the exterior side of the wall, deep enough to some extent to limit the movement of any would-be invaders. Hopefully, it would significantly slow down the speed at which the wall could be set ablaze.

To the soldiers near him, Ulfenkerki stated, "Let's try something out. I see this part of the trench is finished. We'll fill it up with water and see if the soil has good enough water retention to make a moat. When I was digging, I did see some water-retaining clay, but I'm not entirely sure if it was enough. A moat would really help our defenses."

It took an hour to fill the dugout with water, and another hour to realize the water was fleeting much too fast for it to work. But by morning, they did perceive it to be an awfully soggy mess. An advantage, nonetheless.

Later that day, Ulfenkerki decided to test out the range of the catapults he'd brought. He postulated the most likely places for groups of Molisians to form up, and correspondingly situated the catapults into optimum positions.

The General ordered those soldiers within his company who knew anything about blacksmithing to start up fires and whip up the metal components for another catapult or maybe two, time permitting. Since they were in possession of a mine, plenty of catapult ammunition was available.

Every day, troops were dispatched to go out into the countryside for *enemy hunting*. Clusters of these intel-gathering missions departed and returned at all hours of the day.

Ulfenkerki had quite the operation going amid the wilderness.

CHAPTER 16

❧

DURING THE WEEK Ulfenkerki had spent fortifying his base, Mick and Dave continued to organize and execute their battle scenarios. Jason mainly worked with Swidyt and company on the unveiling of the Thorncat Missile. And Yori delved deeper and deeper into the social intricacies of Swyrove. In essence, it was a fairly productive week for the Garobansurovians on Swyrove. Of course, none of them knew anything about what was happening with Ulfenkerki at his newly created base, or if Rowlangiv and the Capital were still out of harm's way. All they could do was hope.

During the evening's game of Fantysy-Escape, the crew found themselves excitingly discussing the upcoming Conceptual Naissance, which was happening the next day.

Thyxer comically noted, "My favorite Naissance was the one a decade ago when Syryx and that one girl both fell in the water."

Syryx laughed. "Yeah, I still can't believe that happened. Those kids who bumped us in, magically came out of nowhere."

"My favorite," stated Yusyta, "was the one when the river was high and spilling over the banks. I thought the show was especially beautiful because of it that year."

"I remember that," said Thyxer, "it was the year it got postponed a day, due to that huge thunderstorm."

Dave asked, "How long is this wonderful sounding exhibition usually?"

"The choreographed part, which is usually set to a story, is about an hour long. But a lot of the aesthetic fires will already be lit upon our arrival. Most people are there for about three or four hours. And some die-hards will hang out on the festival grounds all day, doing various things. It's electrifying, you'll love it!" exclaimed Yusyta.

"Shall we bring anything with?" asked Yori.

Syryx replied, "Only a sense of wild-eyed wonder, a yearning for unbridled fun, and a portable, lightweight chair."

"I think I can handle that."

The next day, the sextet left army training an hour after lunch,—pretty much everyone left their respective jobs early to get ready for and go to the Reflection of Lights Grounds for the big celebration. As a matter of fact, usually half the soldiers, along with many civilian Icytryxans, would go to work late the day after the ceremony as well. A long night of revelry is not without repercussions.

Mick, Dave, Yori, and Jason got dressed up as much as they could—Who knows how many attractive folks would be there, on which to make an impression?

When everyone in the house was ready, they all started for the grounds, which were a mile-and-a-half away.

Even the walk there was eventful, because all of town was also walking there, making for quite the hubbub. Children were everywhere, doing what they do, being loud and innocently rambunctious. Older folks walked slowly, and even older ones hitched rides on carts. A mosaic of activity. The closer they got to the grounds, the more congested the roads were, a good way for a foreigner to gauge how near they were to the epicenter.

Within sight of the grounds, Dave said, "I can't believe we haven't stumbled across this particular locale before!"

"We were close that one day," responded Mick, "the day we climbed the hill."

"Oh, yes. I think we'd crossed the river that flows through the grounds that day. I remember it because I noticed at the time how delightfully clear it was. I wonder if it's the same one that flows through the park encompassing the dark forest we visited."

Thyxer overheard the conversation and remarked, "There are two rivers of size in town. I don't know what park you were at, but I'm guessing that river was different, if it's indeed the park I'm thinking of."

Having arrived at the festival grounds, the group set their chairs down in what seemed like a good spot, adjacent one of the lovely man-made ponds.

The area they were in was once a swamp. It was dug out, transformed into ponds many years ago by very ambitious laborers, workers who more than likely inconveniently went home every night after the job extremely wet and dirty, the kind of manual labor one could be proud of.

Right away the newcomers noticed how beautifully the firelight danced on the waters of the ponds and river. The river had rapids in spots, which really magnified the effect.

"One can only imagine how much this place will come alive with splendor, once everything is under way," uttered Mick.

"Hold on to your hat, *that it will*," replied Syryx, "even though you're not wearing one."

Mick chuckled.

They had an hour to kill before the show began, so Mick and Dave began walking through the grounds curiously. But they only made it halfway around, because eventually there were too many people asphyxiating the walking channels.

Having been confronted by the dead end, Mick and Dave went back to their chairs.

Dave voiced, "I see part of the show takes place in twilight and most of it in the dark."

"Very true," replied Yusyta.

A moment before the show began, the crowd quieted down, clinging to enormous anticipation for what was to come.

It all began with music and the lighting of the great fire in the middle. Dancers wearing reflective dress came out, sparkling and radiant. More and more fires and candles were lit as the show progressed. Even though the show had begun with pleasant music, the *really* good and innovative music would make its presence known later on.

A couple well-performed speeches were given just before the halfway point to commemorate what the spectacle represents—as the name suggests, a celebration of the birth of all the logical concepts the Icytryxans held so dear. Although all the concepts weren't technically realized at the exact same time, they were still celebrated as one.

The second half began in huge dramatic fashion, making for a whole new kind of experience. It was at this point when the flash-type fires were lit. These were the ones that really impressed. The fuel for these fires was composed of quick-burning materials, such as dead evergreen branches with needles still intact; bark from the paper birch trees; and other various lightweight, easily-combustible wood. The flash fires burned explosively, creating very large, brilliantly violent displays. It was one of the crowd favorites, even though they were a bit dangerous. Icytryxans, along with most races, liked a little danger. It made them feel alive. For safety purposes, kids were made sure to be clear enough of the flash fires.

Luckily, the obscuring clouds went away, revealing the celestial bodies, the reflections of which danced rhythmically in the water and other reflective materials.

Mick, Dave, Yori, and Jason could feel the magic of what they were witnessing and would remember the moment for the rest of their lives. They truly knew it was something solely belonging to Icytryxan culture, and they'd more than likely never see anything like it again. Pure enchantment.

The night was climaxing. Mostly everyone could tell the grand finale was near because hundreds of atlytl wielders came out of the woodwork and into view. Each one was visible in the dark, for they had a bunch of reflective projectiles in their hands, plus, they were moderately wrapped in reflective tape.

The atlytl corps lined up in four long rows.

The grand finale music commenced, undeniably the best music of the night, rich in melody and progressive quality. It was also the sort that built up in tempo, volume, and overall grandioso as it went along.

More dancers came out, and more fires were lit.

Choreographed with the unforgettable music, the atlytl throwers began to unleash their reflective artillery into the sky. Each and every spectator was caught breathless, as their heads swiveled, panning to follow the gleaming skylights. All the projectiles were landing in a roped-off area, which was guarded for safety, an area in the same place as it was the year before.

Jason and company knew what was coming and stood up from their chairs. They could tell where the Thorncat Missiles were expected to land, because even though it wasn't roped off like the other area, it had a perimeter of guards—burly individuals whose primary task was keeping kids and straying inebriants away. Jason told those standing nearest him (Mick and Dirax) they didn't rope off the anticipated Thorncat Missile landing zone, to help keep anyone from speculating at the big surprise.

After what normally would've been a great grand finale, the music stopped, the projectiles ceased to fly, and the crowd began to cheer as if it was over—*but it wasn't*. Unexpectedly, the music began again, this time more dramatic than ever. The crowd quieted down with astonishment. Never before had a Conceptual Naissance had a false ending. The atlytls started up again with a few rounds of normal projectiles. Then, another round of normal projectiles was launched as far as they could be launched for a strong lead-in for what was to come.

Jason raised his fist high, in a way that only people who have done it themselves would understand. Mick and Dave understood.

Timed perfectly with the briefest of pauses in the music, the best throwers (including the two that had done the alpha testing) notched and fired their Thorncat Missile projectiles. These had special reflectors put on the tails for different flair. The first wave of missiles took to the air like hungry bats take to the sky from out of a cave at darkness's emergence. The projectiles soared higher than all previous throws. Correspondingly, the crowd looked higher in the sky than they ever had before during a Naissance finale.

With as much grace as objects could muster, the projectiles reached the flight apex, and began the downward trajectory, reflective tails glistening with the utmost flamboyance. They landed way beyond all other landings of the night, about where Jason thought they would. The audience couldn't comprehend what had just happened. It was as if their eyes played a trick on them.

It took a few seconds for them to realize what exactly they had witnessed.

Each and every Icytryxan was taken aback with wonder.

The next wave of Missiles took to the sky, and landed just as far away, proving the first wave wasn't a figment of anyone's imagination.

A total of eight waves of Thorncat Missiles saw action that night. The last wave was the final thing performed at the show and, like the rest of the grand finale, was timed perfectly with the music.

When the last projectile hit the earth, the crowd cheered piercingly, realizing what they witnessed this night was special. Jason Thorncat enjoyed one of the proudest moments of his life. A deep warmth enveloped him, and he smiled at Mick, Dave, and Yori with delight and a twinkle in his eyes.

The show itself ended, but only about half the spectators piled out. The rest stayed, while the festival raged on. Smaller, less elaborate, bands performed. Some fires stayed lit, enough to provide adequate light to see. Groups of folks sang songs of their own. Expectedly, kids played with each other, most of them a game of some sort or another.

Syryx said to the group, "I suppose the betting circles that organized bets on the atlytl distances are going to take quite a while to sort everything out after that unforeseen stroke."

"We'll know when they're done when we see all the losers begin their running laps and pushups of defeat," replied Dirax.

Thyxer said, "Well Jason, I'd definitely say the unveiling was quite the visionary masterpiece. Certainly, an excellent idea."

"The unveiling was Swidyt's brainchild."

Yori asked, "Are we to expect droves of people tonight to come and ask you, Jason, about your invention and applaud you?"

"It's possible, I guess. Not too many know where we are, though, so I think as long as we stay blended in, it won't be too bad."

Jason was right. By the end of the night, only a handful found him and congratulated him. It was hard to locate anyone specifically amongst such a commotion. However, Swidyt was up to the challenge, having made a point to search out Jason.

"Hi-ya, Swidyt, so, what do you think? Your unveiling idea was magnificent, a real sight to behold."

"It couldn't have gone better in my book. Everyone I was sitting by was so surprised to see the projectiles travel that far that they talked about it for a long time. I told them it was you who created it. Most knew who you were. Some of them even began to speculate on what made them travel so far. None of them were even close in figuring it out."

Jason chuckled. "They'll know soon enough, once they see one."

"I wonder if the technology will transfer over to any necessities in Garobansurov."

"That's very well possible. We have many archer detachments, but I don't know if the design will work for arrows."

"I think I'll run the idea across the mold-preparers and see if it'll be a good idea to develop arrows with the Thorncat design for testing. I see no reason why they would decline."

"That's a good idea. My guess is that it would help, but not as significantly as in the projectiles. Never hurts to try."

"That's right. Our mold people love projects like this, so I'm sure we'll be going to the range with Thorncat Arrows before long."

"Sounds exciting," said Jason. "Even just a twenty-five-yard increase in the flight distance of an arrow would be a huge advantage for whomever has the technology."

"That it would," agreed Swidyt. "Well, I'll let you get back to the festivities. Once again, congratulation on the success of the evening. Enjoy the rest of the night, Jason."

"You too, Swidyt. I'll probably see you tomorrow."

"Yup, then we'll further discuss the arrow project."

"Excellent."

One thing the group made a point to do before another Conceptual Naissance was in the books was stand by the big, centrally located fire, where comradery was in no short supply. They joined others in the warmth of the fire and listened to the music. Many sang and many danced, while kids played jubilantly at the periphery.

The Garobansurovians and their hosts enjoyed themselves well into the night and walked home when the children were too tired to play any longer.

On the walk back, they were all bestowed mental pictures of the show's lights skipping across the waters and reflective surfaces. It was as if the pictures were burnt into their retinas. It would take a sleep, maybe two, to be rid of the pleasant images.

The next day, army training was a different story as far as how many people approached Jason to talk about the Thorncat Missile unveiling, many dozens, in fact. Overall, the Icytryxans were extremely appreciative to Jason for such a grand contribution to the army.

The consensus was that the army was no doubt more formidable, but as far as now being formidable enough to sway them *to go to war* alongside Garobansurov, Jason heard no solid evidence of the sort. Nevertheless, he was confident it helped in the mission. So was Mick, Dave, and Yori.

The atlytl corps made haste in practicing with the new toy. Not too many were created at this point, but by the end of the month, many thousands were fashioned and ready to go.

In view of the fact that it was basically a half day, the training session went by quickly.

At the end of the day, Jason went to the metal shop.

To Jason, Swidyt said, "We are indeed going to construct molds for conventional arrows with the Thorncat design. We're also going to fashion wooden arrows with it, which is basically just a procedure of sanding."

"Wooden ones I don't think will work as well as aluminum. You can only taper so much with wood. The aluminum shaft will grip the flights better, so the tapering can be more pronounced."

"True. It's too bad aluminum is rare, though, making it inconceivable to construct a large quantity of arrows of the substance, the metals of which the projectiles are composed are much more common."

"Same for us," stated Jason. "So many varieties of metals. But so challenging to find."

"So much diversification of rigid metals for so much violence. I must propose violence never solves anything. But it is also true, on the other end of the spectrum, talking never solves anything either. Words are empty expressions without true inner belief backing them up. Only by attempting to solve something within your own mind can there be a chance of it truly ending in success. For if a problem can't be solved in the mind, it never really was a problem to begin with."

"Interesting concept. I'll have to ponder that one. Is that an old Icytryxan proverb?"

"Nope," answered Swidyt. "It's a new Icytryxan proverb."

"How new?"

"Oh, about 10 seconds." The pair chuckled.

After his rather entertaining talk with Swidyt, Jason joined up with the rest for the walk back to the house, an action which was turning into one of his favorite parts of the day. The discussions during these walks concerning what each did during the day were surely enlightening and fascinating.

Yori separated from the group at certain a point to go visit with a friend of hers. She was invited for supper and wished to oblige the gesture.

Upon knocking on the door of the home, Yori was greeted by her friend, and introduced to the other two residents of the home.

Supper was nice, but what stuck with Yori the most was a story that was told to her by an interesting lady. It involved how the lady and a group of three others had felt exploratory and spent a long time living away from civilization. It was a good account on which Yori pondered for a long time, although, the story seemed to have missing pieces.

A few days went by and Jason found himself once again at the same testing field the Thorncat Missiles were first tested. This time, it was the Thorncat *Arrows* taking flight for the first time. Jason was right about the metallic shaft's capacity to be tapered better. And because of this capacity, they traveled further than the wooden ones. Both traveled further than the standard arrow, though the distance increase was nowhere near as substantial as the atlytl projectile had received with the Thorncat design. Nevertheless, it was very valuable technology.

Limited by what aluminum could be spared, the new arrow was ordered for construction. Wooden ones were made as well.

Now, along with being a tracker, warrior, and an officer, Jason could label himself as an inventor.

At the time of the testing, Mick and Dave were beginning one of their battle scenarios.

Addressing the crowd consisting of a hundred participants, Dave said, "Today, we've come up with the idea to have two teams face off against each other. Nothing new there, of course. Where it gets interesting is that *shovels* are all you will be armed with. We will trek to the big, abandoned field a few miles east. There, barring the usage of the shovels for clobbering each other, you can use them for anything. Dig trenches for protection, for example. You'll need them, because you'll be throwing balls of dirt and whatever rocks you can find at each other. I know what you're thinking: *Isn't that a bit dangerous?* I won't lie, yes, it is. I guess that's the point of the set-up."

Mick handed each team a flag. "The winner is the one who can capture the opponent's flag, carry it back, and be in possession of both flags at your own base.

"The weak-hearted may quit and walk away whenever they want.

"It's up to you if you want to aim at each other's heads. Dave and I know this could result in serious injury or even death. You participate at your own risk."

Half the day's volunteers walked away immediately. Those that stayed were courageous—or just bored.

At the onset of the match, both teams started at opposite ends of the field. Otherwise, the event would've been a free-for-all, resulting in nothing but essentially a giant wrestling match. Each team had snagged enough rocks off the ground to keep the opposing team at bay for the time being. Either team could have executed a charge at the onset, but not wanting to get hit with a rock, they refrained.

Both teams began digging their trenches for a little cover. Some of the Icytryxans were feeling rather ambitious, excavating with much will.

The trenches grew to decent sizes, eventually.

While digging, they had to avoid rocks and dirt clumps being thrown at them. At such great distances, though, any thrown object could be seen coming, and avoided easily. Nevertheless, the battle arena was sheer chaos.

Different sizes of rocks were collected, some sizes more useful than others. The coveted fist-sized ones were scarce in the field, so each team held onto these valuable commodities until the most opportune time was decided.

It was a fun game for both teams for the first few hours, but eventually, the soldiers grew restless. This impatience soon became the third team.

One-by-one, each team saw quitters.

Ultimately, the teams dwindled down to ten versus ten, then five versus five. And by nightfall, it was three versus two. Luckily by then, only one minor injury had ensued—a cracked rib.

Mick and Dave couldn't help but notice that up to this point nobody had risked a mad dash to the flag, an action which could've easily resulted in cheeky victory.

The team with two participants clung to hope, feeling they could still win for their team. Neither was feeling brave enough, however, to charge at the opposing team of three. They just sat it out.

Once making it this far, the remaining five really wanted to see it through, and possessed the drive to stay awake all night.

In the morning, the victorious team became so, because they basically had the best bladders. The trio had caught one of the enemies with his pants down—literally, foolishly taking a conspicuous piss. With the advantage of three rock wielders versus one, they had run to the enemy trench, dodged the two rocks thrown at them by the one adversary, and grabbed the flag, practically winning before the soldier peeing had the chance to get into the fray.

Mick and Dave congratulated the winners and were happy to start for home to catch some sleep since they had to stay awake for the duration of the competition.

Walking lethargically back to the house, Mick told Dave, "I do have to say I learned something valuable during that display."

"I did too, and I'm guessing it's generally the same thing as you."

"Probably. I gathered you and I could have practically defeated all of them, just the two of us."

"Yup, same thing indeed," asserted Dave. "None of them took any risks."

"Just one rolling of the bones could've been a winning move, but nothing of the sort from any of them."

"Protect the head, everything else heals."

"Affirmative."

Contemplation found its way to the pair, then, sleep.

GENERAL ULFENKERKI LIKED watching Gregg Hogarty's knife-throwing skills. It was the science of it.

"I see you've been practicing your new prowess here quite a bit. I would think there's a certain amount of inherent ability necessary to become so adept at it. I know I could practice throwing knives for many years of my life, and never be very good at it," the General said to Gregg.

"I suppose you're right. It's such a handy attribute to have. If there wasn't an inborn influence in it, everyone would practice it and be great at it. There'd be no reason for a soldier not to."

"You're the best I know of."

"Thank you, sir."

"Like I mentioned before," inserted Ulfenkerki, "I'm planning to fight near you, hoping your talent helps to keep me alive longer."

"I hope you do."

"Enjoy the weather." The Black Bear left Gregg's company amid the backwoods away from the rest of the detachment.

Ulfenkerki returned to the encampment, hungry. Grabbing a quick sandwich and coffee for the road, he started rounds.

Gradually, the newly-acquired military camp had grown in size—not in personnel, but in fortifications, war machines, supplies, and other miscellaneous things. It surely was a testament to hard work.

The wall and adjacent slow-down pit had been completely finished the day before. So, Ulfenkerki had ordered these particular laborers to help in the mine, drawing out materials for the war machines under construction by a different batch of soldier-laborers. Doing it this way was easier than going back to the Capital to get more heavy machinery.

Everything was going well, except for the fact that the—presumably Molisian—army for whom the foundry was previously creating weapons was nowhere to be found. The plan was to stay at the base and search out the army until either it was found and dealt with, or if Rowlangiv were to send emissaries with instructions to return to the Capital.

It was possible for them to return to the Capital due to no hope in finding the phantom army. But Ulfenkerki strongly felt this wouldn't be the case.

At the end of rounds, the General went to help in the mine.

Mine duty chiefly consisted of two independent tasks: one, the actual striking of the cave walls to dislodge the ore; and two, carrying excess stone out of the way and lugging the ore to the foundry. The consensus was that wall-striking was the harder of the two tasks. Ulfenkerki didn't want unhappy, overworked soldiers, so a few hours on the wall was good enough for each, sufficient to break a fine sweat.

Ulfenkerki broke his and left the mine.

Day morphed into night. Gregg Hogarty, the Black Bear, and a few other officers held a meeting in one of the tents, one which contained fancier chairs than what one would expect to see in a tent. The backs of the chairs exhibited intricate carvings which were either carved by a Molisian locally or brought in from afar.

"We'll have another catapult finished tomorrow. Consequently, we'll need operators to practice on it— *green* operators, since all the wxperienced ones already have their stations set," noted Ulfenkerki. "In a couple days, I'm expecting the scouts to return from one of the peaks in the Baustic Mountains. I had dispatched them there because from such a high vantage point I'd hoped they could spot something of value. Enemy soldier-clusters in the area on the move could be easily seen from these heights."

"To which peak were they sent?"

"The Valasat Peak—easy enough to summit, but high enough to get a good view of the horizon."

"I've been there before, you're right," said Gregg. "You can see quite a good ways from up there. If Gamald is mobile, the scouts will know it, alright."

"You can get up there without climbing gear, too. I haven't sent anyone there before because it's so far away."

IN OCCURRENCE A week before the meeting in the tent with the fancy chairs, Ulfenkerki's scouts did reach the top of the Valasat Peak. When they found a rock pile big enough to stand on and see over the trees into the distance, they were a bit surprised to observe exactly for what they were looking. A decent-sized army was heading towards them through the mountains.

However, the scouts also didn't expect to see what was coming at them when they headed back down the mountain to report back to Ulfenkerki—*arrows*.

The scouts from Gamald's detachment saw Ulfenkerki's scouts first and shot them down. Being a step ahead meant life or death during wartime. The Molisian scouts were lucky, for they mainly guessed what they shot at were scouts. Heeding the Molisian way of callously shooting first and asking questions later paid dividends this time. It was a way of thinking regarded as barbaric for most Garobansurovians and other dwellers of the entire Taraosk continent.

AN HOUR AFTER the meeting in the tent with the fancy chairs, the Black Bear took to relaxing with a drink. He needed a moment for contemplation.

The next day, he spent much time giving pointers to soldiers practicing sword work, a department in which he was rather fluent. A general who wasn't was broadly regarded as a *dead* general.

Another day elapsed. Ulfenkerki had expected his scouts to return from the Valasat Peak, but to no avail. He second guessed himself a few times, as to if his estimation of how long the walk would take was correct. But every time he recalculated, he ended up being more and more confident his estimation was accurate.

Two more days elapsed. Finally, Ulfenkerki was positive the scouts should have returned, so he held a meeting, considering the dilemma.

He untraditionally opened the meeting by saying, "It was weird. I thought I was losing my mind this morning. I looked at the ground and it seemed as if I was hallucinating. The grass and earth were twitching in patterns. I looked a few seconds later and same thing. I couldn't figure it out. I thought I was having a momentary lapse of reason. Eventually, I did see what was causing it, though. I should've known. It was a fieldmouse in a path it had made just below the grass roots."

Gregg responded, "Customarily, you see all kinds of mouse paths in the spring once the snow melts, paths they'd created in winter to keep themselves warm in the subnivean zone."

"Exactly," returned Ulfenkerki. "I remember seeing those for the first time when I was a kid. I had spent half a day trying to figure out what they were. I only realized the answer, eventually, when I noticed how much mouse scat was near them."

"I remember asking my father about it when I was younger," said Gregg.

"I could've done that, but I was stubborn and wanted to learn the answer for myself," noted the Black Bear. "It really makes you wonder how many times you've looked at the ground and your subconscious perceived a rodent, but your actual conscious failed to register it."

"Yeah, I wonder."

"But anyways, the reason I've called this meeting is to discuss the fact that my scouts I'd sent to the Valasat Peak definitely should have been back by now. This leads me to believe they've run into some trouble. I'll preface what I'm going to do about it by saying I rarely ever lose scouts, it's not an everyday occurrence. I'm assuming at about an eighty-percent level they met their demise, more than likely by the Molisians. Instead of losing soldiers by sending them on the long, time-consuming trip to the peak, I'm going to start sending recon to the area between here and the peak. It'll cut travel time for them by more than half. I'll tell them to be extra careful as well, because of the recent occurrence."

"So, you think there's an eighty percent chance a Molisian army is heading this way right now?" asked Gregg.

"I'd say there's that much of a chance my scouts got killed by Molisian militants, and maybe a little less that an entire army is on the way here, roughly seventy-five percent."

"That's still a pretty high chance," uttered Gregg. "Are you setting up preparations for battle immediately, then?"

"Well, I wouldn't say *immediately*, but probably in a few days I'll start ramping up the usual battle measures."

"By your estimations, General, how big of an army do you think we can hold off here?"

"Good question. We have five hundred head right now, compounded with all the old and new war machines and wall fortifications, I'd say we could hold off seven hundred without sustaining too many casualties. A small wall and high ground can go a long way. They'll fire at us with their catapults, but we can fire at them from longer range, because of the high ground.

If they come with a massive army, we're screwed. Hopefully recon would see that soon enough, though, so that way we could retreat back to the Capital before they got here.

It's possible a conquering army near the Valasat Peak could be heading to the Capital and not here. If that's the case, we will certainly be going back to the King. I have the bulk of my scouts watching that area, so if a Molisian so much as breaks wind over there, I'll know it. The Capital itself has always been top priority."

"Exactly, General. They'd need many thousands to storm the Capital for sure. An army that large would be seen and heard with ease," said an officer.

Gregg stated, "I'm wondering how a Molisian army even got to the Valasat Peak to begin with."

Ulfenkerki brushed a pesky fly away from his eye, and responded, "I bet they have been trickling through the Baustics in small bands and holding up in one of the ancient caverns rumored to be scattered in the mountains. The King has patrols in the Baustics, but so much of it is uncharted and arduous to guard."

"That's an interesting thing to picture: an army waiting in a cave for the right time to strike."

Ulfenkerki shoed the fly out the door. "Definitely sounds like something Gamald would do."

CHAPTER 17

After another day immersed in their army persuasion task, Mick, Dave, Yori, and Jason started walking together, though they didn't go back to the house with Thyxer and Syryx as usual. Instead they decided to go on a scenic stroll. There were a bunch of trails a couple miles from the training grounds, which none of the four had yet traversed. They were told they weren't groomed trails, but they were mapped and worth the visit. One of the Icytryxan soldiers supplied them with a copy of the trail map. Yori was confident she'd be able to follow it without trouble.

As she led the boys to the left at a fork in the path, Yori said, "Certainly is hilly and gorgeous terrain. Did you guys know there is a trail a few miles from the Capital that directs to a fabled tree?"

"I didn't know that. Did you two?" replied Jason.

"Nope."

"Me neither. What's the story behind this mythical tree?" asked Dave.

"A long time ago, it was said that Garobansurov suffered a great drought. During this calamity, crops withered, wells ran dry, entire forests died, and water reserves became very scarce. The people of the time were dying in droves. This catastrophe went on for many years. Hope was lost.

"Then one day, a certain man, whose name got lost in time, took the initiative to start replanting trees. Apparently, his desire to see living trees was more important to him than his tree seed collection. Why he had amassed a lifelong tree seed collection, no one knows—maybe he liked how they looked. He planted thousands upon thousands of seeds in the arid soil, only to see every single one fail to sprout, every one but one.

"The man was disheartened by the poor result, but he didn't give up on the one tree that'd survived. He tried to keep it watered with the very limited supply of water he did possess. It grew incredibly slow of course, but it did grow. As an earmark of this particular tree species, its seeds had the capacity to be stored for a long time. It was also known to take at least a decade to produce seeds of its own.

"However, the one tree was special, for not only was it the only one to survive, but it also miraculously created seeds by the age of three. I'm sure you guys are aware of this, but it's a known fact that plants and trees of quality stock can hand down their superior genetics to the next generation. And that's exactly what it did. The forthcoming trees all shared the characteristics of the original: hardy and superior reproductive capabilities.

"In relatively not much time, a new forest took shape.

"It was at this time when the drought lifted. It was never really proven that the lifting of the drought was unilaterally connected to the new forest, but most people of the time thought it was.

"From that time on, farmers from all-around considered that one original tree to be magical and lucky. Resultantly, both local and distant farmers started the tradition of venturing to the tree, and touching it for good luck, in the hopes of ensuring excellent crops for the forthcoming years. The tradition has been considerably lost in the vast amount of time, but enough people still travel to it to keep the trail to the tree still recognizable. To this day, the tree is still alive, over four hundred years old."

Mick scratched his chin and said, "This tree doesn't happen to have *black needles* by chance, does it?"

"No, it doesn't. It's an oak tree. The seed was an acorn, I remember."

"Bummer. The black needle enigma lives on."

The four of them stopped walking and sat on a giant log sitting next to the trail invitingly.

"Interesting story. Are there any other trees that old still standing in that forest?" asked Jason.

"The last I heard, most of the older ones had long since fallen. It really is quite the miracle that the original tree is the only one still standing."

"Oaks can live a long time, but four hundred years is undeniably a rather ripe old age for one," uttered Jason. "Beyond the shadow of a doubt, I'm making a point to see it when we finally do make it back to the Capital. Have you seen it, Yori?"

"No, I never made the trip, but I can certainly find someone that knows where the trailhead is. I don't exactly know myself."

"Seems like yet another hike the four of us can partake in together," commented Dave.

"I wouldn't have it any other way," said Yori, while reaching under the log they were all sitting on to grab a funny looking rock. Under close inspection, the rock looked more interesting from farther away. "Sandstone."

"The vestiges of some ocean bottom from long, long ago," added Mick.

"I'm surprised you didn't use that scintillating tree story for Fantysy-Escape. I bet it would've been interesting enough to gain all kinds of points," noted Jason.

"I would've, if I had realized I could've made a story out of it before. It kind of just rolled off my tongue there." Yori chuckled. "Nevertheless, it wouldn't have been enough for me to make a run at the championship. Either Dave or Yusyta pretty much have that in the bag."

Mick came out with, "Speaking of which, championship night is coming upon us here. Looks like we have been here long enough to take part in one."

"Oh yeah, that's right. It should be entertaining. Do you have a good one brewing for title night, Dave?"

"Indeed, I do. Last week, I'd started working on my story's mechanics for the occasion. I'll be ready."

"Well, team," blurted Yori, "shall we continue?"

"I'm ready." The quartet stood up from the log and ventured down the path towards the imaginary point signifying the trail's halfway point.

After a couple more hours of trekking and sparkling dialogue, the Garobansurovians made it back to the house. They were just in time to grab something to eat and join the Fantysy-Escape game already going on in the sub-basement. A few of the neighbor children were already in the pool, enjoying its crystal clear and moderately warm water. The youngsters were no doubt supplying the noise for the evening.

At the end of the thrilling game, everyone packed up the pieces, as Thyxer said, "This is usually the point where Syryx is so far ahead that most of us are out of the running. What happened this time Syryx, did you lose your mojo?"

"I guess it just wasn't my time. Besides, who knew we were going to be blessed with such fine new storytellers." Syryx looked at the guests with veneration.

Dave smiled. "I just really like this game of yours."

Yusyta commented, "You're going to really like it in a couple of days at championship night, when the two of us duel head-to-head for the title."

"I can't wait. It'll be exhilarating, I'm sure."

Mick spoke. "Is there anything special we need to bring for the night?"

Dirax replied, "Nothing really physically speaking. Although Dave and Yusyta might want to fashion their best stories for the event, since they'll be worth massive points and all. We like to bring down a feast of sorts, while we battle it out for the title. But we pretty much have everything needed for that covered."

Syryx added, "It usually lasts longer than normal, so we try to start an hour early. We also like to get dressed up. Some of us even wear costumes. So, feel free to get creative if you'd like. It really is quite the festive affair for us."

"Interesting," commented Yori. "I know exactly what I want to adorn."

"Me too," said Dave.

"I'm certainly glad you guys have been here long enough to attend a championship," stated Thyxer. "It's been nothing but an honor to host the four of you."

"Same for us, truly."

In the morning, things proceeded as normal, another day of the mission. Mick and Dave held another battle ordeal, while Jason and Yori did their thing.

On the walk back to the house, addressing his fellow Garobansurovians, Dave said, "It's not that I'm losing hope we're going to be successful with the mission, but I must admit I'm starting to get the feeling we really are trying to bare-handedly push a mighty river back from whence it came."

"I feel that I know a lot of the soldiers very well," said Yori, "and in that, I'm getting those senses also. We may very well get to a point soon, where we need to set a timetable depicting how long yet exactly we plan to go at this."

"I agree," replied Jason. "There's always a point when one must decide when to pull the plug on things."

"Certainly, but not quit yet," noted Mick, as he opened the front door to the house.

Everyone agreed with Mick and ate supper in the backyard together. They discussed the day, among other things.

"For tomorrow night's championship battle, I'm going to make my special cookies," commented Syryx.

"The peanut butter ones?"

"Yup."

"Awesome, I love those," exclaimed Dirax.

"One thing I do know," said Yusyta, "is that we definitely aren't allowing Thyxer to play his weird music again. Last title night, the stuff he played was pretty bad. I'd rather not relive that again."

"I second that."

"Awe, come on guys, it wasn't that bad."

"Just keep telling yourself that. You're much better on your bass."

"I remember a time when I was younger," put forth Syryx, "playing a title night, and Mom and Dad convinced an entire string quartet to perform while our game commenced."

"I remember that," added Thyxer. "I want to say it was some friends returning a favor for when Mom and Dad went out of their way to help them with something. I can't remember what the favor was, though. That was an unforgettable night and the first time I placed third."

"Too bad we couldn't convince a band to play for us tomorrow," said Dirax.

"Garobansurovians, are you ready for tomorrow's excitement?" inquired Yusyta.

"Like a thunder-clap waiting behind a bolt of lightning," proclaimed Dave.

"Wow, that's pretty ready!"

"Yup, I can't wait."

THE NEXT DAY, while his countrymen, many miles away, were anticipating the evening's Fantysy-Escape title festivities, Ulfenkerki was doing some anticipating of his own. A few days ago, his corps of scouts were dispatched halfway to the area by the Valasat Peak where the other scouts went presumably missing. He patiently waited for the news and couldn't help but be almost certain a battle was imminent.

To ease his troubled mind, he gathered Gregg Hogarty, and the two headed to the nearest tavern.

There was only one town within a reasonable walking distance from the army base, and that town had two taverns, both moderately called upon by the soldiers on their free time. Stereotypically, one or their clienteles was basically older patrons, whereas the other's was younger. This presented a hypothetical conundrum: Ulfenkerki was older, while Gregg was younger. They remedied the puzzle at the crossroads by deciding to go to the tavern currently busier, which turned out to be the younger person's tavern. It usually was busier, not because younger Garobansurovians drank more, but mainly because it was bigger.

Sitting down next to Ulfenkerki on an anything-but-sturdy bar stool, Gregg said, "This is the third time I've been here."

"First time for me. I have been at the other bar in town a couple times, though," commented Ulfenkerki, just before telling the bartender what he wanted to drink.

"I've only been to that one once."

Seeing a couple other of his soldiers in a corner booth, the Black Bear nodded and waived, followed by Gregg, both getting similar gestures in return.

The bartender returned with the beers.

Three beers into the evening, Ulfenkerki and Gregg were approached by a couple strangers aged in their twenties.

The bearded stranger voiced, "Most of us in town have been enlightened of the army stationed in the wilderness." The man looked to Ulfenkerki. "Since you, sir, have the appearance of an officer, I'll ask you if it's possible that my friend here and I join in on the cause."

The other stranger added, "We're aware of the war and how malevolent the Molisians are, and we want to help."

Ulfenkerki turned to Gregg. "It's not the first time I've been told I have the look of an officer." After Gregg's chuckle, the General turned back to the strangers and responded to their request: "You boys look rather capable, and I'm sure your heart be true. Under normal circumstances, I'd be honored to invite you into our ranks. But because of the impending battle, I would be stupid to allow new recruits to join just beforehand. I have no way of knowing you're not sided with the Molisians."

The bearded man said, "I could get half the town here to vouch for us that we've spent our entire lives here in Garobansurov."

"I don't doubt that, but you must understand that it's very well possible that you could've been bribed or something of the sort. I'm not saying that you have, but I must take precautionary measures. However, there is one of two things I would greatly much like for you to do. You can either go to the Capital now and enlist there—tell them I sent you—or you can wait until we all march back, and you can consider yourself a part of my army then. Either way would be equally honorable."

"That's completely understandable, sir." The bearded man looked over at his friend to check on his endorsement, got it, and said, "I think we'll take you up on your proposal, the one supplying the opportunity to join you on the march back."

"Excellent. I'll send someone to town to inform you a day or two in advance when we are heading back. It's a small town, you won't be hard to find."

"That's true. I only live a few houses down and my friend a few more."

"Great. See you then."

The two future enlistees sat back down where they were before Ulfenkerki and Gregg had come into the picture. They enjoyed the rest of their evening, knowing they were mostly successful, as did Gregg and Ulfenkerki. Fresh recruits were always enough to bring a smile to a soldier's face, especially a general's.

SPEARHEADED BY ONE of Ulfenkerki's veteran soldiers, Fjord, the squadron of scouts made haste to their destination. Fjord knew the terrain quite well, for he had done scouting campaigns in the area before for Rowlangiv. Now, he was doing them for Ulfenkerki. He knew there was a bottleneck just ahead, through which an advancing army would have to squeeze if they were headed in the direction of Ulfenkerki's mine/base.

Because he knew the bottleneck was near, he instructed the rest of the squad to keep to the trees staying low and quiet as they walked, and especially to not step on any sticks. He heard what may have happened to the previous scouts and didn't want any repeat occurrences. Fjord had a family who loved him, so he did everything by the book, taking every precaution to ensure both success and continued existence.

Unbeknownst to Fjord, the same Molisian advance party who'd killed the scouts on Valasat Peak was in the area brandishing the same *shoot first, ask questions later* attitude. The Molisians walked the tree line, flanking both sides of the trail. Anyone on the trail was doomed. However, sopping wet and hidden, Fjord's group were navigating the adjacent cedar swamp with eyes on the tree line. No matter how hard you tried hopping from tree root to tree root, you always ended up getting wet.

By navigating the swamp, Fjord, having been under Ulfenkerki's tutelage for a great many years, knew that the much older and larger cedar trees of the swamp provided far superior cover than the scrub trees lining the trail. It made the wetness worth every step.

At point, Fjord crouched inconspicuously behind a two-hundred-year-old monster. He lingered silently and listened for distant footsteps with elevated awareness. Only a true woodsman or crafty soldier knew how to take full advantage of a cedar swamp and its large diameter trees. Currently stationary, Fjord could hear distant sounds better than the Molisians.

Fjord cupped his ear and placed it against his tree. He could hear the unmistakable sound of people coming towards him. He signaled to the rest of the men to remain perfectly still and hidden.

Within a few moments, sure enough, the Molisian advance party came into view.

Fjord let them slip past alive, unlike what the Molisians would've done. If an army were indeed on the way, Fjord knew a dead advance party would attract too much attention. He wanted the leaders of the approaching Molisian army to keep on thinking they were unobserved and sneaky. An enemy's false sense of security goes a long way.

As suspected, half an hour after the Molisian scouts slithered past, Fjord heard the thundering of an oncoming army marching straight down the trail. Ulfenkerki's scouts stayed well out of view from anyone in the army, but within eyeshot enough to get a semi-accurate head count. Fjord realized it wasn't technically a full-sized army, but large enough to wreak quite the havoc. He deducted it was a couple of platoons, eight hundred strong in total. They were equipped with towable war machines and heading straight for Ulfenkerki and the base. Fjord knew that the faster the Black Bear received this information, the more thoroughly the General could prepare.

So, Fjord quickly led his scout-team straight through the thickest, deepest part of the swamp. This way, they could go around the platoons and advance the party, unnoticed. He knew if they could get to the other side of the swamp, the terrain would become less forested, providing topography suitable for running. The faster they would run, the faster Ulfenkerki would get the valuable data. As long as they made it through the swamp without drowning, getting lost, or succumbing to the infamous *quicksand* the area was known for.

CHAPTER 18

JASON SPENT MOST of the day within the confines of the metal shop, where he continued to fine tune the Thorncat Missile. He and Swidyt spent countless productive hours discussing the science of the Thorncat Missile since its unveiling. They also delved quite deeply into the discipline of the atlytl.

Dave and Mick held another basically inconclusive battle scenario at a nearby gravel pit, and Yori met up with dozens of her contacts, sifting through Icytryxan culture faster than water surging over a waterfall.

The day wore on, all of them with the upcoming evening's gala in the back of their minds. The Fantysy-Escape championship night was nearly upon them.

The group did no dawdling in their walk back to the house after army training. Thyxer and Syryx knew they needed all the time they could get for the playing of the game.

As soon as they got inside, all six washed up quickly and joined everyone else already in the basement setting up. A huge buffet of food was all lined up, the gameboard was set, and there were lavish decorations everywhere. Almost everyone was in costumes. Dave had a costume he was going to wear, but he didn't plan to put it on until the telling of his final story, as with Yusyta. In the meantime, they were just dressed fancy.

Dave put forth, "Yusyta, you're wearing a dress that would knock the socks off any man. It really is quite the mystery why you live alone."

"That's me: an enigma wrapped in a riddle."

"Well everyone, are we ready to begin?" announced an excited Icytryxan lady.

"I'm about as ready as I'll ever be, Syryx," noted Yori.

The game began. Everyone playing concentrated as hard as they could, even though most were out of contention. Wonderful music was supplied by a couple of the children. The gamepieces moved without break, as did the pens on everyone's individual game parchments.

At the end of the first hour of play, Mick commented, "No clear leader has been presented, but I see everyone has managed to make a trip to the tremendous buffet at least once."

"Make that *three* trips for me," replied Dirax, as he rolled the dice, resulting in one of his pieces inconsequently crossing a bridge.

Jason walked around the large main table. "I better start focusing my play on this side, or I'm going to find my night to be over rather quickly."

"I'm glad you said that," mentioned Thyxer. "I almost forgot about my warrior piece over there by you."

"Happy to help."

On one of the auxiliary game boards, Dave and Yusyta found themselves going head-to-head for control of a certain area. It was just a matter of chance this noteworthy situation had happened. The rest of the competitors noticed it happening and stopped what they were doing to witness the important aspect of the game. The title wouldn't come down to this part, but it would help in giving an edge to one of them.

In the end, Dave was victorious and controlled the area, a fanciful Aspen forest. He'd reeled Yusyta closer to within striking distance for the telling of the all-important main stories near the closing of the match.

When everyone reached a certain point of the main gameboard, they would tell their stories. Massive points were gained by the tellers through the audience members choosing the story to which they wanted to hear the conclusion. They, then, would go off into a closed room to hear the ending, while those who chose someone else's would never know how the story concluded. And the Icytryxans were very good about keeping the endings they heard to themselves. The storytelling part was fundamentally the bread and butter of the game. The more people choosing to hear your ending, the more points received. The storyteller in ripe form virtually won the season every time.

Yusyta had a decent lead going into the night, but because Dave had just won the small victory in the Aspen forest, Yusyta's lead diminished. Dave had a chance. Unless things changed drastically, Dave would need one more ending listener than Yusyta to tie for the title, and two more to win. A tie had never happened for the household. Nobody wanted one to materialize, because two names, side-by-side, would look silly engraved into the title-plaque forever. But if it happened, it happened.

The children were doing a great job with their music. Nary a soul was disappointed with the performance. The food buffet had taken quite the hit, but was still modestly stocked with food, doing its best to entice with satisfying aroma.

"I'm having one heck of a time," said Yori, dancing to the music, "just like I knew I would."

"As am I," noted Jason. "All our strategizing in these last months comes down to this. Exciting!"

"I couldn't be happier that you all are enjoying this as much as we do," said Thyxer. "The best part is yet to come, though. There's a surprise twist for title night, of which you Garobansurovians are unaware."

"Should we be scared?" said Dave, chuckling.

"Maybe, maybe not. You'll see."

Having heard it was title night, a few neighbors came down to watch. Other Icytryxans held their own championships on the nights of their own choosing. Additionally, on occasion, the winners from separate households would assemble to face off. One year, Syryx did this and took second place overall.

The neighbors had complemented the buffet table with many dishes of their own, furthering its undeniably alluring scent.

A couple hours after the arrival of the neighbors, Dirax noted, "Two more rolls of the dice and it will be story time."

"That looks to be the case," said Yori, as she grabbed the dice and rolled. "Now, one more."

Thyxer took his last turn and the story segment was reached. "Alright, here we go."

A small break was taken before the pivotal telling of the main stories, so those who needed to change their clothes for the stories could go and do so. Plus, who wouldn't appreciate a small pause for dramatic effect?

As Dave, Yusyta, and Syryx went off to change, Jason observed, "The points are pretty much the same since Dave took control of the Aspen forest."

"Yup, so Dave still needs one more ending listener to tie, and two to win. It's going to take a heck of story to do that, I'm thinking."

Dave, Yusyta and Syryx came back in their new costumes. Dave wore a handmade outfit, which resembled what prisoners wore at the Garobansurovian Capital Jail. Yusyta wore another beautiful dress, and Syryx put on the garb of a priestess.

To everyone in the room, Thyxer said loudly, "All of you now know what happens, except for our honored Garobansurovian guests here."

"That's right, we've no idea what this twist of which you spoke was," mentioned Dave.

"And now you shall see. Unbeknownst to you, there's more than meets the eye to this curious abode." Thyxer walked over to the other side of the swimming pool, grabbed the big red rug off the floor and moved it off to the side. To the surprise of Mick, Dave, Jason, and Yori, the removing of the rug revealed a barely noticeable hatch door.

"I would've never guessed that was under there," declared Yori.

Thyxer grabbed the small inset handle of the camouflaged hatch door, pulled it up, and announced to the crowd, "Alright everyone, follow me."

Amused, Jason looked at Yori while heading for the door. *"How exciting."*

"I couldn't agree more."

The whole group, even the spectators, went down the stairs beneath the hatch, descending lower even yet into the ground. Along the way, Thyxer lit the candles inserted into holders situated as permanent fixtures of the walls. The tunnel was obviously a cave passageway, ornamented by ancient wooden paneling. The burrow opened to a room, stocked with chairs, better lighting than the tunnel, and a performance stage.

"Welcome friends," proclaimed Thyxer, "to our championship night story auditorium."

"The acoustics are amazing down here," noticed Jason, "along with the nice, cool temperature."

"I would've never guessed that the house was built over a cave system. There are no rock formations to be seen above ground anywhere near the house," commented Mick.

"Ours is the oldest home in the neighborhood, so when it was built many years ago it was basically built around the cave entrance," noted Syryx. "We are pretty much standing under the backyard now."

Dirax added, "One of our ancestors, I forget which one, found the cave and entrance and built around it a much smaller house than the one current. Since that time, that house has been mostly torn down, and this one built. The original woodwork in here and in the tunnel remains, I know."

Thyxer attached, "A lot of the soil in the yard is essentially fill, along with that in much of the neighborhood. The cave entrance back then was a little more exposed, I understand."

"Why would the whole neighborhood be composed of so much fill?" asked Yori.

"I want to say it's because there was once a large hill nearby, which contained a mineral of some sort. The displaced soil of the mine ended up here," said Dirax.

"It was sapphires," noted Syryx. "The whole thing being really convenient for us in keeping the room secret from visitors for extra dramatic affect. Without the fill, it may be expected for there to be caverns in the noticeable rock formation, and the secret foiled."

Mick laughed. "Yes, had I seen the formation, I may have explored it extensively."

"They may have possibly missed a few sapphires here and there in the excavation of the hill," noted Jason. "Since the back yard is mostly remnants of said hill, have any of you spent any time sifting through the lawn for gems that may have been missed?"

I know I have picked up and examined every reflective stone I've seen shining brilliantly in the sun," said Syryx, "though I've never actually gotten down and dirty, digging up the yard to look."

"Same here," added Thyxer. "I don't think anyone has, because I've never seen any holes strewn all over the yard."

"I have, but I laboriously covered all my holes back up," replied Yusyta.

"Really?" asked Thyxer, dumbfounded.

"Yeah. I was bored one day." Yusyta held firm for a few moments, but eventually released herself from her stance of seriousness. "No, I'm just kidding." The room lit up with laughter.

"Shall we begin, all?"

"Yup," said the players in unison.

To add exhilaration, Dave and Yusyta would go last, being the only two vying for the title. All the other stories were important as well, for everyone wanted to end up with as high of a placing as possible. As worth noting, Icytryxans and Garobansurovians were inherently pretty equal competitively.

Everyone but he who was designated to go first sat down in the relaxing chairs.

Dirax (he who was designated) climbed onto the three-foot-high by twelve-foot-long by ten foot-deep stage. He performed his piece with as much pizzazz as he could muster.

The audience applauded at the conclusion, and the next to go rose from their chair and climbed onto the stage.

A couple hours elapsed, and everyone except for Yusyta and Dave, the only two vying for the title, had performed their reciting. They all told their stories eloquently and enthusiastically.

Some of the neighbors were still there, some weren't.

"Now we're down to the nitty gritty," emitted Thyxer. "Judging by past events, I'm guessing Dave's and Yusyta's championship stories will be around half an hour a piece."

"Making for the next hour to be grand, I'm sure," proclaimed Yori.

Dave and Yusyta drew straws, as was tradition. Dave won, and picked to go last.

How it worked in the end was everyone picked two story endings they wanted to hear. One was from the lot of non-title contenders, and the other from the title contenders. The more people who chose to hear your ending, the more points you got, which were added to the points you'd already amassed. Then, it was pretty much over, just a little bit of formality remaining on the gameboard once the endings were said and done.

In her gorgeous (presumably relatable to her story) dress, Yusyta took a deep breath, went onstage and began her story. She would skillfully change her vocal tone when arriving at her main character's inner monologue parts.

Her story went as thus:

> It wasn't necessarily going to be the best
> day of the year, but Cherryl knew it was
> going to be memorable. She and her

three friends had traveled far, very far, and were in a world almost alien to them. They started the journey because they all wanted to experience life at its fullest. The four women—Cherryl, Mary, Vycki, and Kera—had been in the wilderness the entire trip, and this day was the first they decided to go into a town on the journey.

"It will be really nice to replenish our supplies today," commented Cherryl.

"We've run completely out of fishing hooks, I know. You'd think with as many as we brought, we wouldn't have run out," said Mary.

"There must be more places for a hook to get stuck in this part of the world." Vycki chuckled.

Kera added, "I know I for one have gone through my fair share, half of my losses being on that one stream with the unimaginably thick brush."

"I remember that stream. Yeah, that was a mess," agreed Mary.

"Entanglements everywhere there, but it was certainly a beautiful body of water," said Cherryl. "Deviating from topic, I hope everything thing goes well today in town." Cherryl was apprehensive about going into a town she had never been to before. "Anything can happen in a new place. I know it's just like any other town, but being nervous is just my nature. I'll just slip on my bravest face."

The quad left all their gear and began the walk to the nearest town, an anticipated easy hour walk.

"Hopefully, we can locate the articles we're after. They may not even have them all in stock," said Mary.

"It's a possibility, I suppose," responded Kera, "but my guess is they will."

"It's also feasible somebody steals all our stuff from the campsite while we're gone," said Vycki, pessimistically.

Cherryl replied, in comical tone, "Then, there'll be even more accoutrements we'll need to procure."

"We haven't seen anyone in the area in days, so it'll be okay, I think. Plus, our campsite is considerably out of the way," said Mary.

The ladies had covered ground as well as they'd hoped and saw the town in the distance, as well as the quaint lake beside which it sat. The town wasn't big, nor was it one of those tiny countryside villages that barely had room for a sneeze.

"I'm approximating there to be a couple hundred citizens," proclaimed Kera.

"Sounds about right."

"We are out of flour too, before I forget."

"True. Obviously, they'll barter differently here than we're used to, but I think we'll manage," noted Cherryl.

"I think so too."

Doing so by clearly identifiable senses of adventure, the four women entered town, not knowing what to expect. Right away at the onset they drew attention, not really because they were dressed a bit differently—which they were, technically—but because they were all irrefutably easy on the eyes.

Setting forth on their short-term goals, the ladies wasted no time being distracted by the men of the settlement, men who couldn't help but admire the beauties who'd just entered their town.

"All the commercial buildings look to be pretty close together," noticed Mary.

"That's handy. We won't have to waste much time looking all over town for what shops we need. I think it would also be best if we split up, dividing up among us what we need to acquire," considered Cherryl.

"Good idea. That'll save time. I'd hate to run late and have to walk back in the dark," replied Vycki.

They all agreed to separate, each with a list of what they were responsible for getting.

On her list, Cherryl had the hooks, a blanket, pepper, sugar, and candles, hooks being the hard item to get. As planned, each lady had a hard-to-locate item on her list.

Cherryl switched into her posture of contemplation.: "I think that looks like a place that would have food, over there to the north. There is one thing that might be a hindrance. The gems we must barter with are quite desirable where we're from, but who knows if they are here. This might all go downhill really fast. However, the point of the journey is not to arrive, so this should be interesting. Definitely a memorable day. But I knew this as soon as I woke up this morning."

Cherryl walked into a general store, realized Mary was within, and to her said, "How did you beat me here? It seems like I walked straight here."

"I passed you on the other side of the road when you were peering into the depths of your gem bag."

"Oh yeah, I was doing that wasn't I?"

"We'll grab our stuff and negotiate with the store owner, together, eh?"

Cherryl responded, "Sounds good to me. It should be easy to find my foodstuff. I can already see the sugar right over there."

"Yup, right next to the flour."

Cherryl waited to grab the sugar, so she didn't have to lug it around the store, as she hunted for the pepper.

"I'm thinking my pepper is over here by the rest of the cooking supplies. Yes, I'm right. Here it is. I'd thought of grabbing the sugar last, but I should've thought of getting all the food last, completely. Now I'll have to haul the heavy sugar around town all day. Never mind, I'll think of something."

Cherryl met up with Mary and together the two successfully negotiated with the store owner for the goods, Cherryl's bartering doubts instantly dissipating. It was an easy trade. The shop owner envisioned herself, quite vividly, wearing one of the gems around her neck at church. Most of the gems had been pre-shaped, so any impending onlookers would be astounded by their beauty as much as possible.

Post the exiting of the store, Mary and Cherryl parted ways.

"What's next?" wondered Cherryl aloud. "I think I'll head over to that cute little store over there. It looks like it may even have everything else I need."

As Cherryl approached the store, she crossed paths with Vycki, who'd just come out of it. "Any luck?" she asked.

"You shouldn't have a problem in there with the parley," replied Vycki. "The man running the place is somewhat knowledgeable on the value of precious gems."

"Excellent. The grocery store across the street was an easy barter as well."

"Too bad I have no food on my list."

"Good luck with everything else. See you later, Vycki."

"Yup. Watch your step—the first stair is uneven."

"Thank you," replied Cherryl, who then thought, *This is a rather nice-looking store. The wood for the floors seems to have been chosen from the perfect trees. There's not a lot of merchandise in here, though. I'm pretty sure I'll find a blanket and candles, but fishing hooks, perhaps not.* She combed the place extensively to no avail on the hooks. But like she assumed, she found the blanket and candles. Cherryl exited the store with the newly-gotten goods.

As Vycki mentioned to me, doing business went smoothly. Now, for the tricky part. Fishing hooks are harder to come by because they are crafted in such miniaturization. Furthermore, this sugar sure is heavy, still and all. I wish I could find a place to hide it, since I have the feeling the search for hooks is going to take a while. Maybe, there'll be a nice bush somewhere over there within that little copse of trees. There it is, the perfect place to hide a bag of sugar.

I'll just conceal it a little bit more here with these loose branches. There, a lighter burden. I'm ready to go hook chasing. I just hope there's another store with general wares.

Cherryl walked to the other side of town and found the only other general store thereabouts.

After having hunted in the store for a time, not uncovering what was wanted, she approached the man at the sales counter. "Hi there. I'm looking for fishing hooks. Do you happen to have any in the store, located somewhere I've overlooked?"

"We had some a few months ago, but I think they got sold, and we haven't been able to restock any since. I'm sorry."

"I looked for them at the other store, and they didn't have any either," stated Cherryl, disappointingly. "Would you by chance know of any place in town that would have any?"

The man replied, "Well, that's it for stores, but maybe if you tried bartering with one of the avid fishing enthusiasts in town. It's possible they may have stockpiled a load and are willing to part with a few."

"I'm willing to try."

"There are two possibilities of which I know. The first, you can find across the street in the tan house. The other lives two streets down in the cabin with the tallest chimney. I actually know him well. If he's not there, you can probably find him at his favorite fishing spot, just outside of town at the small lake you probably passed on the way in."

"Yup, I saw the lake. Hard to miss such picturesque blueness. Thank you so much for the help."

"No problem."

Cherryl walked across the street to the home of the first person the clerk mentioned. He was home and had hooks, but dispiritingly, didn't have enough in his supply to spare.

Things aren't looking too good here for me. It seems I basically have only one more shot at it. I'd hate to be the only lady to have not located everything on her list. Maybe they're all running into roadblocks too. I hope not, but it's possible. I'm not discouraged yet.

Here it is, the house two blocks over with the tallest chimney. Here goes nothing.

No answer. I suppose it's to the lake I go. It looked rather inviting from a distance, so I'm sort of glad to be going there. About a quarter mile walk there, I'm guessing. Offhand, I can't remember seeing any place on the lake from where someone would fish, but I suppose when I get there, I'll find things to be less obscured.

It looks like I'll be turning away from the people and wooden constructs of town and traversing a hardly-travelled path towards the lake. Here I go.

It sure is a quaint, little lake. So peaceful, so serene, brilliantly gleaming in the soft, multi-faceted glow of the afternoon sunlight. I wonder if that's my guy there, crouched on the beach, pole in hand.

Curious. He seems to be one with his surroundings, as if an adept artist painted him first onto the canvas, and everything else was painted accordingly around him. Kind on the eyes.

"Pardon me, sir. I don't mean to intrude at your scenic getaway here, and for that I am greatly sorry, but my name is Cherryl, and I need to ask a question of you."

"There's no need to be sorry, dear girl. Nature is possessed by no individual, for its perpetual beauty belongs to us all."

"I suppose that to be true," said Cherryl, as she stepped closer. "I couldn't help but observe and admire how you seamlessly blend in with the world around you."

"Well, thank you. I can assure you I didn't plan it like that. But I do like to merge with the environment. My name is George, and I'm pleased to meet you. A common name, I know, but one easily remembered. You had mentioned a question?"

"I did. My friends and I have been on this adventure of sorts, and we ran out of supplies. We were back-country, so we had to go into town to procure what we needed. I had gotten everything on my list quite easily, except for one thing. A man at one of the stores said he knew you, and that you might have what I'm looking for, maybe enough in abundance that you'd be willing to spare."

"I bet I can guess what that it is. The one thing that's both rare in town and of what an angler such as myself may have a plethora: hooks."

"You're correct."

"For that, I have good news and bad news. The good news is I do have plenty of hooks to hand over. But the bad news is I accidentally left them at a different fishing spot, many miles away. My plan was to grab them the next time I went there, having no timetable as to when that was going to be."

"That's disheartening. My friends and I were just here for the day."

"It is possible, if you wish, for me to make the trip there and be back by tomorrow. You could even accompany me if you'd like."

"That may be achievable. I could go and discuss it with my friends and see what they say."

"Sounds good to me. You want to meet me at my house then, when you're done talking it over with them?" asked George.

"Okay, I will."

"I'll leave here in twenty minutes."

"Alright, George. See you in a bit," noted Cherryl, before aiming towards town.

I must really be smitten with this intriguing man for me to not even think twice about going on a long trek with him. Deep down inside, I guess I genuinely want to go.

Having met up with her friends in town, Cherryl said, "I hope you guys had better luck than I did."

"We all found all our items," replied Vycki. "So, I'm guessing no hooks anywhere, eh?"

"Technically, no, but I do have a chance at getting some, pending tomorrow's events. I met a man who informed me he could venture to get the hooks for us, he having inadvertently left his supply elsewhere. So, I figured maybe the three of you could go ahead back to our campsite today, as we planned, and I would go along with him to get the hooks. And I'd just meet back up with you at the site, either tomorrow or the day after, depending how long the trip ends up being."

Mary responded, "I see no problem with it. But I will say, be that as it may, it doesn't seem like you to be going off traveling with strangers. I can't recall you ever doing it before."

"You're right, it's not something I've ever done before, nor in the past would have seen myself doing. But I must confess, there's something almost magical about this man. I can't explain it. I was enchanted at first sight you could say."

"Well, if you trust him, then, we do too. Have a safe trip and enjoy yourself."

"Thank you. See you soon," replied Cherryl, as she walked away.

I find myself being rather excited. I don't even care how much it may cost to stay at an inn tonight. My heart is beating uncharacteristically fast, as I head towards his house.

George came to the door, just after Cherryl knocked, and invited her in. "Welcome to my home. Please, sit wherever you'd like, if you indeed want to sit."

"Absolutely lovely. Did you paint all these pictures on your walls?"

"I did. Though, it takes me a while to finish a picture. Slowly but surely they get done."

"Nevertheless, they're stunning. Are they places you've been?"

"Some are, others are just loci in my mind."

"Beautiful," noted Cherryl, eying each and every one. "So, I talked it over with my companions, and we've all agreed that me accompanying you tomorrow wouldn't entirely be a bad idea. I actually am a bit animated about it."

"Splendid. I was hoping you would. Not too many people want to go on my treks with me, especially beautiful people."

"We've been on a long trek ourselves, so this one basically strikes as no significant transformation from daily routine."

George angled himself towards his kitchen. "I'm glad. Would you care for anything to drink?"

"I'll have a juice—apple or orange, maybe? I'll have to find an inn for tonight, are there any cheap ones in town?"

George went to the kitchen and swiftly returned with a large glass of orange juice. "There are two places to rent a room in town. But you don't have to go and pay for a room, I have an extra room here for you, free of charge."

"I wouldn't want to impose."

"You wouldn't be. The poor thing never gets used, and I practically feel sorry for it."

"I suppose, since you put it that way, how could I say no?"

Cherryl and George chuckled, and the two of them conversed pleasantly well into the night. Afterwards, having had a fine evening, Cherryl crawled into the usually unutilized bed, and slept wonderfully all through the night.

Marvelous morning. If today is anything like last night, I do believe I'm going to have a spectacular day. What a bizarre time and place to meet someone so amazing. Who would've thought it? I can't recall a time when I woke up feeling so alive. Time stands still.

The pair began the journey just after a large, energy supplying breakfast.

"So how far of a walk is this fishing spot of yours?"

"Five miles there and five miles back. A little hilly, but nothing too bad."

"A decent walk then." Cherryl expressed, "I'm glad we're going to camp out tonight, before heading back. It'll be fun."

"I agree. A night of camping is hard to beat."

"True. How often do you usually go to this place we're going?"

"I'd say half a dozen times a year," presented George. "I frequent locales where the fishing is better, but I do have to say the one we're heading to now is the most visually breathtaking."

"I can't wait to see it."

An hour into the walk, Cherryl found herself alone, as George told her to wait where she was while he went to quickly do something.

I wonder what he could be doing—probably picking me some wildflowers or something knowing him. What an incredibly fantastic man. When this trip is over, I have no idea how I'm going to part ways with him. I'm not looking forward to that at all. But life is too short to worry about things in the future at the cost of living in the moment. And this moment, right here, truly is what life is all about. I'm not about to waste a second of it. It'll probably turn out to be the best day of my life.

Returning to Cherryl's side, George had some things behind his back, something different in each hand. Extending his right arm, he said, "A flower to put in your hair in this hand."

"It's the prettiest flower I have ever seen."

"And in this hand, a snack."

"Thank you so much, I love mushrooms," said Cherryl, as she slid the delicate flower snugly behind her ear. "How do I look?"

"Like that flower was exclusively grown just for you."

Having walked hand-in-hand practically the rest of the way, the pair happened upon their destination. "Here we are. Behold," uttered George.

Cherryl was awestruck. The location opened her eyes as wide as they could go. Deep and clear, the pond was as blue as the sky, and surrounded on all sides by sandy beach. "I've never seen anything like this in all my life. I can definitely see why you would routinely make a 10-mile round trip to come here."

"No doubt. The pond is teaming with fish. You can see them quite easily. But therein lies the problem—they can see you just as easily, making them rather skittish. I suppose if a person wanted, they could heave in a net, and retrieve more fish than they could eat in a week. I prefer my trusty pole. To me, it's more of an artistic expression."

"I can understand that. Netting them is the quick and easy way, but not very sportsmanlike."

George walked to a large rock adjacent the pond and looked down into a crevice. "Excellent! Right where I left them. More hooks than I'll ever use in a decade. I'll keep a few and you can go ahead and take most of them."

"Thank you so much," announced Cherryl. "There are more here than I had envisioned, a couple hundred at least. Where did you get them all?"

"I knew a guy, a friend, that had actually made them. He generously sold them to me at cost."

"Does he still make them?"

"I think so. I haven't seen him in a while, though, mainly because he lives pretty far away."

"Are you sure there's enough there for you?"

"Oh, yes, plus the general store in town does get shipments in a few times a year. I'm sure I won't run out till then. You were just unlucky that someone had come in before you and bought them all up."

"I'd say I was lucky, in more ways than one," expressed Cherryl, grinning. "If there had been hooks there at the time, I would have never met you."

George blushed. "You're too kind. I'm glad they were out too. Shall we set up the tent and go fishing?"

"Sounds wonderful. Be that as it may, I'm going to give you something for the hooks when we get back."

"If you insist."

The pair spent the rest of the day together, enjoying each other's company to the utmost degree. They had a superb day fishing and ate for supper what they caught. They even spent a few hours of moonless darkness in each other's arms, telling ghost stories.

Cherryl lied in her sleeping bag for an hour, thinking, before falling asleep.

It's in the books, the best day of my life. I can't believe how fast the day went. It's too bad these moments must end. I feel so magnificent, spending time with such a compassionate and interesting person. It's as if I've been living in a dream. Oh, to ponder just how good my life could be, having someone to love romantically day-in and day-out. If only I didn't come from so far away, and from such a loving family at home, then I could just stay with him always. If only I had the courage to take a chance. I can't, though. I have too much at home, too many people who love me, too much of everything there. Alas, I admire the brave, those who boldly roll the bones.

In the morning, the two of them packed up and started the walk back,, during which her ruminations from the night before in the sleeping bag circled in her mind with chaotic indecision.

"Choose my story and learn what becomes of Cherryl and the rest of her friends," said Yusyta, as she stepped off the stage. "And learn what events transpire before George's eyes."

Approaching her chair in the gallery, using Cherryl's inner dialogue voice, Yusyta uttered, "Trust me, you'll want to know what happens to me."

Everyone clapped.

"I guess I was wrong," said Thyxer, "that was an hour-long story, twice as long as most stories from the past. Is yours that long too, Dave?"

"You shall see."

"Dramatic till the very end. I like that. A good contest indeed. The theater is yours, Dave."

Dave entered the realm of the stage, wearing prisoner's garb. He cleared his throat and began his story.

CHAPTER 19

ULFENKERKI'S MORNING was a normal one right up until lunch. He managed to cook his stew only halfway before his presence was requested in one of the tents. At least he'd remembered to take his stewpot off the flame before heading out, so it didn't turn into inedible charcoal, *again*.

Entering the tent to which he was summoned, Ulfenkerki gasped, and said, "I didn't expect to see you today, Fjord. You look wet and haggard."

"We've been doing much running and swamp trekking."

"Knowing you then, I suspect you have urgent news to contribute."

"That I do. We tried to get here as fast as we could to tell you a decent-sized army is on the way here to this very spot: eight-hundred strong, probably a couple platoons. They'll be here tomorrow or the next day."

"Did they have any war machines?" inquired the General.

"Yes, they did, but not any more than you have here. It's by no means a full army, but large enough to be daunting."

"I doubt you got close enough to see, but I must ask anyway: Did you happen to notice if General Gamald was present in the party?"

"I tried to get as close as possible to ascertain that. I know how important it is. However, I didn't see him, but I can't be a hundred percent positive."

"You did well, Fjord. Judging by your appearance, I'd say you've been through hell to get here as fast as you did. A day or two ahead of them is a pretty significant amount of hustle."

"Thank you, sir. We had a few close calls with quicksand, but that's another story, one I'm sure to tell you some other time."

"Right, we'll discuss the details later," voiced Ulfenkerki. "I'm deciding to stand and hold the base against this nemesis, so I've got plenty of things to organize now. Thanks again, Fjord, exemplary job as always."

"You're welcome."

"There's just one more thing I have to ask: Did you see any enemy scouts, the ones that probably killed our own scouts?"

"Yes, they were ahead of the army."

"I'm going to find a way to learn precisely what happened to my scouts, even asking the enemy personally on the battlefield, if it's the last thing I do!"

"I can see you doing that, General."

"You know me well, Fjord." The Black Bear exited the tent and began to spin the wheels of battle preparation.

Right away, he held council with the officers, instructing them what exactly he wanted done in the short amount of time before the battle would begin. Without ado, he also ordered scouts, ones other than Fjord and his company, who were obviously exhausted, to go and inconspicuously keep tabs on the Molisian battle force.

Ulfenkerki scrutinized the battle-prep developments, starting with visiting the crew fashioning the new catapults and checking on their progress. After learning one of the catapults was too far away from completion, he changed up the plan, re-assigning the builders to catapults that could be realistically finished by the time the Molisian force arrived.

He made a full lap around the base, inspecting for any possible weak spots in the wall he'd constructed. He also studied the pit in front of the wall for some time. Nice and muddy.

Another vital aspect of battle preparation that was double-checked was catapult placements. Of course, they had been working on this the whole time, but he wanted to make absolutely certain they were positioned as advantageously as possible. They had the high ground and Ulfenkerki knew it.

Every single physical and mental battle preparation Ulfenkerki could think of was put into action. It was a drill he executed many times before, and hopefully would carry out many times again, for an adept general stays alive.

Confident enough in the day's pre-battle routine, Ulfenkerki decided to wind down so he could stay calm, cool, and collected in order to fight the good fight. In doing so, he went for a stroll through the neighboring woods, a half hour walk being enough for his purpose.

Having gathered serenity from a face full of the four-corner winds, he returned to his bed and got a good night's sleep.

DAVE'S STORY BEGAN as thus:

> In both their mind's, childhood was an unforgettable, almost ethereal experience for Roger and Joey. Having a best friend in such a perilous time might very well have been the greatest of blessings. They went everywhere and did everything together. Roger was the taller and stronger of the two. Joey wasn't necessarily the smarter of the pair, but he was one of those types with an excellent memory, both short and long term.

> Roger and Joey, after school one day, decided to spend the money they had earned together raking leaves, on a meal at the town's restaurant. They were only 12 at the time, but everyone knew each

other in town, so it was common enough to see children doing adult things in town by themselves.

"I'm really glad we decided to come here, Roger. They have such good sandwiches."

"They certainly do, Joey. And they are so big. Do you know what kind you're going to order?"

"Not quite sure, they're all good," replied Joey. "I still can't believe how we came from behind to win the football game at recess."

"It was a pretty outstanding victory wasn't it! Your throwing arm looked good out there."

"Well, thank you. Usually, I'm more prone to *over*throwing."

"I'm just glad we were on the same team today," voiced Roger.

"Me too. After we're done here, do you want to practice a few football routes and throws at my house?"

"I was thinking the same thing!" Roger said, enthusiastically. "You beat me by a second, Joey."

The two best friends took their time eating their sandwiches, enjoying their *raking gitis*—which stands for *government issued trading items* in Garobansurov. The pair didn't necessarily feel guilty knowing they didn't have to rake too hard for the gits. But what youth knows much guilt?

They even had some money left over for dessert: ice cream.

When they were finished eating, they paid. Joey went into the bathroom and Roger went out the door.

Upon reaching the outdoors, Roger found himself enveloped by dilemma. A couple bullies rushed at him. Since they had seen Roger come out of a restaurant, the bullies thought he might have some money to filch.

One of the tormentors got behind Roger and held him while the other ravaged Roger's clothes' pockets for money. Because Roger had just spent all the money on the bill at the restaurant, he had none on him.

Finding no money to thieve, the ruffians got livid and started to physically hurt him. They weren't old enough to throw punches with much force, but the kicks to the shin really hurt.

Roger fell to the ground, but before the bullies could fully take advantage of Roger's predicament, Joey came flying out the door, wielding a steak knife he had taken off a restaurant table. He wasn't very intimidating without a steak knife due to his small stature, but with one he was a different story. He ran at the bullies, knife-tip pointed straight at the closest eye. It was enough to make the bullies run away.

Standing up, wiping the dust off, Roger said, "You came just in time. Who knows what they would've done to me!"

"We're lucky the restaurant has a big window, otherwise I wouldn't have seen the scuffle, and known to grab the knife on my way out."

"Good thing. I'm surprised nobody in the restaurant came out behind you. I doubt it's every day someone swipes a knife from a table and runs out the door!"

"Oh yeah, you're right. Nobody followed. I know a bunch saw me grab the knife, they were sitting right there."

"Well, screw them. Stupid, lazy people. I'll always remember what you did. You're a real friend, Joey. I owe you one." Roger put his arm around Joey's shoulders. "Let's go practice football."

"Good idea."

TIME WENT ON, and Joey and Roger remained best friends for the whole of their childhood, having made countless, priceless memories.

But nothing good ever seems to last. Things change. Due to their parent's monetary influence, they grew apart as soon as they reached adulthood. Roger came from a wealthy, prominent family, whereas Joey's was rather poor and insignificant. Wealth got passed down from generation to generation, social classes separated. It was the way of things.

Twenty years after the milestone restaurant incident, Roger was living in a decent-sized town a dozen miles away from the one in which he grew up. He'd received a substantial interest-free loan from his parents, using it to start a rock cutting business. He and his employees carved the stones used in buildings far and wide. Roger grew into being quite admired, just like his parents and grandparents before him, further evidence of money begetting money.

On the other end of the spectrum, Joey's destiny wasn't nearly as grand. He took over the family farm, which for some years lost money. On the average, though, it did generate enough for him to just get by. He spent his days feeding animals and toiling in the fields. Roger did offer him a job but he declined, so as to not see his father's treasured farm dissolve. He knew how much it meant to him, and since Joey's father lost the ability to walk, Joey had to take over.

Twelve long years went by, years which saw Roger and Joey sharing minimal interaction. It wasn't because they lived that far apart, but having more to do with Roger's mindset, his time was better spent socializing with the upper class, a paradigm for the continual purpose of making money. That was just how it worked. An ideology undeniably practiced world-over.

Joey made an effort a couple of times to travel to Roger's home. But upon doing so, he came to the realization Roger just didn't have the time for him. Consequently, these were the last times they spoke. Kind of sad, really.

Sitting in solitude next to a hill, Joey's home was in need of repair. He was working on it, but with all the other farm work needing to get done, the time he had available for home repairs was in short supply.

His mother and disabled father lived in a house just as dilapidated as his own across the field. It was a ten-minute walk there, one that he made for visitation almost every day, and one he was currently undertaking.

The trail to his parents next to the field was awfully grown over this time of year, so he pretty much had to stick to the small footpath within the main trail, the one he'd created by his many treks back and forth. Heightened balance was necessary for such an action.

Closing his parents' door behind him, Joey said, "Lovely day. I'm hoping to finish the east field, today."

Brian, Joey's father, replied, "That always was the rockiest, hardest-going field, I thought."

"Me too," agreed Joey. "Later tonight, I'm heading into town. I must pick up a few things, and maybe stop at the tavern. I haven't done the latter in a while. I figured I'd better, or the townsfolk will start thinking I'm ignoring them."

"Good thinking. I should do it too some time."

Joey and his parents talked for an hour over breakfast. A pleasant talk, like always.

Joey walked back through the tall plants and laboriously finished up in the east field.

And just like he told his father he would, Joey went into town, having arrived just before dark. It only took twenty minutes for him to grab what he needed.

On his way to carry out his semi-annual trip into the bar, unexpected things transpired for Joey. You could call it the epitome of being in the wrong place at the wrong time.

WHILE JOEY WAS buying his necessities, a trio of men were formulating desperate plans. You wouldn't think something as insignificant as beer money would behoove a man to acts of desperation. But the world was full of obscurity, and so the trio concocted.

The three shady characters stood in a back alley. One of them, Allen, said, "I still think the best way to get money is to rob the store."

"No," replied Fred, "none of us are very skilled with our knives. Robbing a store would leave too much opportunity for a hero to kill us as we're doing it."

I agree," commented Harry. "Our scheme of kidnapping someone for ransom is the only thing we can do fast enough to allow escape."

"Alright guys, I'm in," declared Allen.

"So, when we do this, it has to be fast. We'll be wearing masks, so nobody recognizes us. And while doing so, we can't lollygag about, or else someone is bound to think we're up to no good and arrest us. Masked folks always look suspicious."

Harry replied to Fred, "I concur. Remember, snatching a woman or child is our best bet. For two reasons—they'll be easier to grab and restrain, and they'll be worth more to someone, especially a child."

"I'm not doing this for chump change either. If we're doing this, it's going to be for the price of half a town," professed Allen.

"I agree," voiced Fred. "The ransom price is going to be astronomically high. They'll have to sell everything to pay it. It wouldn't be worth it otherwise."

"I'm ready when you guys are. If we happen to split up, let's not meet back up at the campsite, in case we're followed."

"Yes," noted Harry, "meet in the woods at that fork in the trail a few hundred yards from the site."

"Agreed," said Allen. "Follow my lead, let's go."

Having slipped on their masks, Allen, Fred, and Harry crept out from the shadows of the alley. They weren't technically brought up in that particular town, nor did they frequent it, but without the masks they very well may've been recognized. Some people just seemed to have the uncanny ability to remember the names and corresponding faces of practically everyone with whom they came in contact.

Allen took point, briskly walking down the main thoroughfare, Fred and Harry behind, nervously looking down at the ground the whole time. Allen examined the street and shops for a victim. It truly was a horrible, ill-conceived plan. There was nobody even close to being near enough to snatch. They walked the entire length of town and had to turn around and go back. Allen was starting to grow nervously impatient. He didn't care anymore, the first person he saw, he would grab.

Alas, he saw a target. The three of them picked up their pace, beelining straight to the only person they saw on the streets since leaving the ally.

"What? Hey! Who?"

He didn't remember being knocked out, but he knew he had been. Upon opening his eyes, Joey noticed he was tied to a wooden beam in an abandoned shed-type structure. He tried to wiggle free but the attempt was futile.

He scanned his surroundings, trying to make sense of what had happened to him. To the left next to a gaping hole in the wall was a firepit, still hot and smoking. The firepit had a few contoured logs around it for sitting. To the front was mainly just a wall peppered with small holes complemented by sun beams finding their way into the darkness.

Surprised he didn't notice it right away, to the right were three tents along the wall, which seemed possibly occupied. He couldn't tell for sure, as the flaps were closed.

Joey stared at the tents for a bit, and eventually noticed at least one was occupied. It moved a smidge. A few moments later, he saw another one twitch. He rationalized that the occupants' breathing was causing a vacuum and suctioning the tent walls. From his vantage point, the third tent was obscured by the second, so he couldn't see it very well. Joey assumed that since it was there, it too was inhabited.

Along with continuing to watch the tents move in synchronization with deep breathing, he surveyed the room for other minute subtleties.

It took half an hour of observation, but he realized it was morning by the fact it was getting incrementally brighter outside.

He tried again to squirm out of his bondage but stopped immediately when he noticed someone emerging from their tent. It was the leader of the group, Allen.

Allen confronted Joey. "Don't speak at all, otherwise, you'll get hurt. You've been kidnapped and will remain so until someone pays your ransom." Between sentences, Allen made sure the straps keeping Joey to the beam were still tight and secure. "If we see you trying to escape, we won't hesitate to knock you unconscious again."

Fred and Harry woke up and joined Allen by the fire. They stoked it in attempt to reform the flame that was all but out. After babying it with the smallest of tinder, finally, flames appeared.

Harry commented, "I think we'll have to take turns staying awake to watch him from here on out, now that he's conscious."

Fred replied, "Either that or knock him out again."

"If we have to, we have to," remarked Allen, "but I'd rather not risk killing him. A dead prisoner is of no value to us. Moreover, today, we have to write the ransom note."

"To whom are we going to deliver it?"

"I don't know yet. I'm still thinking about it. The price is going to be so high that the whole damn town will have to pay for it."

"Good thinking, Allen."

"I'll write it up after breakfast and deliver it myself."

Joey couldn't believe his ears. He was ruined. Nobody he currently knew well had a gigantic sum of money for something like this. The whole town certainly wasn't going to pool together to pay the ransom. Only making semi-annual trips to the tavern certainly hadn't boosted his popularity at all. His parents, even if they sold the entire farm, were still as poor as poor can be. Joey's heart sank deep into the pit of his stomach.

Time elapsed, and Allen managed to get ransom notes into the tavern. He'd written three of them. One he placed in the latrine; another he slid between some boards in the wall; and the third he put underneath someone's jacket lying about. He'd delivered all three of them in one swift, fluid motion, so he would not be noticed. He wanted to be long gone before any of the notes were found.

An hour after Allen became a vapor trail, the bartender moved the jacket to clean, and saw the note under it.

He read it to himself, then got the attention of everyone else in the bar and read it out loud. "To all the citizens of Veril: We have kidnapped an individual of your village for the means of ransom. His name is Joey and he's short. If you don't comply, we will start to do unthinkable things to him. Place 10,000 gitis by the big pine tree sitting in solitude in the field just east of here. If you do this in two days at noon, we will set him free. And we'd better not see anyone in the area of the pine."

"Who is Joey?" asked a bar patron.

"I know who he is," said the bartender. "He has a farm just outside town and comes to the bar maybe twice a year. He's a real nice guy, actually. That's too bad. All the people in town, combined, wouldn't have that kind of money."

"I know him. I'll inform his parents of this misfortune on my way past their house, later," said Jim, a family friend. "They certainly don't have that much money, that I know."

"A real shame. It sure is astonishing that someone got kidnapped here. This kind of thing usually doesn't happen," noted the bartender. "I think we should organize a posse and scour the area at the proper time the note mentioned. They have to be there, you'd think."

"That's right. We should," uttered Jim. "Nobody is going to have the money anyways. I'll run the posse idea past his parents when I go out there."

"Okay good. In the meantime, the rest of us should spread the word. The more people looking for suspicious activity the better."

Later that day, Jim brought the sad news to Joey's parents. They, of course, were distraught. They did like the posse idea, though, and gave it the go-ahead.

At first, Joey's parents thought maybe it was a different Joey, to which the note referred. But as time went on, they realized it was definitely him, because their son never stopped by, like he usually did daily.

NEWS OF THE KIDNAPPING spread far and wide. In particular, it reached a town a dozen miles away from the epicenter. And more notably, it reached a man who once knew Joey well.

Roger was strolling through the yard at his rock-cutting establishment when he first heard the news. Two of his employees were talking about it, as Roger listened in.

One employee voiced, "Yes, I can't believe it either, a kidnapping truly occurred. The victim's name is Joey. He had a farm just outside Veril."

"Was he a short man?" asked Roger.

"Yes, actually the ransom note mentioned that, I guess."

"Did you hear for how much the ransom was?"

"I have. It was 10,000 gitis."

"10,000! Are you sure?"

"Yes. It is a huge amount, that's for sure. I hear they're forming a posse to try and locate the villains the day of the tradeoff."

Roger was stunned. "I think I know this Joey. I'm going to travel to Veril to learn more."

"Godspeed, boss."

Roger informed the supervisors under his employment that he'd be gone for a few days. His supervisors were more than capable to run the business in his absence.

Immediately after the business side of things were taken care of, Roger started the walk to Veril using the quickest trail. He was pretty sure he could make the 12-mile walk by nightfall. Being in decent shape, he figured he'd run part of the way.

From his childhood, Roger remembered exactly where Joey's parents lived.

Having arrived to Veril just before nightfall like he was hoping, Roger went straight to Joey's parents' farmhouse.

Joey's dad was surprised to see Roger. "Welcome, Roger. I'm guessing you're here because you heard the tragic news."

"Yes. So, it's true, then? I wasn't a hundred percent positive it was indeed Joey who was kidnapped."

"I'm afraid so. Quite the unfortunate incidence we have here."

"And the ransom amount is 10,000 gitis?"

"Yes."

"That is no small amount of money. I'd pay the darn thing if it weren't so extreme. I just don't have that kind of money available. Maybe if I sold my entire business, I'd have that kind of money."

"That's alright, Roger, we wouldn't expect that of you," inserted Joey's mother.

Before continuing in the conversation, Roger took a few moments to think to himself. He realized he could actually afford the ransom, if he sold his business. But deep down inside, where his greed resided, he rationalized out a way not to. He just figured his old friend would end up being okay anyways. Roger was just as weak as the next man. He really loved that rock-cutting business of his.

He jumped back into the dialogue. "So, tell me more about this posse I've heard about."

"Ah, yes. They met up earlier today and are going to meet up again in the morning. I know they plan to search for these bandits at the designated time of exchange."

"I will join them and go to the morning meeting. It's the least I could do."

"Very good, Roger. I'd go too if I could walk. But, anyhow, very nice to see you again."

"You too, sir."

Roger left the farmhouse, weighed by emotion. He felt bad he couldn't help any more than what he was. Though, a part of him didn't think his friend would be harmed.

Having had a good night's sleep at the inn, Roger woke up and prepared himself for what would sure to be a long, demanding day. He did a little stretching and thought.

He left the inn and went next door to meet up at the bar with virtually every man from town between the ages of sixteen and fifty. The posse really seemed to be alive with ambition, all determined as could be to find the villains.

Presumably transpiring at noon, the posse's arrangement was to thoroughly scour the area by the pine tree in the eastern field. Surely, the kidnappers would be there to keep tabs on things. And they'd have to snatch the money at some point or other. Plus, it'd be in the kidnapping scoundrels best interest to know where all potential threats were at all times. They'd probably be watching from high ground somewhere.

The posse meeting ended, but before it did everyone was told to reconvene at the bar at 11:00 to discuss who was to look where. Ultimately around noon they'd set forth to the target area.

Roger had the utmost confidence the gang would be triumphant.

WHILE ROGER AND company were discussing their plans, Allen and company were discussing theirs, Joey still tied to the beam. "Our guest here needs some food. Why don't one of you get him some."

"I suppose."

"Today we need to be one step ahead of the townsfolk, who I'm sure will be looking for us," said Allen. "In order to achieve this, I've inspected the objective area and decided the best place to watch. They'll never expect a thing. Actually, only I will be keeping watch. There's only room for one. And you, Joey, had better hope they bring the money, because if they don't, you're going to get hurt."

WITHOUT A LACK of confidence or the ransom money, the posse started off on the mission. Teams of two methodically combed the area by the east field: near, far, left, right, high, and low. Roger searched with all his might. The day was as grueling as he'd imagined.

Just before nightfall, exhausted, Roger and his teammate sat on a funny-looking log and talked about their failure.

"I can't believe we didn't find them. We scrutinized every single speck of land that we could, still nothing."

"I can't believe it either," let out Roger.

"Now what's going to happen to him!"

BACK AT THE HIDEOUT, many miles from the east field, Allen told his partners about the day. "I watched the field all day long, seeing the townsfolk comb up and down the area the whole time. I couldn't leave until every single person was gone. Like I expected, they didn't have the money this first time around. Now things will get interesting."

"How did they all not see you?"

"The perfect hiding spot is how. I crawled inside a hollow log with a peephole. I capped the end that I crawled into to make it look like it wasn't hollow. At the end of the night, a couple of them even sat on the log I was in. Morons. They're going to pay for the treachery of forming a posse."

"So, what's the plan now?"

"Now, we take things up a notch by sending another note, one attached to a present." Allen grabbed a knife and turned menacingly to Joey. "I'll let you decide what that present is. Which would you rather lose, a hand, a foot or both your ears?"

Clutching the knife, Allen ominously approached Joey.

Joey became terrified. His heart raced uncontrollably. He froze.

"Answer me!" Allen demanded. "If you don't within the next thirty seconds, you're going to lose *all three!*"

Joey thought hard and made the best decision possible. Realizing farm work would be virtually impossible without a hand or foot, and that he could still hear with his earholes, he replied in a stutter, "Ears."

"Ears it is," said Allen, reaching towards Joey's left ear.

DAVE STEPPED OUT of the limelight and announced, "Choose my story, and learn what happens to Joey and his ears. And what happens to the lives of the townsfolk and of Roger."

"Another long, magnificent story indeed," commented Thyxer. "I think this has been the longest championship night in decades. I love it. Wonderful job, both of you."

"Now, for the moment of truth, *we decide the winner*," noted Syryx. "Dave needs *two* votes to win, *one* to tie, so this will be interesting."

Dirax directed Yusyta to one side of the underground amphitheater, Dave to the other and said, "Here it is, the moment we've all been waiting for. You can cut the tension with a knife. Those picking to hear the ending of Yusyta's story, about Cherryl and her friends, go stand by her; and those deciding to hear the end of Dave's story, concerning Joey and Roger, go stand by him. When I count to *three*, choose your winner. *One, two, three…*"

The crowd hesitated, staring curiously at each other for a while, before slowly moving towards their selected storyteller. Some smiled, some laughed, some said a few words, but every one of them loved the moment.

Finally, after they all were standing by either Dave or Yusyta, the winner was clear.

Thyxer shook the would-be winner's hand and spoke. "And the name that'll go on the plaque this time around is… First time winner and hailing from across the sea, Mr. Dave Ghrere!"

"Well, I'll be darned. What a game, what a game!" proclaimed Dave, truly ecstatic for the victory.

"And a narrow victory it was. Dave needed two and that's what he got," emitted Dirax.

"Well, I can't wait to hear the ending I chose, that much I know," said Syryx, excitedly. "Shall we separate?"

"Let's have at it."

Dave and those who chose his story went back through the corridor and to the sub-basement to wait out Yusyta's ending. Since she started first, she'd finish first. The hatch door was closed back up, to be sure there were no eavesdroppers.

Among Yusyta's listeners were Jason and Yori. Throughout his childhood, Jason had certainly heard his share of Dave's stories, so he chose Yusyta. And Yori couldn't help but feel something strangely familiar about Yusyta's story. She just couldn't fathom what that was, though.

Yusyta took the stage, and before she began her ending, she said, "Thank you all so much for choosing my story. It's one that's unquestionably close to my heart. Enjoy, I beg of you."

CHAPTER 20

GEORGE AND CHERRYL couldn't help but walk slowly back to town, they just didn't want the experience to end. They both knew it was only *inevitable* for Cherryl to return to her friends. Along the way, they made a point to stop and inspect every single beautiful thing they saw.

When they did arrive back into town, it turned out to be too late for Cherryl to walk back by her friends, an incident that wasn't so unfortunate, in fact they both sort of hoped it happened.

"I'm glad to be spending one last night with you, however in the morning,

I really must leave," Cherryl, forlorn, uttered.

"Then let's make the best of tonight," proclaimed George, solemnly.

"Sounds wonderful."

They lay together that night. Other than doing the obvious, they talked about the sort of things two halves of a whole would talk about if they knew it'd be the last time they'd see each other. Barely three hours were spent sleeping.

In the morning, they tried their hardest not to cry upon parting ways.

George cleared his throat. "I just want to let you know, Cherryl, there is nothing more in this world I would want more than for you to stay with me. I'm completely in love with you, and I always will be. I certainly understand why you must leave, though. But before you leave, just know that you will always be in my heart, a permanent fixture adhered to my soul."

"Leaving here, right now, is the hardest thing I have ever faced. I may be departing, but I'm leaving my heart behind with you. I love you always and forever." And with those words, Cherryl's attempt at holding back the tears failed. "I told you I was going to give you something for the hooks; here it is." Cherryl reached into her pouch of jewels and handed George the best one she had. "When you look at it, think of me."

George kindly took the jewel, wiped away her tears, and said, "Thank you. I will. Goodbye my dear, Cherryl. I love you."

As she walked away, George also lost the battle of withholding tears. Viscerally, he now knew one could surrender without love, but never ever love without *surrender*.

The walk back to the campsite to her friends felt like it took all day for Cherryl, but in reality, it probably only took her a couple hours.

Upon arriving, Cherryl was glad to see her friends and she greeted them. She also showed them the hooks. She told them all about the trip and of George. It was a hard story to tell—she almost resumed crying—but she managed.

That night, alone in her tent, Cherryl tried with all her might to sleep, knowing that if she fell asleep, the unbearable pain would be temporarily gone.

I feel horrible. Why does this have to be so hard? I know it's out of the question to stay with George, never to return home, but why does my decision feel so wrong? I know my friends will be heading back home soon, and if I don't go with them, I don't have the orienteering skills to get back home at a later date. Painfully, I must close this chapter of my life.

Compounded with the tiny bit of sleep Cherryl got the night before, her current sleepless state would make for quite the lethargic day on the morrow. She just couldn't sleep; her all-consuming thoughts spiraled around in her mind, like a helpless leaf trapped in a whirlwind.

The sun came up, as she continued to stare at the tent wall, thinking.

I know I will never fall in love again like this. I firmly believe love of the highest magnitude only happens once in a lifetime. How long can I hold onto the memories of our time together, see them vividly? Will it be long enough? Long enough for me to live a happy life? I think it all boils down to the answering of this last question. And the answer is: No, not long enough. There comes a time in everyone's life when they must do what their heart tells them, no matter the consequences. This is that time for me. I must stay. My heart compels me so.

Having changed her mind, Cherryl was a new person. All the heartache was instantly gone. She made the right decision, she knew this deep down inside. Her family would understand.

As soon as Vycki, Kera, and Mary were awake and out of their tents, Cherryl addressed them all: "My friends, I must tell you that I made the wrong decision yesterday. I changed my mind this morning. I will not be going back home with you when you decide to leave. I'm going back to George. On the bright side, however, until you go back, I can easily visit with you here, regularly. I understand that I basically will have to stay indefinitely. It's the choice I had to make."

Vycki responded, "I can understand that. I was in love once, and I remember exactly how powerful it was. You follow your heart. The good news is we will probably stay for another month, so the four of us can certainly enjoy that time together."

"That we can! Thank you so much for understanding."

"When will you be going back to tell him your good news then?" asked Kera.

"Probably after lunch, and I will probably run the whole way too."

"I can see you doing that," emitted Mary. "There can also be days when the three of us come visit you there."

"That would be wonderful. His house is plenty big enough to have you."

Joyfully, the quartet spent the morning together. Cherryl exhibited more and more happiness in her resolution, the test of time being the greatest of all tests.

Over lunch, she made plans with the rest to return to camp in a couple days.

Just like she'd intended, Cherryl left right after lunch, running, running *most of the way,* anyways.

George was home. Thankfully, she didn't have to search him out. She didn't know what she'd do if she had to wait any longer to tell him.

George nearly tripped over the floor mat in astonishment, as he opened the door. "Cherryl! I thought I'd never see you again!"

"I did too, *yesterday.* But, yesterday, I made the wrong decision. Lying practically sleepless in my tent, I determined by morning that I couldn't bear the thought of not having a lifetime worth of memories of you. My love for you is just too strong to walk away, letting all that I have of you disappear as the years slip past, like the plummeting sands of an hourglass."

"*Is it true? Could it be?* It seems too good to be. But here you are, standing right in front of me. May it be carved in stone that this moment be the greatest of moments."

"Let us carve it together. I love you. I chose you. I chose you." Cherryl burst into tears. "I chose you."

CHERRYL AND GEORGE got married and lived happily together for more than a decade. In that time, they made a lifetime worth of memories, just like Cherryl wanted. Not just any old memories, but the kind that were more powerful than life itself.

But sadly, there came a time when Cherryl no longer could remain there. It's not that she loved him any less, in fact her love for him only grew as time went on. She had to make the journey back to her family.

This story doesn't go into further why she had to leave, from where she acquired orienteering skills, or why George didn't go with her, but trust that the reason was just, and her heart was true.

George was devastated, but was left with the same powerful and everlasting memories Cherryl took with her.

So, the story ends, although it may seem so, not in tragedy, but in having supplied a window straight to the heart, a window as translucent as the author knew how to fashion.

"I hope you all enjoyed it," remarked Yusyta, after a slight breather.

"It really was quite the unexpected ending," commented Yori. "Very emotional. I can even see the emotion on your face."

"The story means a lot to me."

Yori noticed the Icytryxans who listened to the ending didn't exhibit as much surprise at the conclusion, as she experienced herself. But she didn't dwell too much on it. She did, however, consider deeply the meaning of the story well into the night. It touched her.

Jason spoke. "I loved it, Yusyta. Well delivered. Fantysy-Escape truly is the grandest of past-times."

"Thank you, Jason."

Yusyta and the rest of her party left the auditorium to go back to the sub-basement and the game table, so Dave could have his turn. Yusyta's party further discussed the story, while waiting at the table.

Dave and company went through the trap door and the tunnel to the stage area. Excited, Dave couldn't wait to tell the ending of his winning chronicle. He knew it was a doozy.

He lingered until everyone was settled in their chairs, then went on stage, half-smiled, and began:

> His head bled profusely, but Joey was relieved at least he didn't bleed out and die, and that his hearing wasn't greatly impaired. All things he didn't realize until after the shock had worn off.
>
> He could hear his captors plot, though he might have been better off not hearing.:

"I'm going to have to be a little more creative this time to deliver the new message and the present," remarked Allen.

"Did you have anything in mind?" asked his friend, Fred.

"I think so. I'll have to double check the situation first, before I put it into action."

"Are you doing it alone again?"

"Yes."

At first light, Allen walked to the edge of town and scoped things out from a reasonable distance. Confident in what he saw, he ventured further into town, making sure nobody saw him. He was pretty sure that he, being a new face in town, would be immediately apprehended.

Allen was right, for the townsfolk certainly were on high alert. On multiple occasions, new people to town had been detained and scrutinized aggressively. But having solid alibis and people to vouch for these newcomers, they were released. Allen didn't have anything of the sort. Plus, he knew if he were caught holding a box containing a pair of ears, he'd surely be doomed. As a precautionary measure, he kept the box and the note out of sight, behind his coat.

The evil he intended that day saw no barriers, for Allen successfully navigated to his destination, delivered the package and escaped out of town, unseen.

At almost exactly noon, someone discovered the package, and upon seeing what was inside, fainted. People saw the fainting and as what one would expect, rushed towards the lady on the ground to help.

Once it was determined she was okay, she told those who rushed to help the reason why she fainted. She pointed to the box she found under the bench.

In no time, everyone in town knew about the box and what the note inside said. By afternoon, most of the former posse, including Roger, had trickled into the tavern to discuss what'd transpired. An older, prominent gentleman announced, "They gave us four days this time to raise the money. But that isn't going to help. Nobody here has even close to that kind of money."

"I think," commented a young, well-liked man, "that if we form a posse again, Joey will definitely be killed. I have no idea what to do, though."

The bartender was the next to speak: "I agree. If we summon a posse again on the exchange day, he will be killed. But there is nothing else we can really do. I suggest we put all our efforts into the four days leading up the exchange day. Everyone in town, no matter the circumstances, should inspect as many locales as they can for the criminals. A landowner not showing full cooperation poses possible guilt. Resultantly, said landowner should be subjected to interrogation and trial."

Everyone at the meeting liked the bartender's idea, all agreeing to put it into action. If anyone not at the meeting hadn't seen eye-to-eye, they were out of luck.

Generally, Roger liked the plan. He liked how they all were going to search every possible location, no matter whose land it was. But he couldn't escape the overwhelming feeling that if the fugitives evaded the posse, they could evade anything. Putting it off since he entered the bar, Roger finally decided to stomach looking in the box at the ears. He knew it was going to be hard, but knew it needed to be done. He walked over to the bar and peered into the wooden box.

Seeing his childhood friend's bloody ears flooded his mind with emotion. He was hit like a hurricane by the sheer fright of the display. Incapacitating sorrow rushed at him, making him weak at the knees. Practically all his memories of Joey infiltrated his psyche. It was at this moment when Roger knew he had to be brave and take matters into his own hands.

Promptly, he left the bar on a mission.

In the forthcoming days, the villagers put their scheme into action, searching every single spot there was to search, sweeping through the region. They were confident they could ultimately check every locale there was to check, far and wide. In the timespan of four days a small village of people could really cover a lot of ground.

ALLEN, FRED, AND HARRY seemed stupid on the surface, however they—especially Allen—were adept at strategic planning. They knew very well how many people would be looking for them, so they planned accordingly. Given their rundown barn structure was in the middle of nowhere, more tactics were still required.

Allen and Fred sat by Joey, while it was Harry's turn for guard duty.

Patrol was broken down into three equal parts. As the best possible spot, guard duty took place on a hill near the barn in a tree just perfect for climbing and spying. From atop the tree, you could see plain as day in all directions. If anyone were approaching the barn, someone in the tree would see it. Plus, it would be hard for someone from a distance to spot a stationary person in the tree, since they were camouflaged so well by the limbs and leaves. It was the perfect lookout tower. There were also enough trees for cover the on-duty observer upon discerning an intruder could run back to the barn to report unseen.

Watching, Harry sat semi-comfortably on the limb. To help prevent butt-sores, the limb had been conveniently draped with an old but soft rug.

While Harry took his turn in the lookout tree, Fred and Allen passed the time guarding Joey by playing cards.

Sadly, the criminals had to do away with the firepit. If anyone were to see a firepit, they'd surely grow suspicious and search the barn more thoroughly than they would've if they hadn't seen one. Even the tents were taken down.

"Do you think, Allen, they'll have the money this time?"

"My estimation is there's only about a five percent chance they will."

"Not very high then," said Fred.

"Nope, it's not."

"If we do get the money, then what are we going to do?"

"It is a lot, so we pretty much can do whatever we want."

As soon as he finished his sentence, Allen looked up and saw Harry running to the barn from the tree-line.

Allen knew very well what was happening. Allen gave Fred a signal. The former quickly untied Joey, who was already gagged. Including his bondage straps, Joey was dragged to the thickest part of the forest behind the barn, a real easy place to hide. Fred, meanwhile, grabbed the chairs on which they'd been sitting, and the cards. The tents had previously been hidden under a mat of leaves in the forest.

Harry double-checked the area to make sure nothing was left out.

The pair of villagers Harry had spied came into the barn and searched. Since nothing really seemed out of place they didn't search very long. Having found nothing, they walked on, having not stepped a single foot in the thick part of the forest where the crooks were hiding Joey.

It was the first of three times Allen and company had to execute the routine in the four days leading up to the exchange day.

"Morons."

Exchange day rolled around, Joey hopeless and still in pain from getting his ears hacked off. He had barely said ten words since the incident, suffering utter fear of his captors. Joey did know that it was another exchange day, not that he held onto much hope. He felt any day could be his last. He began contemplating all his life's memories—remembrances of his parents, of his childhood memories with Roger, and of all the other beautiful people and highlights of his life. He closed his eyes and made sure he didn't miss a single one.

Allen crawled back into his log before the sun came up to see if the villagers actually came with the 10,000 gitis. Not the most fun thing in the world to spend a day in a log, but Allen's patience was tremendous.

Just like on the first exchange day, the villagers met up in the bar to discuss matters.

"I can't believe we found absolutely no signs of the kidnappers or Joey," proclaimed a villager.

"We tried, we really did," uttered another.

The same bartender as always, actually the owner of the place, said, "In my opinion, we are definitely doing the wise thing today by not forming another posse, though I am deeply saddened in our overall failure, as incomprehensible as it may be."

Everyone agreed with the bartender and sat silently in sorrow for a few minutes. It was the most soundless the bar had been in its long existence. In the silence, they could sense Joey's imminent death on the air.

One-by-one, they each started to stand in preparation to leave the bar in grief. But just before the place started to empty, a man with a smile entered the tavern, a man who had just ran a long way holding a satchel.

The man, Roger, reached into the satchel, pulled out what was inside, showed the villagers, and said, "It took a lot of grunt work, but I sold my entire business, and got the money to free Joey."

They were all stunned, to a man. The bartender came out from behind the bar. "I don't think I remember who exactly you are."

"I am someone from Joey's past who received an awakening by what transpired, someone for whom it took a great calamity to see he needed to do right."

"It's really all there?"

"Yes, 10, 000 gitis, all here."

"Call me curious, which company was yours that you just sold?" asked the bartender.

"The rock cutting business in the next town over."

"You did a noble thing, sir."

"Let's make haste and deliver the money to the tree," said Roger. "Maybe it would be best if a couple of you accompanied me in doing it."

"Sure, anything."

The bartender and a young, strong man went with Roger on the delivery.

No problems arose during the delivery. The money-filled satchel was propped up besides the tree, and the three of them walked back to town without looking back once.

Allen watched it all unfold, stunned the whole thing actually worked. He waited until nightfall though, to come out of the log. Upon looking in the satchel, he couldn't believe his eyes—*it really was all there.*

Allen sprinted back to his companions, who were even more surprised than he.

"We can practically buy an army with this, and never worry about getting caught."

"Let's not dilly-dally. We should get out of here as fast as possible," instructed Allen.

"Are we letting him go then?" asked Fred.

"We will stay true to our word and let him go. But not right away, so he can't rush back into town and blab where we are. We'll make him accompany us the first night. Then he can walk his way back. Furthermore, we'll be needing to run. It's imperative. I know you two are lazy, but you'll have to suck it up."

"We'll try."

The day after the exchange, Roger and the villager were growing restless. Half of town was anxiously waiting for Joey's appearance in the town square.

"I kind of expected," noted Roger to a few nearby, "Joey to be let go by this morning. But now that I think about it, I bet they toted him along as they fled last night, so he couldn't come tell us their whereabouts right away."

"Yeah, I'm hoping that's the case too," replied a villager. "It would be tragic as heck for them to go and kill him after all this."

"That it would," said Roger. "So, if they fled all night, maybe they did let him go this morning. This way, optimistically, he'd make it back here by this evening."

"Time will tell."

The crowd that had gathered at the square shrunk as the day wore on. Roger had faith he would see his friend soon. Never losing patience, his eyes remained fixed on the horizon. He passed the time by counting sparrows flying seemingly aimlessly through his field of vision.

"Hold on a second, that speck there is no sparrow," Roger blurted.

One man was still waiting with Roger in the town square at this late hour, the bar owner, who said, "And the speck is jogging rather briskly."

"It's him!" proclaimed Roger, nearly tripping over a stone in his excitement.

Joey jogged into town and immediately recognized Roger standing by the owner of the bar, whom he also knew. "It's good to see you, Roger. So, you've heard all about the episode here I take it?"

"Yes, news travels fast sometimes."

"I really am very pleased that you're here, Roger."

Joey turned to the bar owner. "I overheard from them they got their money. How was this possible? My parents, combined with every family member I have don't even come close to having those kind of funds."

"You're standing next to the reason why it was possible."

Joey turned back to Roger. "You! You didn't! How?"

"Well, my old friend, once I realized that hope was lost, and saw your ears in a box, I was driven by my heart to take action. Without delay, I went back home and hustled as much as I could, trying to procure buyers for my rock cutting business. I got lucky that a few were interested. I got the money just in time and hurried back here to deliver the money by the tree."

"I can't believe you did that. What graciousness. What selfless decency!"

"See, I told you I'd pay you back for that time long ago when you grabbed that knife from the restaurant, saving me from those bullies."

"Oh yeah, that you did. You said you owed me one, if I remember correctly. Well, what you did for me was much greater than what I did for you."

"You can equal out the difference by helping me make sure we don't become so distant again."

"Not a problem. Let's begin by scheming a way to get your money back."

"Agreed," said Roger, as he shook Joey's hand and hugged him. "But if I never get it back, I still won't have any regrets."

It was a lost cause, tracking down Allen, Fred, and Harry; they were long gone. Rumor has it they bought a ship and sailed far away to some exotic, uncharted island.

The story is not without a happy ending, however, for Roger and Joey together bought back his rock cutting business, thanks to the fortunate discovery of a rather large gold nugget they simultaneously found one day in a stream bed.

They ran the business together until they were too old to give a damn.

DAVE EXITED THE ARENA, cheerful to have delivered his ending with, what he thought, convincing poise. Everyone in the room expressed how much they loved the ending. They all then went back to join the others. There was still the formality left of finishing the gameboard.

When all the going-through of the motions was said and done, Thyxer proclaimed, "So ends this installment of Fantysy-Escape. It certainly was a good one, thanks in no small part to our supplementary players. The name *Dave Ghrere* will immediately become a permanent fixture on the winners' plaque. Now, we take a couple weeks off before starting the new season."

Syryx commented, "Yes, I concur. This was a fine game period. But, now, I must go to sleep. I can't recall a time when championship night lasted so long."

"Me neither. We were blessed with excellent, long-winded story tellers."

The party left the cleaning for the next day, and all went to bed, exhausted. They didn't get much sleep, but nobody really cared too much. Nobody got less sleep than Mick, though. He lied awake all night, his thoughts having had taken control.

Dave was lying in bed with his eyes open when Mick came into his room in the morning, and said, "After a dozen times of saying no, I now have said yes."

"Said yes to what?"

"Thanks to your story, I now know what needs to be done to convince the Icytryxans to aid Garobansurov in war."

"I'm glad you do, because I certainly have no idea."

"So, for starters, I'll preface by saying please don't feel you have an obligation to also say yes to my idea. It is dangerous. Jason and Yori can be involved, if they'd like too, but this is definitely a Mick and Dave type of an undertaking. It may even be too dangerous for us, which is why I've previously said no myself so many times, but I have concluded that it is the only way. Your story made me see it."

"I'm following you so far; go on."

"In actuality, a while ago, shortly after I said we need to do something of shock value to persuade the Icytryxans, I came up with this idea. But because of its sheer ludicrousness, I kept saying no, having kept the idea to myself. But, then, I heard the part in your story that described the inner battle Roger was going through about Joey's capture, and how it took something as startling as seeing Joey's ears in a box for him to realize just how much danger his friend really was in. My proposal is that we show these foreigners *the ears in a box.*"

"You really have my attention now," said Dave, as he sprung out of bed, having no idea what Mick's next words could possibly be.

Seeing the intrigue and wonderment in his friend's eyes, Mick continued, "I suggest we perform the grandest, most ambitious battle scenario yet. It entails you and I going up against an entire atlytl platoon, while they fire the *blunt but imminently fatal projectiles* at us. If we perchance prevail in the end, they will see the figurative *ears in a box.* And realize that even though their army is powerful, even the most powerful of armies can be vulnerable. They will see that the mere strategy of two can be enough to defeat a much larger force."

"Yes, yes." Dave gained a twinkle in his eye. "They will realize the fact that they may truly be exposed. Their fear will drive them to start seeing things from our point of view. I like it. I like it indeed. I can see the correlation between your idea and my story."

"So, is that a yes?"

"For sure. You're right, it is the only way. I'm in. It is definitely very dangerous. Just looking at those projectiles manifests fright. But I think we can do it. It won't be easy to take on an entire atlytl squad, but I do believe it can be done."

"I do believe it, too. They've shown us their weaknesses in the battle scenarios. I'm confident."

"I remember Jason saying he couldn't imagine anyone ever being fired upon by the projectiles, so I really don't think he'll join us. But we'll ask him and Yori anyways. Even though Yori isn't as battle hardened as the three of us, she definitely deserves the opportunity to participate."

"I agree," said Mick. "When should we do this do you think?"

"I'd say the sooner the better. Every hour wasted hastens Rowlangiv's defeat. He needs us fast, all of us."

"Tomorrow then, we'll begin. Let's go inform Jason, Yori, and our hosts of our devices."

"Hopefully, they don't fear for our lives too much." Dave curled his lip and raised his brow.

"Hopefully, we don't either." Mick curled his lip and raised his brow, slightly more pronounced.

Mick and Dave urged everyone in the house to assemble and told them their plan—the long version. They also asked Jason and Yori if they wanted to participate.

Jason replied to the offer, "Thank you for inviting me, but I've seen those dangerous projectiles, and they were surely a sight to behold. You guys are crazy. I'd like to try and convince you not to do this, but I know it wouldn't work. Nevertheless, I must decline. Hawk and Leopard, the two of you certainly are built from different stock."

Yori took a deep breath and spoke. "I agree. Different stock indeed. I wouldn't know where to begin in such an endeavor. Although I appreciate the offer, I must also decline. But I will say it is a good idea. It may very well be the only way. Good luck you guys, you're going to need it."

"The idea is courageous," noted Thyxer, "I must admit. I'm glad to not be taking part. There is a reason those projectiles have never been used for the purpose for which they were intended. Do you really think you can win, though? It is quite the monumental task you embark."

"The odds are against us," said Mick, "but I believe with the right strategy we can prevail."

I hope you don't get yourselves killed," added Syryx. "I've grown quite attached to you two. Still, I can definitely see how showing the army the proverbial *ears in a box* may result in them finally seeing eye-to-eye with you Garobansurovians. This will be an epic event, and no matter what, it will be remembered for ages."

"Tomorrow, we will begin. Today, we will lay down all the specifics for the army," voiced Mick. "They can all then decide who wants to participate, and who doesn't."

"Will there be a limit as to how many soldiers will be allowed to join?" Syryx asked.

"I think we'll cut it off at one full Icytryxan platoon."

"Wow, really! That many!" cried Syryx. "One hundred and twenty atlytl wielding warriors, eh?"

"Yup," replied Dave. "We've faced that many before and came out victorious."

"Insane."

Later, Mick and Dave amassed the army—*the entire army*—at the main launch field. It was imperative that they all knew what was about to happen.

With composure, the pair delivered the schematics for their ultimate battle scenario to the gathered crowd.

Just like Mick and Dave hoped, virtually all of them couldn't believe their ears. The Icytryxans thought it was a suicide mission. Everyone in the army knew about the blunt projectiles and knew full-too-well why they were never used.

It didn't take long for a full platoon to volunteer for the scenario. It was a rather exciting occurrence they all thought. Nothing of the sort had ever been attempted.

In the end, the soldiers all left the assembly touched by wonder.

Meanwhile, Yori had also been pondering one of the Fantysy-Escape championship stories. She didn't realize it at first, but eventually she felt something strangely familiar about Yusyta's story. After army training that day, she had to make a stop at her friend's house, the same one she stopped at a time ago. There was something she had to know. Her friend may have been a link of sorts.

After Yori parted ways, Thyxer said to the rest of the crew walking home, "I think your address went well Dave and Mick. A lot of the soldiers I talked to about it told me that if by some miracle you guys are triumphant, they will be very impressed, as will I. It is definitely a daring thing you're about to attempt."

"I hope we get a good night's sleep tonight for it, that's what I'm wishing," proclaimed Mick.

Mick and Dave ate supper quickly. They needed all the time they could get to discuss the strategies they wanted to implement.

Sitting in Mick's room, Dave said to Mick, "One thing I feel is vital is what shields we use. We're going to have to deflect a massive amount of weight, so we'll require something both strong and lightweight—lightweight enough so our arms don't get tired, strong enough that nothing gets through."

"Yes. I was also thinking about that. The wood should also be split-resistant. Perhaps poplar, reinforced with a metal band."

"Good idea. Moreover, we could cover the face with animal hide for a little added muscle."

"We'll have to add the hide ourselves. I'm pretty sure we can find poplar shields in the armory, but probably none with both hide coverings and metal band reinforcements."

"That shouldn't be a problem," voiced Dave. "There are plenty of hides here."

"Here's the tricky part of it all, though: We'll need to find a way to split up the hundred and twenty at some point," noted Mick. "There'll be no way we can take on that many head on."

"What if we held the battle scenario at a river setting? This way at some point we can pretend our makeshift raft sank, and we with it. Then, they'd split up in their attempt to try and find us."

"That's brilliant, Dave. It will also add to the spectacle of the event. Projectiles splashing down with report everywhere in the water will be quite the sight for onlookers. Plus, any projectiles fired will be lost to the river, since they can't simply go retrieve them if they're running low mid-battle."

"Definitely. We can also use riverside thicket as cover."

"I agree. I have no intention of going swing for swing with them at long range."

"Yes. The more avoidance of that, the better."

Dave paced around the room, scratched his chin, and said, "Another key aspect for victory will be our melee weapons. Of course, we can't use our obviously deadly *black needle swords*, so we'll need something else."

"Nobody will be able to use metal swords, and similar metallic weapons. To get the opposers to concede fast, we'll no doubt need a powerful, yet still appropriate, weapon."

Dave emitted, "I don't think anybody likes to get hit in the face with a bone."

"Oh, for sure," agreed Mick. "If we go with bone instead of wood, we won't have to worry about the bone getting broken in half by a less sturdy wooden weapon."

"They could use a very hard wood like ash, maple, or hickory to utilize as a club of sorts, but if they do that, I think our bone weapons will be superior, due to the fact they can be swung faster."

"Right, and also our shields will be able to deflect the blunt force of a heavy club."

"The other day, I think I saw some bone weapons stacked in the magazine," commented Dave.

"We'll check it out, since we need to go there anyways tonight to get the shields. We'll also need to cover the shields with hide, tonight yet."

"I'm ready when you are."

The pair jogged back to the army training grounds, directly to the armory. Ironically, they were at the training grounds only a few hours previous.

They were glad to find exactly for what they were looking. It was a good thing they came when they did, there weren't too many bone weapons from which to choose. Any later and someone from the opposing team may have grabbed them. The poplar shields with metal reinforcing bands weren't very plentiful either, but at least there were more than two. And just like they expected, none of them came pre-adhered with a hide shell.

Having gotten what they needed, Mick and Dave hurried back to the house to start fixing the hides to the shields. They worked as fast as they could, so they could get to bed early enough for a good night's sleep.

They executed the shield work, further conferred strategy, and went to bed an hour earlier than they normally did—apprehensive, but confident.

Chapter 21

ULFENKERKI GOT NEWS from his scouts that the Molisian army was very near. He just wasn't sure if they were going to attack the base that night or the next day. Considering this, he only allowed half the army to sleep at a time. Five hours of sleep for each would have to suffice. He didn't want to get caught with his pants down.

Ulfenkerki and Gregg Hogarty stood watch at the wall. They couldn't necessarily stand on top of the wall, where they'd be sitting ducks by enemy arrow shot. Plus, standing on top would present unstable footing. They stood partly up the wall, the part with the best peering holes.

Ulfenkerki perked up. "Well, I can see their torch fires now, just over that hill."

Gregg replied, "Good, at least we know where exactly they are now."

Ulfenkerki informed a couple others what he saw, telling them to relay the information to the officers.

The General returned to Gregg, and said, "There's no real need to hurry, they're still a long way off. But it's certainly time to be attentive."

"You should go get a few hours of sleep, sir. I can come get you when they're much closer."

"Thanks, Gregg, but I wouldn't be able to sleep anyway. This will more than likely be an all-nighter."

"Same for me unfortunately. Partly because I can't help but think about the intensity of the Battle of Sarwa. It's resonating in my mind."

"Yeah, that was quite the bloody fight. This won't be quite like that. We have many advantages that will keep our losses slim, unless something unforeseen happens, I suppose."

"True. Unanticipated developments are always a possibility in war."

"I plan on fighting alongside you, Gregg, desiring to take benefit of your knife throwing prowess. I'd be dumb not to."

"Be my guest, sir. I'm glad to be of service."

"With how many knives are you planning to go to combat?"

"I made a knife-belt, which will hold a dozen. I can probably fit seven or eight more in my pockets, so about twenty in total. Would you like to see?"

"Why not? I have nothing else going on currently," joked the General.

Gregg went to his bunk and grabbed his knife belt. He made like a boomerang and returned to the General. "My favorite twelve are in the belt. I left the lesser quality ones behind."

General Ulfenkerki took hold of the knife belt, slid a couple of the knives out, and examined their features. "These are some pretty respectable weapons. Where did you pick them up?"

"About a third I've had for many years, and the other two-thirds I've bought since I started realizing my proficiency."

"If you lose any in battle, tell me, and I'll make sure the army procures new ones for you."

"Thank you. Hopefully, most of the knives I throw drop their targets, and I can just retrieve them from the bodies in the end."

"A little optimism never hurts," proclaimed Ulfenkerki.

Gregg and Ulfenkerki further discussed the upcoming battle. Gregg practiced a little on his knife throwing as they talked.

Throughout the night, the Molisian contingent inched towards what they still thought was their arms manufacturing facility.

Ulfenkerki never kept them out of his sight.

NOT KNOWING THEIR compatriots across the sea were about to skirmish, Mick and Dave woke up, also about to go to battle. It was an important day all around for the sake of Garobansurov and its King.

Hawk and Leopard had slept as soundly and as long as they wanted to, which was irrefutably much more sleep than what Ulfenkerki and Gregg were able to put together.

Dave and Mick made sure to cook a large breakfast. While they cooked, they organized some snacks for their encounter. They were fairly certain there wasn't going to be any time to settle in for a full-sized meal on the battlefield.

Post-breakfast, Mick and Dave double-checked that everything they'd need for the battle scenario was set and ready.

Everyone who wasn't going to army training sincerely wished Mick and Dave luck, and for them to stay alive.

Mick and Dave shouldered their battle gear, met up with everyone going to army training, and headed out the door.

The party started the walk, but Mick turned around to run back inside and yelled, "I thought of something that may come in handy for us today."

Down the road, Mick caught back up, brandishing a ball of string. "Now this is useful for so many a thing."

"That it is," returned Dave.

Having arrived at the training grounds, Mick said to Dave, "Remember: Protect the head and the heart first. The rest heals quicker."

"And it hurts more."

The platoon Mick and Dave were about to face were waiting fully dressed in their combat attire in the main atlytl launching field along with a whole slew of anxious spectators.

Mick addressed the gathered crowd: "We will hold the battle scenario at a site on the Worod River, a mile to the east, and begin in an hour. When we have all arrived there, I'll talk further as to the specifics. Grab everything you'll need now. I doubt you'll want to come back and get it after we've begun."

Some of the spectators were disappointed the event was taking place a mile away. A small fraction decided to abandon, but most of the audience would've traveled even further to witness such a once-in-a-lifetime display.

Half an hour after the departure, Mick, Dave, and the opposing platoon arrived at the river, including the cart holding all the projectiles. The spectators had walked slower, but Mick didn't wait for them to explain in detail the outline of the battle ordeal.

Addressing the soldiers, Mick said, "There's only one way to win: Get every member of the opposing team to submit. Submission can be done either vocally or by virtue of unconsciousness. You can get as creative as you'd like, but remember: nobody here wants to die today. Nevertheless, Dave and I are completely aware of the danger involved with the projectiles, so don't hold back. We are fully prepared for what is to come. We aren't implementing a time limit, so keep that in mind as daylight wanes. As is optimal, we will begin on different parts of the river. We'll let you choose on which end you want to begin. But it's quite obvious on which side you'll hold the advantage. You'll see what I mean when you go down to the river. When you submit please exit the arena.

And stay honest. Not that we must worry about that with *you*. I'm sure you're aware, but *no metal weapons*, other than your atlytls and the projectiles. Lastly, are there any questions?"

One of the Icytryxans in the front asked, "Are we allowed to reuse our projectiles, once we've launched them?"

"Yes, whichever ones you're able to salvage without getting submitted, you can reuse." Mick scanned the audience for additional queries. Silence. "So, if there are no further questions, let's begin."

The Icytryxan platoon, just like Mick and Dave expected, chose the side with a long, sweeping curve to the right, accented by a steep embankment on the outside of the bend. From the top of the embankment the Icytryxans would be able to advantageously launch their projectiles further. Mick and Dave's starting side was just a straight stretch of the river with normal banks. The starting points were about three thousand feet apart. The river where Mick and Dave would begin was roughly two hundred and fifty feet across. Whereas, because of the sweeping bend, the part of the river where the Icytryxans would begin was wider: four hundred feet across at the apex of the curve.

Each team took their position and the competition began.

Mick took a deep breath and said to Dave before entering combat mode, "Once again, we face unimaginable odds."

"Seems to be our thing."

"The good news at the onset is that we can practically see the whole platoon from our position—their silhouettes at least. And I doubt they can see us. That's our advantage."

"Yes," commented Dave. "So, in essence to win, we must make them come to us, splitting them up in the process."

"We won't be able to use the darkness much to our benefit, I don't think, since I'm sure they'll realize the darkness greatly aids us. To this, they'll adapt."

"Let's just hope they don't realize it then," replied Dave, with a chuckle. "They won't expect us to construct a watercraft to cover some of the distance. When we do our false sinking routine, we should pretend to go across the river. This way, when they come look for us, they'll think they'll have to cross the river too."

"Excellent thinking," asserted Mick. "It'll split them up considerably."

"As is our plan, they probably won't even think to look for us being buried in muck when they do begin the crossing."

"Right. We can attack when many of them are vulnerably in the water. Those who will have gone across the river will be unable to assist immediately."

"I don't see much with which to construct a boat, but I think we'll manage."

"I guess searching for materials will be the first thing we do."

With some effort, Dave and Mick began scrounging up a bunch of wood for the assembly of a crude raft. While doing so, they also made sure to keep tabs on the enemy platoon.

After working for a couple hours, they finished their watercraft. Despite its dilapidated appearance, it held weight and floated. It had a wall in the front and a roof, enough protection to deflect a large portion of the sure-to-come projectiles.

"Good thing you grabbed that string this morning, Mick. It really came in handy with the boat."

"There's enough left over for traps, too."

"Luckily, we aren't going on a day float with this thing. I don't think it'd survive that long."

"If we'd constructed it any sturdier," declared Mick, "we may have found it rather difficult to intentionally sink when we needed to."

"Right. Now we'll just have to cut the string straps to sink it. When we do sink it, I'm just hoping we can make it across underwater unnoticed. I'm not very good at swimming underwater."

"True. You're not. Before we begin, let's go downstream, undercover, and find the best place to beach ourselves after this future underwater swim."

"Right. We don't need them spotting us at that juncture, certainly not after all we will have gone through."

Subsequent the search, they returned to the boat, hopped on, and pushed themselves away from shore.

"Now," said Mick with a look of pure focus, "things will get interesting."

"I'm curious to see as to when they'll start firing. I wonder if they'll waste a bunch of projectiles by starting too early."

"We will know soon, I'm sure."

They nervously floated to the middle of the river, and rode the current downstream, making sure to keep the walled side in the front.

Having floated roughly eight hundred feet, Mick announced emphatically, "Shields up! I can see they started the release."

Mick and Dave held their shields up near their face, an action serving as backup protection to what the boat itself would provide.

"Here they come! The projectiles are within view."

"I'd say about fifty count on this initial wave," returned Dave.

"Damn is this nerve-wracking or what, my friend?"

"For sure. First one hit the water, way ahead of us," proclaimed Dave, peering vigilantly around his shield and the boat's frontal wall.

All the initial airborne projectiles ended up striking the water anterior the boat. In light of this, Mick voiced, "I guess they chose to waste a bunch. They aren't getting those back."

"Right. You know darn well they only did that to heighten tension."

"Indeed. They're perfectly aware of exactly how far they can launch."

Dave added, "Now at least we know where on the water we'll start facing the projectiles."

"Good thing they're not using Thorncat Missiles, otherwise, they'd be hitting us already."

"Oh, for sure."

Just before their watercraft reached the spot on the water where the atlytl projectiles could reach, Dave said, "We're almost there, are you ready?"

"About as ready as I'll ever be," replied Mick, picking back up his shield. "They all fired. Here they come."

"They're launching repeatedly. This will be interest—"

As Dave trailed off his sentence, the metal projectiles commenced hitting the water right in front of them.

Shortly, the pair began to hear the rhythmic thumping sound of metallic shots striking wood. The bombardment was relentless as the boat began to get torn to shreds. The whole time Mick and Dave held their shields in front of their faces and kept the boat facing forward. Results would've been devastating had the boat spun around.

Deadly projectiles crashed into their shields. Mick even had one brush alongside his leg.

Onlookers, of which there were now plenty, saw this part of the river as looking no differently than that of a rainfall, one with big, ominous raindrops.

It wasn't until two minutes into the onslaught that blood was drawn—not a serious injury, but an injury, nonetheless.

Water plumes were rising into the air all around Mick and Dave's boat—it was just about artistic.

Subsequent five minutes' worth of vicious assault from above, Mick uttered, "Almost time to dump this thing. Let's start acting frantic, so they think something bad is happening to us."

"Okay," replied Dave, preparing to flail around and rock the boat. Their acting wasn't pretty, but it was sufficient.

"I think that's far enough. Time to get wet, Dave."

"Here we go. *Goodbye boat.* Nice knowing ya."

In one fluid motion, Mick and Dave sank the boat, took deep breaths and disappeared underwater, weapons and shields still in hand.

They swam underwater as well as they could, shots hitting the water all around them.

Once they got away from where the vessel went down, the projectiles stopped hitting the water near them, which was a tell-tale sign the Icytryxans had no idea where they were.

Luck was on Hawk and Leopard's side during the opening stage, for they surfaced right where they'd wanted—under a tangling of various overhanging bush branches. It was the exact spot they'd pre-scoped.

"Let's bury ourselves here," Dave proclaimed. "When they come look for us, they won't dawdle in this rough terrain. It's human nature to not spend much time in places flourishing arduous passage."

"I agree. Plus, the ground next to the river here is soft and relatively easy to dig."

"But not too damp that the hole will fill in with water as we're lying in it."

Mick found a couple sturdy branches nearby. "Here you go, Leopard. This should work better for digging than your hands."

"Thanks. I see they completely stopped launching into the river. Although, from this vantage point, I can't see if they're all still in the same place yet."

"When I was looking for these branch shovels, I could see them a hair. They all still looked fully together. I'll look one more time, right before we conceal ourselves in this hole."

It took ten minutes and the dirtying of hands for them to dig a pit, one roomy enough in which to squeeze.

Like he'd previously promised, Mick went to spy the platoon before climbing in the hole. He confirmed the best he could they were still all bunched together and not on the move.

Before lowering themselves into the hole, Mick and Dave gathered a spray of branches with which to camouflage their hiding place. They even found a couple dead bushes to set atop. It took some pretty graceful movements, but they were able to get much of the dirt back over themselves while in the hole, along with setting the branches and bushes on top.

Here, they patiently waited for the right time to strike.

A HANDFUL OF HOURS before sunrise, Ulfenkerki assumed the Molisian army stopped to sleep before beginning their attack, so he decided to sleep a little himself, too. Three hours was enough for him to be efficiently rejuvenated for war. The rest of his army, besides Gregg, fortunately got more.

At about the same time Mick and Dave were digging their hole, the Molisians began to get into attack position. Causing death was their objective.

Sipping on his coffee and watching on, Ulfenkerki witnessed his adversaries' state of aggression. The wily General scratched his chin confidently.

Wielding a variation of his usual flag system, he ordered the flag wavers to signal for the catapult operators to get ready to fire.

Like he promised, Gregg started the battle at his commander's side. "I hope you don't spill that when the shots start coming in."

"No loss. It's not that good of coffee to begin with."

The General peered out his spyhole and watched as the Molisian war machines crept closer and closer to the imaginary line signifying time to fire. He knew he'd be able to fire first because of his highground catapult placement.

Once proper time was upon him, he ordered the flag wavers to signal for the catapults to begin launch.

Impressively, a few short moments later, Ulfenkerki's six working catapults began firing, all aimed at the Molisian catapults getting closer and closer to their own point of launch.

The Molisians were caught completely off-guard by the unexpected catapult fire, but they held their composure and kept their lines.

"They're about to unleash their catapults now too, General, sir," yelled a soldier.

"Time to duck and cover," Ulfenkerki said to Gregg.

Gregg and the General took refuge from the aerial assault, leaning beside the part of the wall conveniently situated next to a giant beech tree. The tree canopy wouldn't protect them from catapult fire like the wall would, but it would help later on shielding them from errant arrows. Further down the wall, a couple other officers had trees for cover and spyholes as well.

The first load hit inside the base, landing in the dirt. Seeing it hit, Ulfenkerki became fully engulfed by his intrinsic battle mode. It made him more aware and adrenalized.

When the Molisians were within range General Ulfenkerki initiated his archers. Shortly after, return arrows blurred past.

Ulfenkerki and Gregg utilized bows as well, but they weren't as powerful as the ones of the official archer squad.

Gregg reached up into the tree, un-lodged what his hand discovered, and commented, "Look what we have here. An arrow found our beech."

"Better it than our faces."

Gregg chuckled. "Let me know when we should start throwing our rocks."

"Our pile isn't too big, so I planned on waiting until we can actually physically see them coming over, under or through the wall. Some of the others have much bigger rocks they can drop down the wall when the assaulters are stumbling around in the pit.

"From what I can see, our scouts performed a correct estimation of the opposing numbers. They outnumber us by a few hundred, but we have other obvious advantages." The Black Bear was just then jolted by optimal observation. "We just took out one of their catapults!"

"Add that to our list of advantages!" returned Gregg.

"In comparison, all I've seen them wipe out of ours so far with their catapult fire is one of our tent barracks and they managed to put a hole through a building. All minor damage."

"I saw a couple of our soldiers get stuck with arrows," vocalized Gregg, "but didn't look like lethal punctures to me."

"Good, good. I haven't seen any battering equipment, yet. I have no idea how they think they're getting through this wall."

"They probably didn't expect there to be a wall here."

Ulfenkerki stretched his back and said, "I know if I were them, Gregg, I'd know how I'd try to get around it. With rope long enough and strong enough. They could tie them to the wall and pull."

"If they try to do that, I guess we could continually cut their ropes."

"We may have to. Time will tell exactly what they intend to do. They're getting near now. The weak bows you and I have will probably reach now. Let's start volleying our arrows."

"Sounds good."

Gregg and the General shot their arrows as fast as they could over the wall, not really knowing where they landed. Nevertheless, in their minds they were hitting their mark. They wanted to use up most of the seventy-five arrows they possessed, before the Molisians got to the pit, saving a few arrows just in case.

Once the enemy got to the pit before the wall, the battle would undoubtedly grow in pandemonium.

IT TOOK A LOT longer than Mick and Dave had hoped for the Icytryxans to come searching for them. The waiting was uncomfortable. Lying practically motionless in a hole wasn't ever really on the top of their list of most enjoyable activities.

They would soon find out if their patience would pay off.

Being in a hole, they couldn't see their surroundings too well, but they could tell there were at least a dozen soldiers in their area by sound. The plan was to wait until a good number of them went across the river before springing out from their hidey hole.

There was a lot of land to search before crossing the river, but to Mick and Dave's delight, the Icytryxans did finally decide to go across.

Not wanting to lose the safety provided by numbers, about forty went across at once. Initially, they directed themselves to where the makeshift boat went down.

When the force reached the banks on the other side of the river, Mick whispered to Dave, "I haven't heard anyone near us in a while, have you?"

"No, I haven't."

"Then, I believe now is the time to strike."

Ecstatic to finally stretch their stiff muscles, Mick and Dave emerged from the hole.

Dave said, "Remember, it's possible, although unlikely they'll see us before we see them, so keep the shields up. They can fire the atlytls at close range too."

"That they can. One advantageous thing about being in the hole for so long is that we are that much closer to nightfall."

"Indeed. It'll be dusk in roughly three hours. This is to our benefit."

"Affirmative. We must also try and keep hushed those we're forcing into submission. The longer the soldiers on the other side of the river are oblivious to our whereabouts, the better," added Mick.

"Exactly. Along with whatever soldiers remained at the starting position. I'd rather not have them all rallying together to start shooting at us again, at least not so soon, anyways."

"Me too."

Having switched into stealth mode, Ghrere and Thraiker worked their way along the riverbank. They kept in cover, making sure not to step on any twigs. Twig-crunching: rookie mistake.

They could hear their adversaries across the river making all kinds of mistakes.

Dave walked point and saw movement fifty feet ahead in the thicket. He quickly got behind a tree, Mick following suit. Dave held up three fingers for Mick behind the next tree over. Hand signals were a trick of the trade for the adept. They planned to wait until the three—three fingers for three adversaries—were practically on top of them to pounce.

Waiting closest to the threat, Dave could hear the enemy breathing. He tightened the grip on his bone club.

As soon as the first Icytryxan was within range, in a flash, Dave jumped out and knocked out cold the adversary with a swift swing. Mick followed and was able to put a chokehold on the second soldier for another easy submission.

Witnessing how fast Mick and Dave laid out the two before him, the remaining Icytryxan, seeing Dave's weapon coiled and ready to strike, decided instead of getting hit in the face he'd select the easy-way-out option. He threw his hands in the air signaling his time was done.

"Three down, a hundred and seventeen to go."

"Hopefully, they're all that easy," replied Mick.

Ironically, the next few groups actually were that easy. In no time, Mick and Dave had disposed of a dozen of the platoon—one tenth of the opposition. The pair realized they were getting the hang of their weapons, coming to the decision they picked the right ones. Maybe if they were to get blindsided by one of the heavier weapons, they'd think differently, but they had no real intention of letting that happen.

"If they were more organized, they could've had a system in play, strategically notifying each other when teammates have gone missing," noted Mick. "If they did, they'd realize by now where we were."

"True. Hopefully, we can knock off another couple dozen, before the group across the river realizes we aren't over there."

"I'm actually counting on wiping them out, before they are even able to come back across the river."

"Never hurts to be optimistic," whispered Dave, stepping over a mossy log in his way.

"In the perfect world, we can submit them in the dark, and avoid being fired upon by them."

"That would be ideal, wouldn't it?"

Realizing the thick cover was starting to turn thinner, they slowed the pace and summoned more caution.

"We have a big group up ahead." Dave asked, "Do you think we can take all ten?"

"Not without some prudent planning."

Mick and Dave waited for as long as possible to attack, anticipating a bit more of a breakup in the ranks. When what they predicted happened, Hawk and Leopard went violently on the offensive. The first group consisted of four, all of whom submitted to the wrath of the bone weapons before the second group joined the fray. Fighting the six turned out to be a little tougher battle than all the previous, but still no real threat to Dave and Mick. It was at this point when Mick and Dave were seriously thinking they could pull off the upset. In the next hour, they took out another five stragglers.

"One and a half hours to go, before we gain an ally."

"I'm guessing you're referring to the darkness, Mick?"

"Yes. Darkness, the great equalizer."

"I assume by now they have to know many of their teammates have gone missing."

"You'd think. The group across the river is still over there, nonetheless."

"I have the feeling they will traverse back across before nightfall. They won't want to get caught over there all night."

"True," said Mick. "Also, they probably have a huge supply of food and beverages by their starting base they want to get back to."

"I wish we had a huge supply."

"You win some, you lose some."

Dave commented, "I present a simple but significant reflection, which I'm sure you're already aware, but we should make our way back to riverside. This way we can catch them as they cross, if and when they do indeed cross."

"Right. Yup, I was. Maybe they'll even make the mistake of crossing at twilight or maybe even in the dark. That'd create a huge advantage for us."

"Hopefully. Darkness: our world."

AS ULFENKERKI EXPECTED, the danger and the chaos grew exponentially when the Molisians got into the pit. He instructed his entire army to rally at the wall. At this point, he wished he'd fashioned the sort of wall that could be walked atop.

Those of Ulfenkerki's army wielding big rocks heaved them over the wall. Those with little ones did too, but with less optimism.

Gregg and the General heaved over their smaller rocks as precisely as they could.

Archers continued doing their thing, though now at close range.

Apparently, the enemy didn't have enough strong rope to pull down the wall, as Ulfenkerki had dreaded.

Still reaping the cover of the reliable beech tree, Gregg said to the Black Bear, "We got lucky they didn't end up puncturing the wall with their catapult fire."

"It seems the Molisians are going to try to burn a hole to enter."

"How can you tell, General?"

"A bunch of them are carrying torches, and others are toting canisters, which presumably contain a fuel of some sort. This is an instance, though, not entirely unanticipated. There are tubs of water scattered about, but probably not enough to extinguish any large fires," put forth Ulfenkerki.

"Good thing we're equipped with adaptable battle modes."

The bravest and/or stupidest amongst the Molisians were in the pit trying to start the wall on fire. The cowards and/or intelligent were pretending to be busy on the solid ground just before the pit. The bulky logs of the wall weren't very easy to set ablaze. But using all the fuel they had, buttressed with as much paper birch bark and evergreen needles they could find, the Molisians eventually poked a hole through the wooden obstacle.

The penetration occurred near Ulfenkerki and Gregg, so they used their last remaining arrows on whomever emerged through the burning wall.

Eventually, a second hole was formed by another fire, a hundred feet down the wall from the first. In no time, the invaders collectively funneled through the two holes.

Looking peripherally at Gregg, the General said, "I did a quick estimation of heads, and the wall did its job, as we now outnumber them by a couple hundred."

"I never knew you could count so fast, sir," noted Gregg, just before he threw his first knife of the conflict.

"I can on occasion," remarked the General, still impressed by Gregg's knife throwing. "Did you hit him?"

"Yes, I nailed that willowy-built character right in the gut. May that good throw be the harbinger of accurate throws to come."

"Before we charge in with our newly-sharpened swords, give me a few seconds to mentally maneuver. Maybe I'll come up with something highly strategic via some critical thinking."

"Think away, sir."

At the wall breaches, the Molisians, before any hand-to-hand fighting ensued, had to face the Garobansurovian archer troop. Ulfenkerki's squads had arrows left, but not many.

In no time, the melee began and the archers switched to swords and fought alongside the infantry.

Given enough time, Ulfenkerki almost assuredly came up with a respectable plan, not unlike his far-away compatriot, Mick Thraiker.

The Black Bear voiced, "So here's what we're going to do, Gregg: We need to limit our overall losses, so I thought as hard and as quickly as I could. You and I are going to go stand between the two breakthroughs, behind that hedge plant, there. From there, we will work as a tandem: I the spotter, and you the knife-thrower. I will use my experienced eye to pick out of the crowd the most skillful Molisian fighters posing the biggest threats. Then, you with your arm already grasping a knife will unleash at the target I spotted, like a pre-coiled snake ready to strike. Our gain will be far greater springing this gambit into action, as opposed to us just joining the fray with our swords."

"Good plan, sir. There aren't many worse things in warfare than a misallocation of resources. I have nineteen knives left, so let's go make them count."

Ulfenkerki pointed towards a grouping of tents. "We'll go sneak around that way to the hedge. The hedge should give us three-quarters concealment."

"Right behind you."

DUSK SET IN, but not without Mick and Dave skillfully forcing submissions from another ten opposers.

Waiting at the riverside, Dave whispered to Mick, "I see them over there. They are going to make the swim now."

"We're in trouble if they do it in a solid bunch."

"Indeed. Once that many reach the shore, they can simply surround us."

"I'm going to roll out this string I brought between two trees. Maybe us knowing it's there, and them not knowing, will be beneficial at some point."

Mick spun out his string and returned to Dave, who all the while was spying.

Dave reported, "Favorable for us, I think they're mistiming this. Foolishly, they haven't left the far riverbank yet. By the time they get across the river, it'll be dark."

"It's all coming together, partner."

Twenty minutes into the enemy's crossing—an event which couldn't be seen due to darkness, only heard— Dave said, "I think there's enough separation for us to not be overwhelmed in our onslaught when they reach the shoreline. What do you think?"

"I agree. I think we can take them. There are three main clusters, I've noticed."

"Me too."

Dreadful visions of fighting in the water merrily flew away from Hawk and Leopard's minds. Fighting on the bank was a much better experience they thought. Sure footing goes a long way.

The first wave of soldiers reached the shore—more specifically, the first *two individuals*. They not only reached the shore, but Mick and Dave's weapons. A thump to the face in the dark was the last thing the swimmers expected upon the landing.

One-by-one the Icytryxans terrifyingly encountered Mick and Dave. The entire first wave submitted in less than two minutes.

The second wave could hear something transpiring on the shore but didn't know what. If they thought quicker before beaching, they could've tactically optimized and joined forces with the third river-crossing wave. But in many circumstances panic induces not-so coherent thoughts.

The second wave was a little more prepared than the first and put up more of a fight. There were a few survivors from the second wave left standing when the final group joined the battle—very overwhelming odds for Mick and Dave.

Dave and Mick retreated further away from the shoreline, aiming to take advantage of the string trap Mick had laid out.

Once close enough, Mick and Dave began running so their pursuers would also be running upon proximity of the trap.

Gracefully, Dave and Mick stepped over the string in full stride. Half of the chasers, the front half, met ground, tripped by the string. They immediately fell prey to Thraiker and Ghrere's lightning hands. Most of them gave up before getting smashed on the head. The remaining seven almost managed to flank Mick and Dave post-string incident, but right before they were to succeed in the maneuver, Mick and Dave took off running again.

Due to a lack of coordination in three of the seven trailers, a split formed. Opportunistically, Mick and Dave pounced.

Knowing he had to act fast, Dave aimed and swung his weapon violently. But because of the haste, he received a hit to the leg, causing a temporary limp.

Meanwhile, Mick slashed and hacked with as much precision and power as he could muster. Multiple Molisian submissions were the result.

The three who were in the rear caught up to the tussle, making it *four-on-two* again.

Having ducked, Mick narrowly avoided a weapon thrust. He countered with a solid blow to his opponent's knee, which staggered just enough for the victory.

Dave's limp dissipated, allowing him complete freedom of motion. Using his shield for more than what one was usually intended, Dave, fighting two adversaries, threw it as hard as could at the back of Mick's opponent's head. He knew the scheme would pay off ten-fold, since

Mick could now submit his stunned opponent quickly and come assist.

The stratagem led to total triumph over the river-crossing company.

Dave picked his trusty shield back up and dusted it off. He felt a sense of accomplishment, watching the Icytryxans walk out of the arena. It was dark, though, so he couldn't watch them for very long.

Mick mentioned, "I saw you hobbling around a bit there. How are you doing?"

"It was a little tender for a while, but I'm good to go now."

"That's good. Now, only the cluster that never left the starting point remains."

"The bad news is I don't think they're ever going to leave that station. Sooner or later, I'm afraid we'll have to take them head on."

"Yeah, seeing as they stayed there all day, who's to say they would ever leave. I think those are the individuals who are really attached to their atlytls and the high ground supremacy from which to fire them."

"Whether we like it or not, we inevitably are going to face a plethora of projectiles."

"We'll have to think of something to lessen the blow, before going as it."

"I'm all for that," exclaimed Dave. "Are you tired at all? Should we sleep a bit?"

"That might be best. We'll take shifts. You go ahead and sleep three hours, then I will."

"Okay. There's a spot fifty feet back towards the river that seemed suitable."

"Excellent. When we're done resting, it'll thankfully still be dark. A night attack is usually advantageous."

"Exactly. Maybe we'll even catch them all sleeping, I doubt it though."

Mick concluded, "And I'll try and think of a plan for the assault, amongst many other less helpful things, while I stand watch."

"I wouldn't have it any other way, my friend."

Due to their victory over the river crossers, whatever part of Thraiker and Ghrere thought it wasn't possible to defeat the whole platoon had since vanished.

CHAPTER 22

HAVING GOTTEN INTO position, three-quarters-of-the-way concealed by the bushy hedge, Ulfenkerki and Gregg performed a quick survey of the situation. The former said, "I've seen you make throws at this distance. I assume you still have confidence?"

"For the most part, yes, but anything can happen in the matter of a split second. It is possible, although only slightly, that one of our own guys may inadvertently step into the knife-path."

The General replied, "Risks are a part of life on the whole. We must not shy away."

Ulfenkerki set right into action. "First target: left side, huge man nearest us. He's too adept with that axe to be kept in the battle."

Gregg whipped the knife with passion and precision. The axe man was struck in the back. He didn't go down right away, but his ability to swing the axe with a full arc was affected, stealing the best of him. He was eventually slain by a much weaker opponent than one who would've been able to do so normally.

"Next target: right side, medium build, fancy armor, wielding a longsword. He's fighting Big Jim at this second." Ulfenkerki pointed discreetly.

Gregg aimed at the neck because of the Molisian's well-crafted body armor. It was a tough throw due to the small target. The propulsion was precise, and the target dropped lifelessly in a flash.

Unaware their leader was dictating knife throws from a bush, the Garobansurovians in the thick of things fought valiantly. Parts of the wall were still ominously on fire, but there was no real threat of it burning down the surrounding forest. In the back of some of the soldiers' minds was the hope that the entire wall wouldn't turn to ash, mostly because they didn't want to have to rebuild it.

All arrows were spent, all catapults were out of ammunition (on both sides), making the battle strictly hand-to-hand at this point.

The sound of metallic weapons clashing against each other was so loud that no one noticed the thunderstorm slowly approaching from the west.

"Next objective: the stout guy who just spotted us and is now looking right at you. Left side."

Gregg threw the knife, but the man was half expecting it. The Molisian put up a shielding hand just in time and was only struck by the knife's handle. Gregg threw again, but the fellow sidestepped and avoided the knife once more.

The Molisian soldier took off running directly at Gregg and Ulfenkerki. He was sick of getting knives thrown at him. Taking out the threat would remedy this, the Molisian thought, though sometimes in war, as in real life, someone conceives a plan that is just plain stupid. The Molisian didn't bring an ally with, nor any sort of weapon's advantage. He really thought he could defeat Gregg and Ulfenkerki both in one fell swoop. Gregg and Ulfenkerki drew swords, flanked and stabbed. The Molisian's life left was counted in moments.

"Back to business."

The battle was deepening, numbers dwindling. The two fronts were now one.

General Ulfenkerki and Gregg eventually switched locations from where to throw knives. They were now situated behind a cart.

"Throw at the man with the black gauntlets. I've seen him kill two of our men in the last three minutes."

Gregg hurled with a grunt. *Bullseye, right in the face.* "I have only two knives left."

"I'm glad you have at least one left! I've spotted one of their officers, maybe even their leader. He's the guy in the back who isn't moving much. I've seen soldiers run up to him to report. Bring him down."

Gregg heaved the penultimate knife, but missed on the rotation and it hit flat. He took a deep breath and firmly grasped the handle of his last knife like he would the hips of a voluptuous woman. Curling his lips, he snapped his arm like a whip. The knife flew away spinning.

Gregg grinned, because it was one of those throws he knew was a faultless fling before it even hit.

Hit in the spine, the officer went limp, having lost control of his legs. He went down *bonelessly*.

"Time for us to charge, Gregg."

"Let's have at it."

Running to join the rest of his soldiers, Ulfenkerki shouted to a following Gregg, "I'm going to try my best to capture alive the officer you just hit. I have questions that need answering."

Gregg and Ulfenkerki split up. Gregg dashed into the skirmish head-on, intending to slay at high velocity. The Black Bear rushed directly to the Molisian officer and caught his quarry just in time. Any later and the Molisian officer would have a sword through his heart.

"Leave this one alive! A *prisoner of war*," Ulfenkerki shouted.

The Molisian officer obeyed Ulfenkerki. He was disappointed to have been caught, but content he'd just heard the word alive being shouted by his captor.

Ulfenkerki dragged the completely immobile Molisian officer out of battle's way. "Stay," the General said, ironically.

Post-chuckle, the Black Bear went back to join the fight. He kept a constant eye in the back of his head to watch his POW. He didn't need anyone else trying to kill him.

Gregg and Ulfenkerki basically had fresh muscles, so the two of them joining in when they did was extremely helpful to the fight.

HAVING SUCCEEDED at short periods of sleep, Dave and Mick aimed to replenish lost energy by eating apples they found hanging invitingly on a nearby tree. They had to be extra cautious as to how loud they ate them, however.

"I thought of a plan," blurted Mick. "I'm sure, as we've discussed previously, there is a large open area where they are standing, from where they can easily fire upon us, one that reaps insignificant obstruction. I'd say more than likely this launching advantage is why they never left the area."

"Yes, you can kind of see part of it while in the river."

"The tricky part will be charging at them, as they lob projectiles at us. We must minimalize this aspect."

Dave added, "And do so while ending up in a strong enough position to take on multiple opponents."

"Right," noted Mick. "We'll have the veil of darkness on our side, but it won't be enough. I propose we come at them from the side they least expect: straight up the steep river embankment. They'll still be able to fire at us, but because there's less open area there, they won't have as much time to arouse any sleeping individuals."

"I like it, as long as they haven't stockpiled any heavy rocks to throw down the hill at us. Light rocks we can deflect with the shields—heavy ones, not so much."

"True. I'm one step ahead of you, though. Follow me."

Mick led Dave thirty feet away from where they'd just slept, and said, "I'm surprised you didn't see this while you were on your patrol shift. I made it while I was on mine. I call it *log shield*. Hence its name, the main component is a log. It doubles as an apparatus to hang onto as we float down the river, and a shield we'll hide behind as we climb the bank. Heavy rocks will have a hard time getting at us through this baby."

"I don't think I like it when you're a step ahead of me like this. Frankly, it scares me," said Dave, quietly laughing.

"It scares me too sometimes." Mick returned a hushed chuckle. "We'll carry *log shield* another hundred yards through the brush, before launching it into the water."

"Is it as heavy as it looks?"

"Actually, no. It's pretty dry, but only for now, though. Once it becomes afloat, I'm sure it'll gain some weight."

"Won't it be too heavy then to lift up the bank, while still remaining agile?"

"I guess if it gets to be that heavy, we'll just abandon it and switch back to the poplar shields. I have utmost confidence in *log shield*."

The pair proceeded, the darkness persisted, and the night owls paid no mind to Mick and Dave carrying a handled log through the forest. They continued their hooting regardless.

Following twenty minutes of ducking under limbs and negotiating thick bush with *log shield*, the duo reached the spot by the river where they wanted to enter. Gaining admittance was the easy part—exiting was going to be much harder.

Mick and Dave once more immersed themselves into the Worod River, hoping it would be the last—at least the last of this battle scenario, anyways. With their individual shields and bone weapons firmly attached to their persons by way of string, they grasped *log shield* and began to float downstream. They tried to stay under the water as much as possible to give the illusion the whole getup was just a random log floating down the river, just in case anyone happened to be looking closely.

It took fifteen minutes to successfully reach the steep embankment right underneath the Icytryxans' base of operations. They were a bit surprised they made the whole trip without a soul looking at them suspiciously.

Now waterlogged, *log shield* was thirty unwanted pounds heavier. They furrowed their eyebrows, forced the flow of adrenalin and stretched their arms, before lifting *log shield* and attempting the ascent of the bank.

Most of the Icytryxans were stealing some slumber, but they did have scouts on the lookout watching in all directions.

Mick and Dave made it halfway up the bank before one of the patrols heard sand being un-lodged by the duo's feet and fall into the river below. The scout peered over the ledge and saw exactly for what he was on the lookout. He hollered loudly to arouse the attention of everyone else. Luckily for Mick and Dave, only a couple of the other patrol personnel heard the holler. And even more fortunate for Mick and Dave, they rushed to the scene without arousing any sleepers.

Given the immediate circumstances, the three Icytryxan patrols thought it'd be wiser to take Dave and Mick on themselves, rather than letting the opportunity slip and waiting for everyone else to join in.

Although the patrols didn't have an entire stockpile of rocks to drop on Mick and Dave, they were in possession of a few sporadic stones sitting loosely on the ground. They began dropping them as quickly as they could.

Log shield was serving its purpose splendidly. The Icytryxans heaved the heaviest stones down the bank first, thinking they could bust up the log, or weaken the arms holding it up. They succeeded in neither.

However, eventually Mick and Dave did get to a point where they could no longer climb and hold up *log shield* efficiently, so they ditched ole trusty in exchange for their lighter poplar shields. Just in time too, because the Icytryxans were down to smaller stones.

Mick and Dave just about reached the top when they started facing the desperate kicks of soldiers trying to keep them from cresting. A boot to the face wasn't the pleasantest of experiences, as anyone would say who'd ever received one.

With a face full of hurt, Dave grimaced and rammed his shield into the nearest opponent's leg. Using the slight break in the leg owner's offense, Dave was able to climb to the summit and the flat terrain beyond.

Instinctively, Dave and his bone-weapon first and foremost cleared a spot for Mick to join in at the pinnacle. It was at this point when the three patrols saw how foolish it was for them to not ensure backup when they should have. They were forced to submit in the matter of mere seconds.

One of the patrols had been thinking, though, for she cleverly let loose an ear-splitting scream, just before surrendering. The signal succeeded in getting the attention of the other patrols and light sleepers.

When torches were shone in the direction of the scream, the lot was shocked at seeing prime targets number one and number two in the flesh. They straight-away went to work waking the heavy sleepers.

THE BATTLE FOR THE base was down to the nitty-gritty. However by this point it was essentially just a formality in finishing up the battle since Ulfenkerki's army held a huge numbers advantage. Ulfenkerki's strategies, so it seemed, were going to be superior once again.

The General's final opponent happened to be the cousin of Gregg's final opponent. But other than this sheer coincidence, the fights held no significance. Both Molisians were defeated rather easily. In fact, the last batch of Molisians, minus a few who'd escaped, were so outnumbered that they ended up surrendering, including the officer Ulfenkerki had corralled. There were twenty one prisoners of war in total.

Upon the battle's conclusion, the soldiers worked as fast as they could to put out the wall-fire with dirt. In the end, a lot of it was saved.

Ulfenkerki didn't expect there to be POWs, so he really wasn't prepared for it, having nowhere to go with them. They made do with what they had, transforming one of the buildings into a holding facility.

Time being of the essence, Ulfenkerki desired to begin the interrogation of the officer POW right away. He really only wanted to know one important thing, he pretty much assumed he wouldn't gain any more knowledge beyond that.

He entered the makeshift prisoner building with a few armed guards. To the officer he'd captured, Ulfenkerki said, "I'm sure on the battlefield you'd gathered I thought you were an officer."

"Yes, I made note of that when you wanted me specifically to be left alive," replied the Molisian.

"So, was I right to keep you alive?"

"You were right in that, but not because I'm an officer."

"Why then?"

"Because any man would rather be alive than dead, I'm no less important than the officers."

The Black Bear let a half-smile slip, figuring some lying was afoot. "You're right about that. I can't argue with your logic. On a different note, just so you know, we treat our prisoners well here in Garobansurov. You will not be tortured or killed, and as soon as the war is over, we'll set you free."

"Well, that's good to know."

"I'm sure you know the questions to which I want answers. And I'm well aware any truths that would hinder your country in any way will not be given. Regardless, I will ask anyway. The obvious question is, are there any more soldiers on their way here, right now?"

"Nope, it was just us, aiming to join our compatriots here at our weapons forge," replied the soldier, mustering as honest a face as he could.

"I'm a little cloudy on something, though. Why has General Gamald ordered the construction of so many weapons? Does he intend to arm a much larger army? And if so, where exactly is this army located? It would be really hard to hide an entire army in our country without us knowing about it. These weapons need to be for *someone*."

"Yes, the weapons are definitely for our war effort. But we are just taking advantage of the mineral-rich mine we discovered here. The weapons are, then, delivered back to the homeland to be distributed there."

"You're right about that. It is a pretty fruitful mine. I can see why you risked working it, so far away from your main supply lines."

"Indeed."

"Are you aware of any news from the western battle fronts?" asked Ulfenkerki.

"Nothing really. All I know is that we have soldiers there fighting yours, but I have no idea how many."

"Information on that part of the war is sparse, so that's why I ask." Ulfenkerki scratched his chin.

"I don't blame you. It's the same for us."

"Well, that's basically all the questions I have for you. If I can think of anymore, I'll be back."

"No problem," replied the Molisian. "While you remain hospitable, as will I."

Ulfenkerki left the prisoner building, along with the soldiers who'd accompanied him. Attributable to the prisoner's vague answers to Ulfenkerki's questions, most would think Ulfenkerki left the building with the same amount of information with which he went in. However, thanks to his own ingenuity, he harvested precisely what he sought to know.

After all the dead (including the enemy's) received a proper burial, and the battle zone was tidied up a bit, the General found himself in a familiar position: playing cards in the mine with Gregg and a few others.

Gregg dealt a hand, flicked a nuisance rock off the table and said, "I saw you were successful in capturing that officer, sir. Have you had a chance yet to question him?"

"Actually, I have," boasted the General. "Of course, he thought he wasn't giving anything away in his responses. But what he doesn't know is I tricked him into giving me exactly what I went in there to find out. I led him one way with my questioning, but I was actually going another—a planned misdirection. Because of this, he gave away the fact Gamald was involved with the attack in some form or another. I slipped the word *Gamald* into the questioning, and at no point did the prisoner think to tell me Gamald played no role. I know there's a chance he just didn't think to do so, but I really think he fell for the ruse."

"So, how does you now knowing Gamald was involved alter future planning?"

"Good question. I'll have to ponder on it some more, before coming to any conclusions. All I know is that, yes, we won convincingly here today, but this thing is far from over as long as Gamald is still in the picture. I have the feeling there is a much larger force somewhere, lurking."

An unexplainably eerie and powerful wind blew in through the front of the mine, grabbing the attention of a few. Ulfenkerki associated it with his mentioning of Gamald, his nemesis. A few hairs stood on end.

Gregg collected his winnings from the middle of the card table. His pockets were now heavier than they were a couple hours previous. He remarked, "If that's true, a much larger force *is* lurking somewhere, then let's hope Mick, Dave, Jason, and Yori are successful with their mission with the Icytryxis."

The Black Bear responded, "I think about that sometimes too. It definitely would be of great assistance in these serious times. I can guarantee, though, at this very moment they're attempting everything imaginable to be successful."

Adrenalin was in no short supply.

"Now is when coming up the bank pays off," blurted Mick, running as fast as could, "as we now have a much shorter run to get at them—Which means less time for our sleeping foes to wake up, and less deadly projectiles coming at us."

"Speaking of which, here they come," said Dave. Let's head for that small group of trees near them; it'll give them less room for flanking."

"Yes, on my way. First we have to make it through this open ground to get there."

"Things might get ugly."

Fifteen Icytryxan soldiers made it out of bed in time to join in on the bombardment. Relentlessly, they fired their atlytls as Mick and Dave closed in. A hundred-yard gap of open ground separated Mick and Dave from the Icytryxan grouping.

While running, Hawk and Leopard held their shields up over their faces. This protected the vital area of their heads fairly well. But the rest of their bodies took one heck of a beating during their run through the gap. If the projectiles had sharp, pointed tips (war projectiles), Mick and Dave's bodies would've been torn irreparably to shreds, just like their raft. Some of the projectiles did penetrate the skin and get lodged into Mick and Dave. They'd certainly have to be removed with care at battle's end. Dave had taken a rather painful projectile to the knee, while Mick experienced one lodge itself deep in his quadriceps tissue.

Like a well-established campfire burning in the heaviest of downpours, Mick and Dave endured. It was a true showing of will.

Subsequent twenty seconds of unimaginable pain, Dave and Mick's run was over, having finally made it to the cover of the small but adequate pod of trees.

They took a moment to gather composure, then began work on their opponents. A couple Icytryxans switched to close-combat weapons a little too late and had to forfeit right away. Keeping amongst the protective trees, Hawk and Leopard put their masterful sword skills into full use, even though it was only bone clubs they wielded. The similarity was close enough.

The pair stood back-to-back. Mick cracked his spine as Dave shook the knee that took the projectile hit. They each took a deep breath, and the real tempest officially began.

There were four trees to the immediate left, three to the right, and adversaries all around.

The duo would've gone at this segment of the fight differently if the Icytryxans had decided to wait until they were at full force to attack. If this were the case, it would've been better for Mick and Dave to hunt them down before the numbers swelled too much. But as it stood, the Icytryxans foolishly exchanged advantage in numbers for hasty rage.

Dave blocked a spear thrust, countered, and moved on to the next opponent. Mick swung his weapon powerfully in bursts. Together, the two of them unleashed utter devastation. As each one of their challengers submitted, a replacement (who'd just woken up) joined in. Many times, they each found themselves taking on two and even three opponents at once—never more than three because of the trees, hence their stratagem. Of course, they sustained strikes, some being excruciating, but Dave and Mick fought with the utmost focus and never lost hope.

After ten minutes of fierce fighting between the trees, only fifteen Icytryxans stood between Dave, Mick, and victory. All fifteen were coming at them now, though. It would be a vanquishing most difficult.

Mick gripped his weapon with both hands for the brute-force approach, while Dave made one poor guy forfeit by breaking his nose. He'd broken it with one swing and hit it again with the follow-through. Dave predicted the soldier wouldn't like a third swing to the tender area, so he allowed ample opportunity for surrender, in which the Icytryxan didn't disappoint.

Mick switched back to one hand on shield and one on weapon. He began to surge the last of his adrenalin seeing how very few opposers were left. He surged a little too much, however, having ended up snapping his bone weapon in half. Luckily, a wooden one was within grabbing distance when it broke. He bent down to grab it while blocking incoming blows with his shield—good thing this was still intact. With a new weapon, he was a new man.

The brunt of the hurricane was over. Only four (Mick, Dave, two Icytryxans) remained standing in, this, the grandest of Mick and Dave's battle scenarios.

Mick and Dave separated to avoid any chance for something unpredictable to happen, taking on their final opponents one-on-one.

Dave faced a left-handed foe. All he had to do to win was swing his weapon when the Icytryxan swung hers. He aimed to hit a more vital point than she did. He hit her neck, whereas she hit his shield. The fight was over before the next exchange.

Happening thirty feet from Dave, Mick battled his last opponent, an Icytryxan who knew full well he had no possibility of winning. Knowing and/or seeing his entire platoon go down before him was a clear indication for pessimism. He didn't want to go down without a fight, though. He held his breath and took the largest swing he could muster at Mick's head.

Toying with him, basically, Mick blocked the swing with his weapon, and threw his shield right at the Icytryxan. He would eventually catch it, but in the time it took him to bobble it around, Mick managed to get behind the bobbler and drive his newly-gotten wooden weapon up against his neck. Thraiker deployed a choking maneuver until the Icytryxan threw up his arms in submission.

The scenario was over, the impossible made possible.

Dave and Mick shared an earnest smile.

"Well, Dave, that was certainly an experience."

"We can, without a doubt, add that accomplishment to our mountain metaphor."

"Surely," agreed Mick. "I'll have to think awhile on it to decide how high on the list of our greatest achievements I want to put it."

"I know it was definitely a grueling climb. I just hope it was enough for them all to see that no matter how strong your army seems, anything can happen, and it can be defeated, sometimes under the most unusual and unexpected circumstances."

"This loss will weigh heavily on them, no doubt. There's a strong chance it shocks them enough into thinking that joining us in the war would be wise. A strong alliance is vital for survival in this world."

"Now, we wait patiently to ascertain how much they were affected, and whether or not they're moved to action," noted Dave. "I do know my arms couldn't get any sorer. I'm going to toss my shield and weapon into their wagon over here; I really don't want to carry them all the way back. I don't think they'll mind."

"Good idea. I ended up using one of their weapons anyways."

"Yeah, I heard yours snapping in the heat of battle. How very unfortunate that was."

"It was all my fault. I got a little carried away at the end there."

"You do tend to do that. I remember you doing it at Gravividon too."

Mick chuckled. "I did, didn't I? Good times."

It was almost sun-up and only four spectators remained. The rest had gone home, too tired to watch. The four who stayed didn't for a second regret staying; the demonstration was engaging until the very end.

Mick and Dave walked back to the training facility with the four spectators and the last four Icytryxans who'd surrendered, talking enthusiastically about the event the whole way.

THE BATTLEFIELD took a thorough cleaning in the morning. The soldiers of Ulfenkerki's mine-base were still on an emotional high from the previous day's victory, having had all kinds of energy to whip the encampment back into shape.

By noon, Ulfenkerki had decided how he was going to proceed. He gathered the officers together and held a meeting in one of the outpost's buildings.

Closing the door behind, the Black Bear began, "First off, you all did a great job yesterday. Things couldn't have gone any better. We lost a few lives, but not many at all. I'm glad we stayed and fought. If this battle had transpired at the Capital, who knows what would've happened. One of their soldiers may have gotten extremely lucky and found his way to the King and to his assassination. That would've been a long shot, but I've seen rarer things happen. This was a good place for this skirmish."

"Yes, it was," blurted the nearest.

"So, as most of you already know, I've learned with a decent amount of certainty that the tyrant Gamald is still in Garobansurov and under command. This information is valuable, because we know to prepare for the unpredictable, even more than usual. His style of leading is barbaric and with no reserve. So, in response to this information, and our recent success here, I think it would be best to stop the search and go back to the Capital. Gamald will make himself known sooner or later. I really don't think he will try again to retake this mine outpost, especially not with a strong force. There are uncertainties as to why he sent a squadron here in the first place, but that is another matter. Of course, we will leave a garrison behind to hold the mine and work it. If a large opposing army does come, then it will be lost. But I feel that's not going to happen. Gamald is the sort governed by grander designs than inconsequential mines in the middle of nowhere. Plus, as another reason to depart, we have the prisoners of war, who will be better off kept at the Capital."

"When were you thinking about loading up and heading out?" asked an officer in the rear.

Ulfenkerki replied, "I think we can have everything loaded up and situated by tomorrow. We'll leave around noon. The garrison that stays behind will consist of volunteers. Some will jump at this opportunity. I imagine there are benefits of being here, in solitude, as opposed to the clamor of Myothraces. Also, if there is anyone among you who would like to volunteer to lead the regiment that remains, you can go ahead and step forward now. If not, you'll have until tomorrow when we leave to decide. If no one wants the position in the end, I'll decide myself who stays."

With minimal hesitation, one of the officers (Dan) announced, "I'd be glad to do it. I've enjoyed the time we've spent here amongst the trees."

"Excellent. I'm glad I don't have to select someone for the job. So, basically, your mission is to hold the base against small-unit invaders. If any overwhelming force approaches, just go ahead and retreat back to the Capital. Any valuable information learned can be dispatched by messenger to me. The mine you can continue to operate at your own will. Sell some minerals to the townsfolk if you wish. By all means, make a profit for yourselves. Though, at some point, Rowlangiv may send a mining crew here for his own gain, understandably. Whatever we've mined thus far will be brought back with me, including all the weapons the Molisians had constructed before we commandeered the place. Naturally, enough arms will be left for your squad."

Dan replied, "Very good, sir. How many soldiers will you allow to stay?"

"I'm thinking thirty can reside here, along with an additional scout network. I may change my mind by tomorrow on the numbers for some unforeseen reason, though. I'll keep you informed. I imagine a myriad of problems may arise, which you'll have to deal with yourself, Dan. But I'm sure you can handle it."

"Will do, sir."

Ulfenkerki continued, "You all can go ahead and inform the soldiers of the plan and that they can start packing. And, Gregg, at some point today you can go to town and round up those two civilians who'd approached us that one day to volunteer for the army. They can come join us now for the march back, like I had informed them they could."

"No problem, sir. I'll head there in an hour."

The soldiers had no problem getting all the stuff loaded onto wagons in the timeframe their general had hoped. They could've carried everything by hand, but wagons had proved to be far more efficient for what they had to tote. It would be rough pushing for a bit, but they took solace in knowing once they reached the well-flattened, heavily used main road south, their exertion level would decrease.

Ulfenkerki slept on it and decided his original assessment was correct—a garrison of thirty head would remain behind. Dan, in turn, had no problems coming up with the thirty volunteers. Those who volunteered mainly did so for dislike of the crowds at the Capital's army barracks (introverts).

Gregg was successful in locating and bringing back the two new recruits from town. The pair expressed willingness in taking turns at wagon lugging and would do so all the way to the Capital. They were beyond proud to be a part.

The POWs would not be barbarically chained for the journey. Instead, they'd be guarded and inserted into the wagon-lugging rotation. Pushing/pulling a wagon for three hours a day was far better than being united by chain for the whole day, especially while sleeping.

Led by the advance party, Ulfenkerki and his mass departed the mine-base, heading for the main south road. The walled base was left behind, in operation and in the hands of Dan and his skeleton crew.

CHAPTER 23

AT ARMY TRAINING the day after Dave and Mick's big victory, the pair learned to what degree the Icytryxans were influenced by the events at the river. Thyxer and Syryx had made a point to talk to as many of their fellow compatriots about it as possible.

Dave, Mick, Thyxer, and Syryx met up privately on park benches to discuss matters.

Thyxer brushed a stone off the bench, a painful little annoyance which he first sat on, and said, "So, having spent all morning collecting as much information about everyone's reaction to the favorable outcome yesterday, Syryx and I are ready to give you the report." Thyxer looked to Syryx.

Syryx began, "Overall, the consensus has been complimentary to the cause, without a doubt. They aren't exactly rushing to arms at this very moment, but many are taking the loss at the river very hard. For so long they've looked at their safety as being impenetrable, like an iron shield encased the island. You've definitely shocked them, as was your intention."

"The lot of them, before yesterday, had thought there wasn't a single force in the world strong enough to threaten the IAC (Icytryxan Atlytl Corps). But seeing the two of you whip through an entire platoon like you did has implanted doubt—thoughts that maybe their way of life isn't as impervious as they assumed. If they'd been defeated by a larger force, they wouldn't harbor such feelings, but the fact that it was accomplished by only two individuals, really blew their minds," reported Thyxer.

"We must act quickly to drive the nail all the way home. And in order to do so," proclaimed Syryx, "there is only one way. We must organize an assembly at our most distinguished meeting place. You've been there before, on our very first tour of town: the Javeti Edifice."

"Yes, the place with the stream running through the middle," noted Dave.

"Yup," returned Syryx. "There, with everyone gathered, we can orate with great expressiveness and conviction, in a wholehearted attempt to get them to see that an Icytryxan/Garobansurov alliance would be what's best for all. Anyone who wishes to address the audience may. Of course, having the two of you speak would help out a lot. Additionally, Jason discoursing on the Thorncat Missile he created for us would be of great assistance. Also, this is where Yori, and all her gathered information on our social constructs, can truly shine. She'll know weaknesses."

Mick declared, "I like it. We kind of thought that at some point speeches would need to be delivered. To a certain extent, Dave and I have already been mentally preparing for such an occasion. Although it being such a grand affair never crossed our minds."

"We gave speeches at the Knowing Circle celebration, so you could say we've had some recent practice," commented Dave.

"Very well indeed. Nobody in the army is any more important than the next, so what we'll have to do is invite each and every one to come," said Syryx. "The complex is definitely not large enough to house them all. Not all will necessarily show up, but it's hard to estimate how many actually will. We'll have to think of a way to get around the potential overcrowding, but I'm confident we will."

"Definitively, the sooner we hold this event, the better. Their loss at your hands must remain fresh in their minds, as the occasion gets underway. I'm thinking that even today Syryx, other key figures and I can get the ball rolling on its development. Maybe in three days' time, we can have it all organized and ready to go."

"I think it's a marvelous idea," said Dave. "We might as well not waste any more time talking about it. Go ahead and get things started."

"I agree," noted Mick. "We are at the point, where if this doesn't work, I don't think anything will. We've already been here a long time. What has Jason and Yori said about the idea?"

"We talked to them earlier, out of convenience. They both were on board," Thyxer replied. "We wanted you two to make the final decision, of which in the light, we'll start the organizing right now. We'll search you out if there are any questions or information to tell you."

Having nothing to do with the future event at the Javeti Edifice, Yori came to a revelation that morning. After army training, she had a mission to accomplish. One more time, she stopped by a group of friends, the same confidants with whom she enjoyed multiple visits previously.

During the pleasant visit, she learned what needed to be learned.

Calling upon Yusyta was the next stage of her mission.

At the Narutyx house, Yusyta stood in her room, staring out the window. She heard a knock, turned away from the window, and voiced, "Come on in."

Yori entered, and said, "Hi. How are you today, Yusyta?"

"I'm pretty good. Thanks for asking, Yori. I was just thinking about old memories."

"Do you do that a lot?"

"I guess I do."

"The reason I've searched you out is, I'm sure, one that you probably wouldn't expect. It has to do with your Fantysy-Escape championship-night story."

"Still thinking about it, eh?"

"Yes, I have been. And what I'm about to say, I do it with as much respect as possible. I came to you first, so you can tell me if I'm right or not. I didn't want to bring it up to Mick and Dave first, before I came to you. The whole thing is, however, partly because of a story Mick and Dave told me. Their non-fictional narrative is why I thought of what I'm about to say."

Yusyta chuckled. "Quite the introduction you're giving me."

"I am, aren't I? I guess I wanted to come across as courteous as possible, if I happen to be wrong on my notion—or if I'm right, and you don't want to talk about it."

"I understand. Go ahead and spill your guts, dear girl."

"So, on the boat ride here, crossing the ocean, Mick and Dave spouted off a story to Jason and me. It concerned how they, on their way to the Capital for the Knowing Circle celebration, went out of their way to visit a monastery called Dourinuset. They shared a few stories about that visit, but one was of particular relevance, one concerning a certain monk there. They told us this monk had befriended them and shared nearly his entire life's story, a tragic tale which Mick and Dave relayed to us. I didn't realize it at first, but after much thought, I came to the conclusion that this monk's biography showed a striking resemblance to that of George's life, the George from your story. I would've never thought of relating the two, but I had been visiting with friends, here in Saraty, and they also shared a story, one with no names. This story also lined up with your Fantysy-Escape story. The numbers in the monk's chronicle also coincide with those in your story. You seemed so emotional telling your story—the kind of emotion that only surfaces when something is *real*. Real *and* intimate. So, I guess out of great curiosity, I must ask, are you the Cherryl from the story? And is Alfonso Alardo the George?"

Yusyta looked out the window again in obvious contemplation. Her gaze was powerful. She turned away from the rumination of the window and towards Yori. She hung her head low for a second and picked it back up again to reveal a beautiful smile. "Alfonso always talked about becoming a monk after I left his world. I couldn't really gauge just how serious he was, though. I'm glad he found something into which to put his heart and focus. You must understand how hard it is to be away from your people for so long."

"You don't have to explain a thing to me," said Yori, reaching out her arm to place a comforting hand on Yusyta's shoulder. "I only confront you now, because of two reasons: The most important one is I thought you would want to hear Mick and Dave's story, so you could learn how Brother Alardo has been. From what I've gathered, he thinks about you constantly. And the second reason concerns the mission, the mission regarding why my compatriots and I are here. I don't know if you know, but we are organizing a large conference at the Javeti Edifice in response to Mick and Dave's pivotal victory over the Icytryxan platoon."

"Yes, I've heard."

"We figured that the time for emotional speeches is now. One last big push, if you will. I had just thought that maybe you would like to get involved and say a few words. Perhaps an account illustrating the character you found in the people of Garobansurov. I know it's a lot to ask, but I really do feel it would help."

"I don't know of any Icytryxan who has spent a longer time in Garobansurov than I, so I can see how I could help. Only my family and the friends with whom I'd gone—our mutual friends to whom you talked—know my story. Alfonso actually never knew I was Icytryxan. As you know, we women aren't very distinguishable from your women, like the men are. The little differences he did notice, I just said were because of the fact I came from so far away. Most Garobansurovians basically considered our race nothing more than a myth. As did he, I think."

"That is true. Not anymore, though, thanks to the mission."

"So, it never really crossed his mind that I wasn't human." Yusyta looked out her window, again in deep reflection, and continued. "I don't talk about this much. My family all knew that I was Cherryl from the story, which may have been why most of them chose to hear the ending of Dave's story. They all were aware of my story's ending. I'm surely not taking anything away from Dave's gripping story, though. From what I've heard, I probably couldn't have beaten him anyways. It was exquisite. I could've taken a bigger swing at the title by creating a story to which nobody knew the ending, but the truth is that story is the single greatest part of me. I couldn't resist telling it, seeing as though we enjoyed a larger audience than normal. I think about what happened and of Alfonso almost every single moment of my life."

"It really is a beautiful story. Do you mind if I, or we, share what you told me with Mick, Dave and Jason?"

"Tonight, I will sit down with them, and tell them everything. And I do agree to speak at the assembly. I will do it proudly and can add many beneficial things to the cause. For starters, I can personally attest to just how caring, kind, compassionate, and loving an individual of your country can be. I couldn't agree more to becoming allies with Garobansurov. You can count on me."

"You're a lovely person, Yusyta. I wish you could've had both the love of your people and the love of your life."

"Me too, dear. Me too."

While the two ladies were discussing matters of the heart, Thyxer, Syryx, and a couple other soldiers went to the Javeti Edifice to start getting things in order. Anybody could hold an event there at any time. It was one of the benefits of a world without politics. But it was practical to not double-book. They learned the day they wanted to use the hall was free from any other would-be users, so all was well. The group studied the place to determine how exactly they were going to find enough room for everyone. Thinking back to the past and to large events therein, they figured the best way to enable everyone to participate was to plug the main hall with chairs. There were secondary satellite halls, but anyone sitting in these wouldn't be able to hear the speeches being given in the main hall. Adding extra seating in the main hall would make for less elbow room and overall decreased comfortability. But sometimes you just got to do what you just got to do. They also studied the place for any other arrangements that may need to be done.

The group was confident the event would be nothing short of engaging.

Nearing another day's sunset, Yusyta gathered Mick, Dave, Jason and Yori. They sat comfortably in the living room of her living quarters. She told them all about the conversation she and Yori had shared. Yusyta broke the rules a little by deviating from Fantysy-Escape protocol, the one dictating that only the choosers of a story's ending may hear it. It was an instance where she just had to—the ends justified the means. Everyone would understand.

The men were astounded by what they'd just heard, but in a pleasant sort of a way.

Mick observed, "It's not too often that things come together like this. It truly is quite the cosmic coincidence."

"I remember plain as day," said Dave, "his heartfelt portrayal of how much he loves you. He misses you on a level beyond words. Alfonso seems happy being a monk, yes, but he definitely is living life with his heart somewhere else… still with you."

Yusyta spoke. "I keep it next to me at all times. And I can assure you, my own heart was left with him when I left."

"You speaking," digressed Jason, "at the upcoming assembly will help us beyond measure. You bring a perspective that they certainly will relate to."

"I'm glad I will be able to help."

"If you have the time, Yusyta," Mick offered, "Dave and I will tell you the whole story, and almost every word he said about you. Usually, I don't remember so many words that people say, but he said them with such passion, expressiveness, and honesty I couldn't help but remember."

"Yeah, he definitely had a way of speaking. I remember the day we met so well, and how my heart fluttered every time he spoke. Yes, I want to hear everything that you know."

Eagerness became Yusyta.

Yusyta grabbed beverages for all, and Mick and Dave began sharing everything they remembered about Alfonso. They talked for a long time, right up until they practically fell asleep. By the end of the night, Yusyta had determined it to be the fourth best day of her life up to that point, only beaten by the very day she'd met Alfonso, the day after they met, and their wedding day.

The days leading up to the assembly at the Javeti Edifice went by fast, consisting of the same activities as normal. Mick and Dave continued to have battle scenarios, however, they were small affairs. Jason further worked on the metrics of his Thorncat Missile. And like always, Yori reached out to the people, learning.

And all four spent their nights working on their speeches for the upcoming congregation. Thyxer and Syryx had also since committed to speaking at the assembly, along with a few others. The group had also figured there'd be a few individuals who'd want to speak against joining Garobansurov in war, which the opposition had every right to do. Counter arguments for such parley would need to be generated and practiced. Debate in every sense was always complex. It was never easy. The person who assumed it would be, usually lost.

They all also practiced their vocalizations in front of each other.

The day of the critical assembly arrived. After army training, the Garobansurovians and their host family all began dressing up for the event. It was to be formal (events held at the Javeti Edifice usually were), so they all put on their finest. The children didn't like dressing up very much, but they did, nevertheless.

When they were all ready, they began the walk to the hall, except Thyxer and Syryx, who'd left earlier to finish setting up. There were many other Icytryxans on the avenues heading in the same direction, like the day of the Conceptual Naissance, but to a lesser degree.

They entered the building and walked through the hallway leading to the main hall. They noticed the place was already pretty busy. Plus, they observed the place wasn't without the usual roar created by many people crammed into a confined space.

Those of this story's protagonist party designated as speakers went to sit in the front by the other speakers already there. The rest found seating amongst the crowd. However, they weren't lucky enough to find seats near the stream running down the middle of the room. These were obviously highly coveted. Who wouldn't want to sit by the soothing sights and sounds of running water, clear enough to drink?

To Dave, Mick said, "Who is the loudest among us? We're going to need them to start this thing off, since the volume in here is quite high."

"I doubt it's me."

"There definitely is a good turnout, which is a good thing."

"That it is," returned Dave. "If nobody had showed up, we'd have problems."

"Right. We'd surely get nowhere then."

Thyxer approached Mick, Dave, Yori, Jason, and Yusyta (Syryx was still off finalizing setup), and said, "Unless one of you would rather do it, I'll begin the talks when it's time."

"Funny how we were just discussing that. By all means, go right ahead, Thyxer," declared Dave.

"Sounds good," returned Thyxer. "After me, the order doesn't really matter. The opposition has I think four speakers, so their thoughts will be dispersed into the mix too. When one person is done, the next can walk into position in the front of the stage and begin. Speak loudly, the more that hear you the better. In about 10 minutes, I'll get this thing rolling. Good luck all, and hopefully we're about to play just the right song at just the right time."

"Good thing we brought the good instruments," joked Dave.

Every seat in the place had a butt in it. There'd been almost enough chairs squeezed in, but not quite. A few ended up standing along the walls. The audience was mainly soldiers, but not all—the matter being important for soldier and civilian alike. There weren't many kids. It was expected to take at least a few hours, too long for young attention spans.

Thyxer walked into position and raised his arms to hush the crowd. When the noise subsided, he spoke at length. "Thank you everyone for coming. As you know, we're all here to debate whether or not it's in our best interest to become allies with our neighbor across the sea to the north: Garobansurov. We've aided them in the past, a long time ago, but never forged a strong and permanent relationship. I believe the time for this is now. Currently, Garobansurov is wedged in the clutches of war with their northern neighbor, Molisia. Molisia, throughout history, has exhibited a way of living completely opposite from the ideals and logic we cherish here, whereas Garobansurov is much like us in philosophical beliefs. No, they are not exactly like us, but in the ways that matter most, they are. Such as in the preservation of life, freedom, honor, and honesty. Other speakers will go more into detail on the character of Garobansurov and of Molisia. And some will speak against the overall idea. We're not here to tell you what to do, merely supply you with information, so that you can make the best decision possible.

Four of the speakers are from Garobansurov. They are as follows: Jason Thorncat, first lieutenant, answering to General Ulfenkerki, who is the leader of one of very few Garobansurov armies; Mick Thraiker and Dave Ghrere, freelance fighters of Garobansurov, whose heroics already in the war have merited them the highest award of the country, identified as the Knowing Circle; Yori Rothlin, King Rowlangiv's most trusted adviser, a post she's held for many years. All here on behalf of the King, and of their own free will, because they deep in their hearts believe an alliance between us would save lives.

The other speakers you all know.

Tonight's events are very important. I hope we all have come with minds as open as possible." Thyxer sat down and allowed the opposition their opening statement.

An older man named Fryton stood in front of the crowd and began his introductory statement. "Good evening everyone. I'm here to present an opposing view to an alliance and going to war. We're in no means here to deplete the credibility of Garobansurov, or its representatives sitting here behind me. As far as I'm concerned, they have been nothing but honorable while here, and adhered to our lifestyle without fault. I'm only here to stand for what we believe to be the quintessential Icytryxan ethic—Simply speaking, we don't kill anyone for any reason. We don't do it now, nor have we in the past, minus a few exceptions, of which the reason has been lost in time. We must stay true to our ideologies, for without them we are nothing. Our very lives turn on our philosophies." Fryton continued to lay the foundations for his side's arguments passionately. Upon his completion, he conceded the floor.

Syryx took the stage next. She began by reading the only known information written down concerning the last time the Icytryxans helped Garobansurov in war. It was a write-up that had been on display at the history museum. It contained minimal detail and supplied no reason why the assistance happened, but it did without any doubt prove it did happen.

When Syryx was finished reading verbatim from it, she set the artifact down, and continued, "Even though this happened thousands of years ago, and we don't know why, we do know that at that ancient epoch we held the exact same principles as we do now. They probably held a get-together just like this one to determine whether or not to go to war. We can only speculate, but I'd guess the reason then was not much different than the reason now. The future of our way of life depends on the stability of our surroundings. And for a very long time, Garobansurov has been at our periphery, keeping a peaceful living. I believe it is time to make it official to join sides. By doing this, we establish a future."

Syryx spoke a little more specifically about the advantages of fusing armies with Garobansurov and concluded her turn by talking powerfully on teamwork.

After Syryx was done addressing the crowd, another member of the opposing side spoke, spending 10 minutes on her point of view.

Next, Jason Thorncat advanced onto the arena. He was impressed by the attentiveness of the audience. Having waited patiently and respectfully until a couple of the elderly audience members sitting up front had finished coughing, he began. "Hello all. I have had a lot of time to study the tactical specifics involved with your Atlytl Corps, and especially how your tactics can be seamlessly infiltrated into ours to form an exponentially greater force. The details of my research are too long and complicated to really go into now, but the key factor can be described as such: What's the biggest advantage the atlytl provides? Easy. The huge range it enjoys. An advancing army with atlytls can deal damage way before an opposing traditional archer contingent can. Even more now with the Thorncat Missile. And, no, that wasn't a shameless plea for recognition. Okay, maybe just a little."

Jason chuckled, followed in turn by the addressees.

He continued. "What's the biggest disadvantage now? That's a little trickier. One might say it would be the time it takes to switch from atlytl to close range weapons. But in my opinion, that's not the greatest disadvantage, because it really doesn't take much time to make the switch, maybe three seconds at the longest. Hardly enough time to turn the tides of war. No, the answer is load weight. Lugging the weapon itself and all the projectiles a long distance is a task indeed. Now, moving to the second half of the equation, in discussing the prototypical Garobansurov army, we don't have the range you provide, which very well could be *our* greatest disadvantage. So, obviously you'd help us out in that department, while we'd aid in your weight dilemma, since it'd be distributed amongst everyone, thus lightening your individual loads.

Other, more complicated mutual advantages we'd achieve are in the world of flanking maneuvers. Basically, there are battle formations that can be created with the Icytryxan/Garobansurovian dichotomy that wouldn't otherwise be able to exist. Any wishing to see the diagrams I drew up of these battle configurations are welcome to peruse them at any time. They are all currently posted in one of the other halls—the east one, I believe."

Jason talked for another five minutes about other impending military methods the two cultures could hopefully share. He concluded his speech by saying, "General Ulfenkerki believes so keenly in an alliance between us, he wanted me, his second in command, here speaking with you—right in the middle of war. He saw great importance and value in a partnership in the long run, as do I. And if any of you have studied our history, you would know that the Black Bear, our most experienced general, is seldom wrong about matters of conflict. His judgment to send me here, instead of helping him in the pressing war, speaks volumes."

Subsequent Jason, the third member of the opposing party took the stage and delivered his speech. He was a vociferous, energetic young man that really got the crowd going—a real asset for the adversarial group.

Next in line was Yori. Of all the speakers, she had the longest speech prepared. It covered page upon page, upon page, all of which she had completely memorized— a skill she realized at a very young age. Her speech started off by targeting specific members of the crowd, tailoring her words to what she thought each would be the most affected by. Eye contact was vital, though she didn't single anyone out by using names. It was another skill she realized in her youth. She wasn't Rowlangiv's most trusted adviser for nothing. There was even a point when the family she was gearing towards all came to tears, due to the powerful words she knew would hit them—a forceful hammer-stroke. She achieved this by talking about untimely deaths of children, and how an alliance could help prevent it.

The family had experienced such tragedy, as their three-year-old wandered out of sight and fell fatally off a cliff into the sea.

After they were moved to tears, Yori went straight for the jugular by saying, "Cooperation between us can even be of assistance in preventing loss of civilian life, including children."

In the second half of her discourse she switched to speaking to the audience as a whole. She left no stone unturned, no corner untouched. Sparing no determination, she brought up everything she thought would help. In the end, she was very proud of her contribution to her side's effort, as she should've been, for she touched so many.

Right after Yori was finished, they inserted an intermission, so that way everyone could catch a breather, stretch their legs, and gather their thoughts. It wasn't the midway point, though. This had occurred closer to when Yori began her speech. The intermission also gave a chance for the listeners to share their opinions with each other.

During the intermission, Mick and Dave made a point to not mingle amongst the multitude in the hallways. They hadn't delivered yet, and didn't want to know how things were going, thinking it might influence what they'd say. They wanted to remain true to their guts. Yusyta shared the same way of thinking.

Before intermission was over, Yusyta talked it over with Mick and Dave, and they all agreed she would go next. After her, there'd be only one challenger, Mick and Dave yet to speak. And probably short closing statements, questions and any back and forth debates that would arise.

The audience slowly trickled back in and found their seats.

Yusyta stepped into position. She was nervous, for she was about to tell many what she only had the courage in the past to tell a few. Once the murmur of the crowd subsided, she commenced.

"I'm sure most of you, at this very moment, are thinking, *What is she doing up front speaking on behalf of the pro-alliance committee?* I'm not a soldier in any way, nor am I a weapons manufacturer, war adviser, battle philosopher, or anything relatable. Though, I'm hoping in the end you'll find my reason for speaking to be as just as the rest. Only a very few of you know what I'm about to say. It will surely come as a surprise to most of the rest of you. I'll just come out and say it: I spent over a decade in Garobansurov. I unexpectedly fell in love there and lived happily married for that time. I only came back because I missed my family and my people. He would have come back with me, I'm sure, but I never asked him to out of respect for you, my compatriots. His name is Alfonso Alardo, and I have just recently learned he is now a monk at Dourinuset Monastery in Garobansurov. I am basically here to give my opinion on the character of the Garobansurovian people, those who I knew personally, so all of you can see what kind of individuals with whom my colleagues and I are trying to persuade you to join sides.

I had lived in a small town in Garobansurov and knew all the kind souls by the end. Of course, the village consisted of a few personages not entirely striving for morality, but only a very few. But as a whole, they would've done anything in their power to see everyone in the village made it through the winters.

I remember clear as crystal my first day in the village. My Icytryxan friends who were with me at the time can also attest to this memory if they choose to. We, perfect strangers, had gone from shop to shop to procure supplies in the small village. The shopkeepers all did their best to see we'd gathered everything on our supply lists without any trouble. It was an approach to compassion they resumed my entire time there.

There were countless occasions when they performed favors for me, none more memorable than when I was sick and immobile. And even on one occasion, with Alfonso out of town, a lady named Betty cooked homemade soup for me while keeping me company for days—something friends would do for one another routinely.

It wasn't just the people of my village who went above and beyond. A kind gesture with a smile was common practice for those in Garobansurov.

I've heard many stories about the Molisians, and how these people are nothing like the Garobansurovians, stories that would make you cringe and have sleepless nights. I'll tell you these stories upon the asking. But for now, I'll keep them out of my soliloquy, since there are kids present.

It was also easy to trade for a place to spend the night. And I remember specifically three times when they wouldn't even accept payment for the accommodations.

Another account I must share goes as thus. It concerns a Garobansurovian general and his charge, the same general Jason had talked about earlier.

The General and his army took refuge in our village. It was a winter much colder than normal, and the soldiers had just needed a few weeks respite, before continuing their march. Every single home of our village had soldiers staying it. Alfonso and I took in four. For the two weeks, the soldiers staying with us were as courteous as can be. I imagine they were a little rowdier at the taverns, but while under our roof, they exhibited the utmost respect. They even did all the wood chopping for us. We didn't have to chop any more wood for the entire rest of the winter. Plus, one of them was good at hunting, having supplied us with enough meat to last months. I had even met General Ulfenkerki. He came to the house because he had a question for one of the guys. The man was well-mannered and considerate. On his way out, he shoveled our walkway in the dark—without even telling us he was going to do it. I can definitely see why his soldiers, including Jason (plus Mick, Dave and Yori), speak so highly of him. The soldiers left town with it being in better shape than it was before they came. We were actually all sad to see them leave. And sadder yet, knowing they had to go back out into the cold, unforgiving wilderness.

Up to this point, I have given you a reasonable amount of testimony, depicting what I believe to be the fine moral fiber of the Garobansurovians, but if all I had to say was what I've said so far, I probably wouldn't be confronting you all and revealing my painful secret. Although the former was all solid evidence, what I'm about to get into next is what has principally brought me here tonight. I believe wholeheartedly in the genuineness of what I'm about to divulge. I believe with a part of my very soul—the very best part. My confidence in this truth is so vast it makes the number of stars in the sky seem small. Now is when I will divulge in the exceptional, love-defining spirit of a specific Garobansurovian: my husband, Alfonso. By doing this, I hope you all can vividly see precisely what kind of people with whom we'll be siding, by chance you decide to do so.

I'll begin by telling you about the very first day we met. Like I mentioned earlier, we had gone into town to get supplies for our camping excursion. There was one thing on my list that nobody in town had: fishing hooks. Fortunately, I was told about someone who might have some and where I could find him. Subsequently, I went to search him out. Upon meeting him, I was immediately awestruck. Alfonso had a way about him that made me feel alive. He didn't have the hooks on his person. But having barely known me for an hour, he graciously volunteered to go on a many mile journey to retrieve for me the ones he'd stashed somewhere else. I couldn't resist and went with him. On this journey was when I fell in love.

When we got back from the trip for the hooks, I said goodbye to him, and rendezvoused with my friends with the intention of finishing up the trip with them and coming back home. But I just couldn't leave him behind. I changed my mind and ran back to be with Alfonso, in dramatic fashion. My friends returned home, and I stayed with him in Garobansurov for over ten years.

I'm not exaggerating when I say this, but every day with him was as magical as the first. His ability to let me know I was truly loved was something to behold, a characteristic we here all strive for. He always made me feel that what I had to say was important to him. And equally as important, on a regular basis, he began conversations with me that were specifically created just for me. Knowing someone was saying specific things tuned just for me, and no one else, filled my days with unbridled joy.

There was an incident that happened I must tell you about in order to fully portray how compassionate and selfless he was. Alfonso and I were hiking in an area in Garobansurov known as the Dalart River Batholith, an ancient lava flow cooled a billion years ago. Rock outcrops were everywhere, towering beautifully over the landscape. Some you could walk on, some you couldn't. We'd been walking on a rock platform that gradually inclined upwards when the incident occurred. We reached a point with multiple ledges, where I was on one and he was on another. I took a moment to myself and looked over the trees to the horizon. I guess I looked with a little too much focus and didn't even notice the huge gust of wind that came out of nowhere, on an otherwise windless day. It knocked me off balance. I shifted my free foot onto a loose, unstable rock in an attempt to regain my balance. And because the rock was unstable, it gave way, forcing me to slip and fall. The horrific part was that I was so far off-balance by this point that I couldn't by myself possibly avoid hitting my head on a rock protrusion.

Alfonso witnessed the whole thing happen. Without giving any thought for his own safety, he dove headfirst from off the ledge he was on. Wielding outstretched arms, he was just in time able to get his hands between the rock protrusion and my head, completely absorbing the blow. He saved my life. He ended up breaking a couple of his ribs and nose in the process, both rather painful injuries. Yet, he never let me see the pain. He didn't want me to feel bad for falling. It was second nature for him to do things like that for me. We actually enjoyed the rest of the day, continuing to view as much of the breathtaking locale as daylight permitted. A part of me wanted to go back home, because I knew how much pain he was in, but he absolutely insisted we seize the day. Having just saved my life, I really had no grounds to argue.

I could share countless stories about my husband, but I feel I've already exhausted enough of your time. It's already getting late. But before I conclude my talk, I must say that I would give my life for a particular Garobansurovian, my husband, my legacy. And I would do the same if it meant continued safety for all Garobansurovians. I know Alfonso would do the equivalent for me, and my people, if he knew they existed. These are the kinds of people with whom we'd be siding. I believe in this alliance with great fervor and would sacrifice everything to see it through to fruition. Molisia just can't annihilate them all. I beg you, please. Please, don't let them."

Through a wall of emotion, Yusyta stepped down from the stage.

Yori gave Yusyta a huge, comforting hug, as the audience soaked it all in.

It seemed as if even the opposition's final speaker was affected by Yusyta's passion. It clearly took her a few moments to escape her trance and make it to the stage.

To many it seemed odd how the anti-alliance team didn't save their best speaker for last, as this last speaker read her 10-minute speech almost strictly from note cards. The anti-alliance's penultimate speaker spoke by memory, having stolen the crowd's interest way more. Ending with a bang goes a long way. Perhaps she did have it memorized, but was just that affected by Yusyta.

This miscalculation was undoubtedly good for the citizens of Garobansurov, or at least that was what Mick and Dave were thinking.

For no reason, Mick and Dave ended up going last. They were proud of what they had prepared but knew they couldn't match Yusyta's extremely personal aspect of her soliloquy. In hindsight, they should've had her go last, but nobody had any idea she was going to dig so deep into her heart for her words. Neither Mick nor Dave had any intention of speaking for as long as Yori or Yusyta had, but they did plan on doing so with the same amount of conviction.

Dave jogged out to the speaking podium and began his turn by giving a summary of all the battle scenarios they formed and their outcomes.

After he ran through all these, he began speaking on the key scenario he and Mick had just come out of victoriously against the Icytryxan platoon. "The Icytryxan soldiers, Mick, and I lined up on the river, they on their side, Mick and I on our side. By. . ."—For no apparent reason to the listeners at the time, Dave paused for the briefest of moments after the first word of the sentence. But it was a planned part of the speech for poetic effect—

"... agreeing to the outline, we simulated battle. Each of us not knowing the meaning of the words 'no holding back.' The projectiles flew at us relentlessly; the danger real. My partner and I didn't know what to expect. We were bombarded on both the left and the right side. By. . . the time the pain caused from one metallic peril from the sky subsided, a whole new pain from another arose. Anyone facing the sharpened version of the projectiles would've surely gotten torn to shreds. Soldier after soldier came at us, none without drive, none without cultural pride. Winning for us was so far-fetched that at first it barely crossed our minds. However, eventually the possibility started to seep into our consciousnesses.

Mick and I set out on a mission: We wanted to show you all how very possible it is for the greatest of armies to succumb to one of any stature. And that there is no point at which one can truly feel completely safe under their army's protective umbrella, no matter how powerful an army.

Darkness was upon us. We finally reached their side. By. . . then, their numbers had been greatly diminished. But not their spirit. They unleashed the formidable atlytls at a substantial rate. With no reserve, we charged in." Dave seamlessly relinquished the stage to Mick, an obviously planned maneuver for how fluid the switch-off was. A mere two seconds elapsed during the trade-off.

Speaking in the same poetic fashion as Dave, Mick began. "That last projectile onslaught during our final charge was the worst we faced. We both to this day are still healing from those injuries. They closed in on us, trying to trap. We made our last stand, having established a temporary base from where to fight. A few sturdy trees were on our side. By..."—Mick continued the same brief pause after the word *by* each time, as Dave had. "... the way of determination, we whittled away the opposition, until only two were left. The fight was a true test, a great effort. In the end, Dave and I emerged triumphantly, defeating an entire platoon, strength of purpose at our side. By… perseverance and grit we did it. Now, we just hope that all of you can see that even a great atlytl army is vulnerable, that a permanent alliance with Garobansurov can only serve to patch this vulnerability. I will fight with every ounce of my soul for you. Dave will fight with every ounce of his soul for you. Garobansurov will fight with every ounce of her soul for you. Let us be the ones to aid you, to stand with you . . .”

Dave ran to join Mick on stage. In unison and on beat, the two emphatically declared (this time without the pause after *by*), “. . . side-by-side. Side-by-side, we can preserve our freedom.”

Dave and Mick stood next to each other and would alternate speaking for the next part of their speech. “Side-by-side, our people can be secure,” blazoned Dave.

“Side-by-side, we grow strong by learning from each other,” announced Mick.

“Side-by-side, we have each other's back, until the very end,” Dave transmitted.

“Side-by-side, we'll give it our all, fighting the good fight.” Mick pumped his fist, dramatically.

“Side-by-side, nothing sneaks up on us in the night,” said Dave in crescendo, raising his hand into the air, matching, if not overtaking, Mick's exposure of drama.

Mick realized the crowd was starting to buzz, and he grew in enthusiasm. “Side-by-side, our children grow old.”

The crowd became even louder yet. Dave curled his lips and, again, increased his vehemence. "Side-by-side, our warriors will feel the true meaning of honor and loyalty."

Mick and Dave knew they had them. They clasped hands, raised them in the air, and together hollered as loud as they could over the crowd, "Side-by-side. Knowing we've done everything we could, nothing can defeat us!"

The audience erupted in elation, and chanted repeatedly, "Side-by-side!" Even a couple members of the opposing team joined in on the chant.

During the chant, Jason leaned over to Yori and Yusyta to say, "I guess there will be no Q and A and closing statements." The trio chuckled briefly.

Mick and Dave then knew, seeing the crowd involved at the end, that them giving the last speech worked out perfectly.

The pair enthusiastically went out into the crowd to be a part. The rest of the team followed.

The entirety of the Javeti Edifice was engulfed by thrill. People sang, people danced.

They accomplished the impossible: There would be an alliance.

Chapter 24

THE PEOPLE OF the Capital were happy to see Ulfenkerki was back, along with the segment of the army he mobilized. They were a little less in number, but not much. Ulfenkerki was pleased to learn nothing negative happened while he was away. Nobody, though, was happier about the return than King Rowlangiv. He really did care for and love his citizens, it wasn't just an act. Having Ulfenkerki and the soldiers back meant an even safer environment for the townspeople. Still, Rowlangiv knew Ulfenkerki leaving in the first place was something that had to be done.

The returning soldiers were glad the long, grueling walk was over. They headed straight to the barracks for much deserved rest, while Ulfenkerki headed straight to the King to give the full report.

Rowlangiv already knew about the battle at the mine-base because informed representatives had been dispatched to the Capital ahead of the army. Nevertheless, the General's report would be much more detailed. Rowlangiv was anxious to learn everything.

The King and General met up in the castle.

"Welcome back, ecstatic to see you," voiced a sincere King.

"Thank you, sir. I guess I made it through another battle and ensuing march."

"No doubts. Only the good die young, old friend."

Ulfenkerki chuckled. "Ain't that the truth. So, as you know, we were victorious at the base, with minimal casualties. The bad news is the tyrant, General Gamald, is still at large, whom I'm ninety-five percent sure spearheaded the attack."

"Figures."

"I left a garrison behind to manage the base. If a large force attacks, they were instructed to let it go. But I have a feeling that won't happen. My gut is telling me Gamald is hiding in the wild somewhere, swelling his numbers, and that the mine-base will no longer be significant to him. Trust me, we tried our hardest to find him. But there is so much vastness in the northern mountains that we'd probably need a few years more of constant searching to comb the whole thing."

"Yes, better you came back."

"I'm sure, sooner or later, he'll make himself known. In the meantime, we'll continue to stockpile, enlist, plan, train and prepare. Who knows, maybe we'll even be allied with a foreign race by then."

"Wouldn't that be extraordinary."

"We did end up bringing some prisoners back with us. I think we already coerced as much info out of them as we're going to, but we'll keep trying. They are a pretty well-behaved lot; I'm not seeing us having any difficulties with them. Not like that last bunch. Maybe I'll keep them separated."

"Good thinking," stated Rowlangiv.

"Furthermore, we should have a fair amount of warning if Gamald marches, since I've left a significant scout network back by the mountains. I haven't ordered them to keep searching for Gamald, only to keep watch for mass movement. If an army so much as sneezes in the direction of the Capital, we'll know about it."

Ulfenkerki and Rowlangiv talked war matters for another hour. They ended up eating supper together in the castle's main dining hall.

THE GROUP OF THREE Molisians that had escaped the mine-base battle made it back by Gamald and his main army hiding out in the Baustic Mountains' caves and tunnels. Normally, Gamald killed retreaters, but before they left for battle, Gamald had informed these three specifically (behind closed doors) they could escape to bring back information if things got dire. So, they were left alive. Gamald grew upset about losing the battle so badly. But it was an anger short-lived, mainly because of the fact his main army was starting to swell-up so considerably. He knew it would take a while to amass enough to march on the Capital, but he recognized a march was inevitable. He just hoped it would happen before the caves reached critical mass.

The reason soldiers were now trickling in from Molisia at such a substantial rate was because of a proclamation made by a certain southern Molisian faction. It noted that any soldiers helping in the war would get first pick at the newly acquired land, and that all raping and pillaging during wartime was allowed therein. The second half of the proclamation really rang true for a certain breed—the immoral. The people of Garobansurov were facing a potential nightmare of epic proportions.

But at least they weren't facing it alone anymore.

MICK, DAVE and the rest of the team jovially spent two hours talking with everyone after the assembly at the Javeti Edifice.

When the last member of the audience left the Edifice, the squad cleaned up and walked home. Unfortunately, it was pretty late by this time.

"It seemed," observed Mick, "that a lot of those I talked with were okay with leaving for Garobansurov as soon as possible. They understand the war is escalating, and the fact that things could get dangerously intense rather quickly."

"I talked with an Icytryxan who told me where all the sea-fairing vessels are now and the process deployed to get them battle-ready," noted Jason. "I tried to follow the details, but got lost at some point, due to the complexities. But generally, it seemed that all the ships could be here in Saraty in a week, ready to set sail."

"Yes, we have small cruisers we send around the archipelago with messages," said Syryx. "The network is rather intricate, but it certainly is efficient. A week sounds about right. Half the ships are within proximity. I'm sure all the ships will leave for Garobansurov at once."

"Are there enough ships to haul everyone?" asked Jason.

"I think there are twenty ships, enough to haul a thousand head," replied Thyxer. "Last I remember, we have 2,400 soldiers in the atlytl corps and another 600 in various other military branches. These other branches are mainly geared to operate the defensive systems here, and probably will remain behind to protect the mainland. As for the atlytl company, almost half will come. The number of soldiers desiring to go should almost match the amount of room on the ships. If there isn't enough room for everyone who wants to come, it really isn't that big of a deal; a few of the boats can always make a second trip."

"We'll, no doubt, have to build more barracks at the Capital," said Yori. "There won't be enough room for everyone without doing so. It's an easy task, plenty of wood in Garobansurov."

"I also think it would be wise for Rowlangiv to order the construction of an elevated platform-type structure against the insides of all the walls for the Icytryxans, a strategic place from where to launch projectiles over the wall," commented Jason.

"Yes, that would be a good idea. There are raised sections scattered about, but not nearly enough of them for a thousand additional long-range specialists. The majority of the archer towers are in position to protect the castle itself. We'd probably leave archers as opposed to atlytl wielders in those, since an increase in distance wouldn't entirely be needed there. Where an increase in launch distance is needed the most is looking out beyond the city itself. There are so many tactics we can utilize; it really is kind of exciting. I'm going to get a headache thinking of them all," stated Yori, enthusiastically scratching her head.

"Don't hurt yourself." Jason chuckled. "We'll build grand platforms, large enough upon which the Icytryxans can be distributed evenly, like a thousand finches in a field feeding on seeds."

Yori laughed. "I've never heard that one before. But now that I think of it, yes, finches do tend to space themselves out evenly, as they go at it."

"I think they do it to cover as much ground as possible, while also remaining on the lookout for predators."

"That could be. For the Icytryxan soldiers, the more elbow room they have to swing their atlytls, the better," said Yori. She whimsically jumped through a whirlwind scuttling across the road. "That was fun."

"This whole night was fun. A success to be remembered," noted Mick.

Syryx proclaimed, "You all gave wonderful speeches tonight. It was a pleasure to listen to them all."

"Same to you," responded everyone.

The group arrived at the house and went straight to bed.

At army training the next day, news of what happened the previous night at the Edifice reached all the ears of those who hadn't yet heard. The whole army rallied together excitedly about what had transpired. It was exciting times. They all spent the day organizing themselves for what they called *the great departure*. It was the consensus they could all be ready for the sea-crossing in a week. Also, that day, the intricate ship recalling procedure began.

The Icytryxans spent the day not in fear of war, but in elation of gaining a permanent ally. They all felt safer. Even though they haven't physically seen a threat in many years, they always felt danger could strike at anytime from anywhere. In their hearts they now knew having an entire country watching their backside in the years to come would prove to be incredibly valuable.

Mick and Dave spent the day carrying weapons to the storage sheds situated near the docks. This way the weapons could be loaded onto the ships with ease when the time came.

Jason and Yori spent most of the day unearthing potatoes. A lot would be needed for the trip. In the morning, they would haul them to the available ships' pantries.

Throughout the next few days, things were predominantly hectic on the island of Swyrove. Everyone (soldier and civilian alike) helped to get ready for the departure—ships were loaded, families spent as much time together as possible, weapons were sharpened, armor was polished, plans were finalized. The Garobansurovians assisted as much as they could, alongside savoring what more than likely would be the last few experiences they'd have in the foreign land. Only war would bring them back, a tragedy they would try to prevent as much as they could.

One night, the four Garobansurovians made a point to walk through downtown Saraty one last time together. It was a relishing most bittersweet. They tried to go to as many places as possible, mainly ones they had yet to visit.

Having been washed by new experiences galore, the four had received enough emotion to fill a swimming pool.

Things were all flowing very smoothly. The day before the planned exodus came. By then, all the ships were in the harbor and loaded with all the needed supplies.

Everything was going as planned, everything except for one thing. That night, the Garobansurovians and all but one of their hosts were informed of something none of them expected. Yusyta (the aforementioned one) gathered everyone into the Fantysy-Escape game room. Everyone looked at each other across the game table in astonishment, wondering what could possibly be going on.

Pale as a ghost, Yusyta cleared her throat, and voiced, "Ever since Yori told me about Mick and Dave's experience with Alfonso, my mind has been all over the place. And especially since the Icytryxan decision to aid Garobansurov, certain things have been going round and round in my brain. The alliance has actually allowed something that's never before been possible: me being in the same general area as much of my family, my culture, and… my beloved. Now I know all of you won't be in Garobansurov for the war, which was why the decision has taken me this long to make. Otherwise, I probably would've made it an hour after the verdict at the Javeti Edifice. So here goes…

"I concluded I'll be going along with the army, Thyxer, and Syryx, and stay in Garobansurov as a culture-to-culture translator/interpreter. The cultural gap will be large and having someone there who knows both cultures will help the transition greatly. Though, integrating us all as seamlessly as possible isn't exactly my driving force. I guess what I'm trying to say is that I'm mainly going to Garobansurov to be near Alfonso. I know he's a monk and that he has taken vows, and that things can't go back to the way they were. But seeing both my family and Alfonso from time-to-time will at last complete my soul.

"I am very sad I'll be leaving you all, leaving all but you, Syryx and Thyxer. Let's at least make the best of what time we do have together, in conjunction with making the best of the time we have left with our guests. Considering this, I suggest we all have a final one-day version of Fantysy-Escape."

Dirax couldn't hide his sadness. "I will miss you so much. But don't feel bad at all about going back. If it's what your heart tells you, it's the right thing to do. I love your idea of having one last Fantysy-Escape game. I will enjoy it more than any game we've ever played."

Everyone agreed that Yusyta's idea to play one final game together was fantastic. Although they were stunned, they were understanding and joyous at Yusyta's decision. All those inside the Narutyx house nearly matched Yusyta's excitement on her happy moment.

They would eventually learn that many of Yusyta's fellow Icytryxan citizens were delighted she was going back to be by her husband. Her speech at the Javeti Edifice would come full circle. It was truly a romantic development that touched their hearts.

THE GROUP enthusiastically brought snacks down to the playing board. They played well into the night, and in the end, Dirax was confident it was definitely the best match of his life—he even won. Not once during the game did he think about the pain of losing his sister. He enjoyed the moment. The rest of the family's experience was very similar.

Mick, Dave, Jason, and Yori basked in their last night as much as they could. All four of them were proud, for it was on this night when each of them finally let it completely sink in that they were actually successful in their monumental mission.

They did it.

Departure day came, and before leaving the house, Yusyta and the Garobansurovians all said and received heartfelt goodbyes to and from everyone. The warriors Syryx and Thyxer also said goodbyes, but they weren't leaving permanently… hopefully.

The kids (her nieces and nephews) cried and gave Yusyta one final hug.

Dirax looked at the departing group and announced, "I know it may sound a bit dramatic, but I decided I'm going to accompany you to the ships to wave goodbye as they sail away."

"It's not overly dramatic," returned Yusyta. "It's a very sweet gesture. I'll be sure to wave back with extra sincere flail."

The Garobansurovians had brought most of their stuff to the ships the day before. The only things that were left to grab on the way out were the *black needle* swords—uncharacteristically, two things that'd barely received any attention lately.

The sword handles did feel good nestled in their owners' hands once again.

Everyone volunteered to help carry Yusyta's belongings to the docks. She never got the chance to carry her stuff to the ships the day previous like everyone else, as she'd only made the ultimate decision to depart an hour before telling everyone about it. She traveled lighter than what one would think for a person leaving indefinitely. Visibly, Yusyta wasn't a very materialistic person.

Before leaving the house, the Garobansurovians walked through it one last time, letting all the nostalgia seep in. Their months in the house would genuinely be of the most memorable times of their lives.

Syryx and Thyxer were inevitably going to war, so their spouses had a hard time letting them go, as would anyone suffering loved ones departing for war. They embraced for an extremely long time.

After final farewells, the party started for the ships. But before they were out of eyeshot, the Garobansurovians and the Icytryxans made sure to look back at the family one last time. They never looked more beautiful.

Reaching seaside, Dave exclaimed as he looked around, "Wow, what a commotion! I knew it would be busy down here this morning, but I didn't expect it to be quite like this."

"Just imagine how full of activity it would be here," added Syryx, "if most us hadn't preloaded our stuff."

"I'm glad it worked out that everyone coming could all fit onto the ships," commented Yusyta. "I'd hate to have to wait for a second wave of sea-crossings."

"There actually was a couple dozen beyond max occupancy, but enough had already volunteered to sleep rustically on the big ships," said Thyxer. "We never really had to announce the slight overflow."

"I'm especially glad all of us are able to make the voyage on the same ship," noted Mick.

"Me too," replied Yusyta.

"There is a lot more livestock making the passage than what I had anticipated. I guess some soldiers really like their meat fresh." Dirax chuckled.

Mick, Dave and the rest of the group approached the mighty ship to which they were assigned. They didn't go onboard right away; instead, they spent some time on shore conversing with the other soldiers who'd be on same boat. Some they knew, some they didn't.

By the time the crossing would be over, they'd know them all rather well.

Eventually, the hubbub dissipated, and everyone and everything making the trip was on their respective ships.

Temporarily onboard, Dirax clinched his family tight, last but not least, Yusyta. To his sister, he aired, "I'm very proud of you, beautiful, courageous sister. I know it's hard for you to leave your homeland, but it takes a strong person to not just follow an arduous path but to create their own. I will always think about your happiness, and I will constantly replay in my mind the story of you and Alfonso's meeting. That joy you felt will go on and on in my heart, forever. I love you, sister. Farewell."

"You always know just the right things to say to make me feel better. That's one of the things I will miss most. I'll make a point every day to imagine you happily thinking about my and Alfonso's meeting. This in turn will make me happy."

"I'll do it at sunset every night," declared Dirax.

"As will I. It'll be like we were never parted. I love you dearly." Yusyta smiled at Dirax larger than the ocean she was about to cross.

Dirax bade a last farewell to Mick, Dave, Jason, Yori, Thyxer, Syryx, and stepped off the boat onto the dock, just as its tie-downs were being removed.

Just like he promised, as the ship inched away, Dirax stood with a smile, devotedly waving. Yusyta returned the heartfelt gesture.

It was one of those moments that even the inventor of destiny gazed in admiration.

CHAPTER 25

ALL THE SHIPS were now mobile and sea-bound, staying within eyeshot of each other. The trip was expected to be a little shorter than one coming from the opposite direction, due to favorable ocean currents.

Dave, Mick, and Jason spent that first day onboard doing their favorite thing to do on a boat—fishing. They decided to try to not catch another one of those fish so humongous that the meat took forever to eat. They knew having enough food would never be an issue. They used little baits, and thankfully caught little fish.

That night, the Garobansurovians barely noticed the great size reduction in their sleeping quarters compared to that of their trip to the island—only a greedy person would.

The days at sea went by quickly. Everyone onboard was enthusiastic. Animated discussions and strolls about the ship saw no shortage. Plus, disagreements were few and far in between.

It was learned that all ships had similar agreeable atmospheres—no surprise.

The passengers tried to not spend the voyage talking about military matters; they knew the future would hold plenty of that.

Eventually, a large fish supply did end up accruing, but it wasn't too much to handle—not like before. Mick caught the weirdest-looking fish any of them had ever seen. It had teeth where one wouldn't expect to see teeth. It tasted like crap, but Mick ate it nevertheless; he felt sorry for it because nobody wanted to eat it. In retrospect, he should've let it go.

Nearly a week at sea went by without anything unfortunate happening. A lot of the time, the four Garobansurovians spent their nights on the deck. They talked about the stars and conjured stories of the distant worlds within these stars' gravitational influences. By no stretch of the imagination were these stories lacking in inventiveness. Perhaps they were a little too inventive.

The final leg of the sea voyage wasn't quite as flawless as the rest. A large storm hit, rendering a great diminishment of visibility. The storm wasn't powerful enough for anyone to ever worry about capsizing or sinking, but it was enough to separate the ships. Each boat had an adept sea navigator on board, so the division wasn't too troublesome. In the end, each one found their way.

They didn't all land at the same spot on the Garobansurov shore, but close enough that they only lost half a day waiting for everyone to join up for the march north to the Capital. It was a pleasant wait, as practically all had never been to a foreign shore.

Just like Thyxer, Syryx, and their company utilized to reach the Capital the first time, the Icytryxan army had small rowboats, with which to haul provisions up the Geenhuvagal River. There weren't enough boats for all the soldiers, so half walked. Both transportation methods took roughly the same amount of time, since it was upriver, and the boats were conveniently loaded with most of the weighty supplies.

Being amongst the walking segment, Mick said to Dave, "I'm starting to regret my decision of not putting the Quintaga armor on the rowboats."

"Same here. It really can be heavy, if you know you don't actually have to carry it."

"Sometimes we can be too nice for our own good. Maybe we'll run into one of the emptier boats coming upstream today, and we can toss the suits onboard."

"Yeah, hopefully."

Later that day, Hawk and Leopard were blessed with a bout of luck, for they did encounter a rowboat with extra room and were able to throw the heavy armor onboard.

When the rowboats reached the point on the river that was no longer passable by watercraft, they were beached and tied down. Some time was spent putting covers over the rowboats, because they would more than likely sit there for a while, unlike the sea ships. All but a couple of the sea ships would be brought back to Swyrove for other duties.

It didn't take long for everyone to link together, but they did decide to campout before moving on towards the Capital.

To increase dramatic effect, the Icytryxans chose to not send an advance party ahead to inform of their coming. They thought it would be quite memorable for those of the Capital to see their new allies first with their own eyes, instead of hearing they were on the way. It was Thyxer's idea. He always liked a grand entrance, and this would surely be it.

Of course, the scouts of the Capital would spot them and know they were coming, and therefore Rowlangiv and Ulfenkerki would know. But Thyxer was acquainted with Rowlangiv enough to know the King would understand what was happening and leave the arrival a secret.

The Icytryxan army left early in the morning, planning to reach the Capital by nightfall.

At about the time the army was pulling camp, Rowlangiv's scouts did reach him with the news. And just like Thyxer had thought, the King comprehended their motives for not sending informants and heralders ahead. He kept the great coming a pleasant little secret for his subjects.

Even kings could be graced by whimsy.

Rowlangiv said to himself, *I can't wait to see the looks on their faces. It's sure to be a day of days.*

Just before reaching eyeshot of the city, the Icytryxan soldiers formed ranks to make the entrance just that much more fascinating. Some had a small flag in their hands to add flair. And some had a large one. But none were holding a weapon. They wanted to refrain from looking the least bit threatening. The weapons were stored in carts trailing way in the back.

When King Rowlangiv spotted the Icytryxan mass from the highest window in his castle (the highest vantage point of town), he began rushing to the city's main entrance. Along the way, he tried his best to look casual; he was still trying to keep the secret. Although it wasn't easy—kings rushing down the streets wasn't exactly an everyday occurrence.

Sometimes known to exhibit some otherworldly sense of calculation, General Ulfenkerki was already near the gate, standing under a wooden balcony, when Rowlangiv drew near.

"I suppose with both of us here," said Rowlangiv to Ulfenkerki, "we're going to have to fabricate an excuse for our presence to keep up the secret until the last possible moment."

"If a villager asks," said the General, "we can tell them we are inspecting and discussing the city walls."

"Heck of an idea," Rowlangiv affirmed. "It might turn out to look like a long discussion; the Icytryxans are a couple miles away yet."

"It might, but I'm sure we can pull it off," Ulfenkerki stated, confidently. "Maybe we could actually talk about the wall. It really is quite the wall. And conversation piece."

Rowlangiv chuckled. "That it is, my friend. That it is. You go ahead and begin. I'll jump in when the moment compels me to."

"Sounds good."

"I hope we have enough immediately available beds for them," said Rowlangiv. "We will surely construct more barracks for permanent use ASAP. I guess I'm just a little worried about tonight."

"I wouldn't worry. Judging by my experiences abroad, your people, your commendable patriots, have no problem at all in taking soldiers into their homes. It's never once been problematic," Ulfenkerki said, having no idea of the irony this sentiment was recently discussed across the sea.

"I suppose you're right. I'm just worrying for nothing."

Breaking from his customary stoicism, General Ulfenkerki concocted a comical accent and blurted, "I'll help your nerves... This wall really is great isn't it? Can withstand much damage. Will last many, many generations."

Rowlangiv laughed, and just like that, he stopped worrying about housing.

The citizens of the Capital knew all about 'the mission,' and that it was a possibility they'd receive help from a foreign race. But for most of them, the concept hadn't completely sunk in. The arrival of an army with an appearance entirely different from anything they'd ever seen before took them by total surprise.

The first civilians to see the approaching mass were the ones perched in high buildings with a view looking over the wall. These few started it all with a small cheer. When the rest of the city heard this, they franticly searched out the reason for the noise.

In no time, all of town knew what was going on. The entire Capital was full of thunderous merriment—even before the Icytryxans became an atlytl throw's distance away.

The soldiers within the Icytryxan ranks couldn't help but smile, hearing the commotion emanating from within the city walls. A lot of them raised their flags higher into the air, as some let out yelps of their own. It was one of Mick and Dave's proudest moments—truly one to insert into their ongoing philosophical equation of life.

People of the Capital started to trickle out of the entrance and exit gates to welcome their new allies. Before long, lines of spectators formed on both sides of the Icytryxans. They really were awestruck. Seeing an entire army consisting of individuals so different physically opened their eyes widely. The villagers couldn't help but envision the Icytryxans in action. It was a thought, which instantly made them feel safer. The Garobansurovians were pleasantly surprised when trying to communicate with the Icytryxan soldiers and learning that the two cultures' languages were extremely similar— minus the sounds of a few letters. Some even spoke their language.

Bringing up the rear were Mick, Dave, Jason, and Yori, who were also welcomed with great enthusiasm. Mostly everyone amongst the spectators were well aware of who embarked on the great mission to acquire the allies. There was no failure in a showing of just appreciation for the four.

All the foreign soldiers made it inside the city through the bulk of the commotion. They were informed by officials that they could proceed to the army barracks to unload their provisions.

Instead of going with the Icytryxans to the barracks, Mick, Dave, Jason, and Yori stopped by Ulfenkerki and the King, who were still standing in the shade under the balcony.

"Well done, friends," declared Rowlangiv, earnestly. "I knew the right people were selected for the job. Whose idea was it to stage this grand entrance?"

"It was Thyxer's idea."

"I'll have to thank him the next time I see him. I can't wait to discuss with you the details of how this became possible."

"As do we," returned Mick. "It's quite the story."

Ulfenkerki noted, "If they're half as formidable as they look, the Molisians will have a heck of a time trying to capture the Capital now."

"Oh, trust me," said Jason, "their atlytl projectiles are more fearsome than ten thousand thunderstorms. Just ask Mick and Dave here. They witnessed it firsthand." Rowlangiv and Ulfenkerki quizzically turned to look at Hawk and Leopard.

"We'll save that story for later too," voiced Dave.

"I can't wait to hear all about this. The anticipation is unbearable," noted Rowlangiv. "We'll meet in the castle for stories, tonight?"

"Sounds good. Did anything significant happen here while we were gone?"

Ulfenkerki replied to Dave, "Nothing really in town here, but we had a battle at a newly acquired forward base. We'll discuss that too at our meeting, tonight."

"Excellent."

"See you all tonight then," said Rowlangiv, stepping out from underneath the balcony. He started walking towards the barracks, and hollered back, "I can't thank you four enough for this!"

Much of town met up at the barracks in continuance of welcoming the Icytryxans. It turned out to be an atmosphere very much like that of the night before the Knowing Circle celebration. The Icytryxans were very glad to be there. Not for a second did they regret their decision to become allies.

The two cultures' soldiers got along splendidly, though not seamlessly, as to be expected. Foreign languages were learned quickly by both races.

The quest to procure beds for everyone began. Many of the Icytryxans would bunk in the barracks, while some found refuge with civilians.

Ulfenkerki saw a familiar face in the crowd, (a lady dressed in Icytryxan garb) and said, "I remember you from a long time ago. You and your husband had some of my soldiers stay with you. I forget the name of the little town we were in, though. I had no idea you were Icytryxis. I bet there's a story there somewhere."

Having recognized the voice immediately, Yusyta replied, "I very much remember you. In fact, I've always wanted to thank you for shoveling my walkway that night. I never got a chance to. Thank you so much for that. You would be correct, there is a story. I'll have to tell you it sometime."

"Excellent. Have you found a place to sleep?"

"Nope, not yet."

"I have an extra bed in the officers' quarters. It's yours if you'd like."

"Thank you so much. I'll probably only need it for a night or two on the onset, however. I need to make a journey before I get settled in."

"I bet that journey is part of the story."

"That it is. An important journey a thousand times over."

"I can't wait to hear it," remarked the General. "And you're welcome for the shoveling. I remember doing that too. I have a meeting in the castle to go to shortly, but first, I'll show you to the room. Things may get a little hectic around here, but I hope you make yourself at home while you're here."

"Thank you very much, sir. And I'm sure I will."

General Ulfenkerki showed Yusyta the room, and as she got settled in, he left the barracks for the castle. He met up with Rowlangiv, Mick, Dave, Jason, and Yori. The six of them discussed every detail that'd transpired since the inception of the mission. The conversation lasted for more hours than fingers on the hand. In the end, Rowlangiv was greatly impressed, and felt he couldn't express enough gratitude.

The commotion in town settled down, and the Icytryxans were all able to spend their first night in Garobansurov through peaceful sleeps.

Construction began vigorously in the morning on the new Icytryxis barracks, which would foreseeably take a month for completion. Many of the other militarized assembly projects involving the Icytryxis were now under way too. These included: practice atlytl firing zones, defensive launch-platforms, atlytl workshops, and a mass projectile foundry. Jason was especially delighted to learn his countrymen had planned to craft many Thorncat Missiles.

Through a cool morning breeze, Mick and Dave started walking to Tim Warmane's blacksmith shop. In the perfect weather, they found themselves talking about something they hadn't discussed in a very long time. "When do you think we should head back home, Dave?"

"I don't know exactly, but probably soon. I'm sure people back home are starting to worry about what happened to us. We left for the Knowing Circle presentation, and never came back. I actually have been wondering when Yusyta was going to walk to Dourinuset to share her news with Alfonso. We could possibly coincide our departure with hers and accompany her most of the way there, at least to the Dourinuset hill, perhaps."

"That slipped into my mind this morning too. I'm sure she's anxious to see him and will venture soon."

"We'll talk to her, after our visit with Tim."

Hawk and Leopard arrived at their old friend's blacksmith shop.

Ecstatic to see them, Tim burst out, "There's the two guys, owners of my greatest works! You know, I just missed you the day you left with the foreigners."

"Really? That's unfortunate," said Mick.

"Yeah, I was hoping to catch you guys before you went back home, but a couple guards at the castle told me all about the mission and where you went. I bet that was quite the quest, indeed."

"That it was, my good man," responded Dave. "How's business?"

"Can't complain. I have the feeling it's going to pick up even more, in the midst of the Icytryxans being here and all."

"I'm sure it will," noted Mick. "They'll probably request your expertise and services with the projectiles. And also with the atlytls themselves, since they're made chiefly from metal. I'd recommend getting yourself familiar with their structural mechanisms, the sooner the better."

"Good thinking. That I will do."

"If you're not busy," suggested Mick, "you could come back with us when we leave, and we can introduce you to all the right Icytryxan people, fine folks who can familiarize you with the weapons."

Dave added, "In fact, Jason mentioned to us he brought your name up to their manufacturing team, while on the island. Jason spent a lot of time in their projectile department. He actually developed a whole new projectile for them."

"Amazing. That sounds like him. He always did seem to have the eye for innovation. And, yes, I'll come with you."

"Excellent, we'll head for the barracks then," commented Mick, "but first, I'm sure you'll want to hear all about the mission."

"Damn straight I do."

Mick and Dave took the better part of an hour to discourse on their Icytryxis mission with an attentive Tim.

After which, the three left the blacksmith shop, and went to the barracks.

Dave and Mick introduced Tim to Jason Thorncat's Icytryxan buddy, Swidyt—Jason's partner in crime, more or less.

Upon the meeting, Swidyt said, "Ah, yes, Mr. Warmane. Jason told me all about you. I'm especially delighted to meet the maker of Mick and Dave's black needle swords. I've never seen such exceptional craftsmanship. I'll be looking forward to working with you, no doubt."

Tim and Swidyt got into further detail about the atlytls and their physical makeup. Dave and Mick stuck around during the discussion for a few moments, realized Tim was in good hands, and went to search out Yusyta. Before leaving his company, though, the pair told Tim it was great seeing him, that they'd be leaving town soon, and that they'd see him the next time around.

Next to her bed, Yusyta was pacing nervously in the officers' quarters when Mick and Dave found her.

"Hi guys. Good to see you."

"Hi, Yusyta," stated both voices in unison.

"This is a mighty fine room Mr. Ulfenkerki has bestowed upon me."

"Gotta love the Black Bear," noted Dave, uncharacteristically forgoing real-word usage for whimsy.

"I'm learning that rather quickly."

"So, I guess we came here to see when you were making the trip to see Alfonso. I ask because we will be leaving for Chalatore soon, and if you are also leaving shortly, we could make the trip together, since Dourinuset is basically along the way.”

“Oh, wow. That would be lovely. I planned on departing in a day or two but could certainly leave when your schedule permits.”

“We have no set schedule,” submitted Mick. “Whichever day and time work best for you will be the utmost agreeable with us.”

“Splendid. Can I get back to you later today on the day and time?”

“For sure. We’ll probably be at the castle later, so you can come tell us there when you decide.”

“Perfect,” voiced Yusyta, enthusiastically. “Will they let me in?”

“We’ll inform the guards that you’ll be coming; it’ll all be good.”

“See you then.”

Having left the barracks, Mick and Dave searched out beverages. At a certain point, after every tasty beverage of the Capital, one would’ve thought they’d tried them all, only to find they hadn’t. It was just that sort of a place.

Post the satisfying quenching of thirsts, they ambled to the castle and met up with Rowlangiv.

“We’ll be leaving to go back home to Chalatore either tomorrow or the day after, sire,” communicated Dave.

“Thanks again for your service to the country. I’d give you another Knowing Circle if I could. It really is amazing how the two of you care so much about Garobansurov, without actually having an official title.”

Mick responded, "Wide recognition isn't wise motivation."

"Interesting."

Mick divulged, "Our philosophical journey through life takes us through a world where solving the great riddle of life can only be done so from within. Influence on the riddle's equation derived from the mind of the masses, to a certain degree, impedes the answers for which we're searching."

Dave added, "The sum of all available thoughts is tarnished with the stain of much untruth, so we find that striving to go after the riddle with only our own observations is advantageous. This is why we walk the path abstinent from the influence of anyone but ourselves. And ultimately, we owe everything to Garobansurov, and would do anything for it. For it supplies us with the very freedom needed to embark said philosophical quest."

"Well spoken, you two," replied the King. "More power to you and your quest. Nevertheless, you're always welcome here amongst the masses, at whichever post you'd care to have. Having the two of you around truly is the handiest of the handy."

"Thank you for the honor," Dave responded sincerely. "We will be back at some point, I'm sure. The war is far from over, and Mick and I will continue to do whatever we can to keep your people, our friends, alive."

"And for that, I'm blessed. Have a safe trip, and I'll see you when you come back."

Mick and Dave bowed to their King, and went to their rooms, where just before sunset, Yusyta found them. She told them she chose to leave on the morrow at

11:00. Hawk and Leopard saw no problems with this, so the trio agreed to leave at the time Yusyta suggested.

In the morning, Mick and Dave sought out Jason, Yori, Gregg, Ulfenkerki, Thyxer, and Syryx to tell them all goodbye. They made the farewells comparatively short, because they would more than likely see them all again soon, or at least fairly soon. The task did take a couple hours, though, since not one person was in the same place as another.

Yusyta also did the same with Thyxer, Syryx, Yori, Jason, and a few other kin. She would probably be back before Mick and Dave, so her farewells were even shorter than theirs.

Not exactly idiosyncratic of her normal patterns, Yusyta was ready to go on time, surprisingly even before the pre-agreed departure time. She practically ran to get all her pre-trip preparations completed and awaited her travel companions near the city's front gate. Ironically, she waited under the same balcony Rowlangiv and Ulfenkerki had just utilized. The wooden structure must've really been inviting, perhaps supplying the best shade of the area.

Mick and Dave double checked their rooms to make sure they had everything. Once again, they had full loads on their backs—total combined weight: 190 pounds, a little lighter than when they began the trip to the Capital.

The pair directed themselves toward the castle's front gate.

"Too bad we won't be able to dump off the armor on a boat this time."

Mick waved to the guards posted by the castle gate, then looked at Dave and chuckled. "Yeah, Dave, I'm assuredly going to miss that."

Having crossed the entirety of the castle causeway, the two aimed at the front gateway of the city, the planned meeting point with Yusyta.

Seeing Mick and Dave approach, Yusyta stepped out from underneath the balcony. She commented, amid astonishment, "You guys really do equip yourselves with quite the cargo. I know you told me once how heavy your normal packs are, but my subconscious must not have believed you."

"Believe me, they're as heavy as they look too."

"Oh, I do. I'm just glad my load is much smaller. I have no armor or weapons, except for a knife primarily used for fish-gutting and scaling."

"A tool most necessary," declared Dave. "Shall we depart, fabulous traveling companions of mine?"

"Yup."

The trio took a deep breath, stretched, and left the city behind.

CHAPTER 26

B EYOND THE CITY'S front gate, they walked within view of the recently established, temporary atlytl firing field.

"Projectiles soaring through the air everywhere, just like back home," stated Yusyta. Her eyes followed the full path of a projectile. "Must've been a Thorncat Missile; it traveled further than normal. On a different note, things certainly are going well between our peoples. A lot of the Icytryxan soldiers I've talked to thus far have said they're impressed with how cordially they're being treated. They've also been saying how everything we've said about the Garobansurovians at the Javeti Edifice has so far been quite accurate."

"I've been getting the same reports," noted Dave. "We will be an exceptional team. I do in part regret leaving the Capital, for the reason that I wouldn't mind being a part of the first battle in which our two societies fight together."

"In the ideal world, the battle never takes place, the war ends beforehand. I doubt that, though. But maybe it won't happen until we find our way back," said Mick.

Subsequent inhaling a lungful of farm-modified air, Dave responded, "Ah, farm country. Yup, Mick, that very well could happen. Anything can happen."

It took almost a full half-hour of walking for the trio to be out of the sight of projectiles flying through the air. Normally, you couldn't see projectiles at such a distance, but when there were tons clumped together, you could. Due to line of sight/planet curvature principal, they deduced the firing field must've been on high ground as well.

Overall, their walk to Dourinuset was of the utmost enjoyable. The campouts were all in lovely localities and had the freshest of air, despite the occasional farm-waft. Plus, the weather was nothing to complain about. Trouble of all forms stayed clear—especially from thieves lurking behind trees.

On the campout the night before they expected to reach Dourinuset, Mick asked Yusyta, "Do you know what you're all going to say to him? You know, he will be rather startled at seeing you. Maybe Abbot Ferdinand could tell him about you first, before you go running into his arms. But then on the other hand, maybe that's not the entrance you're going for. You'll have to talk to Ferdinand initially anyways; they don't let many people through the doors, so you'll first need permission. He does know all about yours and Alfonso's history, though."

"I've been thinking about it on our whole walk and have come up with a plan, which I'm sure will need Ferdinand's permission."

"You'll find Abbot Ferdinand to be exceptionally obliging, so I'm sure that won't be a problem."

"Good to hear."

Yusyta sat a little more comfortably in her recently constructed, makeshift log chair, and told Mick and Dave all about her 'Alfonso reunification plan.'

By the end of the telling, all their smiles shone brightly, serendipitously enhanced by romance and vibrant moon beams.

The next day, the three partook in the last leg of their voyage together and reached the bottom of Dourinuset hill by late afternoon.

Yusyta hugged Dave and Mick goodbye, and said, "Thank you so much for walking with me. It really has calmed my nerves."

"It was our pleasure. Please say hello to everyone for us," said Mick.

"Will do."

"We'll see you soon, I'm sure," noted Dave. "Oh yeah, while climbing the hill, be sure to always take the path marked with triple cedar trees when it forks. You'll reach the monastery in hardly any time knowing this."

Mick added, "I'm half tempted to come up with you, just to see how elated Alfonso gets."

"Why don't you?"

"We would, but I think it would feel a little awkward to just go there for the sole purpose of seeing Alfonso's reaction."

"I imagine. And thanks for the triple cedar trick. I'll miss you guys. Have a wonderful rest of your trip. I'm sure the people in your village will get a kick out of hearing where you've been."

"To be completely honest," replied Mick, "I'm still getting a kick out where we've been."

Yusyta chuckled. "Yeah, it is pretty far out. Well, wish me luck."

"Goodbye, good luck, and may the new pages in your book of life be blessed with greatness," proclaimed Dave.

"Same to you."

Mick and Dave split from Yusyta. They headed for Chalatore, as Yusyta began the trek up the steep, foggy hill. Jitteriness crept into her when Mick and Dave were no longer within view. With every passing step up the hill, her heart beat faster. Time was not her friend. By the time she reached the top echelon of the hill, she found herself so flooded by emotion and anxiety that her mind practically became frozen.

She dug in deep for focus.

At last, she was confronted by the monastery's grand staircase leading to the front door. Seeing the building, all her nervousness instantly disappeared. Now, sheer bliss took over. Her true love was just inside, waiting unknowingly.

She finished ascending the stairs and slowly advanced upon the monastery's entry. She held her breath and knocked on the door.

Luckily, Abbot Ferdinand answered. "May I help you? I'm Abbot Ferdinand."

Having remembered to breathe at maybe the last second before passing out, Yusyta replied, "Hello, Abbot. My appearance will come across as unexpected, I'm sure, but my name is Yusyta. I'm Alfonso Alardo's wife."

Quite noticeably, Ferdinand bent over to pick up his jaw off the ground. He shook away the astonishment, and voiced, "You're right, I certainly did not expect to open this door today and see you. I know all about you, however. Alfonso has told us all about his love story— his *tragic* love story."

"I imagine he has. There's much more to the story, but I'll get to that later. For now, I must ask your permission to see him. I know that not many are allowed entrance to the monastery. I only hope for an exception to the rules."

"I'll grant the permission, mainly because I have the feeling you would just hang out on the steps here until he sees you."

"Your intuition serves you well. I would do just that. I have traveled farther than you would guess." She took a second to look contemplatively into the past. "One more thing—Would you mind if I try to make our reunion as special as possible? I would like to try to recreate the very moment I met him. He was fishing, surrounded by nature. He appeared to blend seamlessly into the landscape. I was awestruck at such a sight. I can't begin to explain how he did it. The memory of it has ever since been clear as day to me, carved in stone. I think I can come close to recreating the moment for Alfonso. But, this time, he will be the one stumbling fatefully upon me. Hopefully, he feels the same way I did, all those years ago."

"I hope you're successful. What did you have in mind?"

"I ask to enter your most beautiful courtyard, unannounced," Yusyta inquired, nervously. "There, I will wait until he sees me. Maybe it will be a long wait, for which I'm prepared if need be."

"You're in luck; I've noticed he gravitates towards going to a certain courtyard right after last service, which actually starts here in an hour. It's arguably our prettiest courtyard—not necessarily our grandest, but definitely charming beyond words."

"That sounds magnificent. I appreciate it so much, kind Abbot. About how long is the church service?"

"That particular service usually lasts roughly half an hour. I'll try to steer him to the courtyard somehow, if I see it's one of those rare nights he exhibits no intention of going into it."

"Mick and Dave were right, you really are most obliging."

"Mick Thraiker and Dave Ghrere?" Ferdinand sprouted a quizzical smile.

"Yup, they are a part of this story too, but I'll get into that later."

"Remarkable! Follow me," said Ferdinand, just before beginning to show Yusyta the way to the correct courtyard. "I'll inform the other monks to try their best at not leaking anything to Alfonso about your appearance. I'll also try to keep the courtyard empty of everyone but you until he gets there."

"Thank you so much, sir."

They reached the courtyard, and prior to leaving Yusyta to her moment, Ferdinand voiced, "I wish you luck, and I'll talk to you later."

Yusyta looked around the colorful locale thoroughly, deciphering the best place for Alfonso to lay eyes upon her. A laying that hadn't occurred in a very long time.

After much inner debate, she decided on the best place.

It would be awhile before the service was over, so she trenched in and waited patiently. During the wait, she mentally repeated the words she would say to him. Yusyta wanted it all to be perfect.

Time elapsed. Alfonso, content in being part of another beautiful service, exited the church, and allowed his legs to take him to his normal post late-service locale.

Along the way, he thought about the gorgeous black and red bird he'd seen in the courtyard the day previous, hoping it was there again. He came into the courtyard and smiled, because sitting on the edge of one of the water features was the bird. He assumed it was the same one, since birds of this plumage were too rare for it not to be.

He sat on a bench just far enough away from the bird to not scare it away. He admired its color and large wingspan, especially when it fluffed itself.

The bird apparently got sick of its location, so it flew to the other side of the courtyard. At first, Alfonso didn't follow, to give it some space, but after a few minutes he tagged along after it. He followed it half to continue his gaze at the bird, and half because he liked the part of the courtyard the bird landed in best. It had the oldest trees and captured the essence of natural beauty better than any other part of Dourinuset's courtyards. There was a small hand-dug pond situated like a dream by the side of a very large, flat-topped granite boulder—or at least he always thought it was granite.

Atop the boulder he sometimes liked to sit, relaxingly peering into the pond's perfectly reflective surface. He decided this night would be one of these nights.

Upon the decision, he aimed towards the rock and started to walk around the thick conglomerate of trees guarding the front of it.

Once around the sight debilitating trees, he stopped dead in his tracks. For the first time ever, someone was sitting on the rock, and doing exactly the same thing he always loved to do. This person was clearly absorbing every facet of the ambient natural tranquility. Subsequent a few seconds, he realized it was a woman. There weren't very many women to have ever visited Dourinuset, so it was a bewildering sight.

And after a few more seconds, he realized which woman it was.

Instantly, he was struck by her beauty, but was more so struck by shock. Alfonso's vision went hazy, and he almost fell over at the sight.

Eventually, he regained his vision, approached Yusyta, and stammered, "It's like you magically knew this was my favorite spot."

"I've never forgotten how your mind works."

"Nor I yours."

"I tried my best to arrange a way for you to look upon me the same way I looked upon you that very day we met."

"Honestly, the surprise of seeing you all but made me pass out. Not in a million years did I expect to see you sitting there. I dreamed of this moment ever since you left, envisioning many different ways of how I would react upon seeing you. But not one of them showed me losing my vision, and nearly passing out."

Yusyta jumped gracefully off the rock, placed herself near Alfonso and said, "I've visualized this moment ever since I left too. I just never thought it would be possible. That is, until recent events transpired."

"That's the wonderful thing about life, anything is possible."

"Too true. Now, Alfonso, I'm going to tell you everything about why I left."

Yusyta told Alfonso the entire story—about her being Icytryxis, about her family, about Mick and Dave and the mission, about how an Icytryxis army was now at the Capital due to the alliance. She missed no detail in the telling.

Alfonso listened with his ears as wide open as they could possibly be.

After the story, they embraced. With as much sincerity as she could muster, Yusyta said, "I know you made a vow to the monastery and to God, that you can't leave, and that you have to be chaste. Honorable indeed. But I feel both you and I could be complete, loving each other just the same, if I visited you here from this point on. I'll be helping out our army, probably mainly at the Capital, but I'm sure I can come here to visit you a bunch of times a year. Having you, my family, and my people all in my life would complete my soul."

At that moment, Alfonso realized that the most perfect smile he could ever create was on his face. "Those were the greatest words I've ever heard uttered. Seeing you on intervals would make my spirit sing a thousand songs of happiness, simultaneously. Even the time you wouldn't be here would be spent in elation, just knowing that I would get to see you again soon. This part I have envisioned."

"I couldn't be happier than I am right now," said Yusyta, and she squeezed Alfonso as hard as she could. "I love you."

"I love you too—no less than when you left," declared Alfonso.

They stayed in the courtyard and talked devotedly all night, completely forgetting that a full night's sleep was good for the health.

The pair once again were together and remained so until the day Alfonso died at the monastery at the rather old age (for a Garobansurovian) of a hundred and four. Yusyta would end up visiting Alfonso an average of four times per year, for a mean of five days per time, gaining extremely strong legs from all the walks. The monks were glad and accommodating every time she came, even when she came to visit his gravestone at the monastery, which she did regularly, right up until she passed away at the age (average for an Icytryxan) of a hundred and thirty-seven.

In the end, the relationship was recorded by the planet's gravity as being one of the top hundred most beautiful things it had ever held within its grasp.

MICK AND DAVE both spent the entire rest of the way home in rumination on the bliss and future of Yusyta and Alfonso. It brought cheer and warmth to their hearts, resulting in the last leg of their long journey going by quicker than the other legs, despite it being the most uneventful.

They finally reached their hometown, and on the same day of the year's first snowfall. It wasn't one of great accumulation, but noteworthy, nevertheless. They were gone part of spring, all of summer, and practically all of fall. They were glad to be back when they were, nobody liked walking through snow.

Just before setting foot in town, Mick professed, "I didn't think I would that much, but I'm really looking forward to showing everyone the Knowing Circles."

"I knew I would," responded Dave. "A lot of the villagers told me, before we left, how much they were looking forward to seeing them."

"I wonder if we should cook again for the swooning throng bound to form wanting to see them, sort of like we did before we left for the Capital this spring?"

Dave chuckled, knowing Mick was kidding. "I just hope no one thought we died. We have been away for quite some time."

"I'm sure Old Man Johnson reassured everyone that there just is no killing us."

"Probably. That sounds like him. There are enough hours left in the day; we could yet make it out to his cabin to find out if he did."

"I can see that happening."

As soon as Hawk and Leopard entered Chalatore's town square, a group accumulated to see the medals and hear the story. But what the assembly of townsfolk didn't know was how much there was to the story. By the end of the day, the duo would end up telling the story (at least the short version of) a dozen times to three times as many people. Being one of them, and saving Mick and Dave a trip, was Old Man Johnson. He confirmed to Mick and Dave the fact that he had to convince many of the residents that his young friends were resilient and more than likely alive and well. He also verified that he conjured scenarios for the worrisome villagers detailing what his friends, Mick and Dave, could have been doing during the time they were gone.

He wasn't even close.

ABOUT THE AUTHOR

NICHOLAS WUDTKE, minimalist, naturalist, and ponderer of philosophy, is rarely seen doing otherwise than sitting on a rock or fallen tree somewhere in the still of Wisconsin's vast Chequamegon-Nicolet National Forest, writing. Nicholas is the father of two sons, one who passed away at a young age due to complications of severe brain damage. Nicholas spent the best years of his life caring for this child, whom he named Lifeson, and his current epic fantasy series is being written in honor of him.

Nicholas enjoys trail running, backpacking, bonsai trees, fossil hunting, and last but not least, listening to favorite rock band Rush, his inspiration, insisting one can come nowhere even close to experiencing this rock power-trio enough.

Author of a list of novels—*The Swords: Friendships and Winds of Far-off Places*, and three installments of his seven-novel *Black Needle* series, including: (1) *Parabolic, Magnetic Key*; (2) *Blunt but Imminently Fatal Projectile*; and (3) *Deserved, Contorted Relics*, Nicholas is a free spirit, currently living in a small home surrounded by trees, a swamp, and fresh air. He cherishes his time with his son, his girlfriend, and the rest of his family and friends.

ACKNOWLEDGEMENTS

A great *thank you* to
Jeanne Wudtke
for beta reading.

Black † Needle
Book Three

DESERVED, CONTORTED RELICS

CHAPTER 1

ALTHOUGH THEY HADN'T been there much lately, Mick and Dave lived in a little corner of the world, inhabiting opposite ends of a winter-tinged pond, almost large enough to be considered a lake. The pond was no doubt a natural beauty unmistakable by oral description to those familiar with it. Dave and Mick's houses were small, but the scenery was grand.

There was only one other home on the isolated, unnamed body of water. Ironically, the owner of the house was absent even more than Mick and Dave. Technically, the person was gone so often neither Mick nor Dave had ever gotten the chance to ask them to where they constantly ventured. In fact, Mick and Dave didn't even know what he or she looked like.

Dave lived on the deep end of the pond, Mick the wide. Dave had built a sturdy seawall on his side, making for better pond access. Mick's home was identifiable by the far-from-ostentatious pole pavilion, bereft walls, built alongside the pond. He really enjoyed sitting beside the pond, as it rained, devoid getting wet.

It would usually take five minutes of brisk walking to get from Mick's house to Dave's. Mick had just sluggishly done it in six.

He found Dave sitting by his firepit bordering the seawall. A fire was blazing, and cool air was wafting. "I would guess the ice will be unseasonably off the pond by next week."

"That sounds about right," replied Dave. "Winter has been pretty mild this year, thankfully."

"May I be so bold as to say I could make do without long winters?"

"You may."

The two sat by the fire for half an hour, afterwards, they got to work, doing for what it was Mick had come.

The plan was to leave Chalatore again to aid in the war effort. They determined that while they were away, they'd allow some young men they knew to stay in their houses. Someone may as well use them, they thought.

Dave had one last thing to do to make his house ready for the move-in. With Mick's help, they would repair the chimney. It would be an easier job for two, because one on the ground could hand things to the other working up on the chimney. Undeniably, it was a pain in the butt to climb up and down a ladder repeatedly.

Passing an uninteresting stone up to Dave, Mick commented, "Have you ever wondered if Old Man Johnson would like to come to the Capital with us this time? I think he could handle making the trip, plus, I know he's fascinated with the coming of the Icytryxis."

"That he is. He doesn't have many years left, I don't think, for such a journey. I think we should propose the idea to him."

"We should. And I'd envision we could pretty much carry most of his load, which wouldn't be much, I'm sure. He could sleep in one of our tents with us too."

"We'll ask him next time we see him," said Dave, securing the bland stone into its rightful place.

The chimney was completed in an hour, after which they sat by the fire, watching the ice on the pond get thinner and thinner. It wasn't really something that could be seen, only something that could be imagined. The week previous, they'd done the same with the snow. By that point, the snow was almost completely gone and not expected to return, an expectation not unlike the smoke that'd been escaping through the hole in Dave's chimney.

Yet again, Mick and Dave expected to miss the annual armwrestling tournament in town, beckoned by things elsewhere. They felt bad about it, because they knew how much local tourism could've been boosted just by the Knowing Circle recipients entering. The Knowing Circle was the highest award given by the king of their home country, Garobansurov. Nonetheless, there were more important things than tourism stealing their attention.

Though, they were doing their best to help out the tournament's organizers by hosting a fundraising event for new equipment. The tournament's tables, bleachers, tents, and concession stand were getting old, and funds were needed to repair and replace them. So, Mick and

Dave came up with the idea to host a benefit fish fry. They usually didn't icefish much, but they had spent the last month on their pond catching a rather large supply for the event. To keep the fish fresh, they kept them alive in a makeshift pool temporarily thrown together near Mick's house. The water was kept from freezing by the residual heat of the house and the substantial amount of body heat produced by the many fish.

The event was to take place at Chalatore's only park and was scheduled for the morrow. Dave and Mick had event preparations to discuss.

To Dave, Mick stated, "I don't think we'll have to go very far for firewood with which to cook, tomorrow, as there's plenty of it close to the park."

"That should save some time. We still need to peel and cut potatoes, set up tables and chairs, and clean fish, all by nightfall," replied Dave.

Noticing the wind had picked up, Mick said, "I bet we'd have time in the morning to clean some of the fish, if by chance we don't get it all done today."

"Maybe. We'll see how it goes."

Rare for the season, a leaf plummeted towards Mick's face. He flicked it away, and asked, "How many people do you think will come?"

"I think a couple hundred would be a good turnout. If any more were to show up, we wouldn't have enough fish."

"I think we'll be good. We've got three hundred fish—three fillets and a pile of potatoes for each person."

"I still can't believe how well we did fishing," blurted Dave. "It was almost as fruitful as fishing from the Icytryxan sea-ship."

"Yup, almost. We should make plenty of money for the tournament reparations."

The pair worked hard all day and got everything completed, even all the fish cleaning. Basically, all they had to do the next morning was haul all the fish to the park.

An even warmer weather pattern than the previous moved in, as the morning sun ascended.

The event was scheduled for noon, so Mick Thraiker and Dave Ghrere woke up early enough to tote all the fish and start the fire. They also wanted to get a good chunk of it cooked, before the event began. Their good friend, Old Man Johnson, would help out with the cooking. Plus, a few of the local women had volunteered to help serve.

Calculatingly, at 11:00, Mick, Dave, and Mr. Johnson began to light the fire. Usually, it didn't take three people to get a fire going, but the wind that'd picked up the day prior hadn't yet felt like settling, making for a difficult task. Once the flames reached a desirable height, the trio stopped adding wood.

Dave said to Old Man Johnson, "We were actually wondering something yesterday. Would you like to accompany us on our trip to the Capital this time? You aren't getting any younger, and this may be your only opportunity to lay eyes upon the Icytryxan atlytl corp. You wouldn't have to carry anything."

Mick added, "Trust me, seeing the atlytl projectiles in motion would truly be worth the trip. The spectacle is undeniably mystical."

Old Man Johnson threw a handful of filets into one of the pans on the fire and took a few moments to think. "A few days ago, I had the feeling you would propose the idea to me. I pondered on it but came to no conclusion at that time. But for some reason today, it only took a few seconds to decide. As long as you'll go at a pace I can handle, I would very much like to come."

"We can promise you this, no problem. Though, I suppose I should mention there really is no time frame as to how long we'll be there this time."

"That's fine," responded Johnson. "I have plenty of gitis (Garobansurov's currency) for indefinite accommodations."

"I doubt any of us will have to pay much for lodging."

"I imagine. Also, I'd be delighted to see my old buddy, Tim Warmane, again."

"He actually mentioned during the last time we were there that he wished you'd come someday," noted Dave.

"When will be leaving?"

"Probably next week."

"Excellent. By the way, how did you guys catch so many fish?"

Mick chuckled. "It's a secret. I guess it's a proficiency we only recently cultivated."

The first batch of fish and potatoes were ready for consumption. They began the next batch without delay.

"It must be noon," said Mick, "because our first few patrons are heading this way."

"Let the festivities begin," declared Dave.

Mick and Dave's fundraiser turned out to be a great success. Plenty of people came and filled their stomachs. There'd been enough to feed everyone. A lot of the time had ended up being spent by the villagers discussing what crazy shenanigans Mick and Dave might run into on their next trip. At a certain point in their lives, Dave and Mick would come to learn that the villagers had created a wager system, betting on what exactly would happen to them this time. Old Man Johnson had refrained from betting for two reasons: First, he would be a part of the excursion; and second, he'd learned from Mick and Dave's last cross-country journey that he was bad at guessing such things.

Thanks to the fundraiser, they gathered enough money for everything the armwrestling tournament needed. Mick and Dave were happy to contribute, as they loved that tournament.

Seven days after the fish fry, Mick, Dave, and Old Man Johnson found themselves walking the only road directly connecting Chalatore to the Capital. It wasn't straight, but it was more level than most Garobansurovian trails. Nobody liked a path full of ruts, especially while carrying loads. And like always, Mick and Dave had large ones.

They didn't plan on stopping at any locales for an extended amount of time, as they had during the last trip to the Capital. So, the trio anticipated they'd make decent time—at least decent time for an old man and two carrying large packs. Barring unforeseen incident, they were certain the trip would be pleasant.

Their first night of the trek was spent in a meadow. Normally, Dave and Mick didn't like making camp in terrain without wind blocks, but it was a fairly still night, so they were accepting of it.

While lighting the nightly fire, Dave asked Old Man Johnson, "How are your legs holding up? I noticed you were walking with ease for the most part."

"During the first half of the day, it seemed I was walking like I was fifty years younger. The second half wasn't as friction-free, but I still managed to enjoy myself. My legs are a little sore, but I'm sure they'll be good to go by tomorrow."

"Feel free to tell us to slow down whenever you wish—we're not really facing any deadlines."

"Yup, will do," said Old Man Johnson; a man who, although you wouldn't expect, liked his moniker.

"Excellent."

Johnson kicked an annoying rock out from underneath his feet. "I was wondering, what do you guys think are the chances a battle will transpire while we're at the Capital?"

"Good question. I'd say there's maybe a thirty-three percent chance a battle will occur," replied Mick.

Dave added, "I'm going to say a little higher, a forty percent chance perhaps. I just have that feeling. Knowing Gamald is still at large is a rather ominous thought."

"Those are some fairly good odds," admitted Johnson. "Where do civilians go for safety during times of battle at the Capital? I'm not worried or anything. If I were worried, I wouldn't have decided to go."

"We figured that. There are plenty of places for refuge. The King, of course, can take shelter in the castle's bowels. Civilians could do the same, I suppose. Also, many could take sanctuary in the basements of some of the larger buildings. A few of the smaller homes have basements too, but not many, due to a layer of bedrock close to the surface."

"Oh yes, I remember hearing that once."

Dave commented, "I'm hoping this time around, we hear how the western front is holding up. I'm really starting to worry about that. Yes, the western coast is pretty far from the Capital, but it still affects us all."

"It does indeed."

Dave asserted, "I do know I'm not making the same mistake this time in thinking that nothing hazardous is going to happen."

"Right. Something always happens," said Mick. "I'm prepared, as my sword couldn't get any sharper than it is now."

"Who knows," stated Mr. Johnson, "maybe I'll join in on a battle if one happens. I still have the strength to draw back a bowstring."

"Go right ahead. I doubt King Rowlangiv will stop you," said Mick, following the path of a bat with his eyes.

The trio talked of the Capital for another hour and went to bed.

The next few days of the walk were as smooth as the first. Old Man Johnson had only slowed the pace a handful of times. Mick and Dave didn't care in the slightest when he did. They were more than ecstatic their lifelong friend, Old Man Johnson, was there to share in on the memories.

On the fifth day of the journey, they finally ran into a snag. Despite Mick and Dave walking the road to the Capital multiple times before, they'd never encountered a lone child on it.

When they caught up with the kid, Dave asked, "Hello, where are you headed, youngster?"

"Hello. I don't really know. My father left my mom and I at home, while he went off to war for the King. He said he would be back at some point, but he never returned. My mom has since died, and I don't know what to do. So here I am, wandering aimlessly along this road."

Mick looked at Dave and Old Man Johnson in disbelief, and said, "None of the people in your village would help you? Your mom had no friends?"

"The answer to both is no."

Mick told the child their names and learned his name was Will.

Dave spoke: "We are headed to the Capital now. You're welcome to tag along to see what happened to your dad, or you can walk with us to the next village. These are dangerous roads to be walking alone."

Will replied, "I wouldn't know what to do in some random town, so I think I'll come with you to the Capital and see what happened to my dad."

"Sounds good, Will. We have plenty of food, so you won't have to worry about that."

"Where have you been sleeping, Will, while on the road?" asked Mr. Johnson.

"A few times I found sheds to sleep in, and a few times under trees."

"You can sleep in a tent with one of us, until we get there," commented Mick. "It's a little crowded with two people, but it beats getting rained on."

"Thank you so much. I can fight too, if we run into bandits."

"I imagine you could, Will. I won't stop you."

Fortunately, the party wouldn't run into bandits, unlike the last time Mick and Dave had walked to the Capital. They would, however, run into a lot of bad weather.

One night in particular was especially horrendous. Lightning strikes were so close together there was no clear line separating light of day and night sky. Vein-like bolts of electricity thoroughly illuminated the heavens. The rain came down torrentially, the volume of which was immeasurable. Their tents were exposed to a wind so violent the stakes nearly came undone. Despite the strongest winds the handmade tents had ever encountered, they remained faithfully intact through it all.

Will particularly enjoyed the storm from inside the tent, it was a fresh sight for his young eyes.

Having woken to puddles strewn everywhere, Mick said, "The whole thing was rather reminiscent of the huge blizzard that night by Fort Gravividon. You know, Dave, one of these times our tents are going to lose the battle."

"Impossible. They don't know the meaning of the word *lose*."

"Let's hope you're right. I doubt we'll ever find replacement tents half as durable."

The day after the storm, its aftermath made itself known. It may've stopped raining, but the wind was still gusting ferociously, which made for arduous walking.

The trail could've been considered impassable by some that day, because of how muddy it'd gotten. But Mick and Dave's group were of the hardier sort, not paying the trail's condition much attention. In their minds, they could've run into way worse things than a rainstorm and a sloppy trail.

At the halfway point to Myothraces (the formal name of the Capital), the quartet made camp in the most beautiful place yet of the trip.

"I'm surprised we've overlooked this area for camping on every one of our previous trips through these parts."

"Me too, Dave," replied Mick. "I can't even recall ever sojourning here."

"I know we've seen this ravine before, but I don't think we've ever seen this particular area of it."

"It does seem deeper and more scenic than any memories I have of it. Captivating."

Will spent the whole evening playing near the ravine wall, building forts. Old Man Johnson playfully threw rocks at the forts, trying his best to knock them over. They were having a blast, as a bond was beginning to take shape.

Mick and Dave spent time searching the area for black needle pine trees, since the only other one they'd ever found had been in a similar setting. But the mystery of their swords (which had hilts made from the wood of the black needle tree) continued to be a mystery, as a second tree remained undiscovered.

They made their nightly fire close to a stream trickling through the bottom of the gully. They erected tents uphill from the stream, having gotten lucky in locating the one and only patch of grass. Sleeping on grass was far more comfortable than sleeping on rock, which the whole area was nearly nothing but.

"There must've been a battle down here long ago," observed Mick. "I've been seeing a lot of rusty iron fragments. None of the fragments resemble a weapon of any sort, but there's way more than what could be considered natural."

"I've seen a few too," said Dave. "They must be extremely old to have deteriorated this much."

Old Man Johnson joined in. "It's impossible to tell to whom the weapons belonged, but when we get to the Capital, I'll spend some time researching it."

"As if there was any doubt you would," joked Dave.

Mick, Dave, and Johnson chuckled.

"It is my thing, isn't it? I do love the Capital's library," declared Old Man Johnson.

"Don't we all."

They marched onward. The day's second half saw a little slower going than the first. Old legs were taking their toll. Though, steady progress was surely made, while Mick and Dave allowed Johnson every courtesy he required. Will's pain in having not seen either of his parents in a long time lessened, as having company was a nice distraction. Weather started cooperating as well.

Three nights after the campout in the ravine, the quartet decided that a little respite from the wilderness would be agreeable. They paid for a room in one of the small towns along the way. Will especially liked the idea, for it was the first time he'd ever sleep in an actual bed not his own.

Playing in the garden behind the inn, Will met a few other children staying with their families. They ran and played games most of the night. They would've played *all* night had the other youngsters' parents let them.

Old Man Johnson had also spent some time sitting in the lovely garden, an unusually large creation boasting eight thoroughly maintained sections. Anyone renting one of the inn's three rooms really got their money's worth.

Will came into the room and crashed onto one of the two beds. To him, Mick said, "Fun place eh? What games did you play out there?"

"We played hide and seek, tag, and my favorite: kick the can."

"That was my favorite when I was your age too. It's more fun in the dark though," professed Mick.

"In the dark?"

"Yeah, you play it like you normally would in the daytime, but you do it in the dark. It's fun because you can't see as well."

Will's face lit up with excitement. "That does sound fun. It's too bad my friends can't play anymore. I sure would love to try that."

Dave joined the conversation. "I know how you could play."

Will's face lit up even more. "You do? How's that?"

"All of us here could play—that's if Mick and Mr. Johnson want to play too."

"Count me in," said Mick. "I won't give up the opportunity to finally play kick the can again."

"I'll play too," emitted Johnson. "One is never too old for games at least once in a while."

"There you have it. We can even separate into teams."

"I want Mr. Johnson on my team!" erupted Will.

Enthusiastically, the four went to the garden and played youthfully well into the night. Under the circumstances, Will couldn't have had a better day. He played so hard that he fell asleep instantly upon reaching his bed.

Old Man Johnson wiped his brow and said, "I ran more today than I have in the last three years combined. I will sleep well tonight."

Breakfast was decided at the restaurant across the street.

They sat at the restaurant's only open table and began discussing every facet of the previous evening's game. Will could barely keep his mouth empty of words long enough to fill it with food. He never realized there was so much strategy in kick the can. In the end, Will decided the game was definitely better in the dark, just like Mick had said.

The meal turned out to be identical the discussion: excellent.

Well rejuvenated, the quartet left the inn just after breakfast, and continued their journey to the Capital. The rest of the trip would be spent in tents.

A few days before reaching their destination, Old Man Johnson chanced upon a rather beautiful locality. He'd found it while following the sound of trickling water, as he had needed to fill canteens. The locale contained an impressive grove of trees surrounding a crystal-clear spring creek. The majestic trees seemed as if they'd been placed there for a reason. They stood out from the rest of the forest like an oasis in a desert.

After Johnson came upon his discovery, he beckoned Mick, Dave, and Will, who'd been waiting patiently on the trail. To them, Johnson said, "I know we planned on walking another half an hour tonight yet, but you all have to come see this awe-inspiring grove of trees. I claim we make camp within this mystic setting."

"Lead the way."

Upon seeing to what he was led, Dave's eyes shot wide open. "The trees seem to have been manipulated somehow. The limbs match up more symmetrically than they should."

"Maybe they were wrapped with wires to shape them, like a bonsai tree."

"Good find, Old Man. We'll camp here tonight for sure," said Dave. "Call me curious. I'd like to look around for any signs that someone had indeed purposefully done this to the trees."

"Me too," asserted Mick. "We may find some sort of homestead within the vicinity. That'll supply clues."

Post the erection of the tents, they all scanned the area methodically. However, nothing but natural elements were discovered.

"The trees are old, but not so old that if someone did grow them like this, enough topsoil would've accumulated to cover every spec of evidence."

"That was a mouthful. Are you sure you worded that right?" Mick chuckled.

"I think so. You know what I meant if I didn't." Dave laughed.

"I did, and you're probably right. Oh well. I guess it's another thing we'll never know."

"Nevertheless, it's extremely stunning. Great find, Old Man Johnson."

"Thank you," returned Johnson. "The stream is very picturesque as well. I'm going to fish in it."

"Good luck," emitted Mick. "You probably have an hour of daylight left, I'd say."

"I'm joining in on the fishing," Will announced excitedly.

"Terrific," said Johnson.

Daylight waned, and the duo cheerfully returned with morrow's breakfast, which the four ate at sunrise.

They left the mysterious tree grove behind and walked on.

The final days of the voyage had ended up being an undeniably joyful experience. The miles were steady, and the scenery was noteworthy.

Old Man Johnson was extremely proud he'd made it to the Capital without slowing the pace too much. He figured he'd make it but thought his legs would get a lot sorer than they had.

They approached the Capital from the east.

Hawk and Leopard (Mick and Dave's childhood nicknames) were glad to see atlytl projectiles flying over the tree canopy in the distance, which meant the foreign race of the Icytryxis hadn't gone elsewhere. Deep down inside, Dave and Mick wanted to fight a battle alongside the Icytryxis. Being partly responsible for the Garobansurov/Icytryxis alliance, Mick and Dave felt an affinity towards the foreigners.

"It looks like there's an entire platoon of Icytryxis out in the practice field."

"A lovely sight indeed." Dave turned around and closed the gap to Old Man Johnson, who'd been trailing. "You have to come see this."

Johnson followed.

Dave pointed. "Look there, above those trees."

"It's as magnificent a sight as I'd imagined. They're faster than I pictured. Although, it could be an illusion, since I can't see the projectiles' entire flights."

"It could be. As you'd assume, the projectiles are still governed by conventional physics. We'll be to the practice field in an hour, then, you'll be able to see the full arc."

"Excellent. I do have a particular proclivity for admiring weapons in action."

"We know." Widespread chuckles arose.

GET YOUR NEXT GREAT READ!

VISIT

WWW.NICHOLASWUDTKE.COM

TODAY!